VAMPIRE IN CHAOS
VAMPIRE IN CRISIS
VAMPIRE IN CONTROL

BOOK #7–9 OF FAMILY BLOOD TIES

DALE MAYER

Book in this series:

FAMILY BLOOD TIES BOOKS 7–9
Dale Mayer
Valley Publishing

ISBN-13: 978-1-988315-15-7
Print Edition

Back Cover

Vampire in Chaos

Tessa's life has dropped into chaos. Her father is missing, Goran is unconscious and showing no signs of healing, her mother has taken several steps off the deep end, and David, well, she'll deal with him when she sees him – if she can find him.

Cody isn't sure what happened to the supposedly successful conclusion to the blood farm madness, but he's back in hell and damn it, Tessa is once again leading the charge.

Jared is on the run, again. With no one else he can trust but Tessa's friends and family, he searches them out, determined to help them solve this war – whether he is welcome or not.

With everyone in distress or missing, Tessa struggles to find answers and create some kind of order amongst the chaos – before their attackers strike again.

Vampire in Crisis

Tessa's world exploded.

She survived Deanna's inheritance.

She sees more, hears more ... understands more.

But more is not always better.

Cody doesn't like what's happening around him. Tessa has walked through hell and she has a lot more to go before she's clear. He plans on standing by her side – her guardian – whether she wants him to be there for her or not.

Jared can't believe all trails lead him into trouble. He'd escaped once. Tried to stay out of the mess since. But a friend is missing, and when he tries to get help, the person he confides in goes missing too.

The vampire world was never ready for Tessa before. The new Tessa?

No one is ready for her.

Vampire in Control
Life couldn't be any worse...

Caught in a web of Deanna's making Tessa struggles to find her role in this new reality.

Cody can't believe how quickly his life has deteriorated. He believes in Tessa. Knew she had what it took and is desperate to do what he can to save her.

Only there are secrets, and like poison, they fester until they are released. Tessa and Cody have to find their way through the maze of lies and deceit to a safe haven on the other side.

The whole gang is caught in life and death struggles as they near the end of this war. *But how close are they and who will survive?*

Sign up to be notified of all Dale's releases here!
http://dalemayer.com/category/blog/

COMPLIMENTARY DOWNLOAD

DOWNLOAD a **_complimentary_** copy of TUESDAY'S CHILD? Just tell me where to send it!

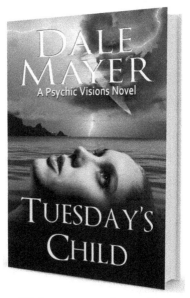

http://dalemayer.com/starterlibrarytc/

Vampire in Chaos

Book #7 of Family Blood Ties

Dale Mayer

PROLOGUE

In Vampire in Conflict we let off with this chapter...

TESSA SAT BESIDE her father as he drove toward the hospital. Cody was in the back seat. She'd been sending texts back and forth between David and Motre and getting them to connect. And to let everyone like Sian know what they were doing and why.

By the time she was done, they were at the hospital. Her father pulled into the underground parking space and stopped the car. The place appeared deserted, but she didn't know or care anymore. As far as she was concerned, this place could burn to the ground.

She'd had enough. Sian hadn't had any luck tracking down Seth, either. And that just sent fear racing down Tessa's spine. She just knew that once he left the country, the chances were very slim that she'd get her brother back. She didn't know if getting him back now would be any different, but to have him go so far away would be terrible. Who knew what these guys would do to him...no. She swore it wasn't going to happen.

That David had taken off on his own was something else she planned to rip him a new one for. He hadn't contacted their father or even Cody to go with him. Like crazy. And stupid. And freaking nuts. She loved both her brothers, but she didn't love what either of them were doing.

Or her mother. In fact, she was pretty disenchanted with all of her family right about now. Except her father, and wasn't that a switch?

They aren't all bad. It's just a tough time. Cody said in a gentle tone. *Give them some space and understanding. Seth isn't responsible, and neither is Rhia. It's a tough time. Hang in there, Tessa. You're tired and hurting emotionally.*

She closed her eyes, loving the way his voice wormed through her heart. It felt so good. It filled the cold empty places inside and made her feel not so alone.

Thanks.

I'm angry, she whispered shamefully. *That this nightmare isn't over. I want it to be over. I want to go out on Friday night with you and your friends and be normal teenagers for a change.*

You might want to be a normal teenager. I'm past that stage, thank you. But his voice was both humorous and wry.

True. She smiled and teased, *You're like really old. Almost your father's age.*

He laughed at that, and she felt infinitely better as his joy lifted her own spirits.

I'm worried about Seth and Mom, she said. *I can't believe Jewel and Ian are once again in trouble. It's always been those two.*

Yes, and I wonder if that is why they've been singled out now, Cody said. *Maybe the scientists want to see the end results. Or maybe they want to move onto the next stage of their testing – whatever that is.*

God help us all if that's the case. She shuddered. *Also, I don't understand what's happening in the human world with Jared finding four bodies today. He has no one left now.*

And that made her sad. She had so much in comparison.

He didn't go back to the home, did he? Cody said. *Surely he's too smart for that?*

He has nowhere else to go. She frowned. *Maybe a friend's house? But how can he? He's expected to be at the home. If he doesn't show up there, they will put out an alarm about him missing. I imagine there is a curfew and possibly some kind of bed check at night.*

I always imagine it to be one step away from prison.

She laughed. *I don't think it's that bad.* Her laughter died and she started texting again. *I'm going to ask him where he is. If nothing else, he can bunk at our house. The thing is empty and there is lots of room. I should have made the offer earlier.*

There was silence. She turned to stare at him. Then got it. She gasped. *Surely you're not jealous?*

He grinned. *Honey, when it comes to other men, I'm never going to be happy to have them sleep under the same roof as you.*

Ha, she motioned outside the car. *See where we are? The only one getting sleep this night will be Jared.*

The gloominess in the underground lot surrounded them as Tessa walked to the entrance with Cody and her father. "Are we going downstairs after David or upstairs to help Motre and Ian?"

"Downstairs after David," her father said immediately. "Then the four of us will go and get Ian and Jewel. Then home. We're not here to fight a battle. Just retrieve a few friends that haven't been able to leave on their own."

Tessa hoped it would be that easy.

It won't be, Cody said with a groan. *It never is.*

He walked over to the big door and pulled it open. "Are you ready?"

Serus walked through first. Tessa next. Cody slipped in behind them. The three of them stared at the staircase that seemed to go on forever. And damn if Serus didn't look up, then down over the railing, then with a wicked grin at Tessa and Cody, he said, "See you at the bottom."

And he dropped over the side.

"What the…" Cody said as he raced to look down. Tessa was already there. She grinned. "He's taken the fastest way."

"Oh no, you don't," Cody said. "I'm not jumping over that edge."

She laughed. "Okay." She jumped to the center of the landing and then down a flight of stairs to the center of the next landing. And repeated it. Again and again.

Cody raced behind her, swearing and crying foul. She laughed and for the first time all day she felt good – in fact, she felt great.

She dropped down several more flights of stairs and realized her father hadn't called up to them. He was long gone. She leaned over the railing and waited for Cody to catch up. There was no visible end to the stairwell. Just blackness.

And her stomach sank. There was no bottom. Her dad had jumped.

But he was a glider. Not a flier.

"Dad?"

No answer.

Her father was gone.

"Dad!"

The cry echoed around and around.

Nothing.

CHAPTER 1

TESSA STARED DOWN the stairwell in horror. Endless darkness stared back. She stretched further out, balancing precariously on the railing, and called frantically one last time, "Dad?"

"Easy, Tessa." Strong arms grabbed her by the waist, tugging her back against a warm chest. "He'll be fine."

She closed her eyes briefly. "Hope so." She rotated in Cody's arms to stare up at him. "We have to find him."

"And we will." He dropped a kiss on her forehead. "But not by repeating his mistake."

Typical. She smirked. "Right. Then race you to the bottom!"

She bolted sideways, laughing down the next flight of stairs. The laughter might not have been appropriate, but it was her way of coping with the fear. She – they – had been through so much. If something had happened to her father...that would be more than she could stand. He was larger than life. He had always seemed indestructible.

Unfortunately, she had proof than no vamp was safe forever. Not even ancients like her father.

She wished he'd waited for her, for them. But he'd always been so in control. So powerful and capable. A take-charge kind of guy.

That didn't mean he was infallible.

She poured her energy into getting down the stairs as fast as she could go. There was a serious silence the deeper they went. She couldn't bear the thought that something might have happened to him. She rounded another flight of stairs, her heart pounding as the tension inside threatened to choke her.

"Dad?" Still no answer. She gritted her teeth, drew in more energy, and jumped again. This time Cody landed in front of her, his hand reaching out to slow her progress. She fell against him as she hit the brakes. "What's the matter?"

"We're at the bottom."

"Really?" She looked around at the empty concrete space. "Oh thank heavens." Her father wasn't lying in a broken heap anywhere. That meant he had to be fine.

"Wher—"

"Shh." Cody placed his finger against her lips and leaned forward to whisper into her ear. "I hear something."

She gasped and spun around. *It's probably Dad.*

With her head cocked, she strained to hear what Cody had heard. She couldn't hear anything. She raised her eyebrow at Cody. *What is it? What did you hear?*

I'm not sure. He slipped around behind her and placed his hand on the wall. *There's no door here, is there?*

Tessa walked closer, shifting her vision to open both her vampire and human eyes. She shook her head. *I can't see any energy on the wall.*

He turned in frustration to stare at the circular stairway they'd descended. *Can you take a look at where we've been? Are we following any tracks? Energy trails?*

She studied the wall at this level. No, nothing. Cody was at her heels, waiting, watching her. She turned slightly to look from a different angle. And stopped. She grabbed his hand

and motioned to the wall. *There is a door here.*

He looked at her as if to make sure. At her nod, he walked closer, his hands slipping across the old surface, looking for the break in the wall.

To the left, she said. *Yes, right there,* as his fingers found the crack. She could see the door shape surrounded in light. And part of the energy in that doorway had come from her father. And…she couldn't be sure, but maybe David as well.

Dad is behind here.

Are you sure? Cody looked over at her, his gaze searching.

Tessa nodded and walked over and kicked the wall where there was a shimmering ball of energy. Cody jumped back as the wall slid inward silently.

What kind of doors are these that they open like this? So quietly.

Old technology. The energy is very young, but the wall is very old.

He shot her a questioning look as she moved past him. *Don't ask,* she said.

She slipped into the space behind the open door. There were no lights shining, but she could see the energy blazing a trail. The corridor ahead was empty and gloomy. Cody moved ahead and led the way.

Careful, she said.

Of course, he murmured, in a deeper tone than he'd used so far. It sent warm tingles down to her toes. If she hadn't been so worried about her dad, she'd be tempted to take advantage of the situation. Cody turned and shot her a look, his steps slowing.

No! She grabbed his shoulder and turned him forward. *Dad comes first.*

First? I like that. He grinned and grabbed her hand. *Let's find your father then.*

But they hadn't made it much further when she heard sounds off to the side. Cody froze, his arm instinctively tucking her behind him.

She snorted at that.

Shhh, he whispered. *Someone is coming.*

RHIA CURLED UP into big wingback chair. Her head pounded and her stomach ached. Something she hadn't expected. Or experienced before. Her thoughts were so confused. Tessa. Seth. Cody. David. There was so much going on in there. Orders. Instructions of some kind.

She buried her head in her hands, the pounding building to the point that she wanted to bang her own head into the ground. She groaned.

"Easy, Rhia," Sian said. "Take it easy."

Rhia's eyes fluttered open, and she gazed into her old friend's face. At least it looked to be Sian. She blinked several times, but it was hard to focus. Everything was blurry. She could barely discern her features. "Sian?"

"Yes." A warm hand brushed the hair back from Rhia's forehead. For the first time, she noticed her forehead was damp, her throat struggling to swallow, the tissues dry and empty of saliva. She choked.

"Easy. Here." Sian held up a glass to her lips. After the initial dryness, Rhia drank with a vengeance.

"Drink it slowly."

Rhia couldn't. She gulped greedily. When the glass was empty, she collapsed backward on the couch. "Thank you."

"Are you feeling better?"

Rhia groaned and closed her eyes. "I'm not sure. Everything is mixed up. I can't make any sense of it."

There was an odd silence.

Rhia's eyes shot open. "What? What don't I know?"

She caught the merest whisper of a grimace before Sian managed to school her features.

"Sian?"

With a heavy sigh, Sian said, "I think you've been drugged – again."

"Oh no." It took her a moment to digest the news. "How? Why?"

Sian shrugged. "We don't know yet."

"How did you find out?"

There was that same ugly pause. Rhia studied her best friend's features, cold fear edging out her confusion. "Sian, What did I do?"

"When we found you, you had chained Tessa up to a bed and were trying to arrange her passage out of the country." Sian paused then added quietly, "You were also trying to inject her with drugs."

Rhia gasped.

Sian, her voice lowered to a hoarse whisper, added, "And apparently you've already arranged to have Seth taken away."

Rhia's chin wobbled. "Oh no. I wouldn't have done that." She stared blindly ahead as multiple conversations rolled through her mind. Bits and pieces were all disjointed and jumbled up. Nothing made any sense. "Where's my son, Sian?"

"Honey, we don't know." Sian shook her head, a sad look on her face. "He was taken to the hospital for treatment after the blood farm."

"Right." Rhia struggled to sit up. "He was getting treatment at the hospital."

"Except the hospital has been taken over by the bad guys. They are holding several of our people in the hospital. We have no idea who is involved."

"No. No. It can't be." Rhia shuddered. "He's supposed to be safe. Getting proper care."

"Yes, and that's what we thought, until you chained up Tessa and started talking all crazy like."

"I'd never hurt Tessa. Not willingly." Rhia closed her eyes. "You know that, right?"

"I know you wouldn't." Sian stroked her hand. "You were doing this so that Tessa would stay safe – at least in your mind. It was the drugs talking, twisting your thoughts, your actions. Making all of it sound very reasonable."

"I didn't hurt her, did I?" Rhia couldn't believe what she was hearing. But she knew she had to know the worst. She had to make amends and before she could do that, she had to know what she'd done.

Sian winced again, her gaze straying down Rhia's body.

And for the first time, maybe because of the drugs wearing off, maybe because Sian had unintentionally brought it to her attention, Rhia could feel the agony rolling toward her head in greasy waves. Her leg was injured, and healing…slowly.

"No, you didn't hurt Tessa, but you fought and she was forced to hurt *you* to protect herself."

"Oh no." Rhia collapsed onto her back, crying out in torment.

DAVID KNEW HIS family was behind him somewhere, but how long until they got here? He had to find Jewel. Who knew what they'd done to her while she'd been a prisoner in this damn hospital?

He was still questioning his decision to go down the stairs. Stairs that seemed to go on forever only to end at a cement basement level showing a huge expanse of open space on the other side of the open door. He stopped to listen, but there was nothing, just an echo of his footsteps. Surely there had to be someone here.

As far as he could see, the damn place was empty. Still, that was much better than being full of assholes. It made no sense that this massive space existed. And as he was lost in all this vast emptiness, Jewel was tucked away somewhere else. Why had he come down here again? Feeling like he'd wasted precious time, he headed back toward the staircase. He should have gone up. Jewel was above him somewhere.

He had to find her.

He stopped and turned to retrace his steps. And heard a voice. He spun around, looking to take cover. He was no longer alone.

JARED STOOD IN the middle of his bedroom and couldn't decide what to do. He hadn't eaten yet. He'd come straight to his room, had a shower, and now he dithered, uncertain of his next move.

He didn't want to be here. It wasn't his room, but it was familiar. He needed food, a place to sleep. He'd spent some time here. Knew some of these kids. But after the last few crazy days, he felt he no longer knew anything. His aunt and uncle were both dead. He tried to feel sorry for them but couldn't. Not after all they'd done to his father.

But they'd been murdered. If it had only been one of them killed, then he'd have been able to toss it off as a random act. A burglary gone wrong. But to have targeted both, well...his mind couldn't help but lock onto the fact that they'd both had regular dealings with the blood farm coalition and maybe with all the craziness there, the men behind that nightmare were cleaning up.

Or the middlemen were cutting ties to save their asses.

Or just as likely the humans busy selling their own people were trying to get the hell free of their own web of deceit.

Either way, he hoped the investigation uncovered a shit ton more people involved. The only way to clean this up was to purge the whole lot from society. He didn't know how far the disease had spread, but they needed to stop it before it spread any further. He hoped that none of his friends and their families were involved but as he stared out the window of his bedroom, he figured that the chances were good that some of them were. This was a relatively small community.

He hoped Tessa was all right.

Of course she was likely out doing something constructive. Something proactive to stop this nightmare. He was stuck here.

"Hey, Jared."

He turned to see a new kid he didn't recognize at his door. "Yeah, what's up?"

"The manager wants to speak with you. He said go down and grab some dinner then meet him in his office right after."

His stomach sinking at the thought, Jared kept his face schooled with disinterest and nodded. "Thanks. Will do."

The kid took off.

And Jared headed down. He might not want to eat, but if he had to take off again tonight, he needed his strength. That meant food.

Then he'd deal with the manager.

SERUS SLIPPED BEHIND the wall. His leg still ached from that crazy ass landing. He thought for sure he'd have ended up at the bottom of the stairwell with both legs broken once he realized how deep the stairs went. He'd lived for centuries – how had he not known about this place? Not that he was in this area all that often. Why would he be? It was a hospital – like he needed that. His body was damn good at doing what it was supposed to do – heal itself.

Besides, who'd have thought this vast dungeon existed below?

Somewhere a hundred years back, there'd been an outcry about needing medical facilities. He couldn't remember the arguments for and against. He'd thought it had been a complete waste, but whatever, if the Council wanted to emulate the humans, so what? He knew Rhia had held the same belief. After Tessa was born, not quite normal but not quite abnormal, Rhia had consulted a few of the older vampires instead of the doctors. Deanna, the oldest of them all, had been one of them. She'd retreated from society soon after.

And always in the background, the hospital had functioned, but more as a developmental place. Or so they thought.

He frowned thinking about that. Developmental? As in researching developments in the vampire genetics? He had to see this for what it was. Likely what it had always been. Was this the original headquarters for the blood farm? Could it be?

It galled him to think that this could have been – no, he had to be honest – *had* been operating under his nose. Because he hadn't *wanted* to see, he *hadn't* seen. And now look.

His beloved Rhia was under the influence of drugs. She'd helped ship his oldest son somewhere 'safe' where he couldn't be found, and he was searching this damn mausoleum for his other son. When would this ever end? He should be tucked up in bed, his wife at his side, with all his kids safe and sound.

It was well past time for this shit to be over.

CHAPTER 2

TESSA SLIPPED INTO the room, close behind Cody. They skulked in as far as they could away from the footsteps to try and come around from behind and catch the person by surprise.

Where did they go? she asked.

No idea.

They can't have gone far.

No. Or they haven't gone anywhere – they are just waiting for us to show our hand.

She froze. *Oh no. That makes way too much sense.*

Shh. He peered around the doorway. *I think I heard them.*

Them? Do you really think it's more than one person? Tessa thought about it then replied. *Let me take a look. I should be able to tell if there is more than one person.* Hopefully it would be her father and brother.

Cody stepped back but stayed close, his warm breath sliding down her neck and under her shirt. And despite the worries, despite the circumstances, her missing brother, her father...she was so very grateful to be here with him. Well, maybe not here...but at least with him. They'd been through so much...and had come out so wonderfully well that she found it hard to regret this.

She made a quick movement and peeked around the corner. Cody squeezed her shoulder in warning. She pulled back, her mind processing what she'd seen. She turned to stare into Cody's questioning gaze. *There are four sets of energy. Dad. David. And two others – I don't know who.*

What? Really?

At her nod and wide grin, he reached out and hugged her.

She laughed silently and stepped back. *The only thing*, she said, *I can't tell if they were all together or if one is following the other. I need to take another look.*

We don't know where they are, and that's a problem.

She nodded and studied the energy around the pair of them. She hadn't seen any odd energy here. So the other two people had arrived from a different direction. *Now what do we do?*

There's really nothing else to do but follow. He stepped out behind the wall, Tessa's hand in his.

He turned left.

Tessa tugged him to a halt. *We need to go this way.*

He looked at her. She nodded to the right. He rolled his eyes and turned right. *It's a little irritating, you know?*

What? But she knew. She tried but couldn't hold the giggle back. Her voice, light as a feather, whispered '*Sorry*' into his mind.

Cody squeezed her hand gently. *Don't be. It is part of the joy of being with you.*

You sure it doesn't make you feel...I don't know... maybe insecure?

No. He shot her a disgusted look. *My self–confidence is not affected by your abilities. I am not that shallow.*

That his voice had some gruffness to it made her glance over. Surely he wasn't really put out by her, was he? She tried to keep her thoughts to herself, but he heard her.

He stopped and turned to face her, a rueful look on his

face. He snagged her chin and looked deep into her eyes. *Never hold back that wonderful light inside you because you think it would upset me. I'm a bigger man than that. And even if I would have problem with it, I'd want to be that better man.*

Ah Lord, he was killing her with his goodness. She was proud to know him. Honored to be with him.

No, you are something. He shook his head, something special shining in his gaze. *You make me so much more when I am with you.*

She smiled. She reached up and kissed him, her lips brushing his with the lightest of touches. *Good. Remember that when you get pissed off at me.*

Cody tried to deepen the kiss, but she pulled back with a smirk. *So not the time. But hold that thought. Let's go after Dad and David.*

Right. He turned her in the right direction. *Lead off.*

"WHERE THE HELL are they?" Ian muttered to Motre. "Surely David and Serus's group should be here by now?"

"They most likely are." Motre pulled his phone out and checked for any texts for what had to be the tenth time in the last ten minutes. "They said David was on his way up here, but look at where we are. We haven't stopped moving. I've given David some rough directions, but it's not like we have a map of this damn place or kept them in the loop of what level we were operating on."

Ian nodded, pulling out his cell phone from the pocket of his stolen pants. Map? That he might be able to help with. The phone buzzed in his hand. He read the text out loud. "Hey, this is Tessa. She and Serus have become separated in the basement."

Motre spun back to face him. "What? Did you say they got separated?" He smacked his hand on the side of his head. "Like what the hell. How do they always end up like that?"

"Easy." With a grin, Ian answered, "It seems to come naturally to them."

With a snort, Motre turned and approached the next door. "Come on, then. Let's get on with it. Before we have to go and rescue the others."

"Ha," Ian laughed. "I wouldn't mind that happening for a change. Usually it's the other way around and Tessa's the one riding to the rescue."

"Too true." With a shake of his head, Motre reached out to turn the knob on the door.

❧ ❧

SERUS STOPPED IN place. There was a sound off to his left. Damn it. He felt like he'd been playing hide and go seek with someone. A game. Not for the first time, he had to wonder if it wasn't his son David. He pulled out his cell phone and sent him a text.

I'm hiding in the basement of the hospital, looking for you. Are you okay?

He stayed in place waiting for an answer, an ear straining to locate the other person. He shifted positions, waiting for his phone to light up. Waiting for something. He heard a noise to his right. He caught his breath and closed his eyes, using all his energy to pick up the stealthy movement.

His phone lit up. David. Then his heart plummeted at David's message. *I'm being stalked. I'm almost at the stairs again.*

Serus spun around. The stairs were on the right.

He grinned.

And stepped out into the open.

"David?"

There was a startled silence, then a hard gasp. "Dad?"

And David stepped out of the shadows.

Serus grinned, stepping forward to slap David on the shoulder. "Glad to see you, son."

"You too. Where's Tessa?"

Serus snorted. "She's supposed to be behind me. I took the fast way down, but I'm sure they are still coming. It's a long way down."

"It is." David frowned and looked around. "But honestly, it doesn't take that long. She should be here."

"She's with Cody. And yeah, it shouldn't take that long." And the fact they weren't here was worrisome. But as he'd been walking forward all the time, it wasn't likely that they'd have caught up to him yet.

David had his cell phone out. "I'm texting her now."

"I wouldn't do that if I were you." The voice came from the shadows. "In fact, you need to hand that phone to me."

And out of the shadows came two old vamps all dressed in black – including black gloves. Serus instinctively shoved his own gloved hand into his pocket, reassured by the feel of the spike he'd refused to hand over at the Council Hall. There were too many assholes roaming around to give that up.

"Who the hell are you?"

"None of your business. You're trespassing, and we don't think much of strangers."

The second vamp stepped forward just as David's finger hit send on the message.

"Too late," he said in a loud voice, pocketing his phone.

"The message is gone."

"Good. We don't have all that much to do lately. Now we can have a bit of sport with whoever you're expecting to join you."

Serus's insides cramped. God damn it. What the hell had just happened?

※ ※

WENDY CURLED UP in the chair in the corner of the Council common room. She'd only been here a couple of times, but never alone. The place was huge, full of official vamps doing important things. There was an aura of secret doings, secret plans. Big things afoot. People rushed from room to room, and still others arrived in a panic. Throughout it all, she sat in the corner, out of the way, and watched.

She understood that David had taken off after Jewel. That Tessa, her father, and Cody had left soon after. She'd wanted to go, but she was tired, scared, and not fully healed from the car accident. And she'd only hold them back. She hated that. She'd gone into the mine after Ian but now that damn hospital...it was freaking scary. Besides, as David had said to her when they were alone, she couldn't go. She'd been seen, and the security staff would be on alert for her. She was better off staying and helping here.

But how? She barely knew anyone. And had no idea how to make herself useful.

Her eye caught sight of one woman walking toward her. Sian. Now that was a scary woman. Anyone who could walk with one foot in the human and vamp worlds was very good at that whole balancing act.

She could teach Tessa a thing or two. She was also Rhia's

friend. Wendy stood up as Sian reached her. "Hi"

Sian's gaze was assessing and concerned. "Hi, Wendy. How are you holding up?"

Wendy's bottom lip wobbled. "I really wanted to go to the hospital to help rescue Ian, but…"

Sian immediately shook her head. "Not until your head heals, and not likely even then. Not if the hospital staff saw you as a threat. They will have your face plastered all over the security screens."

Wendy winced. "Yeah, I figured."

"But there is something you can do for me, if you wouldn't mind?"

"Sure." Wendy was happy to have something, anything to do to take her mind off what might be happening. She kept looking toward the front door, expecting Ian to walk in at any moment. That he hadn't just scared her all the more.

"Rhia shouldn't be alone right now, but I have things to do. Could you sit with her?" Sian made a small motion with her hand. "She's not likely to wake up, but I don't want to leave her alone. Just in case."

"I'd be happy to watch over her."

"Good." Sian led her to one of the private rooms in the back. Wendy tried to keep track of where they were going but quickly became lost. She opened a door on her right, and sure enough, Rhia was asleep in an odd daybed–looking thing. "If she wakes up, please come and find me."

Wendy jolted at that. "Umm, how? I got lost just coming here."

Sian laughed. "Do you have a cell phone?"

"I check it constantly," she confessed, pulling it out. "Just in case Ian contacts me. Stupid, since I know he doesn't have his phone."

"I do understand. In situations like this, logic doesn't matter." Sian read off her own number slow enough for Wendy to add it to her contact list.

"Good. Text me if she wakes up. I'll be back in an hour or so."

And with that, Sian took off and left Wendy alone.

☙ ❧

GORAN SWAM THROUGH the currents. Water washed over his head and into his nose and mouth, filling his lungs. He was drowning...in something. He coughed and choked, gasping for air.

"Hey, sir, take it easy. We're pulling tubes out to make it easier on you," a strange female voice said.

He choked again as something was jerked out of his throat. He jutted into a sitting position, groaning. Opening his eyes, he stared at the female vamp in front of him, then collapsed back again. "Who are you?" he gasped in a raspy voice.

Then groaned at the pain in his throat. It felt like someone had jabbed something down there and drained all the liquid out. He could barely swallow. As he was sure he'd been drowning, how did that make any sense?

"Try not to talk. Your throat is going to feel pretty rough right now."

He snorted but refrained from giving his usual tart response. It would just hurt him more. But as thoughts of fire started to fill his mind, followed by the sensation of drowning again, he had to know. "What happened?"

"You were in a bad car accident. The vehicle you were riding in was hit by a semi-truck."

He lay there trying to cast his mind back to the event she was talking about. There'd been something about squealing brakes and screams, but he didn't remember much more. "And the drowning."

There was an odd silence. He turned his head slightly to see her face, but it was schooled into a professional mask. Damn, he should have been watching her face while he'd asked that question. "Where am I?"

She jumped at that question. "You're in the Council Hall."

"Well, thank heavens for something," he muttered, already feeling his throat start to ease as the saliva slipped down his throat. In fact, most of him was starting to feel better, a long ways away from good...but he no longer wanted to roll over and die. He sat up gingerly, waiting for some body part to start screaming. But there was no more pain. "I feel great."

She frowned. "You shouldn't be moving so much."

"Yeah," he eyed her carefully. "Why not?"

"You've been unconscious for quite a while. We thought you might not wake up."

With one last admonishing look as if that would make him behave, she walked out the room, her hands carrying a tray of whatever she'd taken out of his throat.

Why his throat? If he'd been unconscious, that didn't mean he wasn't breathing. Hating the panic slicking through him, Goran couldn't resist checking his body a little more closely. No broken bones, no cuts or even major bruising. In fact, he didn't appear to be injured in any way – except for a horrible headache. As he lay there, an angry ball in his gut forming, a large male vamp walked in. Dr. Hansen. Goran frowned at the man. "Why the tube down my throat?"

The doctor walked closer. "You were having trouble

breathing. As you were unconscious and showing no signs of returning to us, we took a long term view and made sure to keep your airway open."

"Then you didn't drug me?" He studied the doctor's face, looking for signs of deception. Signs of blood farm bullshit.

The doctor raised his eyebrows but answered mildly. "Your friends noted your fear of drugs on your file. I assure you, the only medication you were given was something you needed." He motioned to Goran now. "As in I administered medication to wake you up."

Goran glared at him. He didn't know what to believe. "How did I get here from the accident?"

At that the doctor grinned. "You were brought here by your son and his friends."

Oh thank God. Cody was safe.

"Apparently you owe your life to a certain young lady who can walk in daylight. She hauled you out of the truck and into the car before they drove you here."

Tessa. Goran grinned. Damn, she was good people. He swung his legs over the side of the bed. "Where are my clothes?"

"You can't leave yet. The drugs are unpredictable." At Goran's flat stare, he added, "You need to stay here for twenty-four hours to make sure there are no side effects."

Goran was on him like a flash. He had his hand around the doc's throat before he had the last word out. "Side effects? What kind of side effects?"

The doctor glared down at him and refused to answer. Goran squeezed his fist tighter.

"Goran?" Sian's voice snapped at him from the doorway. "Stop that. He's been helping you."

"He gave me drugs and won't tell me the side effects."

Sian reached up and peeled Goran's hands off the poor man's neck. "How can he? You're choking him to death."

"Why the drugs to wake me up, and who okayed the drugs?"

"I did, and so did Serus. You needed to come back. We couldn't just let you die from lack of sustenance, could we?"

Goran turned to look at her. She was good people too, but why the hell would she have okayed the drugs?

"Your system needed the shock. It had been under so much stress, so many injuries, that it was just floating. We needed you back so we could get you to feed." She held up a large mug of deep dark blood. "If you'd stayed unconscious, we were going to have to force feed you, and as we tried that and it didn't work out so well…"

"The drowning?" Damn.

She titled her head, her gaze widening in surprise. "Maybe that's what it felt like. We had trouble with the feeding tube."

He glared at the two of them. "I'm awake now, so no more drugs. Shouldn't have been the need for any in the first place."

The doctor stepped back, shook out his coat, and said, "Duly noted. Next time I'll let you die." He spun on his heels and walked out.

"Harrumph." Goran stared after him, a frown between his eyebrows. "What's his problem?"

Sian laughed. "Well, maybe that he's been trying to help you and you decided to almost kill him as thanks."

Goran slanted a sideways look in her direction. "Where are the kids?"

When Sian looked down at her feet, he reached out and grabbed her shoulder. "Sian," he growled. "What's wrong?"

She winced. "Maybe you better sit down."

"I'll stand," he snapped in an ominous voice, taking the mug from her. "Spill."

And spill she did, giving him a few more details of the accident, even going so far as to show him the video that had gone viral of Tessa and Cody rescuing the vamps, then talking about David taking off, Ian and Motre in the hospital, Serus, Cody, and Tessa going after them all. And she ended with the worst. Rhia.

When he heard the last bit, he sat down on the side of the bed and finished his drink in silence. Finally, in a harsh whisper, he said, "Where does all this end?"

∂∘ ∘⋖

JARED SCARFED DOWN the beef and potatoes, wondering with half a mind if the food was poisoned. He sure as hell hoped not but for all the dead bodies he'd tripped over lately, death was hard to ignore. He also needed the sustenance. Not to mention being damn hungry. How Tessa survived on granola bars, he didn't know. And blood. Lord, how could he forget that she drank blood?

Human blood.

Although according to what he'd seen, they fought against having the real stuff in a big way. Synthetic blood had long been the recommended source of food for vampires. Until you factored in the old way of thinking and that massive group of rogue vampires. Yeah, like he wanted to spend more time thinking about *those* assholes.

"Hey, Jared. You look like you could use another plateful."

Jared stopped and stared at his almost empty plate. It had great flavor, and he was still hungry. "Umm, actually, if you don't mind, I could use a second helping."

He hadn't even finished speaking when his plate was whisked away, refilled, and back under his nose. "Wow, thanks."

"No problem. We take care of our own."

There was an overly jovial note in the cook's voice. Jared glanced up casually and tried to read the implication in the other guy's face. But it was hard. He didn't know the people here. Not enough to understand the nuances in their voices.

"Right, Jared?" the cook asked encouragingly. "It's important to stick together."

Jared nodded, and the cook smiled with relief. Now if only Jared knew what the cook was talking about. And what Jared had just agreed to.

He'd just about finished his second plate when the manager stopped at the doorway. "Jared, you done?"

Jared swallowed hard and took the last couple of bites and nodded. He stood up with his plate, but the cook took it from him and nudged him toward the boss. "Go. I'll clean this up for you tonight. You've had a tough day."

Yeah, he had. But from the look on the manager's face, Jared didn't think the shit was over yet.

He followed the manager into the small office and took the seat pointed out to him. "Now, Jared, I just got off the phone with the police. I'd like to hear about what happened in your own words."

Oh, that was a surprise. The police report wasn't enough? Feeling like he was walking through a minefield, Jared carefully retold the same story he'd given the police. The manager frowned, never taking his eyes off him the whole time. Jared could just feel that probing gaze looking for something wrong in his story. A lie? Something to show him that Jared might have seen or done something other than what he'd said he'd done?

When he fell silent, the manager sat there, thinking. He pivoted a pen from end to end on his fingers. "Well, sounds like you had one hell of a day. It also presents us with some problems. As you no longer have any living relatives, that means you need to go into foster care."

Jared's heart sank. He hadn't seen this coming. "Really? Why can't I stay with friends for the next few months until I'm eighteen? That's only like three and a half months."

"With no parent or living guardian, by law you are a ward of the state now. That means a foster home."

"Then I'll stay here," Jared said reasonably. At least here he could go to the same school. One day he'd just not come home.

"No, you can't. We have kids in need here. It's not a group home for healthy individuals as you know. It was a stopgap measure for you while the doctors kept you under observation."

The manager leaned forward and studied Jared closer. "Are you experiencing any side effects from those drugs?"

Jared held his breath, considering. If he said he was, he might be able to stay here, but did he want that? He'd come across two dead men here and there was some kind of revolt going on. If he said no, then they'd ship him off to a group home – and who the hell knew where? He wanted to finish his term at school and then be on his own.

"No, I guess not," he said. "Except the headaches. They are bad sometimes."

The manager frowned.

"Headaches. That can't be good. I've got two doctors coming tomorrow. I'll get them to check you over. They'll have the final say as to whether you stay or go."

Jared stood up, already feeling the small satisfaction of being safe with a roof over his head and a full stomach fading. "Right. I'll head up to my room. I'm really tired."

And he made good on his escape.

CHAPTER 3

T ESSA STUDIED THE energy pathways her father and brother had taken as she and Cody walked forward. From what she could see, they'd been on horizontal pathways, joined up, then joined by someone else – no, two someone else's. She walked in a circle until she understood the pattern then turned back to Cody and explained. She pointed down the direction they'd gone. "They were taken this way."

"Taken?" he asked, slowly staring in the direction she'd pointed. "We don't know that though, do we?"

She studied the energy again. "The newcomers are behind them, pushing David and Dad ahead of them."

"Damn." Cody headed into the darkness. "I wonder if it's the same group as from the blood farm."

"I don't know why it would be. The blood farm isn't operational down here. In fact, this looks like it's been deserted for over a century."

"Hard to say," Cody said. "The hospital above is connected, so it makes sense that anything going on down here is too."

She hated to think that, but it made sense. "Maybe David triggered a sensor when he opened one of the doors. Otherwise, why would there be anyone here on this level? There are what – forty, fifty floors above us?"

"Unless they were here for something else, guarding something?"

"And that just begs the question of what?" She searched the gloom around them. "There's nothing here."

She hated this. "We're supposed to be helping free Jewel and Ian. Not getting caught up in these issues again."

Cody stopped in front of her. "Can you text Ian?"

She pulled out her phone. "Here is a text from David. Saying where they are." She looked around. "Which we know anyway, but they aren't here now." She studied her phone. "We have very limited connectivity."

"Makes sense being so deep underground. It would also explain why David isn't here when his text said he would be. Probably took a while to send."

"I'll send one to Ian regardless and let him know we're at the bottom of the staircase and there are unfriendlies here too."

She hit the send button and the tiny pinwheel started churning, but it didn't send. Damn. She pocketed the phone and looked around. They'd been getting deeper and deeper into the empty building. It appeared to be made from rock and cement. Old, as in very old. "Maybe this foundation is older than what's up top."

"What difference does it make if it is? It's still connected to what's up above," Cody said, almost absentmindedly.

"I'm just thinking that maybe whatever, or whoever is down here is old or has been here for a very long time. They may have been connected to what's above at one time, but there is little to no energy coming down that stairwell, so they aren't going up very often."

"Unless they have an easier way of travelling."

She frowned. "True. Very true. I wonder if they have another entrance."

From behind them came a deep and very old voice. "There's another exit. It helps us to avoid people we don't want to meet."

Cody and Tessa had both frozen at the sound of the voice. As one, they spun slowly around to see a very old vampire in front of them. He held up a finger to his lips for silence and motioned them off to one side. "You must go quietly in here. There are eyes and ears everywhere."

And he moved to the left. "Come, follow me."

And he disappeared into the shadows. Actually, it was as if the shadows closed around him.

❧ ❦

GORAN WAITED IMPATIENTLY for Sian to return to ask about his damn clothes. Taking his off for a woman was one thing, having his clothes taken off him for a damn doctor to run tests while he was out cold was quite another. He still had his boxers on, but he was rather desperate for his pants.

She chose that moment to walk in.

He almost jumped her. "Sian, where are my clothes? Did you take them away?"

Sian frowned, looking around. He thought she'd been about to make some kind of stupid excuse to keep him there, but she'd surprised him again when she said, "They should be here."

After a cursory glance around, she added, "There's no reason for them not to be here." With her hands on her hips, she said, "It's not like this is a hospital, for crying out loud."

With her help, they searched the room.

"Aha!" he said when he opened a bottom cupboard and found his clothes neatly stacked in the back. "Here they are."

Sian stepped out while he got dressed. Which he did quickly. He opened the door to let her back in, but there was no sign of her. He waited for her to return. He would go out there on his own, but he wasn't up to a session with the doctors telling him he needed to stay here. Screw that. He was leaving.

He'd called out mentally to Serus a couple of times, but there'd been no answer. He didn't like that. It took a lot for their mindspeak to not work. And it usually meant one of them was unconscious. Now the last time had been his fault as he'd been the one out cold, but he was awake now and given that, where the hell was Serus?

A rap on the door sounded. He opened the door. Sian.

"Good." He nodded at her. "Now where is everyone?"

Sian wrinkled up her face.

"No idea. Dr. Hansen isn't around that I can see. He's only here to help out, so maybe he left to get some rest."

"Help out?"

Sian searched his gaze. "Remember all the vamps that you were supposed to be bringing to the Council?"

"Oh right. Forgot about those little shits. Are they okay?"

Sian shook her head. "No. One of the three you brought from the mall was killed in the accident. The other two men appear to be enhanced and are slowly dying. We're trying to get what little information from them that we can." She peered around the hallway then gave him the all-clear signal. "The young vamps are in bad shape, but they will pull through. One of them is Councilman Baker's son, and he says they've all been forced to use enhancements or be killed."

"No way. Not his own son?"

"Yes." Sian shrugged. "They were told to think of it as an improvement."

"Seems like lab rat type of experiments to me."

Sian turned a corner. "Absolutely. I think the kids agree. Apparently it was more of a numbers game. Something to do with being short on manpower and needing more men. They weren't given a choice."

"Ha. So we knock out their clones and they just turn to their own families to build up their numbers. That's just sick." And disgusting. Goran made a mental note about Councilman Baker. He'd be sure to find the asshole and pay him back for getting his own son involved. "It's not a shining hour for vampires," he said quietly.

"No," Sian answered. "It's definitely not. Then again, the humans aren't proving worthy either."

Goran shot her a look. Delicately, he asked, "How is Taz?"

"He's fine." She beamed. "I meant all the humans selling their own kin for the blood farm. The Human Council is in a hell of a mess. Between poisoning each other, selling off each other, and generally just being greedy, the human race needs to be culled."

Such violence from one so gentle was unusual. Goran wasn't sure what was going on, but with Sian being the liaison between the two Councils, she must have observed a gutful of nasty behaviors. He decided silence was the best avenue. Then she did it.

"The Human Council," she said, "wants Tessa to go through the human population and sort them out the way she did at the meeting."

"What?"

"Yeah," Sian said, shooting him a dark look. "It worked so well there apparently, they want her to tell them who is good and who is bad. So they can destroy the ones involved."

"Ah hell. They can't use her like that. Especially if she understands what they plan to do with the bad guys. It's one thing to kill during war; it's tougher to be the decision-maker as to who should live and who should die."

"I know," Sian said. "Taz and I have both taken that stance. The trouble is the humans aren't listening."

Goran nodded. "Don't worry about it. They'll have to go through Serus and Rhia before that can happen." He snorted. "No way is she going to do that. Hell, I'll tell them myself."

"I wish someone would," Sian said, fatigue in her voice. "They call almost every hour."

"What does Tessa have to say about this?"

And damn if he didn't see a whisper of something cross Sian's face. His stomach sank. He groaned. "I forgot. They all left without me."

Sian gave a shout of laughter. "Well yeah, you were comatose so they had to go without you."

He glared at her. "I'm never too sick to go hunting."

"Well." She glared back at him. "This time you were. And would have stayed that way except for the drugs that brought you back."

"Then I'm going after them right now." He strode off in the direction of the front door, his mind churning. *Serus? Where the hell are you?*

"Wait. Goran?"

He spun to see Sian running to catch up. She was trying to pull something out of her pocket.

"Here." She held out his cell phone. "You didn't give me a chance to give you this."

He groaned. He hadn't even thought to look for that damned thing. Maybe he wasn't as well as he thought he was. Sheepish, he accepted the phone, noting the fatigue around her eyes. She should be resting.

He checked for text messages. None. Damn. He'd need to send a few of his own and figure out where everyone was. Good thing Sian had remembered.

"Thanks for this." He lifted his phone slightly before shoving it into his pocket. "You look tired. Maybe you should go lie down for a bit."

"I will." She hesitated. "Goran, have you been able to mindspeak with Serus?"

"No." He spun around, his long coat swirling around his legs, and stalked to the front door. "Why do you think I'm going up there right now?"

"Don't go alone," she cried out from behind. "You have no idea what you're walking into."

"I hope it's a trap," he snarled, half turning back to look at her. "I've had a long rest. Now I'm so ready to start kicking some vamp ass."

And he slammed the door behind him.

WENDY LOOKED UP as Sian rushed back inside the room. Oh thank heavens. She'd been sitting here terrified that Rhia would wake up and be the not–nice Rhia. What could Wendy have done then?

The relief must have been obvious as Sian smiled and said, "No worries. I didn't forget you."

"I was just afraid she'd wake up crazy-like and I wouldn't know what to do with her." She glanced down at the sleeping woman she respected more than any other. She reached over to stroke Rhia's hand and said, "I wouldn't want to have to hurt her."

"None of us do," Sian said. "Goran has gone to the hospital to help the others."

"He's that much better?" At Sian's nod, Wendy's eyes filled with tears. Great for Goran, but poor Ian. There'd been no word about him yet. "I thought they'd be back by now. How could this even have happened in the first place?"

"I have no idea. But apparently a lot has been happening under our noses that we didn't know about."

"So true." Wendy nodded. "Tessa had planned to go to the school and talk to the principal. Have him warn the school kids. I wonder if I should instead." She looked around the small comfortable room and frowned. "I feel useless. Everyone is doing something. I'm not even human, but here I am thinking I should go to the school. Or somewhere. Do something to help."

"Not alone," Sian said instantly. "It's too dangerous."

"I'm no hero," Wendy said, "but I don't want anyone else hurt."

"No, neither do I." Sian frowned. "If I got someone else to keep an eye on Rhia, we could both go."

"What time is it?" Wendy asked. "We'd have to wait until the school was open."

Sian checked her watch. "It's evening for the humans. No one will be at the school."

Wendy sighed. "Unfortunately, that just means the asshole vampires are out hunting."

"True enough. We're smart women. Let's see if we can't come up with something helpful for you to do in the meantime."

IAN AND MOTRE pushed the door wide open. And stopped. Two vamps slept soundly. Neither woke up at their arrival.

"Drugs."

"Do you think so?" Both men were lying lax, not a normal relaxed sleep. Ian glanced over at Motre. He shook his head, his hard glance going from face to face. "I don't recognize either of them."

Ian studied the room, but it was much like the others. "Do you think they are on our side?"

Motre shrugged, clearly not knowing the answer.

Ian suggested, "We could wake them up. If they are on our side, they could help."

"And if they aren't?" Motre opened the door again and stepped back out into the hallway. "Besides, drugged like that, they won't be any help. And given that I don't know either of them, I'm not willing to take that chance. Better they stay here and we mark the location of the room somehow. That way we can always come back for them."

Ian nodded, clicking on the GPS to mark where they were. He added a note about being unsure of the men inside.

"Done?" Motre asked.

Ian nodded.

Back in the hallway, a second door opened several feet down to their left. Two male vamps in lab coats with clipboards in hand were deep in conversation as they walked toward Ian. He shoved his fists in his pockets and murmured to Motre, "Let's just walk past them."

"Huh." Motre said. "I was thinking something along the lines of...this." And he lunged forward toward the two approaching men.

Ian watched in shock as the vamps tried to defend themselves way too late for Motre, who'd been primed to beat the crap out of the first decent target. When he finally stood, his chest was heaving and his fists bloodied, his grin happy and wide. "Damn, that felt good."

He reached down and grabbed one man with each hand and said, "Open the door, will you?"

Shaking his head and looking both ways to make sure no one had seen Motre in action, Ian pushed the door open. Motre walked deep enough into the room that he could drop the two unconscious men in the middle. After a moment, he approached the closest bed and lifted a corner of the sheet covering the patient. "Well, that changes things."

The man was shackled to the bed.

"I guess that means they are prisoners." Ian walked over to the other male and checked him over. "Same thing here."

"Can you open them? If so, let's switch the men around."

It took a bit of tricky maneuvering, but eventually they had the two drugged men on the floor and the two medical staff members lying in their place, wearing their shackles. Satisfied, Ian stepped back and laughed. "I'd like to see their faces when they wake up."

"Speaking of which," Motre checked out both of the unconscious doctors and removed two cell phones from their pockets. "Let's delay their rescue for a bit longer."

He motioned to the hallway. "Let's go."

They slipped back out and kept walking toward the next door. The one the medical staff had come out of. Ian pushed it open and walked in as if he belonged there. In his disguise, who'd know?

And he came face to face with Dr. Horander.

The one man who did know Ian.

Shit.

ॐ ॐ

JARED SNUCK UP the back stairs to his room, his mind incessantly hearing the manager and cook's words. What had the cook meant about sticking together? And in that tone of voice as if to say Jared would understand. But the only thing he understood was the creepiness in both the words and tone. Had that been in reference to the vigilante talk – not that he had any way to know that Jared had heard that conversation, or was it in reference to the two dead men Jared had found? But the cook shouldn't know about that either. And if he did, Jared wanted nothing to do with the sticking together part. That was too damn scary. The manager was too damn scary. There could be no sticking together because as soon as something went wrong, there was going to be someone else dead.

Jared had no intention of being the next dead person.

And what was he supposed to do about a foster home? Like really? He had what, three and a half months left until he turned eighteen. He'd started school late so he was older than the other kids. He'd made up for it by working hard. Now he was graduating with the others his age.

Not that any of that mattered. He still had nowhere else to go. And if that didn't make him sick inside...he had friends, good friends, but he'd lost track of most of them over this mess. Surely there was a better place for him than with a foster family. He needed someone in a position of authority, human authority, to lend a hand. He snorted. Too bad he didn't know anyone like that.

He threw himself on the bed and rubbed his hands over his face. He just wanted to finish his schooling and go on to be an engineer.

A commotion out in the hallway was followed by a loud knock on his door. Shit. He sat up slowly and made his way over. "Who is it?"

"Hey, is that Jared? As in Jared who'd been at the crazy blood farm? It's Aaron and Clarissa."

Jared opened the door in a rush. Sure enough, there were four or five faces he recognized from the mine rescue. Awesome! He grinned. "Hey, what are you guys doing here?"

"We came to visit Tobias. He's down at the end of the hallway. He's the one that told us you were here. Come out and join us."

Join them? His confusion must have been apparent as Clarissa hooked her arm through his and dragged him down the hallway. "We're only allowed to be here for two hours, so we can't waste any of it."

Outside Tobias's doorway, she stopped and smiled up at him. But her tone was serious as she said, "Are you okay? I've been so worried. We lost touch after that crazy rescue and I didn't know how to find you. I asked the police, but they said you were getting the care you needed." She squeezed his hand. "I even went by your school but didn't recognize anyone."

She had? Wow. Jared wanted to shout with joy. He hadn't been forgotten by everyone. He grinned at her, happy to know this charming young woman had cared enough to go looking. Some of his loneliness fell away. He reached into his pocket. "I have a new phone."

She gasped, pulled out hers, and they quickly exchanged numbers. "What are you doing here at the home? Are you sick?" she asked as they walked into the room, already stuffed with Tobias's friends.

He winced. "Honestly – I'm not sure." He quickly brought her up to date on the last few days' events. The room fell silent as he stopped speaking, all faces turned toward him.

"Man, you are one bad news magnet, dude."

"Yeah, I know." Jared shrugged. "I didn't do anything to bring this on."

"You didn't have to obviously, trouble found you."

"I am sorry about your family," Clarissa said gently, her fingers squeezing his hand again. He nodded. He didn't think this was the time to tell anyone what his relatives had been like or that as far as he was concerned, they deserved what they got.

"What about a place to stay, surely you don't have to stay here?" Clarissa motioned to Tobias, who was connected to an oxygen tank, a pale grin on his face. "He's here for medical attention. And he's doing great. Hopefully he can go home soon. But you, your uncle isn't there anymore, so what's going to happen to you?"

"Yeah, who knows?" Jared stared down at his feet. "The manager here said something about a foster home."

The room erupted in loud groans, Jared included. "I know, right. I only need a couple more months and then I'm eighteen and don't have to worry anymore."

"Do you get your uncle's place now that he's dead? Maybe you could live there alone?" Clarissa asked, her voice low, intimate.

Damn. He swallowed and said, "I hadn't thought of that. I have no idea who inherits his place."

It's not that he wanted to live there, but if it *was* his, he'd sell it and buy something else. Except this was his uncle he was talking about. He snorted. "But I doubt my uncle left it to me. Most likely to his sister."

"Except you said she'd been murdered too," said someone in the back of the group. Jared couldn't remember his name.

"So maybe you are going to inherit both places."

"Now that would be cool."

Several others popped up with their opinion about that issue and what he should do. He held up a hand to still the flow. "Remember that trouble magnet part?" he said, raising his eyebrows. "More likely they are going to try and pin both murders on me, and I'll spend the rest of my life behind bars for something I didn't do."

Silence descended.

Jared understood. After all, what could anyone say to that?

CHAPTER 4

TESSA STARED AT the retreating figure.

In her mind, Cody murmured. *We don't have much choice. We need to follow him.*

I know, but I don't like it.

She stepped in behind Cody as he cautiously followed in the stranger's tracks.

Who do you think he is? Tessa whispered.

No idea. I've never seen him before.

He looks...old.

Ha, don't they all?

Yes, but he looks old old, like he has existed for a long time in this desolate space. No fresh air or maybe not even enough sustenance. A meager life. One of lack.

He shot her a sideways look. *You can see that from his energy?*

She shook her head and answered him in a low voice, "No. Physically, he's gaunt, crippled almost."

"He's moving damn fast for a cripple."

"Hmm. That's not quite what I mean. If he were human I'd say anemic, as if he hadn't been out in the sun for centuries. But as he's a vamp, that should be a good thing."

Cody stopped suddenly.

Tessa bumped into him gently. She reached out to grab his arm, her gaze locked on the energy swirling ahead of her.

He's being attacked.

What? Really? Cody launched himself forward.

Tessa followed. She had no idea who was fighting who. *Careful. The attacker could be David or Dad.*

Cody never slowed down. Closer, Tessa could see the energy firing in all directions. She didn't recognize the new energy. But it was stronger, more powerful than that of the frail old vamp. He was going down…

Or not.

She grinned. Cody had entered the fray, and damn if the attacker wasn't beating back a hasty retreat. Only Cody wasn't having any of it. He went after the retreating male as Tessa ran up to the injured vamp, who had collapsed on the floor.

"Easy," she murmured, trying to stop him from jumping to his feet so fast.

"No time," he choked. "I'll heal, just slowly. Come. You must come now."

He struggled to his feet, pushing away her hands. "We have no time."

"No time for what," she cried out softly. "Who are you?"

"One of her protectors."

Her? Tessa cast a quick searching glance around. Who were they running from? Who were they running to? Off to the left, she watched a spark of light glow then blow up. She called out, "Cody? Is that you?"

"Yeah, the asshole pulled out some kind of weapon. I had to take him out." He walked toward her, holding some kind of small handheld weapon. Bigger than the spikes they'd been using, but smaller than a flashlight. It didn't look lethal. "This is the weapon he was holding."

It looked odd.

"What is that thing?"

"I don't know. It's weird." Almost in front of her, he held it out so she could see the button. "It's like a UV light and silver combined. Maybe it shoots silver droplets with the initial force of light?" He studied the weapon grimly. "Let's keep moving. We don't know how many others are down here."

She picked up the pace to keep up with the frail vamp, who she'd thought would be too injured to move as fast as he was, but he was scuttling along at a pace she was having trouble matching. Like what the heck?

Her astonishment transmitted to Cody. *I know. He's really moving. I wonder what the hell is going on down here.*

And where is here? she cried. *It seems like we've been moving underground forever. We've lost track of Dad's energy too. And David's.*

Do you think this guy is leading us to a trap? Cody asked, reaching out and grabbing her arm. She slowed down slightly.

I don't know. She hated to lose her father's energy trail. *I don't know if my father and brother are prisoners down here or if this guy may have contacted them too,* she said as frustration rolled over her.

A weird birdcall whistled through the blackness. She cocked her head and whispered out loud. "Was that him?"

"I think so. We've fallen behind."

"Crap. How is he moving so fast?"

"No idea. The ceiling is too low for me to fly, so running is my only option." Cody picked up speed and took off in the direction where they'd last seen the vamp. Tessa shook her head. Like what the heck. She took one leap then another and then a third, catching Cody on the third. She passed him on the fourth.

"Hey, that's cheating," he cried out.

"Sucks to be you," she said, laughing as she lost him in the distance on the fifth. A wall came out of nowhere. "Oh crap!"

In the back of her mind, she could hear Cody sniggering. *Tessa, watch out for that w—*

—all

Just before she hit it sideways.

"Ooomph." She slid to the floor, Cody's barely restrained laughter in her ear.

"No time. No time." The frail vamp shuffled along the wall beside her. "We must go."

And damn if he didn't turn and skittle off into the darkness again.

Cody reached down and helped her to her feet. "Are you okay?"

Tessa gave herself a good shake. "I'm fine. Or I will be if we find out what's going on."

Still holding hands, Cody tugged her forward. "Let's go. We can't lose him."

And the chase was on.

☙ ❧

CODY DIDN'T THINK much of this latest development. Or the strange ghost-like vamp. And definitely not that these people knew about Tessa and him.

What the hell was going on?

All he wanted was to get Jewel and David and the rest and get the hell out of here. Get home where they could rest, relax, and be together. He wanted to take Tessa out on Friday. Enjoy an evening just being normal.

"Come on, Cody." Tessa tugged on his hand. "Cody, are

you okay?"

She stood in front of him, a confused look on her face. And he realized that he'd come to a complete stop. Like an idiot. A lovesick idiot.

The light in her eyes warmed and a twinkle lit up the bright depths. He didn't know if she'd heard him or not. And he no longer cared.

He bent his head and kissed her. The touch of her lips against his was so sweet. So tender. So perfect. He couldn't resist, he wrapped her up into his embrace and held her tight. Then he deepened the kiss.

"No, no. We don't have time." The frail vampire raced toward them.

Cody groaned. *No. No.*

Yes, Tessa whispered. *He's here. We must go.*

Damn it. Cody loosened his arms and stepped back, already feeling the loss in his heart. The emptiness in his arms.

No. Not in your heart. Not in your head. Not in your arms. I'm always in there.

"Hurry," the old vamp snapped. "We are late."

Cody grabbed Tessa's hand and turned to follow him once again. Their short interlude was already over.

Only for the moment. And Tessa laughed. The sound was light and airy as it flew through his heart.

She was making him nuts. And he wouldn't want it any other way.

৵ ৻

DAVID WATCHED THE knowing smirk cross the big asshole's face. Crap. Why hadn't he gone straight to Jewel? They'd obviously tripped over something else going on here. To make matters worse, his own sister was on the way.

David had screwed up big time. He faced the two men. "What do you want with us?"

The first man never even glanced his way, dumping David into the category of 'can't be bothered to answer.' And that pissed David off. "Hey, I'm talking to you."

The big man suddenly extended his arm and plowed David in the chest. David grunted, falling back a step from the force.

The other man chuckled. "Maybe that will teach you to keep your smart mouth shut."

David straightened slowly, holding his chest, wondering how the tank had moved so fast. Surely that wasn't normal. Not that there was anything normal about this scenario.

He looked over at his father. Serus, a bored look on his face, studied their opponents, his arms crossed on his chest as if to say they weren't anything to worry about. Only David knew he was seething on the inside. He looked so calm. So in control. Almost disinterested. As if these men weren't worth bothering about.

Too bad David hadn't thought to emulate his father. Damn, his chest still hurt.

"Now move."

The two men pointed in the direction of the darker shadows to the left. Serus raised his eyebrows and asked, "Why should I?"

The second man spoke up, "'Cause we'll kill the pup if you don't."

"In which case, I'll kill you both," Serus said, his voice so calm, his words spoken as if fact. There was no way the men wouldn't have believed his threat. The men looked at each other then back at Serus. The first man opened his mouth when there was a shout coming from the opposite direction they were being pushed.

"Bloody hell. It's Lamar. What's the idiot up to now? He was supposed to be watching the left gate."

Left gate? David filed that tidbit away. Good to know there were other exits to this mausoleum.

A third man, much smaller than the first two, arrived, out of breath and panicked. "Degan is dead."

The two men stared. "What the hell are you talking about? There's no way. No one could kill him. He's too big. And he's too mean."

"He's dead. Some punk ass kid managed to get the weapon away from him and turned it on him."

Serus piped up. "Boy or girl?"

Lamar looked at him briefly and frowned. "Boy. The girl was standing and watching."

David grinned. Damn good news. That had to be Cody. And Tessa. Some things just never changed.

"I hope to hell you killed them both?"

Lamar shook his head and stepped back. "No. They were with a ghost."

The two men gasped. "What? Not possible. There aren't any of those left anymore."

Lamar shook his head vigorously this time. "There is. I saw him. And man, could he move."

David had a dozen questions he wanted to ask. A ghost. Like what? And one that could move fast? These men were scared of it. He studied the look on his father's face. If he'd heard or known about ghosts, he never said a word...except he'd lost the look of casual disinterest. Now his fists were clenched and he was glaring at Lamar like he'd kill him if he got the chance. Because he'd seen Cody and Tessa? Attacked them both perhaps? Or was something else going on here?

Either way, it wasn't good for any of them.

GORAN ARRIVED AT the hospital within ten minutes of leaving the Council Hall, and he was pissed at that. His damn wing. Had the doctor even mentioned it? Goran didn't know if he'd broken it in that crappy accident or something else had happened, but he'd listed to the side more than normal while flying. He hoped no one had seen him. He'd be mocked for life.

With the hospital parking lot below filled with parked vehicles and vamps moving freely around, he opted to land on the roof where he couldn't be seen. With his luck, the wing would give out just before landing and he'd tumble to the ground. Definitely not a good start to this operation. He snorted. Listen to him. It wasn't like he was a soldier on a secret mission...yet he'd *been* a soldier, and this sure felt like a mission.

He just hadn't figured out his priorities. Rescue Jewel. Find Ian and Motre, find David, find Serus, or go after his son and Tessa? Although the last one pulled at him the strongest, he figured that one he could easily slide to second place. Those two kids had proved to be remarkably resourceful and could take care of themselves. At least he hoped so.

It really bothered him that he couldn't hear Serus in his head. Like any sense, when it was cut off, the sheer absence of it made it sound so much louder in his head.

Where could that damn idiot be?

He looked down over the edge of the hospital roof to stare at the vamps crawling around like ants below. For all their coming and goings, he didn't sense any panic. Any sense of alarm. Any sense of urgency. They were calm. Organized. He studied as they moved vehicles to and from. It was almost like a military shift change. Dozens leaving and dozens arriving. An exchange of notes in the meantime. Weird.

He turned back to studying the side of the hospital building. He needed a way in. And preferably without setting off any major alarms. There appeared to be a dozen floors to the building. On this side, there were no decks or verandas that he could land on. Although he could always bust through a window. That appealed somewhat but with his gimpy wing, he was afraid he'd smack into the wall and miss the window altogether.

Wouldn't that be a picture?

He was almost glad Serus wasn't here. He'd have suggested they aim for the windows just to watch Goran crash into the wall. Feeling grumpy and not sure of his next step, he turned and walked to the far side of the roof. There had to be a way down. A way to get up.

Then he stopped and laughed. He was an idiot. The roof had to have access for maintenance.

He studied the large vents sticking out of the roof. Not that he planned to go down one, but there had to be a door for workmen to come up here. He strode to the largest mass of pipes and vents. Sure enough, he found a door on the far side. It was locked, but he made short work of that – by knocking the door clean off the hinges. Useless things. Who needed them anyway? Sometimes he wondered about all things man–made. They weren't the brightest of species.

With the door open, stairs leading down appeared. With one last look around at the night sky and the empty gravel rooftop, Goran took the easy way down and jumped to the landing. With the exterior door closed, there was a flat hush to the air. And an antiseptic smell – even here. He reached for the door to the top floor.

∂∞ ∞

AFTER HIS FRIENDS left, Jared felt lighter and more at ease than he could remember. And he had Clarissa's number. Of course he had several of the other people's numbers too. But as he couldn't have Tessa, it helped to know that Clarissa was interested. She was cute, nice, and seemed to genuinely care. There was a momentary qualm as he realized that the only people who appeared interested in his life had double-crossed him – then he remembered Tessa and her family and realized the vamps who'd appeared interested hadn't. Just the humans. Clarissa had also helped him rescue the other humans and vamps. She'd already proven to be different. Besides, it sucked to be alone. He stared down at the cell phone when it beeped in his hand.

It's Clarissa. Missing you already.

With a silly grin, Jared texted back. *Me too.*

As he hit send, he heard footsteps approaching. His stomach sank. It wasn't late, but he was worn out. The best thing for him was sleep. In fact, as he looked over at his bed, he realized he should at least pretend to be sleeping. He turned out the light, crept to his bed, and slipped fully dressed under the covers…and waited.

The knock came again. But no one called his name. The footsteps carried on down past his door. He closed his eyes and relaxed until he realized the footsteps were coming back.

And damn it, it stopped in front of his door again.

This time, under his watchful gaze, the knob turned and

the door opened.

JEWEL OPENED HER eyes, glanced around, recognized a hospital setting, and slammed her eyes shut. She struggled to control her breathing. Act natural. Breathe normally. Let no one know she was awake. *If* there was anyone around watching her. She cast her mind for some clarity on the situation. She remembered surfacing once or twice to see David, usually asleep with his head on his arms resting on the side of the bed. She must have given him a scare.

Then again, as visions of that damn blood farm filled her, she realized she'd scared herself, too. She'd felt so funny, as if her dreams were trying to take over again. Horrible feelings of fighting. Something being off in her psyche, her mind split into two parts and both of them fighting each other. As dreams went, that one had been kind of horrible.

As more and more images slipped into her brain, she realized that those dreams were actual memories. She'd been drugged again. She remembered meeting up with Rhia and Wendy…that brought a smile to her face. Wendy and Ian. Who'd have thought? Tessa had been right again.

At Tessa's name, Jewel opened her eyes slightly and looked around. She was alone in a small room, a chair beside her. Empty. She frowned. This room was smaller. She was alone now. She hadn't been before. Creepy. She didn't want to be here. She hated being separated from the others. And where was David?

She shifted her position to something more comfortable when she realized it was hard to move. Her body didn't want to respond. With a mounting panic, she focused on taking a deep breath. *You can't be that badly hurt.* That didn't make any sense. Likely just more drugs. She shuddered at the thought. She'd had more than enough drugs to last her a lifetime.

Take it easy. She took several deep breaths then opened her eyes fully and assessed her body. She was lying on her wings. Not the most comfortable position to begin with, her body was stretched out fully and she was covered in blankets. She lifted a hand to brush her hair back off her face, only to realize it had been braided down one side. She frowned. How long had she been here? With her other hand, she lifted the blanket and realized why she couldn't move.

Across her legs, hips, and chest were bands keeping her immobile.

To stop her from hurting herself? To keep her from damaging something they'd fixed and hadn't finished healing yet? Or just to keep her a prisoner?

At the sound of the doorknob turning, she dropped the blanket and closed her eyes at the same time. She'd wait to see just what the hell was going on before she let anyone know she was back.

At least until she found out which side was looking after her.

So far her luck hadn't been too good in that department.

CHAPTER 5

TESSA RACED BEHIND the stranger. She had no idea how deep this space went. They were still in the cement building, yet it was empty. They might be going around in circles, though she couldn't be sure. The darkness deepened up ahead. How could that be? They'd been running headfirst into complete darkness for what seemed like forever. *The air up ahead is different, Cody.*

Yeah, not sure why.

They hit the darkness at that time and she understood. There was no longer any cement and without the gray walls, there was only dirt, which explained the shift in the shade of black.

Instinctively she slowed, coming to a halting stop just inside the dirt walls.

"What's the matter, Tessa? Tired?" Cody gasped, coming to a stop beside her.

She shook her head. "I'm tired, but that's not why I stopped."

Cody looked down the dirt hallway. "The stranger went that way."

"Did he though?" she asked. "The shadows shifted here. I don't think he did. It was an illusion."

Cody stared at her for a long moment then turned to look down the hallway and back at her. "Can you see his energy?"

This was where it got tricky. "Um, not really."

He frowned, his gaze narrowing. "What does that mean?"

"His energy was getting thinner and thinner a long time ago, I barely saw anything to begin with. Now it's non–existent."

"Meaning he didn't come this way, or you can't see him for some reason if he did."

She wrinkled up her nose. "I saw him come this far, I think," she admitted. "But it comes to a stop now. So either he's still here and isn't showing any energy for some reason, or he's taken off so fast I can't even see where he was."

"Both," said the stranger coming out from the shadows to the side. "I needed to observe you. See if you really are who you are."

Cody stepped forward. "What?"

Tessa placed a gentle restraining hand on his arm. "You need us to be Cody and Tessa, right?"

At the stranger's nod, she added. "Did we pass the test?"

Cody growled at her side. The stranger took a long slow look at Cody to make sure he wasn't about to attack, and nodded. "You are indeed Tessa. Your watchdog is Cody."

"And you doubted us, why?" Cody snarled.

"Because it's too important to get it wrong."

The stranger spun on his heels and called behind, "Come. There is someone waiting to see you."

"We're not going anywhere until we get an explanation," Cody snapped.

Tessa stepped forward. Cody hauled her back and snarled, "Who are you? Who wants to meet us, and where are David and Serus?" At the stranger's blank stare, Cody growled, "Don't pretend to not know them."

"Of course I know them. Our spies keep us very well informed," the stranger said impatiently. "I am not allowed to explain. You'll have to speak to she who waits for you."

She. Tessa rolled that around in her head. A woman waited for them. One the stranger revered, if his tone of voice was anything to go by. Interesting.

She stepped forward. "Take us to her."

The stranger bowed slightly, turned, and walked ahead in an unhurried pace.

Ah, Tessa…this isn't a good idea.

I know, but we need to find out who she is and what's going on here.

I get that. You notice that he's not rushing anymore. There's no panic apparently now that we're here. Where ever that is?

I know. I think the shift from cement to dirt allowed us to enter… she stopped and considered, *or maybe left a force field of some kind? It's like we're behind it all now.*

He shot her a sideways look. *You're starting to sound pretty far out there. Force fields? Next you'll say all that cement building was nothing but a mirage.*

She gasped as the bits and pieces of the puzzle fell together.

That's exactly what it was, she said excitedly. *An illusion. No, not all of it,* she said at the confused look on his face. *But at the end where it seemed like it went on forever, that was the illusion. We were just going around in circles.*

Maybe, he said doubtfully, *but why?*

"She is waiting for you. Please don't delay." The stranger appeared in front of them, reminding Tessa that they'd come to a stop while they discussed the issue. She flashed him a bright smile. "Sorry."

He nodded his head in a regal manner and turned once again.

We need to go to her and find out what's happening down here.

So you say. But I'm all for getting David and Serus out of here and heading back to the surface. What in all of this looks normal to you?

She smiled at the dirt walls. *Nothing. Except it looks like a mine, and that is enough to make me want to find out what's going on.*

At the word *mine*, she felt his spurt of shock.

Ah hell, he whispered. *That can't be.*

It not only can be, I wouldn't be surprised if it was.

She took a step forward when a booming voice filled her head. *You know nothing!* It was so loud, so dominant, so controlling, she cried out, her hands clapping over her ears as she fell to her knees.

"Tessa?" Cody cried, "What's the matter?"

"Someone is in my head," she gasped. "Can't you hear it?"

"No. I can't hear anything."

You must come to me. Hurry. It's not safe.

And the voice fell silent.

❧ ❦

CODY HELPED HER back on her feet, but she bent over and took several large gulps of air.

"Are you okay?" What a stupid thing to say. Of course she wasn't okay. She wouldn't be looking shell-shocked if she was. "What did the voice say?"

"Something about needing to hurry. That we weren't safe." On the last word, she lunged to her feet, looking around warily. "We need to go."

"Go where?" Cody motioned to where the stranger had

been. "He's gone."

She blinked several times, then pointed. "He's waiting for us up ahead."

Cody peered into the darkness. He couldn't see anything, even with vampire night vision. "If you say so."

Keeping a firm grip on her arm in case she collapsed again, he walked toward the waiting stranger. A stranger who was getting stranger all the time.

They hadn't gone a dozen feet when the stranger appeared in the mist, his features working in agitation. "Hurry, we must hurry."

"Yeah, so she said," Tessa muttered.

The stranger looked at her shock. "You have spoken to *her*?"

"I didn't get a chance to say anything," Tessa snapped. "She did all the talking."

A beatific smile crossed his face. "Truly you are blessed to have heard her voice."

He reached out a gnarly hand. "Let me help you. We'll go faster."

Cody opened his mouth to protest, but Tessa already spoke. "I'm fine. Let's go."

He smiled again. "Indeed, you are worthy."

Tessa raised an eyebrow at Cody. He shrugged. He'd always thought she was worthy.

Really?

He snickered. *Always.*

A tiny smile wrinkled through his mind. He squeezed her hand in response. How did one ever get used to that intimacy? That level of knowing someone so well that you could hear their very breath in your mind?

Feelings overwhelmed him, and all he wanted to do was

pick Tessa up and carry her away to keep her safe. To keep her with him from this day forward. Like his primitive ancestors, he wanted to find a hidden lair for just the two of them.

Her gentle voice rippled into his mind. Shock, laughter, and was that a warm hug at his words? He hadn't meant for her to know the depth of his feelings, but it seemed like it was almost impossible to hide it. He hadn't closed the door between them in a long time. He hoped she never did.

And just like that, the door slammed shut.

Snick.

He stared at her in disbelief. Not only had she closed it with way more force than necessary, she'd locked it. As in locked him out.

She turned to face him, her head shaking rapidly. "It wasn't me," she said. "It was that same being who yelled in my head earlier."

"But why?" Already he was frantically trying to open it. But the door refused to budge. The stranger waited impatiently for them.

"I don't know," she said. "We need to go and find out."

"Oh, we'll do that, all right." Cody glared at the stranger. "Why aren't we there yet?"

"We are here," he said with a nod behind Cody.

He spun around, immediately tugging Tessa closer. Before them sat a vampire he'd never seen before. But she – if it was a she – was so old, it was as if she was one step away from being dust.

GORAN OPENED THE door and peered around the corner. The hospital hallway was empty. Good. This place was big, like seriously big. He didn't really expect to meet many people up here. And certainly none he knew. There were many doors on both sides of the hallway. He studied them. Should he explore? The last thing he wanted to see was more people or vamps hooked up to tubing where they were being fed drugs. Still, any number of his friends and family could be in here. Damn. Making a decision, he walked to the first one and opened it. Empty. Good.

He walked to the next one. Empty. Feeling much better, he walked to the next and then the next. On the last one, he was already closing the door when he registered it as full of people. Shit. He paused and pushed it open again. And that was when he realized he knew two of the people.

"Well, well, well." He walked over to Motre and slugged him on the shoulder. "It's good to see you."

Motre's grin was wide and wonderful as always. What the hell was going on? As his gaze wandered the room, he caught sight of Ian, standing in the corner, two big vamps in white lab coats pinning him in place, and finally he understood. "Looks like I came just in time, Motre."

Motre snickered. "We can handle it. These guys aren't going to make us break a sweat."

"That's all right," Goran said with a ferocious grin, "I've been looking for something to pound into the ground since I woke up."

"Wait," said one of the two men standing in front of them. "No pounding required. I'm Dr. Horander."

Motre snapped, "Right. You're the doctor who kept Ian a prisoner here."

"No, you don't understand. Ian is on special medication. He's reacting to the drugs he was given in the mine," the doctor cried. "Don't you understand?" He motioned to the big guards holding Ian. "They need to take Ian back so he can get his next dose."

"No! No drugs." Ian cried. "Besides, you wouldn't let Wendy see me."

"Of course we couldn't let her see you," Dr. Horander said. "She wouldn't understand. Then she panicked and started this chaos." He calmed down and turned that genial smarmy voice on Goran. "Don't you see, it's all a big misunderstanding."

Goran smiled and stepped closer. "I understand perfectly."

He reached out an arm and placed it across the man's back. As it slid across the man's shoulders, his fingers splayed out like claws and he grasped the one spot at the back of the doctor's neck and squeezed. Hard.

The doctor went down without a fight. Motre took out both orderlies who'd been holding Ian. They never felt a thing. They both dropped to the floor. Too damn easy. He turned back to the second doctor, who now held a syringe in his hand.

"No, don't come any closer. Or I'll have to use this."

Motre took one step closer.

Goran eyed Motre. He had on a thick leather coat and his shirt under that. It would have to be a very sharp needle to go through to his skin, so as long as he could keep his face and neck protected…

"What's in the syringe?" he said in a conversational tone that had the man shaking in his boots.

"It's a weapon," he cried out. "It's new, just out of our labs."

"And what labs are those?" Motre asked in a hard voice. Ian joined them a few moments later, his color back now that he wasn't in danger of being drugged again.

"Our testing labs," the man said. "It's to make you docile."

"Really? That doesn't sound like much of a weapon to me," Motre said, his voice cold and clear. "If you mean knock–out drugs, then that would make more sense."

"That's what it's going to be," Ian said. "Knock-out drugs that make you docile."

He snorted. "Think of the mind control drugs. They use this and give you a new program," the doctor said, "As long as you are receiving the drugs, then you are going to follow the program."

Ian added, his voice curiously detached, "Is that what you gave to me?"

The doctor shrugged. "Everyone gets a certain amount of it. It can't be helped."

"Ah." Ian smiled, then reached out and snatched the syringe out of the man's hand.

The doctor backed up. "No, wait. Don't hurt me."

"Why not?" Goran asked. "You had no problem hurting any of us."

"No, you don't understand. I could be useful."

Motre stepped closer and he cowered back. "No. Don't let him hurt me."

"What kind of help could you be to us?" Goran asked.

"I know things," he said. "Big things."

Motre stopped and stared at him. "What kind of things?"

The doctor smiled. "For starters, I could tell you about what's beneath this hospital building."

Motre stopped and stared. "What? There's something under us? What the heck?" He turned to the other two. "Now what do you want to do?"

Goran glared at him. "I already know what's under here. We don't need you."

Motre stepped forward.

"No, wait. There are cameras down there. People."

With a shrug, Goran figured Serus could fill him in later. He motioned to Motre.

Motre was on him in an instant.

∂ ∽

GHOSTS? SERUS COULDN'T believe what he was hearing. Somewhere in the recesses of his mind, he remembered hearing about such vampires. You only saw them if they wanted to be seen. There were whispers about Ghosts living where they wanted, how they wanted. There had only ever been a small group of them. He remembered that. He thought they'd all died out.

Interesting twist. He wouldn't mind having a talk with one of those Ghosts himself. They were supposed to be the eyes and ears of vamp society. That was another reason their presence gave vamps the willies way back when they could be in places where you least expected them – and often were.

They made the best spies.

Then suddenly they were gone.

He couldn't remember why.

He studied the three men more panicked than he'd seen them before. He glanced surreptitiously over at David to see him tense, muscles ready to attack. They had their diversion.

He jumped without warning and hit the bigger of the two men sideways. His attack was so fast, he had the vamp knocked down and out without warning. He hopped to his feet and spun around. David had taken out the other large vamp, a spike in his hand still smoldering.

Serus eyed the weapon. "I thought we'd left all those at the Council."

David gave him a savage grin. "I was never asked to hand mine over." He pocketed his spike while Serus watched, his own in his hand.

"Just be careful with that thing," he growled, already studying the mouse of a man who appeared to have lost his wits after seeing the Ghost.

He quaked in front of them. At least he hadn't bolted. Then again, the Ghost was out there somewhere.

"So," Serus said, walking around the smaller male. "Where the hell were these guys trying to take us?"

David interjected, "And why?"

The man's Adam's apple bobbed up and down as he swallowed nervously. "Anyone who comes down here is taken prisoner."

"And why is that?" Serus asked in a pleasant voice. "And when was the last one taken?"

"Oh, not for decades. It's really unusual for anyone to come down here. And then you lot show up today. Well, they couldn't let that alone, now could they? Not you guys." As if that made perfect sense, the man fell silent while Serus was still trying to figure out just what he'd said.

"You're watching us?" David asked, astonished. "How would you know who we are?"

"The video cameras."

Shit. Serus hadn't seen any cameras on the way down or anywhere in this mausoleum. From the look on David's face, he hadn't either.

"A video would show our faces, but not identify us," David said slowly, eyeing the man who'd started to quake again.

"Why would anyone know who we are?"

The man looked nervously from one to the other. "'Cause you're on the wanted list, of course."

Serus's eyebrows shot up. He'd only ever heard of a wanted list in terms of humans and crimes. Never for vamps. "Wanted for what?"

The man swallowed, then swallowed again. "For your DNA." He said it in a harsh whisper, as if the words would choke him on the way out. "The bosses want your DNA."

WENDY DOZED OFF and woke up with a start, realized the room was dark and silent except for Rhia's heavy breathing, and dozed off again.

When she woke the next time, it was to find she was alone. Crap. So much for babysitting Rhia. It looked like she woke up and left Wendy to nap. Straightening up, Wendy groaned at the sore muscles and the kink in her neck. Stretching gently, she made her way to the door, wondering if she should text Sian and let her know Rhia was gone. When she opened the door to the hallway, she realized there was no point. Rhia and Sian were having a heated discussion in the hallway.

Rhia caught sight of her first. She broke off in mid–sentence. "Wendy? How are you feeling?"

Typical. Rhia always thought about everyone else first.

"I'm fine. My head is better," Wendy was quick to add as Rhia reached up to lift her hair back and expose the damage from the car accident. She did feel fine. The sleep had helped a lot.

She smiled reassuringly at Rhia then turned her attention

to Sian. "Any news? Anyone back yet?"

Sian shook her head, concern whispering across before being replaced by a bright smile. "Not yet. I'm sure someone will check in soon."

"Not likely," Rhia snapped with enough force. Wendy realized this was the conversation she'd interrupted. "You know what it's like, Sian. They are in battle, hunting. They aren't going to take the time to let us know if they found someone or had reached the roof and found no one." She threw up her hands. "They are going to keep fighting, keep hunting, and keep searching until they have found everyone."

Wendy had to admit, Rhia was right. Checking in with the others in a timely manner was ideal but hardly feasible.

"And that's why I'm going up there," Rhia announced.

"What?" Wendy stared at her in alarm then switched her gaze to Sian. Only Sian was rubbing the side of her face as if she'd run out of arguments.

"You can't," Wendy said bluntly.

Rhia rounded on her. "And why not?"

Subtle wasn't going to work. Maybe it was because she was still punchy from her nap, but Wendy snapped back, "Because you were drugged again, and you are more of a danger to them than a help."

Rhia's gaze widened to huge orbs and she blinked once…twice.

"Look, what you did to Tessa means you can't be trusted right now. Maybe the drugs have worked their way through your system, and maybe they haven't," Sian said quietly.

At the mention of her daughter, Rhia's face cracked and tears started to run down her face. "Why do you think I have to go help? She was trying to get away from me."

"No," Wendy stepped forward and clasped Rhia's hands

in her own. "I'm sure Tessa understands. But it happened so fast. Like Jewel and Ian in the mine. Everyone is going to look at you sideways and wonder if you are going to go off again. They won't be able to focus on what they need to do because they'll be worrying about you." She didn't add that they'd be concerned about her attacking them from behind, too. Rhia could figure that out herself.

Sian stepped in, "Rhia, you need to help your son Seth."

Slowly, Rhia lifted her head, confusion on her face. "Help him how?"

"You said when you were under the influence of their drugs that you shipped him out of the country."

Pain rippled across her beautiful features, her shoulders slumping in defeat. "Did I really? Where to? Why? I remember something, but I'd thought that was all part of the nightmare."

"So figure out where you shipped him so we can get him back," Wendy suggested. "It would also help us to see what other countries are involved with the blood farm."

Rhia's eyes filled with more tears. "I can't believe I did that. I must find out where." She brushed the tears back. "But if I do that, who is going to find out what's happening with the others?"

Wendy and Sian exchanged glances. Sian looked at Rhia, "Can't you talk to Serus, ask him for an update?"

Rhia looked at her blankly. "Who is Serus?"

JARED KEPT HIS eyes closed, his breathing stable, as the intruder studied him from the doorway. He desperately wanted to open his eyes and see who it was, but he didn't want anyone to know he was awake. He deliberately shifted in bed and in the process managed to peer through his lashes. But his intruder was already closing the door.

Damn.

Should he call out? He had to do something. He slipped out of bed, crossed the room, and opened his door just a crack. He peered around the corner to see the manager standing outside the next room. He turned to stare at Jared.

"Something wrong, Jared?"

Jared managed a fake yawn and shook his head. "I thought I heard something, but I guess not." He rubbed his eyes as if still half asleep and withdrew into his room, closing his door solidly behind him. And waited.

Had it been the manager who'd opened his door? It wouldn't have been out of the realm of possibility. After all, checking to make sure Jared was in his room was within his responsibilities. Considering all the shit that had happened in Jared's life, that was almost a requirement.

And if they'd thought Jared might have been uneasy over this evening's conversation, maybe he'd figured Jared would bolt.

Struggling to still the unease in his gut, Jared climbed back into bed. He hated this. Hated the uneasiness. Surely there was somewhere else he could stay? He tried to text Tessa again. He didn't know what to do about food at Tessa's house, but he'd feel safe there. And didn't that beat all?

Then another name popped into his head. Someone respectable. Responsible. Position of authority. And human. Dr. Taz.

He grabbed his cell phone and realized he didn't have the contact number, but Tessa would. He texted her, asking for it. Surely she wouldn't mind. Just in case, he sent another long text explaining why he needed the number.

Maybe that would do it.

He didn't know where she was or what she was doing, but he hoped she was getting the rest she deserved.

CHAPTER 6

TESSA STARED AT the faded, aged–beyond–belief vampire. She stepped closer. The ghost immediately stepped between the two women in warning.

"Hortran, it's fine."

Hortran bowed and retreated.

Tessa watched his smooth movements that made him seem to slide and glide more than walk.

"How does he do that?" she murmured, studying him as he stilled in place.

"How does anyone do anything they are good at?" the old woman answered. "It's natural for him. It's who he is."

"A ghost?" Tessa said, switching her gaze to the woman. "Someone said he was a ghost."

"Not a ghost…a Ghost." A dry cackle filled the air followed by a painful fit of coughing. "A big difference. Although soon, I'm afraid they might be one and the same."

"He's dying?" Tessa asked hesitantly, wondering what was going on.

"Aren't we all? Even you, my dear, are dying. Some of us are closer to the end than others."

"At least you aren't completely at the end of that road," Tessa said politely. She heard a half snicker from Cody beside her.

"Yes, I am. Maybe not today or tomorrow or even this

year, but it will be this century."

She stared at Tessa, then motioned with her hand. "Come closer."

Tessa stepped forward two steps. When the woman repeated her hand motion impatiently, she walked right up to her.

And stopped. The woman's skin was almost scaly from age, her eyes deeply set into her head, but there were indications that she'd been a beauty at one time. Likely a thousand centuries ago.

"Who are you?" Tessa whispered.

"Ah, I wondered if you knew me." She shrugged, a slight movement that still made Tessa wince as she heard bones creak and skin scrape across each other.

"Your father knows me. So too does your dear mother."

At the mention of her parents, Tessa reared back slightly. She studied the old woman as if the face would shake something loose in her mind that had stayed hidden for the last twenty minutes. "Really?"

She turned to see Cody still standing back where he always was. "Cody, do you know her?" She motioned to the Ghost. "Or him?"

Cody frowned and approached slowly. "I have never seen Hortran before, nor yourself, but from old conversations between my father and Councilman Serus that I vaguely remember, you must be Deanna."

Deanna? Tessa turned to see the old woman beam at Cody. "Indeed I am."

And all the memories of one of the oldest vampires still alive today surfaced. "You're on the Council but don't attend the meetings any longer. In fact, you're never seen in public anymore either."

"Bah, Council. Those mealy–mouthed useless imbeciles. The 'we must keep up tradition and do things the way we've always done them garbage.'"

She shook her head. Her hair, long but in a single braid, flung around her shoulders. "As if that logic holds true through centuries where everything else changes except for the Councilmen's attitude."

Tessa grinned. She liked the woman already. "Is that why you don't show up anymore?"

"That's one of the reasons. The other is much simpler." She glanced over at the Ghost and smiled. "I can't. I am a prisoner here."

"What?" Tessa glanced around. "How is that possible? We came here, so surely you could leave."

"I can't. There are special walls designed to keep me here forever. It's Hortran that makes my life here easy enough. Besides, as my captors can't find me, I've turned the tables on them too. And that suits me just fine."

While Tessa tried to muddle through that speech, Cody was the one asking for clarification. "So you are someone's prisoner, but they can't find you?"

At Deanna's nod, he motioned to the Ghost. "Hiding you is part of what he does?"

She grinned. "In part, yes."

Tessa shook her head. "Surely if you can camouflage the appearance of this place to that extent, you could have left?"

"Oh sure. I should have said I *was* a prisoner. Not now. I can come and go as I please, but I've decided as my time is near, this place suits me just fine. Besides," she said, a crafty look coming over her eyes, "It keeps them guessing."

Cody said in confusion, "So you aren't a prisoner?"

"That's what I just said, didn't I?" she snapped, glaring at him.

"Actually, you said you were a prisoner then said that you weren't. Sorry if we're a little confused," Tessa said with a gentle smile. "This is all new to us."

Deanna sniffed then motioned to the Ghost. "He can explain."

The Ghost stepped forward. "We were prisoners. After we explored the tunnels, we found a way to escape but still had to stay out of sight so our captors didn't know. But as long as the captors thought we were here, they left us alone, so we made this our headquarters and came and went as we pleased, allowing the captors to think we were still here. However, we also camouflaged the area so they couldn't find us." He smiled a small smile. "Knowing I'm a Ghost, they knew that's what we'd done, so they could believe we were always here but they had no access to us. That suited us too."

"And the camouflage…how did you do that?" Tessa asked.

"Easy," Deanna said. "Energy."

Tessa gasped. "Energy?"

"Yes. Why do you think I hoped to meet you once I heard about all the weird things you were doing up top, my dear?"

"You know about that?" Cody asked. "How?"

"We have eyes and ears all over the place," the Ghost said. "We know what's going on everywhere."

"So you know about the blood farm?" Tessa asked cautiously, unsure of whose side these two were on.

"Of course, I'm thousands of years old. Blood farms aren't new you know. Synthetic blood is new. I don't mind it actually. It has a certain ambiguous flavor. After tasting several horrible batches of bad blood from some men carrying nasty diseases that I had no idea beforehand, I'm happy to have the synthetic stuff."

Tessa exhaled noisily. "So you weren't part of the group that created the blood farm?"

"Bah, of course not. I'd have had all humans strung up like that if I were. Besides, like I said, humans don't taste the same anymore. Gross tasting now if you ask me." Her gaze sharpened. "That doesn't mean I don't know who is running it though. Like I said, we keep tabs on everything."

Cody, his voice hard, asked, "Then who is behind it all?"

CODY STARED AT the ancient crone and wondered what game she was playing at. Who'd stay a prisoner in order to turn the tables on their captor? Then again, as she could come and go and her captor was forced to keep guards here to watch over her, it might just be damn clever. But it was a twisted kind of clever. And said much about her relationship with her captor. "And is it the same person who imprisoned you?"

A smile whispered across her lips. "My husband is the one who imprisoned me."

Cody heard Tessa's gasp of shock. His own mind was scurrying through his memory banks, looking for the name of her husband. And came up empty.

"I hadn't heard you were married."

She laughed. "It was a long time ago."

"Why would he do that?" Tessa asked, anger in her voice.

"For the best of all reasons," Deanna smirked. "To get back at me for imprisoning him."

Dead silence.

Tessa said cautiously, "You imprisoned him, he escaped and turned around and imprisoned you, you escaped but he doesn't know it." She shook her head. "You do realize that none of this makes any sense, right?"

Deanna chuckled. "Oh, it does to us, child. You just have to understand we've been married for over nine centuries. Sometimes games liven things up."

Amusement whistled through Cody at the thought. How bloody fascinating. And intriguing and yet…sick at the same time. From the look of incomprehension on Tessa's face, Cody realized she wasn't understanding at all.

"I don't suppose you are here…some of the time… are you? As in the odd time when he comes to check up on you personally, perhaps," Cody asked, humor threading through his words.

Deanna gave him a droll look. "You do understand. How very interesting. It must be Goran's influence. That man does like a good time." And she smiled in such a way that Cody was sorry he'd broached the conversation.

Tessa, however, didn't appear impressed. "And why are we here? You said there was danger and we had to hurry."

"Ah, right to business. You could do well to spend more playtime with Cody here."

Tessa, her voice hard, snapped. "Any playtime I have with Cody is my business and not up for discussion."

Deanna rolled her eyes. "Lord, so young. So vehement. So passionate. You two must have fun." She gave Cody a single, slow, up–and–down look that actually made him embarrassed. "Ah well…"

Until Tessa stepped in front of him and blocked him from Deanna's view.

Cody hid his grin. Oh, he did love this girl.

JEWEL OPENED HER eyes again. Awareness hit faster than the last time, making her alert and almost cognizant of her surroundings. And her situation. She was in a hospital, but the jury was still out as to why she was still here. She got that she'd been drugged. Understood that she'd taken a turn for the worse and knew the doctors were keeping her under observation. But if all the above were true, where the hell was David?

She sat up slowly and paused, realizing something had changed. Her restraints were off.

Or had they been part of her nightmares?

With effort, she made her way to the laundry tub and took a drink of water. When she was done, she stood in the open doorway and surveyed the room. She was only wearing a hospital gown, so where were her clothes? More important than those, where was her cell phone? She went through the cupboards systematically, feeling her strength slowly seep away as she finally opened the last cupboard. And found her clothes. "Of course. I should have started at the other end. Damn fool."

She straightened with her clothing in her hand and stacked them on the counter. They hadn't been washed since the mine. Gross. She wrinkled up her nose and wished there were other options. Still, she wasn't leaving right now. Maybe she could at least hand wash these and lay them on the railing in the bathroom to dry.

Feeling better, she searched her pockets for her cell phone.

Nothing. She turned to the rest of her clothing. Also nothing. She cast her mind back to the mine. Did she have a phone then? Sure. But...the battery died. At least she thought it had. Things were still foggy. The bottom line was, she didn't have a cell phone. There was no phone in the room, so the only way to contact anyone was to go out in search of another phone to use. That meant clothing. And that meant her old dirty clothes.

Or not. She assessed her own health and sinking energy level. If she could wash her clothes then sleep for a while, her clothes could dry in the meantime. She'd have asked about laundry here if she'd seen anyone, but outside of remembering seeing David, she didn't think she'd seen anybody else.

A horrible thought struck.

Was she all alone? She knew it was a foolish thought, but it was a hard one to shake. She stumbled to the door, hating the fatigue once again catching hold. She turned the knob to open the door. Only it wouldn't budge.

It was locked.

She dropped her forehead against the wood in front of her. *Please, not again.*

SERUS'S GRIP TIGHTENED convulsively. His DNA? Seriously? This bullshit again? "Who is behind it?"

The man's eyes bulged. "I don't know. We don't know who is really behind this mess. There is almost no one down here. You triggered the alarm, and that's the only reason the alert went out."

Serus released the man so he could catch his breath. The man bent over coughing and choking. When he finally straightened, his face no longer looked like a beet, but didn't look quite normal either.

"Is this place completely uninhabited?" David asked. "It doesn't feel like it."

"It's not supposed to be. But I haven't been down here in

decades."

"And then there's the matter of the Ghost," Serus snapped. "If he's here, then how can it be empty?"

"He's a Ghost. They aren't real." The man shook his head in confusion. "I don't know. It always is empty though. That's why the alarms." He turned on the charm with a hopeful smile. "You entered and that triggered the alarm. The camera feed picked you up and the security men told the bosses. Your faces were visible and when they saw who you were, they sent us down to get you." He shrugged and looked around. "There have been odd rumors about this place for decades. I've not been here in so long, I'd forgotten how creepy it was."

"Why was it built? It's too big to be a hospital."

"Originally, I think it was supposed to be an end of the world bunker with room for most of us to hibernate here for decades until the humans killed themselves and everything else off." His face twisted oddly at the idea. "But that never happened. Most vamps have forgotten about the place."

"I did," Serus said, nodding. "It's been more than a few decades." He frowned as he stared at the cement. "Looks like it's been refinished somewhere in the last couple of years though."

The other man nodded. "It wasn't cement originally, but as new material became available..." He motioned toward the darkness behind him. "This doesn't go all that far into the mountain before it becomes dirt again."

"Like a mine tunnel?" David asked, his tone hard.

The man looked at him nervously. "Could be, but the whole area is full of those."

"Easy, David. There's not likely a connection."

"Really?" He looked at Serus. "What about that whole DNA collection thing?"

Serus's jaw tightened. "Why do they want our DNA?"

"For the database," he cried. "But I don't know what that means. They don't have you or your line's DNA on file, and they want it."

"And for the last time, who is the 'they' you are talking about?" David cried impatiently.

"I don't know," he whimpered. "I only know my immediate bosses, and you just killed them."

Serus glared down at the two dead men. Or rather the one dead and the one burned in a pile of ash. "Damn it."

"Yeah, next time ask your questions before you kill people indiscriminately," the man cried.

Serus slowly raised his gaze. "Right, and now...now that you've answered our questions and are of no use to us, what should I do with you?"

"You could let me go." He gave his most winning smile.

Serus wasn't fooled. He glanced over at his son. David shrugged. "You can't kill him for being a weak weasel."

The weasel shook his head in horror. "No, you can't. I'm being helpful, I am."

David turned to study the empty space. "It's creepy down here. If Tessa is here, she could be anywhere."

"Tessa?" the weasel asked. "You mean the young girl causing all the trouble?"

Serus spun so quickly, the weasel backed up several steps and cowered.

"Sorry, I'm sorry," he cried out from his crouching position. "You don't have to answer that question."

"Stand up, man." Serus knew many vamps like this one, but they weren't usually in his presence. He hated weasels and weaklings like this one. But occasionally they were useful. Like maybe...now.

"What do you know of Tessa?" he asked deliberately, lowering his voice to a calm, even tone. If the man was too scared, he'd never answer.

"I just know she's a priority for the bosses. They want her DNA very badly."

RHIA SAT IN solitude, wishing her brains would unscramble. She'd thought she was normal again. Back to normal as Sian would say. She remembered Sian, Wendy, and her children, but there was a blank space in her head where Serus should be. She understood he was her husband. Understood she loved him, had been married to him for centuries, but there was a giant empty darkness she couldn't fill with memories when she thought about him. Although that was getting better.

That was the first tangible proof she had been drugged.

Her mind shifted through what she knew about drugs. It wasn't likely that they'd been able to target a particular person in her life to wipe out. No, chances were that part of her brain had been the unlucky area affected. She rubbed her face, feeling old and tired.

Then again, that was likely the drugs, too. She remembered the blood farm and all the horrors held within. Another name popped into her mind. Goran. A good man. A best friend. He'd been such a huge help over the years. She could see him easily, so why not Serus? She struggled to see the man always at his side, her side, but his features stayed just out of reach.

She wished he was here so she could fill in those blank spaces in her mind. As warmth wrapped around her heart, she realized she might not know this Serus, but inside she *knew* him. The feelings were there, getting stronger, closer. She smiled.

She might have forgotten some things, but her heart hadn't.

Now if she could only talk to him. See his face and know he was hers.

Then she'd feel better.

JARED WOKE TO darkness, surprised he'd slept at all. He swore from the grittiness of his eyes that he'd not gotten a wink of rest, but apparently he had. He checked the time on his cell phone and realized it was just before five in the morning. He was loath to get up and take the chance of finding more dead bodies below. If he waited until everyone else got up, they could find the bodies this time. Presuming there were some. Still, he wished he'd slept longer. He'd prefer to not be awake at all right now. He was still tired, his body aching. From what? He'd done nothing out of the norm, so maybe just the restless night? As he lay there, willing himself back to sleep, he thought he heard stealthy footsteps out in the hallway.

He tensed. Was it just one of the guys going to use the bathroom at the end of the hallway or something else? It seemed as if the footsteps slowed outside his door. He studied the chair he'd jammed under his doorknob as an early warning system and waited, his breath choked back in his throat.

The steps, after what seemed like a long pause, moved on. He released his pent-up breath slowly, silently, as if afraid they could still hear him outside. If someone was using the bathroom, they'd have to come back the same way. For a long time he heard nothing, then what he did hear made his blood run cold.

The steps were heavy, loud and awkward. As if someone carried a heavy weight. A weight that was almost too much for one person.

A dead weight.

He shuddered and stared at the door, terribly afraid. And once again hating his choices. He slipped out of bed and raced silently to his door where he quietly removed the chair. When the person had gone several steps past, he turned the knob and opened the door a crack, just enough to peer down the hallway.

And watched as one of the orderlies carried Tobias around the corner, the boy's limp body hung like a carcass over his shoulder.

CHAPTER 7

TESSA CAST A glance over at the Ghost who stood, head slightly bowed, immobile in a corner. Was he sleeping?

Wanting to walk over and poke him, she instead turned back to Deanna. "Are you going to tell us who is behind the blood farm?"

Deanna shrugged. "I don't know that he's in charge. He's also old. Almost as old as I am. He'd created the blood farm because he believed in the system. Not to harm the humans, but because they never mattered in the first place."

Anger rippled through Tessa. "That's not how the rest of us see it."

Deanna bowed her head, then lifted it slowly as if the weight of her years made it almost impossible to do so. "No, you wouldn't. But times have changed, and he hasn't."

She waved an arm around the room. "Lots has changed recently. And most of it isn't good."

"You said we were in danger," Cody said, his tone impatient. "From what? You?"

Deanna laughed, or at least that's what Tessa understood the wheezing to be. "No, if that were the case, you'd be dead already."

Cody glared at her.

"No, Hortran here has found cameras in this place," Deanna said. "They might have been here for a long time, I couldn't say. But now that they have been installed, the game has changed. My husband didn't put them in here."

"How do you know?" Tessa asked, not sure she wanted to know any more about their strange marriage.

"I asked him," she said candidly. "He was quite put out that our dungeon," she gave a coy smile that had Tessa's gaze widening, "had been invaded." She turned to stare throughout the emptiness surrounding them. "He was investigating who did this, when…" she swallowed hard and said in an icy cold voice, "When he disappeared. I don't know if he was called for an urgent matter or was taken."

"Disappeared." Tessa gasped. "Is he dead?"

Deanna gazed at her, sorrow and pain filling those black eyes. "I'm so afraid that he might be."

"That would be terrible. Why kill him?" Tessa cried. "He's old already. Why not let you both live out your lives until your time has come?"

Deanna stared at her. "I think that's where the blood farm comes in."

And Cody spoke up. "Right. Not the blood farm itself, but the experiments they were doing. They needed your husband's – all the ancients' DNA." He turned to Tessa, "Remember, they had Moltere hanging and were looking for both our fathers…and you for just that reason."

"Exactly," Deanna said. She nodded toward the Ghost. "He is the last of his kind. They want him too. I am the last of my family line, although there are some of mixed blood below me."

Tessa tilted her head and asked, "What is your family line? I'm not sure I know it."

"Well, you should," Deanna snapped, shifting her moods once again. "You are one of us."

"What?" Tessa shook her head. "I'm a jumbled mix of too many things," she cried. "I don't belong anywhere."

"You are wrong. It doesn't show up in every generation, and lately it hasn't shown up for centuries, but you definitely have Leant in you."

Leant? "I think my great grandmother was a Leant," she said slowly, remember something her mother had said last week. "But I know nothing about them."

"Of course, your great grandmother was related to my sister, who's been gone for a long time."

"But still," Tessa said quietly. "I am only a little bit Leant."

"Maybe. But they want me. And if they can't have me, they'll take you. I know of no others showing the Leant heritage who is still alive. We're a dying breed, our pure heritage diluted."

"If this place is dangerous now," Cody said. "Why are you still here?"

Silence.

Studying the wash of grief on the old woman's face, Tessa understood. In a quiet voice, she said, "It's because you hope he'll come here, don't you? That he'll find you here. And if he doesn't, you feel closest to him in this place."

Deanna raised her gaze. "Yes and yes. I can't sense his life force anymore. The mindspeak is quiet. I'm afraid he's gone. And if he is…" Her smile grew cold, hard… "Everyone who comes down here might be the one who planted those cameras. Everyone that comes here is suspect. Anyone could have something to do with his death." Now her gaze turned lethal sharp as she studied the two of them. "Including you."

91

CODY GLARED AT the old woman playing games with them. "Well, we didn't have anything to do with it. I haven't seen anyone close to your age, and I have no idea who might have killed him."

Deanna never took her gaze off Tessa.

A heavy silence filled the air. Cody looked from one to the other, wishing he understood the heavy undercurrents going on between the two women.

Were they speaking telepathically?

"Tessa?"

He studied her face, her gaze locked on Deanna's.

"What did I miss?"

Tessa tore her gaze free and took a deep breath. "There was one old ancient…"

"Really? Where, when?"

She winced. "Think power struggle. Think of your brother. In the mine. We found him dying."

Cody cast his mind back. There'd been so many. And he remembered the wizened ancient who'd been attacked by his young apprentice – Cody's brother.

"Oh no."

She nodded. "Maybe."

She turned back to Deanna. "He was one of the top bosses with the blood farm, wasn't he?"

Deanna dropped her gaze. "Yes, but he was fighting against the testing. He wanted to see vampires returned to pure bloodlines, like he was. Not the monstrosities that they were working on. He knew his time was up in many ways, but he'd been trying to stop the clones. He wasn't against the DNA database. To him, that was just good sense." She stared moodily at the two of them. "He's dead then? You know that for sure?"

"Yes." Tessa said gently. "We did not kill him. He said he'd been attacked by two young vamps possibly following orders by his upcoming—"

"Tyson," Deanna growled, rising up from her seat until she towered above them. "It was that little prick, wasn't it?"

Cody stiffened.

Tessa answered. "Yes, we believe so."

"My love thought it might happen, but not this soon. I will have my vengeance. He will not live through this night," She spun to face the Ghost. Her face worked with the emotions and confirmation she'd expected but had hoped not to get. Her mouth opened to issue orders to the Ghost, who was now awake and ready.

"Wait," Cody said. "The job is done. He's dead."

She froze. Her body vibrated with unnamed emotion. Slowly, she turned back to Cody. "Did you do it?"

Now what the hell was he to say? He wished he'd done it, but he hadn't. As this woman was already unbalanced, if the truth came out, would she take it out on them?

Then the decision was taken from him.

Tessa took a half step forward and said, "No. He didn't. I did."

Deanna stared at her in shock and anger, then the anger faded and a weariness like he'd never seen replaced it.

"Then I owe you." She collapsed back in her chair as grief rolled through her.

Tessa stood quiet, as if not sure what she was to do or say.

Cody knew she'd killed Tyson out of necessity and had hated doing so. She didn't want to be thanked. He asked, "Can you tell us about any of his colleagues? We're trying to clean up the group so that humans can live free again."

Deanna wasn't so lost in grief that she didn't snort at that.

"Mayhap you should look to the humans involved," she said with a heavy sigh. "My love always said that he was going to keep an eye on the humans. He worked with one or two he didn't trust. And several he said deserved to be strung up in the very farms they were profiting from."

"A bit of superiority in that attitude?" Cody asked, his voice hard.

She gazed at him. "Meaning that he could laugh at others profiting? Except you must remember, we've been drinking human blood since we were born. This was a simplistic system that's been tried many times over the centuries."

"Times have changed," Tessa said smoothly. "I call many humans as my friends."

"Really?" The concept appeared to be odd to Deanna. She raised her eyebrows. "Whatever. I wouldn't trust any of them."

"The question is, can you identify some of them for us to capture?" Cody asked.

She nodded, looked over at the Ghost. "Hortran can take you to their headquarters. As they use fake names, the ones I know them by won't help you."

Tessa started. "Thank you, that would be helpful."

"Go now. I'm getting very tired."

No, not tired. Cody studied her face that was ravaged by emotion, the tsunami of grief no longer capable of being held back.

It was definitely time to leave.

Cody turned to face the Ghost. Only to find he'd disappeared. He turned around, looking behind him. When there was no sign of him, he turned back to Deanna.

"He'll meet you outside." And she turned away.

Dismissed. Tessa reached out for Cody's hand to find it

already reaching for hers. The door between them clicked open. Tessa smiled at him. They walked straight back, expecting to see the Ghost arrive from somewhere. But the further out they walked, the less they saw. It was back to the mirage of the cement building.

"Creepy. You're right on that point."

"Yeah, but did any of that make any sense?" Tessa asked. "It's weird, like we're peeling back layers. It seems the more problems we solve, the more we find."

"Dad. David." She came to a dead stop.

She felt sick to her stomach. "How could I forget?" she cried out. "We must go back and ask Deanna about them." She didn't give him a chance to argue; she turned and raced back. Cody pounded the cement behind her.

They raced back the way they'd come. She stopped a moment later. "Surely it was here, wasn't it?"

They were standing in the same place where they'd spoken to Deanna. She turned to glance at Cody for confirmation. He walked around and appeared to fix his gaze on a mark on the dirt wall he'd seen earlier. "Yes, I think it was."

"If it was, where are they?"

GORAN SMACKED MOTRE on the shoulder. "Let's go. There should be a mess of people out here that need saving."

The look on Motre's face was scary at best, but it was definitely heartwarming for Goran. He did love a good fight. And there were a few due to come. Like himself, Motre was looking forward to it. He looked at the crumpled doctors. "We need to secure these men. Make sure that they can't come after us."

Motre's grin turned ferocious. "Vamps don't need doctors." He pulled something out of his pocket and stabbed the remaining men.

Ash filled the small room.

Goran watched as some of the savagery retreated from Motre's face. With his sleeve covering his face, he choked out, "We're all good then?"

Motre nodded.

Ian walked over the door and after a quick look at the other two, he opened it. They filed out to the silent hallway and quickly checked the rest of the rooms. There were a few men, drugged and unconscious, but that was all. They unplugged the men from machines and undid all the restraints. They couldn't wake the men, so they left them alone to rouse when they could. And they headed back out to the hallway. And proceeded to the next floor.

It was a systematic search they had down pat by the time they made their way back across that floor. Goran was primed for a fight, and he couldn't find one. All they could see were drugged vamps. Just the thought made his stomach cringe, but to know that they were all here and kept prisoner where they should have been safe just made him angry. He stepped back out to the hallway ready to open the next door and hoping for something more violent when he came face to face with several vamps. Men in lab coats. Large men. As in too large men. They had to be enhanced.

He grinned. "Finally. A worthy opponent."

They reached into their pockets, intent on pulling something out. He didn't dare give them time to use whatever they were planning on using. He cried out a war cry and jumped the first man, a fist jabbing in the closest man's jaw. The man stumbled back, but he didn't go down. His head barely shook from the blow. But the unholy grin on his face was terrifying.

"What the hell are you?" Goran cried out.

"I'm the wave of the future, old man. Any day and time, you can come and fight me." And he dropped whatever had been in his hands, reached out, and punched Goran.

It must have been due to his earlier injury that had his body being picked up as if by a huge cannon ball and tossing him ten feet down the hallway. He lay there stunned for a long moment. He could hear sounds of a fight going on around him, then a cry and the sound of another body landing beside him. He looked over to see Ian, crumpled and unconscious. Damn.

"What's the matter, old man? I thought you wanted to fight."

The snigger was the final straw.

Old man? Goran felt that same old bitterness rise up from where it normally lay quiet and calm inside. He said, "Old man?"

He bounced to his feet. The man had turned partly away from him, giving him his back. Dismissing him. "I'll have you know," he said, "That I'm not even close to being an old man."

And he launched himself onto the mammoth–sized vamp's back and found the spot on the back of the neck. The man collapsed to his knees, but he wasn't down and he wasn't out. He roared as he fought against the hold.

Goran squeezed tighter. It was hard to hit the sweet spot with so much oversized muscle in the way. He looked around for a weapon, but there was nothing.

And caught sight of Motre suspended off the ground, held in a death grip by the other man. There was no help for it.

Goran bent his head and used his fangs to hit the sweet spot. Just like that, the huge male was out. Goran got up in time to see Motre's legs kick the air in a macabre death dance.

Goran launched himself on the back of the second man and bit him in the neck. He roared like the dying bull he was then dropped like a mountain, Motre still clutched in his hands.

Motre crashed to the floor and lay there gulping like a fish, staring up at the ceiling. When Motre could finally speak, he asked, "What the hell are these guys on?"

"I don't know," Goran replied. "But I want some." He collapsed to his knees beside Ian. He checked, grateful for the pulse beating strong in the kid's neck. He sat beside him to catch his breath. He motioned to Motre. "If you want to finish them off, I'd really like to not have to do that again."

"With pleasure." Motre scrambled to his feet, pulled the stake out of his pocket, and turned both men to ash. As they lay burning, a weird hissing and awful smell taking over the air, Ian woke up choking and gasping for breath. Goran dragged Ian, Motre hobbling slowly behind him, to the stairwell where the air was fresher. "I don't know about you guys, but I'd say we got our asses well and truly kicked."

"Not so," said Motre. "We're alive and they aren't."

"True. But it was close. Too damn close."

DAVID TURNED FROM the vamp in disgust. His father could deal with him. He was more concerned with finding his sister. And there was no sign of her.

He walked around to the other side when he heard murmured voices.

"Shh," he hissed to his father. Serus immediately froze, every inch alert. He grabbed the other vampire by the back of his neck in warning, leaving no doubt what his fate would be should he displease Serus.

David slipped back into the shadows, straining to hear the conversation, the tone of the voices. And then he knew. He smiled. "Tessa?" he called out. "Is that you?"

There was a shocked silence followed by a shout of joy and running feet. He'd barely turned to the sound when Tessa bolted from the shadows and launched herself into his arms.

"There you are," she cried. "We've been so worried."

We? David looked over his sister's shoulders to see Cody sauntering toward him, a big grin on his face.

Tessa backed up slightly and spun to the side after hearing something. She gasped in shock. "Dad!" She launched herself into their father's arms. David could only shake his head. A couple of weeks ago, this would never have happened. It was a good thing to see.

Cody walked closer. "What the hell happened to you?"

David winced. "Yeah, I wasn't sure what was down here, and instead of meeting Motre and Ian up top, I decided to make a quick trip down."

Cody shook his head. "And you never said a word."

"The reception down here is crappy. No one can send or receive properly. It takes like ten minutes to send out a message if you're lucky."

Cody nodded. "I haven't tried honestly. Been a little too busy." David watched Cody's gaze narrow as he studied Serus and the vamp he was holding onto. "Who's the extra?"

"Who knows? He's trying to save his skin by offering us information."

"Hmmm."

Serus stepped closer. "Cody, what took you so long?" His grin flashed deep and wide.

"Good to see you didn't smash like a bug on your landing, sir. As Tessa was afraid you'd done."

Serus gave her a startled look then laughed uproariously.

"Well, you didn't answer when I called," she said, flushing. "I was afraid you were seriously hurt or dead even."

As he laughed louder, she added, "Obviously I knew you hadn't died when we got here," she said in exasperation, "But you were nowhere to be found."

Still grinning, Serus reached back to tug the stranger forward. "That's because we found this guy's buddies. Only they weren't very friendly."

"But I am," the stranger said. "Lamar is my name."

David snorted. "Whatever. Let's move. I've wasted enough time down here." He looked up the long stairwell above him and groaned. "It's going to take forever to get up here."

"Wait," Tessa said. "The Ghost is supposed to show us another way."

"So was Lamar." Serus shook his new friend hard. Then he stopped, glanced over at Tessa, and said, "A Ghost? Did you see one?"

Lamar cried out in fear as if the Ghost was going to come and get him personally.

"Yes," Tessa said, "And Deanna."

Excitedly, with Cody interjecting when she missed a point, she told them what had happened to them.

David, still standing on the second stair, stared down at her. "Really? So that really old vampire we found already dying was her husband?" At her nod, he whispered, "Holy crap."

"She immediately knew it would have been Tyson that had attacked him."

When his father was quiet, too quiet, David glanced over at Serus to see him staring at Tessa, a really odd look on his face.

"And Deanna talked to you?"

Tessa nodded. "Yes." When he didn't say anything, she asked, "Why?"

He shook his head in wonderment. "She doesn't speak with many, and even then she only speaks with the elders."

"There were no elders there." Tessa shrugged. "Besides, she seemed to think I have some of her genetics in my blood."

Serus frowned. "Some, but I doubt much. You must have caught her on a good day. She is one of the most powerful vamps of all time, and very cranky."

"She's also dying," Tessa said.

"But is she?" Cody glanced over at her. "She's old, but do you really think she's dying?" His voice said he was doubtful.

David wished he'd seen her. Met her. She was a legend in her own right. "She likely still has another century or two left in her," he scoffed.

Tessa stared at him. "No, I'd say days."

"And you'd know this how?" Serus asked.

Silence.

"I don't know. Something about her energy. It didn't look...right?" She shrugged. "Not sure how to explain it. But it's like the energy was fading. Not black like the energy of the enhanced, I saw no sign of that, more like a dying out. As if she was done. Inside and out."

"She doesn't want to live now that her husband is gone, that's for sure, but I wouldn't count her out," Cody said.

"No, I'm not," Tessa said. "She has something she wants

to do. Something she needs to do, and it's not revenge, but when she's done, I suspect she will die."

"She's a tough old bird." Serus snorted. "It will take a lot to kill her off."

"Maybe," Tessa admitted. "Her Ghost was as ancient a being as I've ever seen, too."

"And that's a second very odd fact," Serus said, "I'm not sure I've seen a Ghost in many a century."

"I never have," David said.

"I got the impression they were rare now," Cody said.

"And I got the impression he was in fact the last one." Tessa said. "He's supposed to meet us outside. Show us the headquarters the humans involved in the blood farm used. But..." she looked around. "I'm not sure where he is."

The stranger started to shake. "If a Ghost is coming, I don't want to be anywhere around here."

"And why is that?" Serus growled, squeezing the man's neck.

"He'll kill me," the vamp cried.

"So will my father," David said calmly, "So what's the difference?"

The man started to shriek loudly. Serus sighed and shifted his grip. Instantly the vamp went limp and silent.

"Should have done that in the first place," he muttered. He glanced over at David. "Let's go, son, you can lead off."

Out of the darkness came a long hollow cry. "No. You must not go up there."

RHIA WOKE SLOWLY. It seemed to be all she did these days, waking up and trying to assimilate her surroundings with her pothole memory banks. Still, she came to faster and more alert than she could remember doing in a while. Thank heavens. She had a lessening of the brain fog she'd been fighting. She thought about her son Seth, wondering what she could possibly have done to him. She understood she'd done it for his own good – but what did that mean? Especially in her drug–induced mental state. And where had she sent him, if she'd sent him anywhere? Maybe she only thought she had done so. Maybe he was still in whatever was left of the blood farms – like the hospital. That made her sick to her stomach. How could she have trusted those doctors? She lay back down on her bed. Her mind swelled with confused memories. Had she trusted them? She must have. She'd been there. Gitorria and Rosha had both been there earlier. They must have trusted the men too. Was her family in on this? Who could possibly have drugged her again – and how?

She hadn't eaten anything or drank anything that she knew of.

It boggled the mind to think she'd been so susceptible.

So vulnerable that she'd have been slipped more drugs.

It made her sad.

And it really made her angry.

JARED STARED OUT the doorway to the now–empty hallway. Should he sneak downstairs and try to help the kid? Did he even know which boy it was? He'd thought from that quick glance that it was Tobias, but had it really been him?

He turned to look down the other end. He cast his mind over the bedrooms to the side and mentally tried to match up the glimpse he'd caught to the kids he knew here. Then he realized that the door at the end of the hallway was open. That was Tobias's room. He was sick but getting better. At least that's what Clarissa had said last night. Was that only last night? He hoped so. The days were all mixed up. He couldn't remember what day it was or what date it was. But Tobias had been in good shape last night when he'd seen him.

He had to make sure. He tiptoed down the hallway to Tobias's room. And found it empty, the blankets tossed to the floor.

Confused, Jared wondered if the boy had any medical treatments happening at nighttime.

Damn it. He walked quietly to the top of the stairs and cocked an ear. There were voices talking quietly downstairs. So now what? He crept down a few stairs, hoping to hear things. But the sounds were no clearer. He crept lower to the corner and peered around. He could see the manager talking to another man he didn't recognize. There was no sign of Tobias. He couldn't go any lower without being seen.

Tilting his head, he waited, trying to hear the conversation.

"Tonight…"

"Delayed…"

"Not sure this is a good idea…"

"Bosses don't care. He's not sick, and the kid's not…"

Jared tried so hard to hear…he's not what? But he couldn't hear anything else. The two men moved further away. He thought about the layout of the downstairs and figured they'd likely gone to the office. But where was the kid? He had to find him.

At the bottom stair, it hit him. What was he going to do if he did find Tobias? If he was unconscious, Jared was hardly going to be able to carry him away. And neither could he do much against the manager and his cohort in crime. But damn it, he had to do something. The kid could be taken anywhere and they'd never know.

The voices rose in anger.

"I understand that, but we promised them a quota."

Quota? As in needing to supply a certain number of what? And then he knew. Bile rose up his throat, threatening to choke him.

They had to supply a quota for the blood farm.

CHAPTER 8

T ESSA TURNED AT the raspy sound of the Ghost's voice. "Where should we go then?"

"I will take you to the other exit."

She started forward and stopped when her father grabbed her arm. "Who speaks?"

Silence.

Tessa whispered loud enough for her group to hear but hopefully not loud enough for the Ghost. "He's the one we told you about."

Her father let her arm drop. She watched as he peered into the darkness. "I can't see him."

"I think that's the point," David said in a low voice.

Tessa strode forward. "Hortran, why shouldn't we go up?"

"They are waiting for you."

"Ah, that whole camera thing." Cody caught up to Tessa. "Makes sense."

"Hey, I wasn't looking forward to going up those stairs again anyway," muttered David. "If you can't fly, walking would be a bitch."

"There is another way, but you must hurry," the voice called back, faint and distant. Tessa groaned. "You guys have no idea what it's like to follow Hortran. David, the stairs will start to look mighty good in a few moments."

Cody laughed and took off. Tessa, already knowing what

was to come, took long springing steps to keep up with him, but not so fast she couldn't stop if she saw a wall coming.

She focused on keeping the Ghost's faint energy trail in front of her. As usual, he was so far ahead he was hard to see.

"Can you still see him?" Cody asked.

"Yes, he's still ahead."

"Who is this guy?" David asked from behind. "How can he possibly move like that?"

Tessa was about to explain when her father did. She looked at him to make sure he wasn't getting as tired as she was, not surprised to see him jumping in long lean graceful steps, the unconscious vampire over his shoulders.

"The Ghosts were known for being the best hunters. Their speed and ability to disappear into the surroundings is what gave them their name."

"Then if they were so good, why aren't there more of them?" David asked.

"There were never many of them to begin with. They were so good at what they did, all their genetics went into their skill rather than in another generation."

"And now they are almost all gone."

"A dying breed, like many other genetic traits," Cody said. "Deanna said something about him being wanted by the blood farm people."

"Of course," her father said, "with those genetics, they could make vampires move faster than ever, and the ability to disappear like they do would be tempting for any vampire."

"If he's the last one…"

"Even if he's not, he's the only one I've seen in over a century."

Tessa hated to think that Hortran's people were all gone. "He was with Deanna. Friend, mentor, or slave, I don't know, but there was no question he was loyal to her and her alone."

"Then let's hope she's friendly with you and Cody as this Ghost has the ability to kill you just by walking past you. Something to do with his energy."

"Energy?" Tessa's steps slowed. Deanna never had explained that aspect. "He works energy?"

"I'm not sure how he does it." Serus laughed but it was grim, hollow. "Maybe similar to what you've been doing lately with your slicing movement."

Tessa wondered. "If he does, I'd really like to talk to him about that."

Her head filled with Deanna's voice. *He won't talk to you. He won't talk to anyone but me.*

Is he not the one that called us to follow him?

Yes, but he won't speak of other things.

Can you help? Ask him to speak to me about his ancestors. I can do so much, but I don't know why and what else there might be yet to learn, Tessa cried in her head. She hoped no one else understood that she was speaking telepathically to Deanna – especially Cody. If he understood, he might try to stop her. Still, having a conversation with Cody and Deanna was next to impossible. She gently closed the door to Cody. She recognized the confused glance he sent her, but she wasn't about to stop and explain.

You should keep that door closed. Don't be so open, so vulnerable that you can be attacked.

Cody would never attack me, Tessa said. *I know he wouldn't.*

You are too trusting. Like a child.

To you, I am. Is Hortran helping us right now?

He is. Careful where you go – there are eyes and ears everywhere.

Why are you helping us?

It's you I'm helping. Her strident voice rose to the point of making Tessa wince. *No one else.*

And...you didn't answer why?

"Tessa? Are you okay?" Cody asked at her side. She puffed her breath in and out and gave him a reassuring smile. "I will be when he stops."

Cody laughed. "He's much slower this time."

"Yeah," she puffed. "But then so are we. I'm assuming that's why."

It is. Deanna said. *He could leave you all in the dust.*

And back to that question, *Why are you helping me?*

You're being tested.

And with that, she disappeared.

"Is that Deanna again?" Cody asked.

She nodded. "But she's gone now."

Knowing he was going to ask anyway, she explained Deanna's short message. "I just don't understand why she'd be testing me."

"Neither do I, but I don't like the sound of it."

She shot him a long look. "She hasn't done anything but help us."

"I don't know if she can be trusted."

"The Ghost would say she can be."

"For him, I'm sure she can be," Cody said. "Obviously there was a lot of trust and loyalty between them. They are also both very old and likely to be coming to the end of their road. We can't say for sure when or what method that road will be. We have to remember her husband was one of the big bosses from the blood farm."

True enough, and Tessa hated the reminder. "True. Even if he wasn't interested in the genetic modifications and enhancement they were doing, he was quite happy to run the blood farm."

"Exactly, and she was most likely happy to drink the product. So how much can we trust her?"

"You know something, with all the experiments they were working on, I wonder if they found a way to stop vampires from dying at all. Just because we live for thousands of years, we do still die…"

"And maybe they were working on something like that. Her husband might have seen that as a viable experiment. No way to know. He's gone, and she certainly won't tell us."

Hortran stood in front of them.

Tessa could make him out in the darkness, but she didn't know if the others could. She heard the rest of her family come to a halt behind her.

"Is this the exit?" she asked him. He nodded and pointed to the left. She could see light ahead.

"Go now." The Ghost stared at Tessa. "Deanna will see you later."

And he stepped back deeper into the shadows and disappeared.

❧ ❧

CODY WATCHED AS the man vanished. The group walked forward to where the Ghost had stood, realizing he had really left. Somehow. He turned to Tessa. "Do you see his energy?"

Tessa frowned at him, then realizing why he wanted to know, took a slow look around. She shook her head. "It was faint to begin with, now it's dissipated completely."

"He couldn't have just vanished like that," David exclaimed. "Surely they aren't real ghosts."

"No. But they are damn good at what they do," Serus said.

"Nice to know they are aptly named." Tessa motioned to the exit. "Let's go."

Cody led the way, his mind churning. If the man had the ability to disappear like that, he could understand how valuable they'd been in the wars. And why the enemy would target them. It hurt to think a whole species of vampires would become extinct. But maybe, the Ghosts were an ancient people with ancient thinking. Maybe it was time for the younger generation. And new thinking.

Ahead of him was a steel wall. And wouldn't you believe it. Elevators.

David crowed. "Yes. This is so much better."

Cody punched the buttons and the double doors opened. He stepped in and to the side, waiting for the others. Tessa was last and looked hesitant.

"Tessa? What's wrong?"

"Everything." She gave him a shaky smile. "Where does this go?"

Cody read the buttons on the panel in front of him. "It offers fifteen floors and the parking level."

"Go to the parking level first." Serus said. "Let's make sure we know where we are."

"Done." Cody hit the correct button, reaching out to tug Tessa closer. He didn't know what was bothering her, but he wanted her close.

The doors slowly slid shut, and with a noisy groan, the elevator started to rise.

GORAN HATED THE fatigue rippling through his body. That last fight had been too close. He couldn't help but wonder how long they could keep doing this without losing one of their friends and family.

"What's the matter, Goran? You're getting too old for this shit?" Motre laughed at his own joke.

"Who the hell isn't?" he muttered, glaring at the man he was proud to have fighting at his side. "I've had enough of this whole damn mess."

"I hear you there." Motre reached over and smacked Ian on the shoulder. "What about you? You're just a little kid yet, you should have lots of fighting spirit in you."

"I do," Ian snapped, "But I'm not into war. I'll be happy to get the hell out of here. I'm all for blowing this whole building up."

"And the vamps within?" Motre asked curiously. "Are you ready to blow them all up too?"

Goran watched Ian struggle with his emotions. He understood. There were innocents in there, but there were way too many bad guys too. When did the good outweigh the bad?

"I say we release the ones we can and then drop the entire building."

"And that's the end of it?" Motre pushed. "The end justifies the means?"

Ian dropped his head. "I wish. But I doubt it."

"We still have the human element to deal with." Goran filled them in on what Sian had told him about the humans.

"They shouldn't be our problem," Motre argued. He stopped and sighed, "But as long as they are dealing in human flesh and supplying them to the vamps, they are our business." He glanced at the other two, "So what – are you ready to clean out another floor?"

"Want to – no. Need to…" Goran nodded. "Yeah, we need to. Time to make another dent in their numbers."

Silently, the three pushed open the double doors and walked through.

WENDY LOOKED UP from her spot on the couch, sorting through the list of humans that they'd received from the Human Council. Rhia reclined, weak but aware on the opposite side of the room. Sian had just arrived. She held out another sheet.

"Can you cross reference these names against the list you have? We're sorting through the files from Gloria's laptop, looking for names to match to the blood farm victims and cross–referencing with the ones Taz has identified at the hospital. Most are in drug–induced comas and aren't likely to pull out of this, but if there is any way to know who we have, how they arrived at the blood farm, then we need to know, especially if the humans sold their own kin."

Wendy swallowed and accepted the sheaf of papers. "That's disgusting."

"It is, but it's human nature – apparently." Sian looked over at Rhia's sad face and added, "I'm not sure it's all that much better than our own. Look at what we did to each other."

"I've been trying not to," Wendy said. "But then I think of Jared and what he went through…"

"Exactly." Sian frowned. "Do we have an update on him yet?"

"I don't have one. I don't have his number." Unfortunately. She'd have texted him a long time ago if she could have.

"Tessa will."

"And have we heard from them yet?" Sian pulled her phone out and looked to see what texts she had.

"No," Wendy said in a low voice after taking a quick glance at Rhia. "Nor from Ian."

A grim look on her face, Sian nodded. "Not surprised. All hell is breaking loose and we're in command central again."

"I was in the trenches last time," Wendy said half-jokingly. "As much as I want to be in the middle of it, I'm actually happy to be here."

Rubbing her slightly rounded tummy, Sian nodded in agreement. "There is much to be said for doing our part from here."

∂ ∞

SERUS WATCHED TESSA stand at the front of the elevator. It was bothering her for some reason. More than usual. Considering the amount of deadly things she'd been through in the last couple of weeks, it intrigued him. What about this elevator bothered her so much? And why?

Just then the door opened.

He was watching her face and saw the last thing he expected to see. Relief.

As they exited the double doors, he asked her, "What were you afraid you'd see?"

She half laughed. "Snow."

Serus winced, remembering her trip down the mountain after escaping her captors the first time. The underground parking lot was dark. He flattened against the first barricade and surveyed the area. There were a few vehicles entering and another leaving, but he couldn't be sure who was driving, and they were far enough away that they weren't likely to be driving toward him. He hoped. He glanced around to see if anyone walked from the building out to their vehicles. But there weren't any that he could see. He could see the name on the glass doors up ahead. It looked like where he'd entered earlier. He searched the area and smiled. His car was just where he'd left it. He walked over to it and dumped the unconscious vamp in the trunk. Lamar wouldn't escape that. Then he called the Council Hall to come and pick him up. Once done, he took another careful look around.

"Dad?"

He nodded. "Looks clear."

They walked toward the underground entrance of the hospital. "Plan of action, Dad?"

He grunted. "Why ask me now? You three seem to be acting on your own these days. Maybe you should all fill me in."

"I want to go and get Jewel," David said.

"And I'm here to help get them all free," Tessa piped up.

"We need to meet up with Motre and Ian." Cody strode forward ahead of them to pull the door open for him. "That's where we need to start."

Serus glared at him. "I can open my own doors, thank you."

Cody's eyebrow shot upward. Tessa slipped around him and entered first, called back a cheery "Thanks" to Cody.

Serus rolled his eyes at the kids' antics. That he agreed with Cody was beside the point. It would never do to give the arrogant pup any more reason to inflate his ego as it was.

"So, Dad, we'll defer to you." Tessa spun and flashed her grin at him, her eyes alight with love and laughter. Damn, she was a special kid.

But there was no way he was going to be able to get control of her now. The genie was out of the bottle, and she'd proven to have magic none of them could match. In fact, she was the treasure promised by the genie. Whoever caught that genie and won Tessa as the prize would be the luckiest man alive.

That it was likely Cody was still something he was struggling with, but given the way life had shifted these last few days, he might just be good with that.

At least this way he'd be around to make sure Cody took care of his little girl.

Or else.

❧ ❦

JARED SLIPPED AROUND the corner and walked casually through to the kitchen. There was no sign of anyone. The lights over the stove appeared like a bright beacon in the dark gloom. There was the green light on the coffeemaker. He walked closer and touched the pot, swearing as his fingers came in contact with the hot glass. So they were expecting to be up long enough to drink a pot. Or had gotten up so early as to start the day.

He wondered about that. When he'd gotten up last time, there'd been only dead people around. No one else had been awake. At least not that he'd seen. He tried to come up with an excuse to being up so early in case anyone caught him. It was half past the hour now. If it were six, he'd have no trouble. Before then was a different story. He vaguely remembered hearing a house rule about up by seven but not downstairs before six. He walked into the big room they used as a dining room. It was empty and clean, as it had been left last night. He carried on into the big living room that functioned more as a game room.

It was also empty. Everything had been turned off for the night. He frowned and searched the rest of the downstairs, avoiding the manager's office. The big window leading to the backyard and the wrap-around driveway was on his left. There was an ambulance parked. His heart pounded. Is that where Tobias was? Had he needed an ambulance? No, he tossed that idea away. If that had been the case, he'd have had a stretcher to take him away, not tossed over an orderly's shoulder like he'd been.

There was no one in the cab of the ambulance. Should he look?

He had to know. He opened the side door leading to the large garage and slipped out. It was only after he entered the garage that he remembered the security system. He looked up, but it wasn't even on. Which meant someone had turned it off for the ambulance driver to enter. He walked to the door on the far side, leaving the big garage doors down. They made a racket when they were being raised.

Out at the ambulance, he raced around to the far side to look in the window. A male was there strapped into a stretcher. Jared checked the passenger door and it opened under his hand.

He slipped inside.

He had to know if Tobias was dead or alive.

As he made his way to the back where the stretcher sat, he heard voices coming toward him.

Shit.

CHAPTER 9

TESSA STRODE AHEAD, coming to a sudden stop at the stairway that had given them so much grief. She peered over the railing to see the depth of the building. How odd that they'd gone all the way around in a circle coming up in that old elevator. That it even worked had been amazing. She headed up the first set of stairs, the others following close behind.

"Tessa, we have reception again. I've texted Motre to see what floor they are on."

"Great." Turning the corner to go up the next flight of stairs, and pulling out her own cell phone. She grinned then frowned at Jared's text waiting for her. She gave him Sian's number and told him to contact her as she was easier to get a hold of her than Taz. Raising her gaze from the others all checking their phones. "David," she asked, "what floor is Jewel on?"

"She was on nine. They might have moved her now."

"Motre just responded saying they are on the eleventh floor – and…" Serus's voice rose in shock, "Goran is with them!"

Tessa spun around to see Cody frozen a step below her. She squeezed his shoulder as she asked excitedly, "Really? He's awake?"

"Apparently not only awake but in fighting form."

Cody looked at him, a puzzled look on his face. Tessa wondered what the problem was.

"You didn't sense him, sir?"

Serus glanced up, frowning. "I hadn't tried in a long while as we were so far down I figured, like our cell phones, there'd be no reception." He grinned at that last bit.

Cody laughed. "True enough. It will be good to see him on his feet again."

"Then let's get moving and find them. Level eleven then?" she asked as she continued the slow climb. She wasn't tired, but she was starting to hate stairs of any kind.

"Nine," David said. "We get Jewel then we meet up with Motre."

"And then what?" Serus asked, his voice flat. "Leave with the ones we came for or clean house?"

There was a long silence only broken by the sounds of the footsteps hitting the metal stairs. Tessa was interested in hearing David's words. As much as she wanted to go home, they were in a position to do so much more. "While we have access, we need to contact Councilman Adamson and Sian to see how the others are. And how their plans are moving forward."

"I already have," Serus growled. "Wendy is watching over your mother, who is awake and back to herself with a few missing spots in her memories."

Tessa snorted. "I can imagine."

"No, not the way you're thinking. Although she doesn't remember how she was drugged or when, she's also unaware of what arrangements she made for Seth."

Tessa spun around. Cody, who was behind her, grabbed her arms to help steady her.

"Dad, if she doesn't remember, how can we find him?"

she cried. "He's been through so much. We have to stop them from making the drugs and brainwashing permanent."

"Sian is working on it, Rhia is trying to regain her memories, and we have to trust the Councilmen are trying to clean house – on both sides."

They ran up the next few flights of stairs as Tessa pondered the mess. "I never made it to the school to ask the principal to warn the kids either."

"Sian is trying to work something out."

"I should have gone."

Her father growled behind her, "No. You won't be dealing with the humans again for a while."

There was an odd note in his voice. Odd enough that she slowly turned to look at him. "What's wrong?"

He glared her and slipped his phone into his pocket. "Nothing."

She stopped, making everyone else stop, too. "Dad?"

"I thought we were in a hurry." He started to walk around her, but she stepped in his way.

"Except that something is wrong and you're trying to hide it from me." Oh no. "Is it Jared? Has something happened to him?"

The others gasped and looked at him expectantly. Serus rolled his eyes. "No, nothing is wrong with Jared. At least as far as I know."

Tessa had barely given Jared a thought until she'd just seen his last text, looking for Taz's contact information, but that could have been sent hours ago as he should be sleeping at this hour. She glanced up at her father and caught that bit of relief in his eyes. She narrowed her gaze. "What is it about the humans you are trying to avoid talking about?" She sharpened her tone like her mother always did and said,

"Spill."

"Nothing," he glared at her, but then his gaze slid away.

"Aha," she crowed. "You are hiding something."

She crossed her arms and refused to move.

He threw up his arms. "It's nothing."

"Good, then you might as well tell us." The others circled him.

"It's just that they want your help again." His gaze whispered between Cody and her and back again. "They want you to determine who is enhanced and who is poisoned."

"Really?" She didn't know what to think.

"They are calling Sian constantly." He sighed. "She's trying to dodge them, but they are persistent."

She frowned. "We can help." She looked over at Cody. "Right?"

"It's your call. I'll help sort; you just tell me which ones to coax into the right groups." His feral grin said all too clearly just how much he'd enjoy it.

She eyed him carefully. "Nicely?"

His gaze widened innocently. "Of course."

"No. There are too many of them. They don't want you to just sort a few of them; they want you to look at each and every one of them." Serus shook his head. "It will be too big a job."

"Sis, he's right. There are too many."

"But if she could," Cody said, "It might be the way to clear out the problem of the humans once and for all. We could pull them in groups in a big hall and do a few thousand at a time. She would just have to motion which goes left and which goes right."

"And the odd cases?" Serus snapped. "Remember her trying to figure out why each of those men had been poisoned?"

Tessa sighed. "I'd like to be able to help. I'm just not sure I can."

"Exactly." Serus swept past her. "Now forget about it. We have a job to do and we need you to be focused."

She would focus on the job at hand, it was suicide not to, but she'd never forget. There had to be something she could do.

Cody grabbed her hand, squeezed it, and pushed her up the stairs.

❧ ❧

CODY WATCHED TESSA move ahead of him. She'd almost caught up to her father. He wondered if she'd push the issue right now. He hoped not. Serus appeared fairly adamant at this point. He understood Tessa wanted to help and he'd go with her, even though it would likely take days. They had to find a way to speed that up. He just didn't know how. He watched David and Serus jump up to the next landing and stop.

David said, "It's the ninth floor."

"Good." Tessa looked longingly up the next couple of floors. "Where are Motre and Ian now?"

Serus pulled out his phone and tapped out a message quickly. "We'll wait here until I hear back, oh—" his phone beeped. He read out the message. "They are on the tenth floor."

"Maybe we should get them first. If they are almost done, we could join up before going through this floor."

Serus nodded. "That's probably a good idea."

"No. We can't." David shook his head violently. "We don't know what's happening to Jewel. They can meet us here." He opened the door.

Cody groaned. "Serus, make sure you tell my father. Although if they are fighting, maybe just send a text."

But Serus was already texting. Cody didn't even know if his father was in good enough shape to mindspeak, but of course he had to be in the middle of the fighting. And Tessa being Tessa had bolted into the hallway in David's wake. And Cody was damned if he was going to be left behind. He raced up the last couple of stairs and pulled the big door open. He slipped inside, hearing the metal door clang behind him. He hoped Serus was coming soon.

Tessa and David had raced down the hallway. He could see them striding ahead of him. There didn't appear to be any staff visible. How could that be? Weren't hospitals full of them? Frowning, a last glance behind him, he raced behind Tessa. That girl could get into trouble like no one else.

He had a whole lifetime of trying to keep her out of trouble. He hoped.

Are you coming, slowpoke?

Tessa's laughter rippled through his mind.

God, he was so hooked on her.

If that were true, you'd be here at my side instead of wasting time and mooning about.

Mooning? Mooning? Me? he asked, affronted. Then he realized he'd come to a dead stop in the middle of the hallway like a lovesick child. He groaned and picked up his feet. *I wasn't mooning.*

Sure. That's okay though – as long as you're only mooning over me.

He grinned. *Only you, Tessa...forever.*

He hadn't meant to add the forever part, but it sounded just right to him.

❧ ❦

"THEY ARE JUST a floor downstairs? Really?" Goran grinned. "Let's go get them then."

Motre shook his head and waved his phone back and forth in front of him. "Serus says David is trying to find Jewel. They want us to sweep this floor first then go join them."

Feeling lighter and more connected than he had in a long time, Goran said, "Then let's go."

He called out mentally to Serus, *Hey Serus, old buddy, is that you?*

Damn, it's nice to hear you again. Are you sure you should be out of bed?

Goran's smile fell away. *I'm fine,* he growled. *I've been calling for you for hours. Where the hell have you been?*

In the basement – and what a hell of a basement it is. Must be a quarter mile deep. Met a few interesting people down there too. He laughed. *You missed all the fun.*

Goran frowned. *Damn it. We've been busting asses up here too. Met a couple of monsters that we could barely drop.* Realizing how that sounded, he quickly added, *Of course we took care of them.*

Serus chuckled. *Yeah, us too. How come we didn't meet this size in the blood farm?*

I think they are smarter than that lot. Goran growled. *They are here at the hospital area doing whatever bullshit they are doing here.*

But they are bigger, stronger than the others. Shit. I'm getting tired of going against genetically modified vamps.

Yeah, I hear you, but the good news is we keep winning. The more they throw at us, the more we knock them down.

At least he hoped so. Goran walked down the hallway

125

behind Motre, Ian at his side. Motre opened the first door. Goran glanced inside. *More drugged vamps. And one of them Councilman Bushman – the councilman Motre was protecting when they all ended up in the blood farm. He's hooked up to drugs again.*

Damn. Serus said. *He wasn't supposed to be anywhere around here. I thought he'd gone to some damn Council meeting?*

Meeting with the Human Council? Goran asked sharply.

No. Other clans. He was attending the International Council.

Goran stopped Motre from closing the door after pulling the tubes loose from the men. He strode closer. *There are four men in here with him. I don't recognize the first couple, but they are old. As in very old. Not sure about the last one.*

What's the chance the Council meeting was targeted? A way to collect a few more specialized vamps for their damn experiments?

That would be unbelievably wrong. If you're right and these other vamps are from the International Council, then these are heads of their own clans. That's bad news.

And will bring down the other clans on our heads because we let this happen.

I know.

Would you recognize the men from that meeting? Goran walked from one to the other. At the fourth man, he stopped and swore loud and long.

Motre asked him, "What's the matter?"

"I recognize this man. He's the head of the German Council."

JARED HUNCHED IN the back of the ambulance, his head low so no one could see through the window. He pulled the blankets down on the boy's face and checked for a pulse. And let his breath out in a rush. Tobias was alive. As relief shuddered through him, he realized he hadn't expected that. With all the dead bodies racking up, he'd half expected him to be dead. He twisted around to look outside. The voices were closer. Shit. How could he get out? He shifted back to the front passenger side and opened the door quietly. He slipped out and ran into the bushes lining the parking lot. His heart yammered so loud he couldn't hear anything. Had they heard him? They hadn't called his name. Then again, maybe they hadn't been able to recognize him. There. His gaze darted to the driver's side of the ambulance and the heated discussion going on between the manager and the driver.

Still, that wasn't his prime problem. How to get back inside the home was. He needed to avoid these men. And he needed the license plate of the ambulance to track it. Although what good that would do, he didn't know.

Another option was to stow away inside the ambulance. At least then he'd find out where they were taking Tobias.

He stared at the ambulance in frustration. From his position, he couldn't hear the conversation, and that just pissed him off. He didn't want to let Tobias be taken away but if he was sick, maybe he needed help. Only sick men weren't hauled out like a sack of potatoes.

He so didn't trust the manager. He was damn dodgy. Hence Jared's need to sneak back into the home without being seen as he'd left his stuff inside. How could he get out of the bushes? He turned around and searched the neighboring yard. Could he sneak around back and get into the house that way? Or come into the property from the far side? Realizing he was running out of time to act, he picked up his feet and ran around the back of the home and over to the far side where the shrubbery was closest to the door and raced to the door. He slipped inside, pausing for a moment before running upstairs to his room. He closed the door and jammed the chair under the doorknob again. His heart clamoring and his blood pulsing, he slipped under the covers and closed his eyes.

He could hardly breathe for the panic choking him.

Had he made it without being seen?

WENDY SAT BESIDE Rhia and did the slow, tedious cross-checking for Sian. She couldn't help but constantly check her phone. She knew Ian didn't have his but surely if he was free, he'd managed to get a hold of someone's phone. Just then it buzzed. Ian. She read the incoming text and gasped.

Rhia sat up from where she'd been reclining. "What is it?"

Wendy turned to face her, a huge smile on her face. "It's from Ian. He's with Motre and they are waiting for the rest to meet up with them." As she finished speaking, another text came in.

"Goran is there too." Wendy sat back and pinched the bridge of her nose, willing the tears to not fall. She was so damn grateful Ian was okay. She quickly texted him back asking for more details and when he was coming home.

When he didn't answer right away, she didn't know why. Just when she was starting to worry again, another text came in. *Lots of fighting. We're coming down the hospital and searching room by room. So far, it's mostly drugged vamps. Not sure about some of them. It's really weird. For a hospital, there is no staff to be seen. No noise even. It's like the dead are the only ones here.*

"Wendy?" Rhia asked gently. "Can you let me know what they are all saying, please?"

Sian walked in just then, carrying a big tray of blood slushies. Wendy took a tentative sip while Rhia told her what had happened.

"That's excellent. As soon as they meet up with the others, then all will be well."

"Except they are searching the hospital room by room."

Sian frowned. "I guess that is the orderly approach. Do you know what or who they are looking for?"

Wendy read the next text then looked up. "David is trying to find Jewel. She'd been close to Ian last time he'd seen her, but they haven't found her yet."

She looked over at Rhia. "Ian says he saw me leaving earlier but couldn't get out. Motre rescued him."

"Perfect. Motre is a good vamp. With him in charge, they should be just fine."

Wendy studied her face. "I hope so," she said quickly. "I'd like to see them turn around and just come back here."

The smile on Sian's face was gentle and compassionate. "For the same reason you want Ian home, David won't leave Jewel behind and in danger."

"I know." Wendy gave her a tremulous smile. "That doesn't stop me from wanting something different."

"Keep trusting in Ian and those helping him. So far we've all been lucky. Maybe that luck can hold out for a little bit longer."

She hoped so, but like everyone else's thoughts, she knew no one's luck held forever.

CHAPTER 10

TESSA FOLLOWED DAVID to the room he disappeared into. She stood at the doorway, waiting for Cody to catch up to them. She started when a strong hand slid around her waist, tugging her backwards against a large warm chest.

Hi.

Hi back. She smiled. *I gather my father isn't right on your ass?*

He stiffened and his arm dropped away.

She giggled.

Think that's funny, do you?

Yep, and then some. But that's okay. Our time will come. She watched David walk through the large ward checking the beds, so when the silence was a little awkward, she could forgive herself from missing it initially. *What?* she asked mentally. *What did I say?*

Nothing, he muttered. She turned to look up at him, noting her father's approach from several feet away. *Something is.*

Just your comment that our time will come. Will it?

She knew what he was asking without asking. *Yes, it will. Soon? Yes. Today? Given our situation, so not.*

He grinned. *How about next week?*

Ha. I wanted to go to the hangout this Friday.

His voice turned serious. *And I want that too. All we have to do is get Jewel and Ian out of here. Then we can go home, rest, shower, feed, and still have the next few days to ourselves before Friday.*

"Hey, move it you two," Serus barked. "You're standing there mooning at each other."

Tessa snickered at the word he used.

Cody stepped back and gritted through his teeth, "I am not mooning."

Serus growled as he walked past them into the room, "Were too."

At that, Tessa broke out laughing, her voice free and easy.

Until she saw David turn around at the end of the room and come back slowly, checking out the beds on the other side. As she'd seen him glancing at both sides as he'd walked down, she had to assume he hadn't found Jewel. Every step he took toward her, the grimmer his face got. Every step he took, the more her heart sank. What if Jewel had been moved, the same as Ian had? They couldn't just isolate her friend – there'd be no point to such actions. Her friends were no more dangerous than other vamps. So why move them?

David met with Serus and the two bent heads, the conversation fast and furious. Tessa stayed at the doorway with Cody. David's face and clenched fists told the story. Jewel wasn't here.

As they approached the doorway, David said in a harsh whisper. "She's not here. No one is."

"No one," Cody asked, motioning to the closed curtains. "What do you mean by no one?"

"I mean all the beds are empty. As in completely empty."

"What? That makes no sense."

"No," Serus said, adding, "But from what I can see, the beds are all made and prepped as if waiting for an influx."

"Aren't hospital beds always ready like this?"

"No idea." Serus shrugged. "Why would they need to have so many beds?"

"More than that, what happened to those that were here? This ward was full when I was here last time," David snapped. "Where is Jewel?"

"Could they have gotten better?" Tessa asked with a faint hope.

"I know you don't want to consider this, but do we know for sure that she's still here?" Cody asked quietly. "Is there a chance Jewel is on her way home, or already at home and sleeping?" He threw up his hands at David's glare. "I just want to make sure that she's not before we go half-cocked with more conspiracy theories."

David shook his head violently. "She's here," he said harshly. "I'd know if she weren't."

Tessa stared at him. She understood what he meant but didn't want to put him on the spot. She heard Cody swallow back his own comment. She slipped her arm through his, grateful he was at her side and they weren't once again split up and trying to find each other. Cody squeezed her arm tight against his body.

He understood.

"Dad," Tessa said, "Have you asked Motre to look for Jewel?"

"Goran knows already, but I'll remind Motre," he said, already texting. Tessa backed out of the room, tugging Cody with her. "David, let's do a systematic search," she suggested. "Jewel might just be in one of these rooms."

She was surprised they hadn't met any staff since they'd arrived on this floor. Surely if they had video cameras in the depths of that basement, they'd have similar cameras on these floors. As she walked to the room beside the one they'd been in, she noticed a camera, the same color as the walls. She turned to the next room, and said to Cody, *Smile, we're on camera.*

His step faltered. *Where,* he hissed.

In the corner, the walls with a doorway arch. They are the same color as the hall so they blend in well.

Damn, his harsh whisper raced through her mind. *I suggest we check these rooms quickly before we have company.*

She agreed. The next room was full. Of vamps. Connected to tubes. In a grim voice, she asked, *Who are all these people?* Tessa assessed the occupants. All males, roughly late teens to late twenties as far as she could tell, although males that age kept their looks for a long time, making it hard to guess their age as they could be a couple of decades older. They all appeared to be in fine physical shape. There were no broken bones or visible injuries.

"They are being drugged. I just don't know why."

Serus came to the door behind them. "Let's go. Goran says they haven't seen Jewel, but there are foreign delegates being held upstairs."

Tessa, in the act of checking out the other occupants, froze, her mind racing. "Why would that be?"

"There is a huge international meeting happening this week. Between all the clans. And now the head of the German clan is here, and he's drugged. There are a few men with him in the same room. Likely the entire German party."

"Does Dad suspect that there might be other delegates here?" Cody asked, striding toward the door. "Is that what we're thinking? Someone is kidnapping the delegates and keeping them here?"

"Isn't that a bit much? Why not take the drugs to them?"

"Because they'd have to infiltrate the clans. And you know

clans are very protective."

In fact, Tessa remembered from her history lessons, the clans were more warring than peaceful. Peace, tentative at best, had happened several centuries ago. Now the clans met yearly to make sure all treaties were still being met.

"If they kidnapped the Germans, then chances are the other clans are in trouble, too."

"Or maybe the Germans signed up for this willingly. They'd get enhancements and then be superior to the other clans and be able to dominate them if another war happened."

Tessa winced. That was the last thing she wanted to consider, but it was all too possible. The clans' peace treaty was a little ragged around the edges. It wouldn't take much if someone wanted to make a power play and take over the others. Especially if they had enhancements for their people well before anyone even realized what was happening. It wouldn't be a war – it would be a non–war – over before it had begun.

The humans would be the fallout in that case. And everyone's way of life would change.

❧ ❧

CODY HATED TO hear this new twist. As far as he was concerned, all this bullshit could disappear so he could go and play – with Tessa. Immature maybe. There was no doubt his relationship was getting stronger, but he hadn't had any time with her alone.

And damn it, he wanted that. He needed that. So did she.

He strode out of the room, leaving the others behind. It was only as he swung into the emptiness of the long hallway that he realized his hands were clenched into fists. He stared down at his fingers, opening and flexing them in frustration. He'd rarely known such emotion. And no target to hit out at. God damn it. He swung out and punched the wall in front of him.

And barely strangled back a scream. That hurt! What the hell. He stuffed his fist into his mouth and bit back the moan of pain.

Idiot. Tessa's concerned voice whispered through his mind as the pain swelled and ebbed.

Ya think, he snarled. *I want this bullshit over.*

Me too, she said soberly. *We all do. Let's find Jewel and Ian and go home.*

Promise? He smiled at the warm hug that he swore he could feel in his mind from her thoughts, her emotions. She was so expressive.

Yeah, I just choose not to punch out walls. And she laughed out loud.

He turned, caught her close in his arms, and hugged her tight.

As he released her, he started to turn away but she stumbled. He reached out to steady her. Her knees buckled, the color drained from her face, her eyes great orbs of pain.

"Tessa?" He tried to hold her up against him, but she'd gone completely limp.

She moaned deep inside her throat. He tried to contact her mentally to see what she was feeling, sensing. And couldn't gain access. The damn door was closed again.

"Please don't shut the door, Tessa," he begged. "Please. Stay in contact. Tell me what's wrong," he cried, seeing her gaze fog over.

"Tessa?"

Her father rushed over to Cody and grabbed Tessa around

the waist, throwing her arm around his shoulder. "What happened, Cody?"

"No idea. She just collapsed."

"Tessa, stay with us."

She groaned and with the barest of a whisper, she said. "It's Deanna. She's in trouble."

Then as if a string was cut, Tessa collapsed.

SERUS GASPED AND shifted his weight to catch his daughter more securely. "What the hell…?"

"I don't know," Cody cried out.

"What did she mean about Deanna being in trouble?" Serus snapped, trying to get Tessa on her feet again. He considered laying her down until she came out of her faint but didn't want to let her go.

"Earlier, Deanna spoke to Tessa telepathically – and slammed the door shut between Tessa and I. I couldn't open it at all."

"What?" Serus stared at Cody in shock, his mind racing.

"She's really strong."

Serus started. He considered how strong someone would have to be to do what Deanna had done to Tessa and how strong Tessa would have to have been to survive the on-slaught.

"Did she collapse then like she'd done now?"

Cody shook his head like mad. "Not like this. It hit her hard for the initial moments then she was fine. She had a conversation with her. Several in fact."

Serus studied his young face. "And she didn't show any reaction?"

"A mild one, but not like this." He shifted his weight. "How long is she likely to be out?"

With a frown, Serus had to ask that question himself. He didn't know. "Shouldn't be long."

"Why would Deanna have called Tessa?"

David, having checked out the several rooms around them, returned to lean against the wall and said, "Because she could. Either Tessa's door was open so she could talk to her, or she was the only one close enough to hear Deanna's transmission."

Tessa moaned.

"Easy, Tessa," Serus crooned against her head. He shifted her weight slowly, trying to get her to tilt her head up.

"Tessa. Wake up."

She moaned again louder.

Serus studied her face, her head tilted to his side, her pallor ashen and her cheekbones strong and lean. Damn Deanna. What was her game? And why his daughter? He didn't have a reason to not trust her, but he wished she'd contacted anyone else but Tessa.

Still, it was Tessa who'd been the one to step in Deanna's space. And no one could call Deanna stupid. And neither could anyone ever say Tessa was weak. A few weeks ago, a few people might have made that mistake – not him – he prided on knowing his daughter had always been stubborn and strong–willed. Right from birth, she'd been determined to follow her brothers in whatever trouble they'd gotten into. They'd tried to discourage her, but she'd never listened. They'd had a hell of a time with her. Like the first time she'd gotten loose while they'd slept and had run outside the house – in the daytime.

To this day, he didn't know how she'd managed to open

the door. The security system had been on and the light said it was working. Rhia had gone to bed, but he'd been in the study. Until he heard the door and had raced out to the hallway to find Tessa laughing and dancing outside – wearing only a diaper and the biggest smile possible – in the bright sunshine.

He'd screamed for Rhia. As she'd come running, so had her brothers.

They'd stood in shock and terror as Tessa had run and jumped in joy, enjoying her first time in the open sunlight – something no one else in the family had ever experienced.

Rhia had stood by helplessly, confusion all over her face. Her brothers had been shocked to silence. Serus, well, he'd grabbed up his coat, hat, and gloves and had gone out into the sunshine to play with his daughter.

As he stared at her, so grown up and so confident – at the same time – so vulnerable at this moment, his heart ached for the little girl he'd spent so much time protecting from sunlight only to realize she hadn't needed it in the first place.

As if on cue, she moaned again and this time her eyes fluttered. She was a long ways from being alert. He glanced down the hallway. "We should move into a room and out of the public eye."

Tessa shook her head, more like a puppy shaking off water, as if shaking off Deanna's voice. "Too late," she muttered, her voice slow and slurry. "Cameras."

"Shit," Cody said. "I never gave them a thought." With his free hand, he pointed up to the corner of the wall arch. "She pointed it out earlier."

Cameras? Serus hadn't considered that. Not that it made much difference at this point. "David, let Motre know about the cameras and about Tessa."

Mentally, he gave Goran a quick rundown.

"I already have." David motioned to Tessa. "Is she going to be able to move anytime soon? Or should we lay her down in one of the rooms and you can stay with her while Cody and I search the rest of the floor?"

Cody opened his mouth to protest but choked back the words.

Serus gave Tessa a shake. She mumbled, "I'm fine."

"Like hell you are."

David's phone rang. He pulled it out while Tessa made an attempt to stand. She gave another shake of her head. And this time, she struggled to lower her arms. "I'm going to be fine. I just need a moment."

"Or ten," Serus snapped, but he kept a supportive arm around her waist. He watched David grin and close his phone. David turned to the end of the hallway and motioned. Motre, Ian, and Goran were standing there.

Tessa took one step then another on her own. Serus watched the color come back to her face and awareness back into her eyes.

She smiled at Cody. "Good, now we're all here, we can go help Deanna."

In unison, all three men said. "Like hell."

∞ ∞

JARED LAY SHAKING under the covers as the clock slowly turned. He couldn't help thinking that he was in danger again. He was already cursing himself for being a fool. And yet what were his choices? What was he supposed to do at this point? He didn't want to go to a foster home. He wanted to stay with the people he knew. The people he trusted. He pulled out his phone and checked to see if he had any texts.

He needed to contact the group of friends who'd been here last night. Let them know that Tobias had been moved. If he was being moved. Had the ambulance even left? He couldn't get rid of the feeling that they might have seen him. And what was he going to do about it? Shit. He looked around his small room and took a deep breath. He got up, packed up his few belongings, and sat on the bed. He'd love a shower – but was it safe? It seemed a long time ago since it was safe. Undecided, tired, but too wired to relax, he rocked back and forth, a blanket now around his shoulders as he tried to concoct a plan. Like what the hell was he supposed to do?

Just when he'd started to relax and figured out that maybe he was going to be okay, there was a soft knock on Jared's door.

He swallowed hard, a nervous panic filling his blood. He didn't answer.

"Jared? Are you awake?"

He huddled deeper into the corner of his bed, his gaze locked on the door handle and the chair jammed underneath.

"Jared? You there?" This time, there was no pretense at being quiet. And it was definitely the manager's voice. "Jared. Time to get up for school."

Jared looked at his watch.

Shit. It was seven. How the hell had the time gone by so quickly? He must have dozed off.

The manager was right. It was time to go.

The only question remaining was time to go where?

CHAPTER 11

TESSA COULDN'T HELP the shudder of pain that raced down her spine as the voices around her rose. She wished she had a way of explaining, but the fact that Deanna had almost crippled her with the force of her entry and exit said a lot about the vamp's methodology. But the men weren't listening to Tessa, and neither could they hear Deanna. And she had no choice but to listen, otherwise Deanna could cripple her again.

There'd been no malice in Deanna's actions. More fear. Panic. Desperation.

Tessa reached up a hand to rub her temples, her nerves ragged and frayed, screaming at her now. They had to go help Deanna. There was no option here.

Just then David snapped, "We have to find Jewel first."

"First, yes," Ian said. "But I want to go and see Wendy."

"Tessa needs to lie down for a bit," Cody said. She rolled her eyes at him.

"Forget the others," Motre growled at everyone. "This is bigger than before. Like way bigger now."

Finally, her father snapped. "Enough!" he said in a roar loud enough that the rest of the German delegates should have been able to hear him in their home country. She couldn't hold back the cry of pain as his voice thundered through her head.

Instantly, Cody wrapped an arm around her shoulders and tugged her closer.

She nestled in.

Into the silence, she whispered, "If you want to split up, fine, but I have no choice. Deanna is going to be able to cripple me no matter what I'm doing if it's not what she wants me to do. And I don't think distance is going to help."

The others stopped their muttering. Serus said, "Fine. Deanna really has left us no choice then."

"And the Germans?"

Cody asked, "Any idea if the Nordic clan is here? Or the Asians? What about the African clan?"

Tessa turned slightly so she could see Motre's head shake. "Would you know?" she asked in a quiet voice. "Could you recognize them all?"

"All of them? No. Some of them, yes," Motre said. "So far I've only seen the German group."

"We've only checked part of this floor. While I stay here and rest, you should do a fast sweep of the floor, see if Jewel is here or anyone else we know so we can see what we're dealing with. There's no way the others don't know what we're up to with the cameras running the whole time."

"Let them," growled Goran. "I'd be happy to tell them how I personally feel."

He walked over to the first door, Serus at his heels, and in a systematic method, the four men carried out a search of the rest of the floor. As the hallway was broken into long segments, and from the size of it, could likely house a hundred and fifty or more patients to the floor, she highly suspected that there could be other delegates found soon too. She could believe that the Germans would willingly want the offer of superiority through enhancements, but she couldn't be sure they were here of their own free will. They could just as easily be prisoners like her friends had been. If the blood farm assholes managed to collect all the DNA of all the ancients available throughout the world, who knew what kind of nightmare they'd create in the name of science?

"Are you okay?" Cody had kept his arms around Tessa, holding her up.

She straightened again and moved her head around slightly. "Yes, for the moment. It's scary though. There's nothing like knowing someone can jump into your mind and take you out without warning."

"And given that she can do that, she's got a hell of a weapon to use on anyone. If she can use it on anyone – it's a crazy good self-defense, too." He waited a bit then said, "So why does she need you to help?"

"I *think* that's what she can do, but I'm not sure." Tessa stopped to consider what she instinctively understood but was struggling to put into words. "I think it only hurt because she more or less shoved her way in. In her panic, she blasted at me instead of spoke to me." She shrugged. "Like a slap in the face instead of a *hey you*."

"So that's why you didn't get knocked out the first time she talked to you?"

"Exactly." She smiled up at him. "She's powerful. Incredibly powerful."

"I think I remember my father mentioning her and her husband in the past. Something about being the strongest of us all. And the oldest."

"That's what she said. The oldest generation being the strongest, with all others becoming more diluted as each new generation came along," she murmured. Experimentally, she took several steps around him, her hand on his arm for support just in case she needed it. She shifted her body and neck from side to side. "I think I'm back to normal now."

"Good. Any idea how to help Deanna?"

"Not really. She told me where she's being kept." She stretched, only to step back in surprise as Cody stepped in front of her.

"Really? Why didn't you say something?"

At his raised voice, she groaned slightly, her hands coming up to clasp over her ears. "Shh. And the answer is because I haven't really had a chance to recover yet." Then she sighed heavily and added, "And because of where she is."

That stalled the words about to explode from his mouth. Instead, he sighed. "Sorry." He dropped a kiss on her forehead. He stepped back and eyed her carefully. "So where is Deanna?"

Tessa stared at him, then sadly said, "She's in the morgue."

❧ ❧

CODY STARED AT Tessa, not sure he'd heard correctly. "Are you telling me she's dead?" And how that could be, he didn't know. But there was a surge of relief washing through him at the thought. He didn't like her being able to slam the door between him and Tessa closed like she'd done. Hurting Tessa was another big no no. Still, given the atrocities he'd seen, he wouldn't wish her fate on anyone. He doubted she'd gone down easy. "She might be just a prisoner in that room."

Tessa stared at him, and damn if her bottom lip didn't tremble. He tugged her back into his arms. "You think she's dead, don't you?"

Tessa's slim shoulders shifted. "I don't know," she said,

her voice muffled against his shirt. "But something is very wrong. And I know time is an issue."

The others were almost done. "We'll be able to go soon."

Sure enough, the ancients walked back toward them, with David and Ian, heads bent, trailing behind.

"There are many vamps here. Same as upstairs," More said, "I don't recognize any of the foreign delegates, but I can't be sure."

Serus said, "There's no sign of Jewel."

Cody waited.

Serus looked at Tessa and frowned. "I know you want to go off after Deanna, so David will join Goran and Motre and keep going floor by floor, I'm going with you and Cody to find Deanna if..." he paused and fixed his long considering gaze on her wan features. "If you know where she is."

Tessa winced, but in a clear strong voice, she explained the little bit she'd heard from Deanna.

"The morgue?" Motre exclaimed. "Damn. I never even thought to look there. That's a great place to start."

"And as such," Serus said, "We'll go to the bottom where the morgue level is and slowly work our way up."

Goran stared at Tessa's face before switching his gaze to Cody. "Son, you okay with this?"

Cody nodded. "Yes, sir. She thinks Deanna is still alive but that she's running out of time."

"And she could quite possibly be. Let's go." Serus headed down the hallway, calling back, "And you guys, check in constantly. Goran, keep the mind link open. We need to know where each group is and what they are up against at all times."

Tessa ran to catch up to her father, a smile on her face. "Thanks, Dad."

He shrugged. "You were going to go no matter what I said. This way I can at least try to keep an eye on you – maybe keep you safe."

Tessa tossed a rolling eye look at Cody. He laughed.

"At least he knows you, Tessa."

"That he does." She reached out a hand. Cody grabbed it and they headed to the elevators.

JEWEL PLACED HER ear against the locked door. She heard loud voices outside, but they were far enough away to not identify the tone or the speakers. She shuddered. She'd been curled up on the corner of the bed, wondering, worrying when she'd heard voices.

She glanced around the small room, thinking there couldn't be anything good about waking up in a small room on her own.

What had happened to the nice big room where there'd been lots of other people to see and feel comforted in knowing she wasn't alone? She looked around her room once again. There were no windows, just empty shelves as if they'd hastily converted this room for her. Why? She hadn't done anything to them.

Of course she'd been involved with Tessa and that whole blood farm mess, but waking up isolated like this was the first indication that she'd been in trouble. At least she couldn't get the concept that she was in trouble out of her head. However now that she'd said something about being isolated, she had to wonder if that was exactly what they'd done. But for a good reason. As in she'd been infected. Or contagious, or they were concerned that she might be.

There was no name on her bed or the wall. No buzzer to contact anyone for help. There was nothing. She sat back down on the corner of her bed and wondered something else. She'd been here for hours – without a bathroom. In her old room, there'd been a large bathroom with a shower. Now… there was nothing.

The only door in and the only door out was the one right in front of her. She didn't need the bathroom yet, but now that the concept had been brought up, she'd have to go soon. A loud noise outside had her racing to the doorway. Crap. Why couldn't they speak louder so she could hear what was going on?

"Then again, Jewel, why haven't you called out or pounded on the door so someone lets you out of here?" she whispered out loud, finding comfort in the sound of her voice.

Because she was afraid. If she was here and forgotten, then she was safe. If she brought attention to herself, then she had no idea who'd open the door.

The voices grew louder. She got up and crept into the corner of the room.

She had no idea who was coming, and she had no weapons but her own brains. However, as she'd found out this last couple of weeks, thanks to Tessa, that was more than enough in most cases. She shrunk into a tiny ball and waited for the person to unlock her door.

This was her ticket to freedom. She'd be damned if she'd waste it.

GORAN HATED TO see them split up. *Are you sure this is a good idea, Serus?*

149

Hell no, it isn't. But if she thinks Deanna is either dead, dying, or lying in trouble, she's going to go regardless of what I say. I just want to keep her safe, and the only way to do this is to go with her. I'm hoping we can be done in a half hour. Be back here soon.

Yeah, but I doubt it.

Serus snorted. *I know. Nothing is ever easy.* He hesitated.

Goran's senses sharpened. *What's up?*

I'm wondering if one of the men from the second to last room wasn't part of the Nordic clans. He looked familiar, but it's only as we were walking past that I considered it again. I'm not sure what's going on here, but it's bad news. If there was just the German clan here, then I'd likely think that they got greedy and are once again planning a full takeover of the conclave, but if there are more than one of the clans represented here – well, I'm not so sure.

Damn it. I wondered myself when I saw that guy. He's like seven feet tall.

Yeah, all the vamps in that corner are. Must be their early Viking beginnings.

Who'd know?

I don't know, Serus said. *Our Councilman was supposed to go, but he's upstairs like you said. If you could wake him up, he'd know. Maybe haul him back down and go room by room with him.* Serus's tone brightened. *Actually, that's a hell of a good idea.*

Yeah, but David is pretty set on going down another floor and finding Jewel.

I know. But I'm not sure she's in a ward. Look where they moved Ian. A small dinky room on his own. Check the broom closets, what should have been laundry rooms, etc. She's more likely in there. I don't know why they are doing this, but it's a better scenario with what's going down so far.

Goran stopped and spun to the opposite end of the hall-way. "David, did you check the linen room down the hall?"

David frowned. "It was locked."

"Exactly." Goran grinned, striding back the way they'd come, saying, "Ian, didn't you wake up in a similar type of room?"

"Yes," Ian said. "It was some kind of supply room."

"We've come across a couple of linen closets in the back of several rooms," Motre said.

With a shake of his head, Goran said, "And you didn't think that meant the locked rooms were more valuable?"

"Shit. Ian, come with me, there is another one of those locked rooms at this end. And I think a couple upstairs. As the rooms that were open were so big, the space in the closets so little, it never occurred to me that there'd be anything in there."

Satisfied that they were at least going to make sure they hadn't missed anyone and not ready to suggest that they wake up their own dignitary yet, Goran motioned to the locked door he'd just reached with David. David tested the door. It was locked. He pulled out his wallet, removed a credit card, and played with the lock. There was a loud snick.

With Goran standing ready, David opened the door. He did a quick sweep and stopped. Huddled in the far corner was – Jewel.

❧ ❦

JARED DRESSED QUICKLY after his shower. He'd taken a chance on that, not knowing when he'd get an opportunity for another one. As he dressed, he decided to go to see Taz and tell him everything. He couldn't likely go to Taz's house as he was married to a vampire, but the idea was one he couldn't let go of. He felt safer with the vampires he knew at this point.

He wished he was just a few months older. Surely someone couldn't take his family's property from him in the meantime. If he was getting either of the places. He deserved them, but then again...that didn't mean anything. He did wonder about trying to live in one of them on his own right now. His uncle's house was the best option as his neighbors were already used to seeing him there. He'd lived there since he was just a kid. He just might try it...as long as the house was no longer a crime scene.

After school, he'd run by his uncle's house and see what paperwork he had lying around. With the body gone, he'd really like a chance to pry into his uncle's life some more and maybe find the asshole who'd bought his father. Then he could do the same with his aunt's place. He didn't know if anyone was allowed in either house, as technically both people had been murdered and he was pretty damn sure there was a process involved in solving such crimes, but it was his home. Maybe. It had been his home before that damn movie night. Surely it would be again. Now all he needed was to be eighteen and he could do what he wanted.

Except if this whole mess didn't get solved fast, it wouldn't matter what age he was, the danger would exist regardless. He packed up his stuff, made his bed, and left the room spotless, as if unoccupied. He might be back. He just couldn't be sure. If there was any other option, he'd take it. He'd have slept on the streets if he thought that was better. But with the vampires hunting, he didn't have a chance. He'd fall asleep and wake up strung up again. They'd brought down the one blood farm, but he doubted they were all gone.

There was too much money to be made in fresh blood. And it was always a problem with supply and demand. Always. With a last look around his room, he closed the door firmly and walked down to the kitchen. Pretending to stifle a yawn as he walked in, he took his seat beside two other boys and snagged several pieces of toast off a platter in the center of the table. Who knew when his next meal would be?

"Hungry, Jared? Looks like a good night's sleep woke up the appetite in you."

Jared smiled at the kid joshing him. "Yeah, no kidding. Kinda feel like I missed a lot of meals lately."

The cook brought him a plate of pancakes and eggs. He took one look, smiled, and dug in. Perfect.

He looked up, his mouth full, to take a sip of milk from the glass in front of him, and saw the manager leaning against the doorway. Staring at Jared. Jared dropped his gaze and continued to chew as if everything was normal, but it was damn hard. And even harder to swallow the food down. With the glass of milk, he got it down. He stared at his plate and knew he had to eat it. But it was nerve–wracking with the asshole standing there. He glanced over again to see the cook and the manager speaking in low tones. Shit. He couldn't help but think it was him they were talking about. His backpack at his knees, he wondered how he could sneak a little food and get the hell out of here.

Like a fly knowing he was caught in the spider's web, Jared couldn't get rid of the idea that he was about to be pounced on. He forked up another bit of egg, chewed, then repeated it until his meal was gone. He looked casually over to the side and realized both men had left. He relaxed slightly. Now to escape. He stood up, took his plate into the kitchen, grabbed a couple of granola bars and stuffed them into his pocket, snagged two apples and grabbed several muffins, then headed back to the table for his backpack.

With a fake cheery grin, he waved at the other kids, slung his pack over one shoulder, and walked out the kitchen door. Once outside, he raced to the side where the garage was and bolted into the bushes. He stood there out of sight and shaking with nerves. Thank God no one had come after him. He waited a long moment and just as he was about to step out of the trees onto the neighbor's property, he heard a man call out angrily. "Where the devil did he go? I didn't take my eyes off him but for a second."

"In this case, it seems our intrepid Jared only needs half that time to disappear. Something to remember next time."

Next time? Jared gave a silent snort. Like hell. If he couldn't stay with friends or Taz, then he'd hide in the bushes until nightfall. There was no way he was returning to that home.

Especially not now that they were looking for him. He checked the view all around, hoping no one was watching from the window, and he slid to the back of the neighboring property and bolted to the far side and around, racing to the street. Safe on the other side, he started off down the road. It was early and there was little traffic.

That was fine with him. He'd had enough of people for a long time.

He didn't trust any humans at this point. And very few vamps.

❧ ❦

RHIA STARED AT Wendy, then glanced at the phone in

Wendy's hands. It was the lifeline between them and the rest of their friends and family in the hospital. Sian wasn't here at the moment. She should be resting, but chances were good she was working on the Human Council issue. She didn't know what to do about that going forward and was very confused as to Tessa's capabilities that she'd seen while there. She couldn't believe what her own eyes had seen. It was all too impossible. She understood that much of what she'd seen Tessa do had been the catalyst for Rhia's actions while under the influence of the drugs and the brainwashing triggers, but she wasn't clear enough in her own head to work through it all. The brain fog was improved, but not enough to sort through the convoluted mess going on with the humans. She'd let Sian deal with them. She seemed to be so much more patient than Rhia could ever be. Taz must have had a major influence on her.

Rhia had enough to deal with like – like the latest text from Ian.

She struggled to deal with the latest bombshell.

"Did you say Deanna?" Rhia said in shock. "Tessa is going after Deanna because Deanna jumped into her mind and insisted?"

Wendy winced, held up her phone, and in a deliberate voice, she read the message out loud. "We're splitting up. Tessa, Serus, and Cody are going to the morgue to find Deanna. She jumped into Tessa's mind and insisted. David, me, Motre, and Goran are continuing with search for Jewel floor by floor."

When she stopped, Rhia groaned. "Deanna? Oh dear God. Why Tessa? This is just wrong. She shouldn't be able to do that. Not with Tessa."

"Rhia? Are you feeling okay?" Wendy asked. "You are not

making sense."

Rhia stared at the young vamp who'd missed so much of the ugliness Rhia had seen. Wendy only knew the new traditions, not the old ones. She had no idea the power the old ones had and what they could do with it. Like Tessa, Wendy was innocent. But unlike Wendy, Tessa wasn't safe. She was looking to find Deanna. The most powerful female of the entire conclave. Not just this clan. She was the most powerful female in the world. And she was dying. Or dead.

Dead would be better. Much better.

Dimly she recognized Wendy dialing on her phone while she collapsed back onto the bed. Her daughter was in trouble. And she didn't even know it. Deanna would kill her. That she hadn't done so already only meant she wanted Tessa for something else.

God help them all. Rhia didn't think she'd survive if something happened to Tessa.

Sian appeared suddenly. "Rhia, what's the matter?"

Rhia reached up and grabbed Sian's arm, clutching her best friend hard. "It's Tessa," she said in a hoarse whisper. "Deanna has contacted her."

Sian gasped in shock. "What?"

Rhia watched her friend look to Wendy. Wendy held up the phone and said in a quiet voice, "There's a text message to that effect from Ian."

Sian held out her hand, and Wendy gave her the phone to read the message herself.

In a tentative voice, Wendy asked, "Who is this Deanna, and why is it a problem that she's contacted Tessa?"

"Because she's one of the most powerful vamps in the entire conclave – if not the most powerful." Sian collapsed beside Rhia, her face drawn and pale. She mustered up a smile for Wendy. "And because Deanna plays games. Deadly games. She deals in information on anyone and anything. If she's involved, this is way bigger than I expected." She shuddered. "And it's way more dangerous, too."

CHAPTER 12

TESSA BYPASSED THE elevators. She knew they'd be faster and she was definitely tired of the stairs, but with all the cameras they'd showed up on, chances were good there were teams waiting for them. "We'll be trapped in the elevators," she said as she ran past her father, opening the stairwell door and bolting through.

"Tessa, wait up. We go together." Serus jumped down the flight of stairs to land ahead of her. "No running off crazy–like."

She sighed. "I wasn't, Dad. But Deanna's in trouble."

"So is Jewel," Cody said. "Remember that."

She nodded, feeling chastised. She did have a tendency to become so focused on the problem at hand and forget about the rest. And Cody was right. There were a lot of people in trouble. "I know," she said, "It's Deanna who has the power to make sure I follow her orders…and if I don't, I'm going to crash and burn again."

Serus shook his head as he dropped to the next landing. "She might not be able to do that anymore."

She understood what he meant, and it didn't help. She didn't want to consider that Deanna might be dead. It's not that she'd had a chance to get to know Deanna in any meaningful way, but she'd connected with her. Had made a lasting impression. And she wasn't one of the bad guys. And that mattered.

She was also a Leant. One of Tessa's family bloodline. That mattered too. Tessa tried to shake off the heavy worry in her mind over Deanna's fate. In truth, she'd lived longer than ninety–nine percent of other vampires. She thought about all the piles of ash she'd seen this past week and realized that Deanna's passing was hardly something to mourn. It was a rejoicing of a life well lived. Not that she expected Deanna to agree with her assessment.

They passed landing after landing after landing. On the few doors with windows, her father took a quick look inside to see what type of activity was happening. But he never said anything. Tessa took only a passing glance. All the hallways were inevitably empty, with just more long white walls leading to multiple rooms. She shook her head. As they'd seen above, so many rooms were empty. Were they prepping for an influx or had they just moved out a large group of people? Her father stopped at the next landing and turned, a big grin on his face. "Goran says they've found Jewel."

"Oh thank heavens," Tessa cried. "Is she all right?"

Serus nodded. "David is with her right now."

"Good. That's one major worry off our plate."

"Especially if she's okay." Cody added. "I was afraid they were doing more brainwashing on her like they did on Rhia."

"Speaking of which," Tessa turned to her father. "Dad, any word on Mom?"

He frowned and looked away from her.

"What?" She hated that he'd still try to hide information from her, but considering it was her mother, she understood.

"She's awake and more or less normal," he said reluctantly, "and some of her memories are coming back, but it's spotty."

"Memories coming back?" Tessa asked cautiously. "What is she not remembering?"

Serus winced. "Apparently me." He lifted his shoulders in a forlorn movement. "I can hear her meander through the mess in her mind, but she isn't seeing me. Nor is she hearing me."

He jumped down another landing. And stopped.

Tessa, moving slower as her mind wrestled with what he'd just told her, came to a stop at his side. They'd reached a very large set of doors and a series of elevators. Not pretty elevators that they'd normally see in a hospital or an office building, but large service–looking elevators. Cody strode forward and clicked the button. The closest one opened immediately. It was empty. He stepped inside and checked out the numbers and names of the buttons he had available. "Looks like this goes down to the morgue."

She nodded. "I think I still prefer the stairs."

She walked away as he jumped out, the door closing on his heels. At his exclamation, she turned to see what had happened and realized his coat had gotten caught in the doors. She ran over and hit the button again, opening the door and releasing him.

Glaring at the elevator, they walked over to join her father standing and waiting for them. "They are big elevators. Likely to move gurneys full of bodies," Cody said. "There was also a laundry level listed on the elevator buttons, so that's another reason for the size. Some of those laundry carts are huge."

"Tessa," Serus asked, "Any word from Deanna? We're close enough that you might be able to hear her."

"Oh." Tessa paused, her foot on the stair below. "I hadn't considered that. I've never tried to contact her myself." In fact, she'd avoided even thinking about that connection. It had been horrific. She kept descending the stairs. In her mind, she tentatively called out, *Deanna, are you there?*

No answer.

Yet there was a tingle. She frowned.

"Tessa, you okay?" her father asked.

"Yes, I was just trying to contact Deanna. There's no response, but I can feel a weird tingle as if there is a connection but she's not capable of answering."

"We'll be there soon," he said, motioning to the stairs.

Tessa didn't think it would be soon enough.

~ ∞

CODY COULD SEE the worry settle on Tessa's face. They were almost to the morgue level. In fact, as he came to a shuddering stop…they were already there. He peered through the square glass windows of the door. There were some kind of mesh in between the glass impeding his view, but he could still make out the large room full of gurneys and the walls full of cupboards.

"Is there supposed to be some kind of viewing room where they move the bodies into?"

"I think you're talking about the human system where they raise and lower the bodies so families can see just their loved one."

Serus growled, "Maybe, but the real question here is why are there dozens of gurneys just sitting there?"

Tessa frowned as she studied the sheet–draped gurneys. "And are they dead?"

"What else would they be?" her father asked.

"I don't know," she said, "But are there really that many dead vamps? And why do we need to have them on gurneys.

Why not just turn them to ash?"

"Biohazard most likely. Just because we did that to them when fighting doesn't mean it's the best solution for a large amount of dead vamps."

"But why are so many?" She turned to her father. "You know we don't die easy or young." She motioned to the scene beyond the doors. "This is quite likely what a human morgue looks like – but not a vamp one."

Both men were silent as they stared into the room. "Do we know for sure that they are vamps under those sheets?"

Cody winced at Serus's question. The same thought had occurred to him, but he wasn't sure Tessa was ready for the answers. Still, they needed to find out. He pushed open the door and strode in. He searched for staff, but no one moved. Wasn't that odd? He'd never heard of anyone doing an autopsy on vamps like they often did on people, but like Tessa said, vamps didn't die young and rarely died at all. He lifted back the sheet on the gurney closest to him. It was a male vamp. He frowned and studied the young features. The man's face was contorted as if he had been in extreme pain. He pulled the sheet further down to see the man's hands splayed out like claws. "Serus, look at this." He pointed out the man's hands and faces to the other two. "Whatever killed him, it wasn't an easy or fast death."

"Drugs," Tessa said instantly.

Cody looked over at her. "Can you see that, or are you just guessing?"

"I was guessing." She stepped back and nodded. "But even though he's dead, the temperature in this room is cool enough to keep the energy low and heavy." She spun to look at the other gurneys. "There is a darkness surrounding all of them."

Serus systematically walked over and flipped back the sheet on every one. "They are all vamps," he announced. Cody walked to the wall of drawers. He didn't know if they were full, but if they were, it would make sense why these were just lying in the room instead of being taken care of properly. Whatever that meant.

He clicked the latch on one and pulled it open. It was full. Only it wasn't a vamp.

The body inside was human.

And he might just know him.

"Tessa, come here," he said quietly. "Tell me if you recognize this man."

SERUS STRODE OVER just ahead of Tessa. They both stared down at the young male in the drawer. Serus shook his head. "I don't remember him."

Tessa frowned. "I don't know. There's something familiar…"

"Think back to the rescue in the mine where Jared showed up with all those other young people," Cody said in a grim voice.

Serus looked up at him. "You remember him?"

Cody nodded. "He was with the group Jared brought that day. I can't remember his name though."

Tessa nodded. "There were several young men. We found several of the same group later in the mine – they'd been locked in one of the rooms. We let them out."

"And they were in that last group that Motre had his group of vamps haul out of the mountain before it blew up."

She studied the young man's face. "I do hope all of them

weren't caught again."

Serus move to the next drawer and opened it, then on to the next and then the next. He systematically opened every door so that they would know exactly who was here and who wasn't. At an odd sound, he turned to see Tessa taking a photo of each face, walking along the line behind him. The drawers were stacked three high. When she was done, he walked back the other way and closed the drawer that sat open while opening the drawers on the next row. She repeated the process. He wouldn't have bothered, but for some reason she had a need to memorialize the dead. Maybe so the others could find out about their missing loved ones. He had to admit, knowing there were this many dead humans in the vamp hospital was very concerning. Finally, he turned to the third row and once again repeated the process. By the time he was done, Tessa right behind him, there was only grim silence. Fifty–seven dead humans, all young. Why?"

Cody cried out. "This makes no sense. They didn't appear to have been in any accident or show injuries of any way."

"Only one," said Tessa. Her voice gentle, grieving. Serus watched her, seeing the tears collect in the corner of her eyes. She was soft, this daughter of his. Even after all she'd seen, she mourned for those who would never be again. He turned his attention to the walls of bodies and had to admit he was feeling pretty despondent himself.

"What do you mean?" Cody asked.

But Tessa was flicking through the pictures. She stopped. "This one." And held up her phone.

Cody studied the image. The man's arm was turned outward, showing the smooth inner skin. "I don't see any injury."

Serus saw it and said softly, "Damn. I'm going to be so glad when this is over."

In the picture, clear as day, was a set of needle tracks running down the man's arms.

"Drugs."

Tessa shook her head. "Maybe some was, but I think this was something else. I think this was the short-term answer for the blood farm not being up for production."

"What? Oh no." Cody stared at Tessa in shock. "No. That would be too gross."

Cody looked at Serus. "Sir?"

Serus contemplated the selection of healthy young males and their alabaster white complexion in the drawers. "Unfortunately, I'm very much afraid that she might be right." He ran his hand over his face and in a hard voice, he said, "I think the men were bled out."

"Until they died?" Cody asked in shock. "Surely it would be better to have kept them alive."

"We took down the blood farm, remember?" Tessa said.

"Without the facilities to keep them alive, they had to turn to other alternatives." Serus reached out and kicked the bottom drawer – hard. "In the short term, they took the ones they wanted and bled them until they had no blood left to give."

⌒ ⌒

GORAN STOOD IN the open doorway watching David calm a weeping Jewel down. He turned to Motre. "That ends this search."

Motre nodded, his face grim. "I do not like any of this mess." He said. "It makes no sense that they separated her from the rest."

"That's what they did to me," Ian said from behind them.

Goran turned to look at him. Tall and lanky, he was no poster boy of fitness and health, but he didn't look as bad as he had earlier. "Speaking of which, how are you feeling?"

Ian shrugged. "I've felt better, but knowing we've found Jewel and that Wendy is safe, I'm good."

Motre shifted, accidentally bumping Goran as he turned to study Ian's pale features as well. "You don't look it. You look terrible."

But there was nothing weak or tired in the glare he flipped Motre's way. "I'm fine. I just haven't eaten in a while." Goran frowned, studying the pale color of Ian's skin. He looked dead. It could be from lack of sustenance. After all, they had fought pretty heavily recently. His own reserves had filled quickly, but Ian had been drugged too many times for his system to recover that fast. He looked around, wondering if there was blood. "You need to eat."

"Don't bother. There's nothing here for me." Ian exclaimed. "At least nothing I care to eat."

Goran couldn't blame him. It wasn't exactly confidence building to see all the vamps connected to tubing.

Just then, Serus checked in. *Goran, we're in the morgue. You're not gonna believe this mess.* And proceeded to tell him.

"Serus is in the morgue," Goran told the others. "They haven't found Deanna yet, but there are a dozen dead vamps on gurneys and fifty-seven dead humans in the drawers down there." He lowered his voice so Jewel wouldn't hear him. Motre and Ian leaned in. "They are thinking the humans were bled dry."

Ian gasped.

"Shit," Motre said. "That's not good."

"No, but as we took out the one blood farm, they need stock while getting back up and running or to increase their supply at a different blood farm."

"Wouldn't they have taken these fifty–seven men and taken them to the new blood farm instead of killing them off?"

"If they had equipment up and running for these numbers. If not, they still have a lot of people needing the blood in the short term."

"And there's no doubt they are going to consider the humans disposable."

Goran nodded. "Cody recognized a couple from the group that came with Jared to the rescue at the end."

"Ahh hell," Ian said. "Those kids were young."

"That means their blood is all the sweeter," Motre said.

Silence ensued.

Ian said, "I wondered about something." He opened his mouth then closed it.

"Go on," Motre said. "Wondered what?"

Ian stared down at the hallway, moody and unsure. Finally, he looked back at Goran, his gaze sliding to Motre then back to Goran. "I was wondering why all the vamps we've seen so far are male."

He waited a beat then added, "Where are all the females?"

❧ ❦

JARED WALKED IN the direction of the school grounds with a whole new viewpoint.

He'd been worrying about the license plate number all night.

He pulled out his cell phone and texted Sian asking if Taz could help with tracking the license plate number and Tobias.

Glancing around at the empty streets, he realized it was early. Like really early. He didn't need to be here just yet. He could go to his aunt's house first. It was closest to the school and just a block out of his way. Maybe see if there were any papers in there to find.

Considering the distance, he checked his watch and realized he had close to forty-five minutes to spare. That wasn't tons of time, but impatient to figure out what was happening in his world, he turned the corner and changed directions. Acting as if he had the right to be there, he walked up the stairs to his aunt's front door. The door was locked. Crap. He stepped to the side and lifted the front door mat. Perfect.

That spare key had been there for as long as he could remember. He used it to open the front door and pocketed it afterwards. As he entered, it occurred to him belatedly that maybe someone else had moved in. But the sight of the familiar furniture eased his mind. Surely the police wouldn't have this mess sorted out so quickly. At least not the police he knew.

The living room appeared untouched. Except for the bloodstains. He swallowed hard and skirted around them. There was no business type of furniture in the living room. The coffee table didn't even have drawers. He carried on to the dining room and found the same old table he remembered since he'd been a kid. An overstuffed cupboard with glass doors sat on the side. It had drawers. He thought they were full of dishes, but walked over to check. Sure enough, it was the matching set of dishes to the china set showing in the cupboard. Probably her mother's. He doubted she ever used it. But maybe she did if she entertained.

He carried on into the kitchen and realized that room would likely take longer to search than he had at the moment. His aunt's bedroom was likely the best bet. He raced up the stairs to the spare room and realized it was a pristine, empty room. Good. Made it one less that he had to search. He walked over to his aunt's bedroom, realizing this house was quite a bit smaller than his uncle's. He hadn't considered that before.

In the bedroom, he turned on the light, seeing the heavy drapes closed and the bedding tossed from the bed. He stayed in one spot studying the mess. Had she done this before she'd died, or had the killer done this after taking her out? The drawers of her dresser were pulled out and dumped. Jared walked further inside so he could see her walk-in closet.

Someone had been looking for something.

She'd always kept several hatboxes stacked on the top of the closet. He'd watched her box up papers and put them away several times when he'd been younger and had gotten roped into helping her to spring clean the house. At least one of his more distant memories said that. Interesting. He stepped further into the closet and studied the mess. Some stuff was still on the shelves, like several hatboxes, but there were several cardboard banker boxes tossed on the floor. He didn't see papers anywhere.

If she had a huge boxful, he'd have no way to carry them. He reached up and carefully brought down the stack of hatboxes at the far end. He vaguely remembered the purple and yellow polka dots pattern. He turned and set them on the bed. And opened the top one. A hat. Well, what did he expect?

Just to make sure, he lifted the Sunday hat that she'd always worn to church. And how he knew that, he didn't know. It seemed like he remembered her more than he thought. And with it came a certain amount of nostalgia. If things had been different...

There was nothing under the hat. Good. He opened the

second box and found a different hat. Black for funerals. But it wasn't very big, and he could see a big packet of something underneath. Excited, he pulled it out and opened the tape sealing it closed. He should probably be handing this over to the police. But how? They wouldn't believe him, and he highly doubted that any of them were going to be looking out for his interests.

He carefully dumped the paperwork on the bed, gasping when several bundles of cash fell out with it. At the very end, a large yellow gemstone fell out as well.

How had his aunt collected so much money? This was just what she had hidden here in *this* spot – was there more? He glanced around. Maybe this was what the intruder had been looking for. He flicked through the wad of cash and realized there had to be several thousand dollars. He quickly stuffed it back into the envelope, and then picked up the large multifaceted jewel. He couldn't imagine her not wanting this set into something special to wear. He presumed she couldn't afford to set it the way she wanted to – or she couldn't wear it. As in it wasn't hers and she might get caught if she wore it.

He voted on the last one. He carefully unfolded the paper. One appeared to be the deed to the house. Reading the name on the paper was like being stabbed in the heart. He sat down in shock.

It was his father's name on the papers.

This wasn't even his aunt's house. It was his father's.

She'd not only sold him to the blood farm, but she'd moved in and taken over his home.

CHAPTER 13

TESSA WINCED AS her father's boot connected with the heavy metal drawers. She turned to study the far wall of drawers similar to the first. She hated to think it was full of dead humans as the other drawers had been.

Still, how could she find out if she didn't look? She walked closer, studying the weird energy pattern outside. There was a lot of black on the bottom. She spun around and checked the bodies on the gurneys – they had similar energy surrounding them. She suspected they'd died from the drugs they had been given. Either from being given too much or some new drug that they hadn't tested fully to make sure it was safe before administering it to others. The last drawer on the right held the biggest mystery. There was energy there, but it was...odd. She strode forward, her hand outstretched to open the drawer when her father called out, "What's the matter, Tessa?"

She motioned to the drawer. "The energy here is unusual. I suspect that all those victims," she motioned to the drawers covered in black energy, "and the ones on the gurneys were administered lethal doses – quite probably by mistake."

"Mistake?" Cody asked. "How could anyone have given them too much of the drug accidentally?"

It was Serus who answered. "They were likely thinking that bigger and better was best and gave too much or didn't have time to do proper testing and found out too late that the drugs were killing a high percentage of the patients."

Tessa nodded, hating the thought, but given the panic the assholes had gone into, she could see something like that happening. A small sound wafted up to her. She turned her head slightly. The noise came again.

"Cody? Dad? I just heard a noise from inside this unit."

Both rushed to her side. Cody pushed her back and pulled it open for her.

Deanna, her arm moving slowly as if to hit the wall again, took a deep breath.

Tessa dropped to her knees beside the old woman. "Deanna, are you okay? It's Tessa."

"Tessa?" The woman's feeble voice was hard to understand. It was so weak.

"Yes, you called to me," Tessa said, studying the other woman's faded features. She looked even closer to death – if that was possible. "You told me you were in trouble, so we came to find you."

"Thank you." Her eyes fluttered open. She saw Cody and Serus and she reached up a hand. "Help an old woman to sit up."

With Serus's help, she sat up and rested for a moment before swinging her legs over the side of the drawer. She sat like that and rubbed her face. "I don't ever want to go through that again. Being locked up alive is not the end I'd envisioned." Her glance went from one face to the other before she added in a conversational tone, "The bastards caught me."

Tessa sat back in surprise. Outside of being very tired, she didn't appear to be injured.

"Did they get Hortran, too?" Tessa asked quietly. She turned to study the drawers beside the one Deanna sat in. It looked suspicious, too. She motioned toward it and Serus opened it. There lay Hortran, and this time he was older and more frail-looking. He appeared to have succumbed to old age. Deanna looked over at him and grinned. "Hortran, wake up, you old bugger."

Hortran's eyes popped open, and he stared at her with his ageless look and smiled slowly. "So it worked?"

Deanna nodded. "Looks like it. Tessa heard my call and came to rescue us."

The Ghost sat up and nodded at Tessa. "I am, we are," he corrected, "indebted to you."

Serus straightened and walked over to stand beside Tessa. "Explain what happened."

Deanna frowned at his tone, but she obliged in a grudging voice. "They caught us. Being both so old and frail, we pretended to die during the fight, knowing we were outnumbered."

Tessa gasped. And what started out as a tiny smirk ended up in a full-blown laugh. "Oh my, that's priceless. Why didn't you just project that voice of yours into everyone's minds and knock them all out like you did me?" she asked, still giggling.

The Ghost stared at her in confusion, then his whole face changed as he smiled at her in wonder. "It's almost as if you understand."

She grinned back, loving the wrinkles and the man's strange appearance. She was starting to think these two had tricks she'd do well to learn. "I do. I've never tried such a tactic before," Tessa said. She glanced over at Cody. "Mindspeak is new to me."

"That you can do it at all is wonderful in one so young," Deanna said. "That makes you way ahead of the curve."

Tessa snickered. "Yeah, that's me. Not."

Deanna stared at her. "But you are. In many ways. You just don't know it yet." She stood up and stretched, then carefully took a few steps forward as if testing her balance and stability. She then strode forward to the wall, turned around, and walked back. She looked over at Hortran. "Are you ready to go?"

He nodded, but he didn't get up. Tessa didn't know if he needed help.

As soon as the thought crossed her mind, he turned and gave her a sharp look. *You can read my thoughts,* she gasped silently. She felt Cody stiffen at her side. *It's okay, Cody.*

Is it? he murmured softly.

Hortran stared at her with that ageless look in his eyes. She smiled in understanding. In her head, she said, *It's all right. I won't say anything.*

What if I want to? Cody asked.

As his response rippled through her head, Hortran raised one eyebrow.

She couldn't read his thoughts, or at least she made no attempt to. But as she stared at him, an image of a door appeared in her head. She frowned, tilting her head slightly. *Is that you,* she asked him.

There was no answer. Still, she grabbed the knob and pushed the door open. There was a bright light on the other side. She smiled and stepped into the doorway.

Cody said, *Umm, Tessa, are you sure you should be doing that?*

She laughed and walked in further. The door closed behind her. She turned, saw the door closed, considered the issue, reached out, and pulled the door open. On the other side she found Cody, a worried look on his face.

It's okay. The door isn't locked.

What's over there? he asked curiously.

Not sure. She started to close the door. *I'll let you know what I find out.*

Wait. Leave the door open – just in case.

She considered, realized where he was coming from, and left the door open enough he could see her. Then she turned and walked into the light. And realized it was like a mindspeak highway. She could go anywhere she liked. At least she thought she could.

GORAN STUDIED IAN'S face, his mind churning with the reality of his question. "That's a damn good question," he looked over at Motre. "Outside of Jewel, who'd been segregated, we have only found males."

The silence stretched as each of them considered the ramifications of such a selection.

"I can't see any reason for that. Maybe it's random."

"If it were random, then it wouldn't be only males. The law of averages would say that some would have to be female." Goran looked back at David and Jewel and realized he had her on her feet, though she still looked washed out.

"I'm wondering if we shouldn't send these two, potentially Ian as well, back to the Council Hall, and you and I can join up with Serus." He added, "I'd feel better if we were working together as it is. I really don't feel comfortable with that Deanna stuff."

"I wondered about her. I haven't met her, but I've heard the horror stories."

"Yes, she's been around long enough to be an icon herself.

She'd been a reigning queen of terror in her time. Now she's old and supposedly mellowed." He snorted.

"Can someone like that mellow?" Motre asked.

"I don't know."

A sound behind him had him spinning around. It was David helping Jewel over to the group.

"I need to take her back to the Council Hall. Sian should be able to help her there."

Goran nodded. "We were just talking about that. The three of you need rest." He glanced over at Motre, adding, "We'll meet up with Serus and stick together."

Ian and David looked at each other. David said, "I can drive us there."

"Oh, thank God," Jewel said. "I just want to go somewhere where I'll be safe."

Motre nodded. "And that means the Council Hall."

"I'm game. I could use some blood," Ian said, leading the way to the elevators. "Can't say a nap would hurt either," he muttered, loud enough for Goran to hear.

"I know the break you had was short," Goran said. "It was nowhere near long enough for all the shit going on here. Still, you were sleeping most of the time here anyway. Thought you'd have been fine by now."

Ian shook his head. They reached the elevators. He pushed the button to open the door. "No, it seems like I never got any sleep. Crazy dreams and with the adrenaline rush and panic of trying to help Wendy and not being able to…yeah, I'm pretty wasted." He yawned.

"The same for me," Jewel said. "The drugs don't help that way. I'm exhausted."

"We'll get you checked over by the vamp doctors at the Council Hall then we'll eat and rest. Hopefully Goran and

Motre will return with the others in no time," David said.

"The rest of them? Who all is here?"

Goran looked over at Jewel and realized how much she'd missed. And so had Ian. "David can fill you in later. After you are back at the Council Hall."

They entered the elevator and dropped to the garage level. It was empty. With Motre and Goran on guard, they waited while the three youngsters got into the car and drove away.

"Do you think they will be okay?" Motre asked as they stood there staring into the early morning. Goran studied the sky. It was not safe for any vamp to be outside now. That was good. With the tinted windows of his car, the kids should be able to go straight to the Council Hall and not be followed.

"I don't know. I think this latest turn means none of us will be okay ever again." Goran turned and headed back inside.

❧ ❦

SERUS STOOD OFF to one side and studied the Ghost. He already knew Deanna. She'd been on the Council since forever. And he'd seen her many times. She'd been impassioned for the vampire lifestyle. Not a heavy supporter of the vampire database, and happy to leave the day–to–day running to the Council. She was a staunch friend and supporter and a very dangerous enemy. It was that enemy part that worried him now. For some reason, she'd latched onto his daughter.

And that couldn't be good. Still, she was a known element.

The Ghost wasn't. He was something Serus had never seen or known. And he was very close to Deanna. That alone made him very dangerous. And wasn't that a weird thing?

The two of them were an odd couple. There was almost a worshipping look on the Ghost's face when he looked at Deanna. And a look of respect when he looked at Tessa. That was also concerning. Or rather disconcerting.

"Why did you call for Tessa?" he asked Deanna.

She turned slowly to look at him. He refused to back down. It would be suicide to do so. She'd rip his throat open if he did. In a heartbeat.

She glared at him. "Councilman Serus, why are you asking?"

"Because I know you."

She straightened up, insulted.

He straightened up to match, struggling to not show his nerves. Goran's voice rippled inside his head. *Watch it boyo, she'll take your head clean off.*

I know, he answered, *but I need to know that Tessa is safe.*

Let me know how that works out for you. By the way, we're on our way. Motre and I will be there in five. Sent the kids back to the Council Hall. Jewel is fine but weak and exhausted.

Good.

It was hard to keep up the internal monologue with Goran and stare Deanna down. But he wasn't Serus for nothing.

After a moment, she relaxed and chuckled lightly. "You haven't changed much, have you, Serus? Still stubborn and pigheaded."

He shook his head. "That's my child you're dealing with. No setting her up for a fall."

Deanna shook her head. "No, I won't. I actually need her more than she needs me. I can't afford to hurt her."

"And *her* is looking for answers as to what you want with her," Tessa said in exasperation, stepping boldly between them.

Deanna looked startled, then she laughed, a great booming laugh that rang loudly throughout the room. "Oh Serus. You did good."

The Ghost walked over to stand beside Deanna, but he had a grin on his face. If that was what the cadaver scrunched–up look meant. Serus watched him carefully. "And yet you don't answer her."

Deanna's grin widened. "I am not sure this is quite the right time."

"There might not be a better time," Tessa said coolly. "I certainly don't want you screaming through my mind and knocking me unconscious because you feel like it."

The look on the Ghost's face was a combination of shock and respect. As if he wasn't used to seeing anyone stand up to Deanna. Or question her.

Deanna was a force to be reckoned with regardless of her age, position, or status. She had power – megawatts of it. And she had no compunction about using it.

Deanna stared hard at Tessa. Serus watched Tessa relax and cross her arms across her chest. Instead of straightening in a show of power, she'd gone the other way and relaxed completely, dismissing the concept that she was in danger. And as a result, she had defused the tension.

Serus shook her head. Was Tessa that smart? Or had she not understood the consequences of her actions? He couldn't help wonder if she hadn't done it naturally – as if instinctively understanding that with all the power floating around the room, another power play wasn't the answer.

Damn. She was good.

CODY HAD WATCHED the interplay quietly. He knew Serus wouldn't let anything happen to Tessa. He knew Tessa had no clue who or what Deanna was. She'd been kept out of the loop from most of the Council stuff. Whether right or wrong, she was never included because of her heritage. But it was too bad right now that she didn't have some idea of just how dangerous Deanna actually was. That the Ghost was her defender or protector and obviously loyal dog made him an unknown, and in Cody's estimation, that made him much more dangerous. Particularly when an order from Deanna would be carried out without question.

He wondered how this stalemate was going to end when Deanna started to laugh again. She walked closer to Tessa. Cody shifted his attention to Tessa. There was no artifice in that girl. No way to hide her as being anything other than what she was. Happy and content in who and what she was. Now. Not who she'd been. Now she faced Deanna and didn't seem to know how dangerous a rattler was when cornered.

He swallowed, wondering what to do. His muscles bunched. His jaw locked.

"Down, lover boy," Deanna said, "I'm not going to hurt her."

Cody switched his gaze to Deanna, instinctively holding back the snarl clogging up his throat. He had much he wanted to say, but Deanna wasn't even looking at him. She was studying Tessa.

"Well Tessa, I see you have a couple of champions."

"So do you," Tessa answered coolly. "Not that either of us need them."

A smile whispered across Deanna's face. "Isn't that the truth. You are lucky, you know?"

Tessa tilted her head, a gentle smile on her face. "I know."

Another long moment passed where Deanna studied Tessa's face slowly, carefully, as if she was searching for answers.

Cody wished he knew what she was looking for.

Tessa, do you understand what's going on?

No, she said something earlier about testing me.

Right. He'd forgotten that.

The door beside them burst open. Goran and Motre rushed in. Sizing up the scenario in front of them, the two men immediately flanked Serus. Cody happened to glance back in time to see an odd look cross Deanna's face. He wondered at it, but then he saw the Ghost ready.

Deanna threw her arm out to the left in front of the Ghost.

Stopping him.

Tessa looked at the Ghost and said mentally, *It is all right. They are not here to hurt you.*

The air buzzed with odd energy.

Cody realized suddenly that Tessa was talking to the Ghost mentally. *How are you doing that?*

Having walked through the weird door in my mind, she said, *I can now speak to the Ghost. And maybe other people.*

Damn. "Tessa, I know you are talking to the Ghost and likely Deanna mentally, but the rest of us need to hear words out loud. It makes us all worried when the silence gets big and awkward like this."

Tessa looked startled, then she laughed. She walked over to Cody and slipped her arm through his. "It's all good. Deanna isn't quite ready to tell me. She's not sure about me yet."

Cody wrapped his arm around her and pulled her close. He couldn't help the whole protective male thing. He knew she didn't need it but at the same time, he did.

She patted his chest. "It's fine."

"Hi, Goran. Motre," Serus said easily. "Good to know you found Jewel."

Goran never responded, his glare locked on Deanna.

Cody studied Motre. He was just as silent, only his gaze, shocked and confused, had locked on Hortran. Maybe he had never seen a Ghost before.

Neither had Cody, but that was the way his life went these days with Tessa. She made life interesting. Then he realized she was leaving the circle of his arms. He tried to pull her back. She shook her head, gave him a smile, and walked over to stand between Deanna and the Ghost.

Damn it, Tessa

It's fine.

You don't know that. Cody said. *She's got plans for you. You can't trust her.*

I don't plan to. And she took another step closer to her father.

"It's all good, Dad." She smiled cheerfully, switching her gaze to Goran. "Goran, Motre, can we lower the guard dog modes down a little?"

Goran switched his gaze to Tessa. She brightened up her smile.

"Do you have any idea what you are up to?" he growled. "Or with who?"

"Not yet, but I won't find out if things don't calm down." She spun around to face Deanna. "Who locked you in the morgue drawers?"

Deanna sighed, her aggressive stance easing. "It was Rexy, a punk that reports to Stanley. He came with a dozen others. We chose the easiest path."

Tessa motioned to the gurneys surrounding them. "Do you know what happened to these men?"

Deanna's gaze hardened. "They were dupes. Volunteers for the new drugs. Drugs that were not ready for circulation. My love warned me of it before he disappeared."

"He couldn't stop it?"

"No." Deanna said sadly. "He said it was out of control as vamps were volunteering all over the place to get enhancements."

JARED SAT ON his aunt's bed. He was stunned by the depth of her betrayal. He had to wonder about his uncle's house. Was it his? Or had it been his father's house as well? He glanced through the rest of the papers, but he hadn't had time for a real look. He stuffed all the contents back into the brown envelope and put it inside his backpack. Then he repacked the hatboxes and replaced them both. He checked the night tables on both sides of the bed and couldn't help bending down to look under her bed. He wanted to have more time – do a better search. Be more thorough. As in tear the place apart. He wanted to flip her mattress and rip it to pieces. He couldn't forget the idea that if she had this hidden, there was likely a whole lot more hidden as well. And he wanted to be the one to find it. Just in case someone tried to take his father's house away from him. Again.

He slipped back down the staircase and into the kitchen. He looked out at the morning. It was time to get moving. He walked through the kitchen to the back door. He gave a quick glance through the cupboards before opening the top drawer. It was full of papers. There was a manual to the washer and one for the dryer. And something that looked like a manual for the coffeemaker.

There was lots of other little manuals plus the odd receipt. He rifled through the mess but couldn't see anything important. Then he stopped. She'd been killed in the house, so where was her purse? He walked to the long cupboard that had been converted to a key and catch–all cupboard. There, on the bottom shelf, sat her purse. Therefore, she'd been home long enough to put her purse away instead of having just walked in the door. So who killed her, and had she let them in? Had they just knocked on the door or snuck in through the back?

She'd lived on the criminal edge. She hung out with unsavory people, so she must have known that she'd be in danger. Or she'd become so smug she'd discounted her position as dangerous. As disposable. He pulled out her purse and opened it on the counter. There was makeup, a notepad, and several candy bars. Those he pocketed. He opened her wallet to find her credit cards and several twenties. He didn't know what to do, but he didn't want to leave her wallet behind for someone else to steal. He stuffed it into the bottom of his backpack. Then took it out and stared at it. What if he left it here but in a different location? One no one but him would know about? That felt like a better deal than getting caught with it and making it look like he'd been stealing. He glanced around the kitchen, deciding to hide the wallet in the very end of the pot cupboard inside a stack of pots.

Done, he then slipped out the back door. It was late now. If he hurried, he'd be just in time for school.

CHAPTER 14

TESSA LOOKED AT the young men on the gurneys. There was sadness but also stupidity in their actions. She hoped they'd enjoyed life before it had been snuffed out at too young an age.

The humans were a completely different matter. They'd had no choice. They'd been bled dry like cattle and their bodies in cold storage for further disposal. She wondered how they would dispose of so many bodies. Were they in cahoots with a funeral home? Maybe that was an angle to look into.

She filed away a note then realized she was better off letting Sian know. Maybe they could track back faster. How many funeral homes could there be? She quickly wrote up a text to Sian and copied Wendy on it. Maybe one of them had time to do some checking. When she hit send, she looked up to find the group all staring at her.

"Well," Goran snapped. "Do you think you could put your social life on hold for a few moments so we can figure this out?"

"As I was texting Sian to search for connections to funeral homes to find some of the humans in cahoots with this mess, given..." she swept her arm back, "the fifty–seven human bodies that are here waiting for disposal, I hardly think my social life is involved."

At his mollified look, she sighed and asked, "Where do we

go from here?" She turned to Deanna. "Where are you planning to go now?"

Deanna stared at her. "I was going to go into hiding, but if you are all here, I suspect something major is going on."

Serus spoke up just ahead of Goran. "We found several members of the German delegation upstairs, connected to several machines that we believe are pumping them full of drugs."

"Believe," she snapped, using that same autocratic voice that had terrorized everyone else at the Council meetings. "What do you *know*?"

"Not enough," Serus answered readily. "Our own delegation has also been found connected to similar machines."

"He was supposed to be back in a few days." She glared at Serus as if he were responsible.

Tessa wondered at the razor–sharp mind and what conclusion she'd come up with after all this. How much did she already know? How much did she care?

There was an odd noise buzzing in the room. Tessa turned to stare at the Ghost. She reached for the door in her mind, but it remained locked. She couldn't enter. The conversation was between him and Deanna.

Goran stepped forward. "I think the Nordic Council rep is up there as well."

"Njordvik?" Deanna said incredulously. "No one could have taken him out." She amended that with her next breath. "At least not easily. He's over seven feet."

"Exactly. And there are several of his clan up there as well."

"What of the other clans?" the Ghost asked quietly. "That is three so far."

"I know," Goran said, his voice sharp. "We haven't made

it through the entire hospital yet."

"I have a question, Deanna," Tessa said quietly. "What about the women. Why are there only men here?"

Deanna frowned, but a light shone from the back of her eyes, giving them an odd feral look. "Interesting."

"What is?" Tessa asked. She studied Deanna's face intently. "I don't understand."

"What do men do that we don't?"

Tessa frowned. "Not much."

At that, Deanna snorted with humor. "Okay, so reverse that – what do women do that men don't?"

Cody snorted. "They bitch."

Deanna narrowed her gaze at him. "Men fight. Women don't unless pushed to do so. They use words. Men use their fists."

The group went silent as the truth of her words hit them.

"So they don't need to enhance the women, just the males as they are the soldiers."

"Exactly. There is also a surplus of males in our society, making them expendable."

Tessa hadn't thought of it that way. "That makes sense."

"And the odd female who is caught in their net? Chances are they will be used for special projects. Use her for some kind of experiment."

Tessa looked over at Goran and her father. "Would that fit Jewel?" she asked.

"Unfortunately," Goran said. "Yes."

"Does that mean that Jewel is in trouble still?" Cody asked. "That she might have been selected for some special project?" His voice hardened. "A project that may have already started?"

Deanna shrugged. "Depending on her genetics. If they

have her DNA, they might want to test more drugs on her genetic line. See if her wings fly stronger, or weaker, or make her bigger, thirstier…" She glanced at the men, adding, "The options are endless."

"But they'd have a program listing what had been done to her and when and why, surely." Tessa nudged Cody. "We need to get our hands on those programs and patient files so we know what's been done to our friends and family."

"I wish David was here. He is the best at the computer stuff."

Tessa understood. David and Ian were both techies. "We'll have to do the best we can."

"What are you planning?" Deanna asked curiously. "You can't begin to fight them all."

"No, and I don't intend to. But you know who all the bosses are, and if we take them out, the underlings will be easier to control."

Goran nodded. "I like that idea."

"Of course you would. All brawn and no brains," Deanna snapped. "Hortran, explain the system in place so Tessa can at least understand what she's working with."

The Ghost stepped forward, his voice hollow and faint, but the words were easy enough to understand. "They are operating in cells. Each with a blood farm connected to the other yet operating independently. You might cut off one head, but short of taking them all out, another will grow in its place."

"How many cells?" Serus asked his voice cold.

"Five that I know of."

"And Moltere's Mountain? Was that one or two?"

Deanna laughed. "That was the main cell. You did well there. But now the other four cells are vying for top position."

"Where are they?" Cody asked. "One is here at the hospital, I presume."

"This is the smallest one. They do more experiments and selective processing to keep the supply fresh and the vamps coming in."

"And the other three?" Tessa asked impatiently.

Deanna smiled, a secret smile twitching at the corner of her lips. "Where do you think?"

Tessa studied her. She thought of all the places they could be. "The mall." she said suddenly. "Where Wendy was."

Cody spun back to her. "Why there?"

"Because it leads to the underground city."

"Underground city?" Goran growled while her father started at her in shock, his mouth working but no words coming out. Goran asked, "What do you know of the underground city?"

"I know that there is a large underground movement of vamps who wished we lived in the olden days. They would be prime buyers of the blood," Tessa said coolly.

"You are right in that the underground city is a cell. They have a small blood farm there. Not enough to supply everyone, hence the need for more people and instant blood supply." Deanna smiled, a movement that was both icy and terrifying. "The underground city is likely where they get their biggest pool of vamps looking to enhance themselves."

"I wonder. Those men are already living on the edge of life. They could just as easily be recruiting from the college and getting the smaller, less popular males from there. Offering them bigger muscles, more women and skills that would allow them to finally be superior to their peers." Cody said. "That would make sense, too."

"True." Deanna dipped her head in acknowledgement.

"The trouble with all the cells is supply and demand. As you took out the biggest supply, they are scrambling to set up new ones. Quickly."

"Quickly? Where could they possibly find people to fill such a warehouse again so quickly?" Tessa turned to the drawers so full of bodies. "And if they needed people for the blood farm, then why kill these ones off?"

"Because it's all about balance. They could afford to lose these people for their short term needs while having picked up equal numbers, if not more, for their long term numbers." Serus strode forward to stand at Tessa's side. "Right, Deanna?"

She shrugged. "I believe so."

"And all the foreign dignitaries. Why are they being drugged?" Motre asked. "Do you know if they are willingly getting enhancements?"

"No, I doubt it. They are pure bloods – all of them. Like me, they don't want anything other than pure strains to be born." But she hesitated as if undecided. She took a deep breath. "What I don't know is if this group had another motive. They might have taken down the entire conference. It wouldn't have taken much, particularly if they had the men in place inside the organizations already."

"So that our clan is the ruling clan?"

"Exactly."

"Do you know if the blood farm extends beyond our borders?"

"I don't know for sure, but I've heard talk that each clan has their own blood farms. Underground of course. And likely all connected."

"We have to stop them," Tessa cried.

"You can't stop everything, and first you must stop what's

in your own backyard if you are going to bother." She shrugged as if to say why you would do that.

She swayed suddenly. Hortran rushed to her side. She waved him off. "I'm fine. Just tired. I need to feed and I need to rest. Somewhere I will be safe for a long time."

"And what will you do?" Tessa asked curiously. "Go to sleep for a decade or two and see who of us is still alive when you wake up?"

She heard her father's quick intake of breath and felt rather than saw Cody take a step forward. She didn't take her gaze off Deanna.

"I wish I could. But I doubt I have that many years left."

"Not wanting to try your husband's live forever drugs?" Tessa asked. "Or did you not know that he was working on one like that?"

"I knew, but it's not stable. If it was safe, given my age, I might try it. But if they don't fix it in the next twenty years, then who knows if I will be here by then?"

She walked slowly over to the double doors where they entered. "Now if you'll excuse me, I have places to go. People to see."

"You haven't told us where the other two blood farms are," Serus said in a hard voice.

She smirked as she pulled the door open. "It's not that hard for you to figure out. Shut this hospital down, then the underground city, and you'll have no trouble finding the rest."

Tessa, are you going to let her walk out without telling you what she wants from you, Cody whispered in her mind. *Don't you want to know?*

Damn it, she did. "Deanna, why did you want to test me?"

Deanna froze. She bowed her head as if thinking. The

Ghost walked closer, offering silent support. She looked over at Tessa. "I have a very important job I need to do. I won't have time to make that decision when it's time to do it. I'll need to have the person I choose there at the time. Everything will happen fast."

She took a deep breath. "It may not work at all. There can't be any practice run." She glared at Serus and Goran. "If I can make it happen, it's important that I do it properly."

Tessa shrugged, not sure she was bothered. Her life was crazy enough. "What kind of job? Why would I suit or not suit?"

"Ha. Curious, are you?"

"I am," Tessa admitted.

"Good. Keep that thought and stay focused." She stepped into the doorway, the Ghost running ahead and opening the door in front of them. "I might need to test my choice earlier than later. Stay alert."

She walked out the door and disappeared from sight.

❦

CODY WATCHED THE ancient woman leave as confident and strong as he'd ever seen. Even though they'd just released her from the morgue drawer. Not that she'd let them know too much information, just enough to keep them busy and the heat off her. But she hadn't shared who the bigger bosses were, and more importantly, who had done this to her. And why. There'd been no explanation of the hate behind the act.

Plus leaving the group with such aplomb had her once again firmly in control. As always. He both respected and dreaded her. Although she'd done nothing to deserve either, he couldn't help but think she'd been running circles around his kind since forever.

He was glad that he was too young for her. She'd have been hell on wheels in her prime. Eat up young males and spit them back out when she was done, regardless of the fact that she had a husband.

Cody didn't want to know what she'd done to deserve such a fate, but he didn't want the assholes to get away. He motioned to Tessa, "Shall we go, too?"

She shook her head as if to clear her thoughts. "No point. She's already gone."

"I didn't mean to follow her, but either we're going back to our floor by floor search or we're going back to the Council Hall."

"Floor by floor search," Motre spoke up. He'd been silent for most of the time spent with Deanna, but now he looked ready to get the hell out of there. He held the door open. "There are likely more delegates here. We need to segregate them. Move them to the Council Hall and put them under guard until we know what they are up to. Willingly or not."

"How many men are you expecting to find?" Serus asked, leading the way back to the elevators. "Twenty is doable, forty or up to sixty is not."

"We can move them in relays."

"Then we need men."

"Councilman Adamson could help," Cody suggested. "At least for manpower. He's also a friend of Councilman Bushman, who was supposed to be in the conference."

Motre agreed. He stepped into the elevator and stood at the very back. Cody and Goran entered. Tessa was last. Cody reached out a hand. "It's okay, Tessa."

"Is it though?"

But she entered and stood close to him. He wrapped his

arm around her waist and tugged her back against his chest. He dropped a kiss on her ear. She turned slightly in his arms so she could see him. And gave him that smile. His insides melted a little more.

I'm fine.

Are you though? he asked quietly.

Yes, but her smile was tired, sad.

He leaned his head against her and just rested like that until the elevators came to a gentle stop. The double doors opened and the men started filing out.

Cody waited for Motre to walk past him. He reached up and grabbed Tessa's face with both hands and lowered his head.

WENDY STUDIED THE text that Tessa had sent.

She'd forwarded texts from Jared.

She understood the text, she just didn't believe it. She opened the door to the hallway, wondering if Sian was around. She could just forward it to her and hope that she knew how to help find Jared's friend. The thought of the blood farms recruiting anyone else for their new blood supply requirements made her stomach knot. She'd seen the horrors from Moltere's Mountain and to consider that there were others – that had been hinted at – but not confirmed – made her skin crawl. Those teenagers who rescued them were her age. Human or vamp, it didn't matter – they were young people trying to have a life. The damn assholes were putting a crimp in everyone's plans. She looked back down the other way and sure enough, there was Sian racing toward her.

Wendy held up her phone.

Sian mimicked her actions. "I have Tessa and Jared's messages now, too. I just got the text about the missing ambulance – did you?"

"Yes."

"Why would they take a kid out of the home in the middle of the night?"

"I don't know, but I think that if he didn't show up at any of the local hospitals, private or public, we have to assume something bad has happened to him."

Wendy snorted. "I assumed that as soon as I heard he'd been taken out while sleeping."

"And over a man's shoulder instead of carted out on a gurney."

"So…?" Wendy took a deep breath and voiced her worst fears. "Are we thinking blood farm?"

Sian shrugged. "Not for sure. They might be part of an experimental group. We don't know for sure what Tobias was doing at the home in the first place. We already know that place needs to be shut down. We can't prove it, but I believe Jared's story that he found two dead men there. Bodies that no one else saw."

"Damn. So they are using the home to find victims for their purposes?"

"It could be worse. Those people in the home could be ongoing experiments."

Wendy stared at her. "That's horrible." It was, in fact, much worse, but words failed her. She shook her head mutely. "How can we find out?"

"I'm going to give you access to some databases and see if you can track down the ambulance. Who owns it, who used it on the day in question. If there is a driver listed. Etcetera. There could be even a pick up and a drop off point."

Wendy brightened. "I'd like that. I'd love to be able to nail this guy."

"And hopefully recover those kids."

Wendy smiled grimly. "Even better if we can catch the assholes that did this to them."

GORAN GRINNED AS he caught sight of his boy staking his claim. Not that Tessa was doing any fighting. She was looking all too happy to be in Cody's arms.

Good boy.

He chuckled as he walked back to the ninth floor. One below where they'd been last time. Serus went to turn around and check on Tessa and Cody's progress, but Goran hooked his arm around his and led him forward.

"They are coming."

Serus grumbled but walked forward. "Yeah, before or after he kisses her."

Goran's laughter rippled free. "They are who they are. And it's going to be good to watch them grow together."

"Says you."

They were so engrossed in their conversation that Goran didn't realize until it was too late that they weren't alone. He looked up in surprise to see several vamps relaxing along the walls. His steps slowed. "Well, well. Who do we have here?"

JARED PICKED UP his pace, trying to stick to the one side of the sidewalk, and made his way to the school. His mind churned. His gut was twisting with what he'd learned about his aunt. He desperately wanted a chance to study the papers and see what else he could find out. He wanted someone in the legal world to help him out. He needed help, and he didn't know how to get it. Surely there was someone he could trust in the human realm. Maybe Taz knew someone? Would Tessa? Or would it be out of her league? What were the chances that a vamp would know a human lawyer?

"Damn." There had to be a way forward. There had to be someone out there.

"Hey, Jared."

He spun around to see Clarissa running to catch to up to him. "Hey," he said, "I'm surprised to see you here."

"Yeah, I was going to bring Tobias some of his work from school. But they said he wasn't doing well this morning." She frowned. "He looked so much better last night and when he asked for it, I thought I'd drop it off on my way to school."

"Who said he wasn't doing well?" Shit. Should he tell her? If so – tell her what?

She frowned and shrugged. "A different man than I saw there before, but I didn't know him." She grabbed his arm and tugged him to turn and face her. "Why?"

Worriedly, he stared at her. "I don't know what it means."

"What is it?"

He searched around the area, making sure no one was close enough to hear them. He lowered his voice. "They took him out of the home early this morning by ambulance."

"What? Really?" She spun around to stare back the way she'd come. "Are you sure it was him?"

"Yes."

"You saw him on the gurney? Close enough to make sure."

"Yes. It was him. I know it."

"Why wouldn't they say something?"

Jared shrugged. "I don't know? It's possible they brought him back this morning, but I doubt it."

"Why would they not tell me?"

He winced. "I just know I saw him taken away."

"Okay then, I want to go to the hospital and find him." She glanced down at her watch. "This really worries me. I think I'm going to go there now and see what I can find." She turned around as if to reorient herself and figure out what direction she was trying to go. "I'll be late for school again, but if he's in trouble..." her voice trailed off as she took several steps in the direction of the hospital. "Look, I'll see you later." And she gave a half wave and walked away.

"Wait," Jared called out.

Clarissa turned to look at him, but she continued to walk backwards. "What?"

"I'm coming with you."

CHAPTER 15

TESSA STRUGGLED AGAINST Cody's embrace, afraid they'd be seen.

Shh. They're gone.

She stilled. Breaking contact, she snuck a look around behind her then over Cody's shoulder. They were alone.

"I told you so." Cody hauled her back into his arms. And laid his lips against her temple.

She peered up at him under her lashes. "I can't believe they're giving us a moment to ourselves. My dad has been watching us constantly. If he isn't, someone else is."

"To be expected. Besides, your father is handling us much better," Cody said with a smile. "He's worried about you."

"True." She twinkled up at him, "But he's more worried about you."

Cody chuckled. "And so he should be."

She gasped, laughing.

And he couldn't resist. He tugged her close, pinning her from thigh to shoulder and lowering his head once again. This time, knowing that she was alone with him for just a few moments, she returned his lighthearted passion with a fervor of her own.

She slid her hands up his chest to wrap around his neck and pressed herself closer. He coaxed her lips open, sliding his tongue into her mouth to tease and dance with hers. She lost herself in this world of heat, touch, sensations. Her blood pulsed, her heart swelled.

He deepened his kiss.

She moaned softly against his lips.

At the almost imperceptible sound, he eased his embrace, his lips no longer so demanding. They soothed as they stroked across hers, now swollen from his touch. Finally, he withdrew altogether to drop tiny kisses on her cheeks and closed eyelids. He buried his face in her hair and just held her close.

She shivered in the aftermath. "That was magic," she murmured.

"No," he murmured, a gentle laugh rumbling through him. "That was the merest of fairy dust. The true magic is yet to come."

She tilted her head back so she could look up into his dark eyes and smiled. "In that case, I can't wait."

Heat flared in his eyes. As he went to lower his head again, she stepped back with a regretful smile. "I know you could make me forget where we are and what we are here for, but we shouldn't…"

He closed his eyes, took a deep breath, and dropped his arms. "True. And since I can't have you where I want you, I suggest we catch up with the others."

"You mean before they come looking?" she asked dryly.

Chagrin washed over his face. "Definitely before then."

She hooked her arm through his, and giggling like kids, they raced to catch up with the others.

∂∞ ∞

THE MEN STOOD up to attention.

The aggressive look on their faces had Goran's muscles

bunching, and he could feel his jaw locking. "Looks like we're going to have some fun."

"Good," Serus snarled. "I could use a good fight right now."

"Hold up." Motre said from behind them. "We let those guys off the tubing."

Serus sighed. "Really? That's no fun."

"Damn," Goran said. "We could use a good fight."

"Then again," Motre said, "Have you forgotten the size of that last group we tangled with? We got our butts kicked."

"Hey, they weren't that big." Goran snorted. "I was fine."

"Flat on your ass, you were fine." Motre grinned at the glee on Serus's face. "Especially once Ian landed beside you."

"Harrumph."

With the casual conversation keeping the other men confused as to why they were there, they reached the men before they had time to react.

"You guys look much better on your feet instead in that bed hooked up to a mess of tubes."

The first man looked confused.

"That's okay, you can still say thanks," Serus said, a big grin on his face.

The first man smiled and nodded. "If you are the guys that woke us up, then thanks."

"The real question is why you were there at all." Goran asked. "Followed by the next question – why are you still here?"

The two men exchanged glances before looking back at Goran. "We weren't sure if there was a reason why we were here. We can't remember anything about how we got here. We aren't injured as far as we can tell."

"Besides," the second man said, coming over to stand beside the first one. "Some of our friends are in there still. They are waking up, but slowly." Lines of worry filled his features. "Maybe too slowly." He spun around to look down the empty hallways. "Where are all the doctors? What kind of hospital is this?"

"A nasty one," Goran said. "Now tell us what happened to you."

"I don't remember much." The first man shrugged. "We were at a school pub having a drink or two. Just relaxing and having some downtime."

The second man picked up the story. "Some other vamps joined us. We'd seen them around the campus, but like I said, we didn't know them."

"We had a couple of drinks," the first man said, "And then it's like a big blank in my mind."

"Would you recognize the men again?"

"Sure." They both nodded. "We've seen them around." He frowned. "Why? Do you think they slipped something into our drinks?"

Goran nodded. "It would have been so easy."

The two men looked at each other then over at their friends. "What are they doing to us here?"

"You were probably getting an injection of drugs."

"Drugs?" The two men looked shocked and horrified. One of the other men, who'd been listening in, walked closer. "We don't do drugs of any kind."

"You wouldn't have had much choice in this case. You'd have been given drugs that you'd have quickly become addicted to, and that would have changed your basic physiology."

"Whoa, is that the weird enhancements we've been hearing about?"

"What have you heard?"

"That for a price, you can get bigger and better and smarter."

The first guy said, "Actually, it's more like they are trying to sell the program to us. I think some of the guys at the university were recruiters."

"Were they the guys you met at the bar?" Serus asked.

The two men looked at each other in surprise. Then looked back at Goran and Serus. Both shook their heads.

"Will you help us find the ones who you knew as recruiters?"

The second man took a step back. Goran nodded. "Yeah, see, you aren't in any way pissed enough. You haven't seen your friends murdered or transformed into something they don't want to be without their permission."

The young man in front frowned, his gaze going from one to the other. Then his gaze locked on someone behind him. "Cody? Man, is that you?"

Goran turned to see Cody and Tessa standing behind them. At least they'd finally managed to join the rest of them. His son's face lit up. "Malcolm."

"Yeah," Malcolm's face brightened. "Cody, what are you doing here?"

∂ ∽

CODY SNORTED AND made his way forward. "Maybe I should be asking you that question." He turned to his father and said, "This is my father, Councilman Goran, and our friend, Councilman Serus. And that's another friend, Motre." He grinned at Malcolm. "I believe they unplugged you guys from the tubing."

"Are they serious about the drugs, Cody?" Malcolm asked, his troubled gaze searching Cody's face.

Cody nodded. "Unfortunately, yes. Have you heard about the blood farm mess?"

The second guy winced. "Heard horror stories. Surely they can't be right?"

"They are, and there are worse ones, too." Cody's face lightened as he recognized the two men standing behind Malcolm. He grinned. "Hey Charlie, Eric. Good to see you on your feet."

"Yeah, but Andrew isn't moving well and Harry is worse." Charlie motioned back to the room they'd been guarding. "Any idea what to do to help them?"

Cody led the group into the room where two other vamps lay stretched out on the bed. Tessa said from behind him, "Oh no."

He turned and shot her a hard look. "Oh no, what?"

"This is what we just saw downstairs."

"But these ones are alive."

She walked over to the first one and laid two fingers on his neck then shook her head. "Not this one."

"Really? Harry's dead?" The shocked question came from Eric, who was standing by the doorway. Goran walked over and checked the young male over himself. "She's right. He's dead."

Cody stood at the end of the bed where the second male was. His chest rose and fell in a heavy labored motion. "This one is still alive."

"But dying." Tessa murmured. She stood beside Cody, trying to study something. Cody watched her as she shifted slightly, probably to see the energy layers. "Can you help him?"

"I don't know, he's pretty far gone."

Eric stepped forward. "He's my brother. Please, if there is anything you can do…"

Tessa nodded and walked to the side of the bed. Cody knew that to the others she might look odd and slightly looney, but he knew what she was trying to do. When she sat down and started scooping in the air, he glanced over at his friends to see the shock and dismay on their faces. They thought she was nuts.

"I'll go get a doctor," Eric said hurriedly, his voice hard.

"No, you won't." Serus stepped in front of him.

"He's my brother," Eric said tightly. "If he's dying, I need to find someone who can help him."

"He's getting the best help he can have right now. Whether you understand what she's doing or not. Besides, haven't you realized that the only doctors in this place are the ones that hooked you all up to the drugs in the first place?"

"That makes no sense," Eric cried. "Why inject us with something that can kill us?"

Cody snorted. "Because if it doesn't kill you, it makes you stronger."

He turned to partially block his friend's view. He knew Eric couldn't possibly understand what Tessa was doing but as the young man was already seriously ill, he might very well blame her if he died.

There was a tense silence in the room as they all waited for Tessa to do whatever she was doing.

Cody just hoped her method worked. Like she said, he was already dying. She might be able to help someone in trouble, but she couldn't bring them back to life.

Or could she? He paused, remembering the number of times she had knocked men out – killing them – then brought them back.

He turned. "Tessa, can you bring them back to life again?"

"Again?" Malcolm said in shock. "What the hell, Cody?"

"You have no idea what we've seen and done these last few days."

"Why are they picking on us?" Charlie asked. "We didn't do anything. We aren't part of this war."

"No, you didn't *used* to be part of this." Cody snapped. "You are now."

Goran reached out a hand and squeezed Cody's shoulder. "Easy." He turned to the other men. "They are after new recruits for their soldier program. They make you bigger, better, and hook you on their drugs." He took a deep breath, "Then they send you out to fight the rest of us."

The men stared at Goran. "Seriously. Why is this happening?"

"Because they are trying to take over, to lock up the humans and bring back the old way of life."

"And in case you don't know what that means, school becomes only for the privileged – if at all, and your friends and family are divided into two separate camps. Those in and those out."

"Not possible. These are like seriously ancient issues." Malcolm groaned and threw up his hands. "I don't know any humans personally, but my friends do. We deal with them on a business level all the time. We have partnerships and business arrangements. Why would we turn them into blood factories?"

Cody grinned ferociously. "Because these vamps want the real stuff and not the synthetic blood."

"I like the synthetic blood."

"I don't care either way, but I'm not interested in the human's blood if they aren't willing to give it. Why can't people get it that way?" Charlie said, "Hell, they used to sell it to us."

"And then the vampires decided that they shouldn't have to pay anyone." Serus said in a hard voice. "They want what they want and they want to have it easy."

"So they decided to take it." Goran smiled at them, the viciousness in his face making the others take a step back. "And we're stopping them."

"So will we," snapped Eric. "They attacked us, drugged us, and killed my friends."

The other men crowded around. "Our friends. We want to fight too."

Cody appreciated the sentiment. "We've released a lot of men from this floor already, but I only see you standing outside. Have you seen others?"

When he didn't get an answer, he turned his attention to one of the other men. But he quickly realized they were all staring at something going on behind him. He spun around to see Tessa helping the one young man to sit up.

"Andrew?" Eric rushed to his brother's side. "Andrew, are you okay?"

"Oh, I don't know man. I feel so...odd." Andrew looked around. "What the hell happened?"

"We were knocked out and drugged, brought here, and hooked up to some crazy drugs," Eric said.

Cody watched as Tessa, a frown on her face, walked back over to the dead man. She studied him and then cleaved her hand down at an odd angle as if seeing something in a specific spot that no one else could see. He half expected the guy to gasp and wake up, but he didn't. She stirred the air around in front of his chest.

"Cody," Malcolm asked in a heavy whisper. "What is she doing, man?"

"And who the fuck is she?" Charlie snapped, confused fear warring on the young man's face.

"She's Tessa," Serus growled protectively. "And she's my daughter."

Cody walked over to Tessa. "What's going on?"

"I'm not sure he's dead. Well he is, but there is energy flowing through his system. His body is still churning up the black stuff. Oh…" and she started madly wiping the air about the man, scooping huge armfuls of something away from his chest. Then she stood up and did the same all down his trunk. The guys whispered behind her.

"Weird."

"What the fuck…"

"I don't know man, but look at Andrew; he was a goner for sure."

Tessa walked back over to the man's chest and laid her hand directly over this heart.

Cody knew what was going to come next – if she could.

There was a spark in the air.

And the guy gasped, his chest rising massively as his lungs fully expanded and he took in much needed air. Then his eyes opened and he groaned, a long slowly agonizing moan.

"What the hell," cried Charlie. "How did she do that?"

It was Goran who answered so aptly. "I have no freaking idea."

☙ ❧

SERUS, NOT BELIEVING what he'd seen with his own eyes,

walked to stand beside his daughter, staring at the man lying on the bed. "Did you really just bring back a man back from the dead?"

Tessa laughed, her voice light and beautiful. "No, I think the energy was about to finish him off, but it was such a heavy black cloud that I couldn't see underneath. Once I saw a twinkle of light under there, I thought he might be still alive. Dying definitely, but with a few bare threads of life." She grinned. "Left for me to pull."

"Threads that you could actually stimulate back to life," he asked in bemusement, studying the not–so–dead man. Tessa returned to the young man, busy pulling and twisting and brushing over the man's body. "I guess. I pushed some more energy into his system, and he responded to it. I figured this might work."

The man lay on his back, his eyes searching. They landed on Tessa's face, and Serus watched the panic in them calm.

"Hey, nice to have you back," she said gently. "Take a moment to come to."

"Harry?" Malcolm asked, rushing forward to stare at his friend in disbelief. "Are you okay, man?"

Harry switched his gaze to the men now circling him. "Hey Charlie, Eric, Malcolm. What the hell happened? I feel really odd."

"Yeah, we thought you were dead."

"I thought I was, too." He grinned boyishly as he stared up at Tessa. "I guess I was saved by an angel, huh?"

"Except," Tessa laughed. "I'm no angel."

"But you did save me, right?" Harry asked.

Tessa paused then shrugged. "I guess so."

She finished doing whatever she was doing to his energy then stepped back. Immediately, Cody wrapped his arm around her. "Are you okay?" he asked in such a low voice Serus barely heard him.

"I am. Glad we got here in time." She twisted to look out the doorway. "I guess we should check the other rooms in case there are other men who need help."

Willingly, the other young men moved out of the way, only Tessa looked like she wanted to sit back down again. Cody said something to her that Serus only caught a few words of; something about using his energy if she was tired.

He had to stop and consider that. She had given some of her energy to this young man, Harry, who even now was sitting up and swinging his legs over the side. He'd obviously put it to good use, but who gave Tessa energy when she gave hers away? He walked over to stand in front of her. "Do you drain your own system when you do this?"

"I don't think so," she said, but the fatigue in her voice said something was going on.

"Maybe not," Cody said, "but it does tire you out."

"True." She shrugged his concern off. "However, I recover fast."

"Not really." Serus frowned. "Can't you find a way to not get so exhausted? There could be another thirty men in trouble here, you know."

She gave him a wan smile. "I hope not."

"That's why you need to access some of my energy to help yourself if you need to," Cody insisted. "I have lots, use it."

"And mine," Goran said, stepping forward. "I'm pretty damn sure every one of us would be happy to share. Just don't get so worn down that you can't heal."

She smiled such a beautiful smile, Serus was shocked. She looked…stunning, and strong, and so angelic it made his heart hurt. How could he have fathered someone so special?

"I'm not sure how it all works yet. If I could use your energy when mine gets low," she admitted. "That would be great. I have to see if I can figure that out."

"If you can give him some of yours, I'm sure you'd be able to just reach out and grab some of ours," Cody said, reaching out a hand to motion her forward.

Goran went out of the room ahead of them. Tessa turned, smiled at both men she'd helped, and said, "Take a few moments to get back on your feet. Your friends can fill you in on the mess going on."

They both nodded, their smiles bright and adoring.

"Thank you so much," Andrew said. "I appreciate it."

"We both do," Harry said. "I know I wouldn't be here right now if it weren't for you."

Serus watched as Tessa gained two more loyal admirers. At the rate she was going, Cody was going to be beating them all back with a big stick. He grinned. Damn right. The kid was going to have to work for his daughter. And so he should. She was a prize worth fighting for.

As the two young men followed Tessa's progress out the door, Serus chuckled. They looked besotted. He caught Cody's questioning look and nodded toward the men. Cody turned, saw the looks on their faces, but instead of getting angry, he sighed and wrapped an arm protectively around her shoulders.

Serus chuckled louder.

Cody glared at Serus. "Why is this funny?"

"The sweetest fruit is that at the top of the tree," he murmured to Cody as he walked past. Cody narrowed his gaze. "You just want me to sweat a little."

"Nope. I want you to sweat a lot." And he laughed and laughed.

❧ ❦

"ARE YOU SURE?" Clarissa smiled hopefully. "I'd love the company and the help in finding Tobias. But I don't want you to get into trouble with school."

Jared snorted. "And that is so not an issue."

"Are you sure?" she repeated, but her tone was light and breezy. He laughed. "So we're going to the hospital?"

"That would make sense, wouldn't it?" She frowned as they walked. He sighed happily. "It's great that we reconnected."

"I know. I was afraid that I'd never see you again." She reached out and hooked her arm though his. "I do hope Tobias is fine."

"I do too."

"Was he awake when you saw him?" she asked. "Was he in pain?"

"No, he appeared to be unconscious." He deliberately didn't mention how Tobias was carried out.

"Oh dear." She unconsciously squeezed his arm tight against her. "Maybe it was better that way."

"As long as he is getting the help he needs."

The walk went by too fast, and before long they were turning the corner to the hospital block. Sounds of ambulance sirens rent the air. He winced. Jared thought he'd never get used to the sound of those damn things. They always meant pain and anguish for someone. He just didn't want that someone to be him anymore.

The hospital was a hub of activity. One he'd like to avoid but given the circumstances, it wasn't possible. Neither was it sensible. He might be lucky enough to find Taz. Ask him some questions. Maybe find a private moment to ask him about his residence issues.

"Ugh. I hate these places. I was so happy to see Tobias in the home. It was always nice to see him there than at the hospital."

"Did you get a chance to see him here?" Jared asked as he opened the front door for her.

"Yes, we saw him several times. He was on the second floor." She led the way forward. "I don't think he'll be back in the same place, but it's possible."

"Do you want to check there first? Or should we go to the front desk and ask someone there for help?"

"Maybe." She smiled. "That's why I'm glad you're here. We'll figure this out together."

She walked up to the reception desk and said politely, "Hi. A friend of mine was brought in early this morning. Could you tell us what room he is in, please?"

"Sure, what's his name?"

Jared stood off to the side, not paying attention to Clarissa so he could check out if Taz was anywhere around. And sure enough, he was walking out of Emergency. "Clarissa, I'll be right back."

He raced toward the doctor and called out, "Taz!"

The doctor froze then turned around.

CHAPTER 16

TESSA STRODE DOWN the hallway, Cody and her father on her heels. She was elated with having saved the young man, but she wished she understood how and why it had worked. As she didn't know, she couldn't count on it working every time. And she didn't want other people to think she could.

The process *was* wearing her down. She hadn't said anything to Cody because she knew he'd try to stop her. The drain on her own personal resources was hard – harder than she was expecting. She kept telling her vampire genetics to kick in and they had, to some extent, but not enough.

Surely there couldn't be too many more men dying. It would devastate her to not be able to help those others because *she* wasn't strong enough.

At the men's urgings, she raced into the closest room. There were three men hovering over another man. Several more lay or reclined against the walls, looking alive but exhausted or still wiped out from the drugs. She headed for the man on the bed.

"He's in a bad way," Goran said. "Tessa, he's our own Councilmen Bushman."

She got the message. That didn't mean she could do anything about his condition. The councilman looked familiar. She thought she'd seen him in the blood farm.

At her say so, Goran moved the others back and she dove in, sweeping away the black energy that choked his life force. She didn't even know where the words she'd used came from, but it seemed to fit. She was neither a doctor nor a specialist in vampire genetics, but somehow she'd become a specialist in energy.

There was a deep angry black lying against his heart, and that was the one killing him. She focused and pulsed lighter energy from her own system under the blackness. It gave his system something alive to use while she worked to cleanse that heavy blackout of his chakras. That was another word she'd read about somewhere that seemed to fit. She just hadn't heard it often. Head down, she kept her eyes focused on the job at hand even as her ears heard muttering behind her.

"What is she doing?"

"How is this going to help our Councilman?"

"Did someone call for a doctor?"

It was getting irritating. She glanced over at Cody and rolled her eyes.

He grinned. "Everyone might just want to give her a little peace and quiet to work."

"What work is she doing? This is not normal, Cody. I understand that you know her, but..."

"Isn't that Tessa? David's weirdo sister?"

As if everyone knew a line had been drawn, a pregnant silence that filled the room.

A couple of weeks ago she'd have been devastated. Right now? She'd let the others take care of this guy. When there was a shriek followed by a heavy thud against a wall, she grinned.

"This is Tessa," Cody snarled. "She *is* David's sister." His voice rose in volume. "However, she is *not* a weirdo."

Her father picked up the conversation. "And she is *my* daughter," he roared. "That kind of talk will get you an ass–kicking like you've seen before."

"Damn it, Serus," Goran groused in glee. "How come you get all the fun?"

There was a rumble of raised voices behind her, but Tessa lost interest as she pulsed a little more energy into the man's chest and watched it rise then fall...and then nothing. She pulsed a little more. Same thing. She frowned and shot a heavy bolt of energy into his chest and damn...he gasped, groaned, and opened his eyes as he gulped for air.

"Holy shit."

"She did it?"

"What did she do?"

"I don't know, but I'm a believer now."

"Told you, man. Same thing she did to Andrew and Harry. Hell, Harry was fucking dead and she brought him back to life."

Tessa reached down and helped the Councilman into a sitting position, shifting so she crouched in front of him. His face had a peaked look to it, but his eyes were bright. Clear. "Take it easy, your system is weak and still fighting off the drugs. You will need a day or two to recover."

She glanced back at Goran, seeing the relief in his eyes. "Goran, he needs to be moved to safety." She motioned to the hallways. "Same as the other two men. They need rest for their systems to recover."

Goran nodded. "I'll take care of it."

Tessa watched him face the group of young men.

"We're going to split you into two groups. One group is going to take the three men that Tessa worked on – and any others she says needs to – back to Council Hall. The second group is going to run interference for the first group to make sure they get out of the hospital safely. Remember, you were all drugged and kept prisoner here. We trust no one who isn't here working to free everyone." He glared at them all. "Anyone *not* understand?"

There were no dissenters. Tessa held back a smile. Goran was the right man to organize a large group of rowdy males. This group wanted to fight back against what had been done to them.

She stood up and gasped as the room wavered. She reached out a hand.

A dozen hands reached back.

Cody was first. He wrapped a gentle arm around her. "Tired?"

"I'm okay," she whispered.

He gave her a doubtful look.

In a stronger voice, she responded with, "I'm better this time. Is he the only one that needs help?"

"No. There are two more."

She winced. "We'd better go then. I don't know how long before I crash."

As they walked out of the room, she heard Goran organizing the men into groups. She asked, "Cody, do you know these guys?"

He nodded.

"Are any of these men going to be there on Friday's hangout?" she asked curiously.

"Likely all of them."

"Well, maybe it won't be so scary then. I'm no longer a stranger to them." She laughed. "A weirdo, but not a stranger."

"He's going to regret saying that," Cody snapped in a

hard voice.

"Don't punish him anymore," she said quietly. "He didn't know. He's just saying what everyone else has been saying for years."

Cody, silent at her side, walked her down to where several other men were waiting impatiently for her.

She smiled at them.

They smiled uneasily, their gazes shifting to Cody. "Cody? Is she the one? She's just a kid."

"Yeah, she's the one."

"And I'm no longer a kid." She brushed past them, leaving Cody to the explanations. She couldn't blame them. She *was* young. She was someone new to them and what she was doing was a kind of magic – but it was also new to her and she couldn't give anyone an explanation. The more men she helped, the more she worried about the men she'd ignored in the morgue. Had she missed a chance to help them? Considering what she'd seen, she realized there'd likely been no live energy surrounding those gurneys. They'd been dark and heavy with the black rot of death.

In the next room, she stood, shocked to a standstill. There was a massive young vamp on the bed, his knees at the end and his lower legs hanging off the end. She'd never seen one so big.

"Who are you? We requested a doctor, not a child," snapped a huge older vamp standing protectively in front of the collapsed male. She studied his features and realized they looked close enough alike to be family, quite likely father and son. She could probably check that information through their energy but honestly, she didn't have time. The younger man on the bed had no time.

"I'm not a doctor," she snapped, tired and fatigued and

not up to warring with someone that probably outweighed her three times over. "I'm Tessa, and I'm what you've got."

A guttural spat filled the room. Her jaw dropped. She didn't recognize or understand the meaning, neither did she recognize the language. Talk about foreign dignitaries! What language was that anyways?

Cody answered in her mind. *It's Nordic.*

Two massive men from the same clan approached.

Cody stepped in front of Tessa. Instantly the two men were on him.

She hissed, the odd sound filling the room.

Two more men approached her, intent on protecting their leader. She understood, but that couldn't happen. She glanced over at the young man on the bed and sighed. He was already mostly gone. If she wanted to save him, she didn't have time for this crap.

Shifting slightly, she could see the father guarding his son. "Okay, don't call them off, but don't say I didn't warn you."

Lowering her hands, her claws extended inches past her fingertips. The men's gazes widened, but they kept coming.

"Wait!" Serus shouted from the doorway. "Don't attack her."

Tessa laughed. "You're calling out to the wrong person, Dad. You should be asking me to stop. Not that I will after they attacked Cody."

The men launched themselves at her. She crossed her arms across her chest, bright red claws extended, and checked out their energy. She realized that given their size, her trick wasn't going to work at the normal height. She waited until they'd almost reached her then crouched and jumped up as high as she could, then slashed her hands sideways into the energy over their hearts.

Both men stopped as if they hit a wall. The look of their faces shifted from anger to shock to horror then… nothing. They both collapsed.

"Shit." Serus raced into the room. Tessa crouched, her breath locked into her chest, a feral grin on her face…waiting. Were more men going to attack?

The massive male standing guard over the dead man started screaming and shouting in his language as men rushed towards them, but the noise was driving her crazy. For some reason, the tone and the decibel level was like a hammer going off in her head.

"Shut up," she screamed at him.

Easy, Tessa, Cody said. *Take it easy.*

But the noise continued. Tessa reached out mentally and slammed a door on the man's mouth.

I. Said. Stop. It, she screamed.

The man stopped screaming – the noise cut off like a knife. A blank look of shock filled his face and his gaze widened as he stared at her.

I'm here to save your son. But if you don't want that, then I will walk out of this room now. She waited a long moment. *But if you want me to see what I can do, call off your men, let Cody go, and get the hell out of my way.*

∂◦ ∽

CODY WATCHED AS the seven foot Nordic giant's face went ashen and he slowly fell to his knees on the floor, face first. He turned to Tessa. She had her hands over her face, whispering, "Oh thank heavens."

Tessa, he asked gently, hating the whiteness to her face and that horrible bruising around her eyes. She was paying a high price for helping these men. These strangers. And facing a difficult wall of rage, fear, and scorn. Once again, life had asked much of her. *Did you do that?*

She peeked at him between her fingers then gave a short nod. *I don't know what happened, but he was screaming and my head was hurting so I screamed at him to stop it – but I think I screamed in his mind.*

He took a moment to assimilate that. *So you did to him what Deanna did to you?*

I think so. She nodded and dropped her hands. *I didn't mean to hurt him though. I needed him to stop screaming. I don't know what's wrong with me, but I'm so tired and everything is amplified.*

Cody studied her, worried. She looked to be barely holding on.

"Tessa?" Serus asked. "Can you fix these two guys?"

She glanced over at her father, tears appearing in the corner of her eyes making Cody want to take her in his arms and hold her close. She was exhausted. Damn it. She'd worn herself down. Cody couldn't imagine any other instance when Tessa would have snapped like that.

She gave a weary nod. "Cody, can you turn them over please."

The room had somehow filled with vamps silently watching her. The men were so big, Cody and Serus struggled to turn the two Nordic men who had attacked her onto their backs. She studied them carefully, then reached down and filled the energy channel she'd created with her own positive energy. Instantly both men opened their eyes, saw her, and backed up in confused panic.

"You're fine," she said in a hard voice. "And as long as you don't attack me again, you'll remain fine."

She walked over to the leader, checked his pulse, and realized he was just unconscious, much as she had been after Deanna's entrance into her mind. She nodded. "Move him back please so I can work."

Again, silently, Serus and Cody struggled to shift the huge man's weight. Goran entered the room and shoved himself front and center. Watching the other two struggle, he reached down and helped. "Is he okay?"

"He is. He's just unconscious. Now please keep the rest of the goons off my back. We've wasted too much time. I don't know if I can save him as it is."

"You can save him?" asked one of the men who'd attacked her. "How? I thought he was dead."

"Given that his father's reaction was based on the fear of having just lost his son, I will forgive you for what you did, but I won't be so happy if you try a repeat performance," she snapped. "I'm tired and low on energy. If you want him back, I need every bit I have available."

With that, she sat down beside the dead man. Cody watched her giving the male a careful once over, hating that the work had taken such a toll on her. She reached up a trembling hand to her own temple. She didn't know if she could do this.

A warm hand landed on her shoulder. "Use my energy," Cody said calmly. "Make sure that as you give, you also take."

"I might take too much," she whispered. "I don't know what I'm doing."

He smiled. "I'm willing to risk it."

She gave him a small smile then reached out and got to work. Cody stepped back to give her some room.

No one made a sound. She worked tirelessly even though her arm shook at times with the effort of holding them up.

Cody wanted to help her but didn't know how. Her color faded and her shoulders drooped.

Taking a step forward, Cody laid a hand on her shoulder again, willing his own energy to the forefront to help her out. He didn't know if he was doing any good, but she seemed to perk up.

He glanced around the room to see several dozen vamps' gazes locked on every movement she made. If she saved the young man, she'd become a legend in her own right. A hero of the people as this man came from one of the ancient lines. If he died – which technically he'd already done so before she'd ever entered the room – they'd hold her responsible.

The Nordic Councilman sat on the floor, slowly recovering. His gaze too was centered on Tessa. But there was no hope in his gaze. Only defeat and grief.

But he didn't know Tessa like Cody did. Cody had faith in her. He glanced over at his father to see worry etched in every line. His father knew Tessa too, but that he was so worried said much about how important this man – this scenario – really was. Serus stepped over to Cody and stood with his back to his daughter. Cody understood he was standing guard in case things went bad.

Which, as Cody watched Tessa's shaky movements, he realized was all too much a possibility.

Call on your vampire heritage, he whispered.

She faltered as if surprised, then straightened her back. As if her genetics did indeed kick in and give her more power, more energy, her movements sped up, her actions more decisive.

Then she was done. Or rather she was done in. Her arms dropped. Her head bowed and a heavy sigh escaped.

Silence.

Everyone waited.

Tessa? Cody asked. *Is he dead?*

She reached down to the man's chest and did something odd. Then as if not liking something, she reached up and grabbed Cody's hand and repeated the motion. This time there was a spark between Cody's hand and Tessa's. The young man's body jolted. Hell, so did Cody. She repeated the spark thing. The young man took a deep, life–saving breath.

She repeated the spark one more time and nodded in satisfaction, studying the young man. Cody switched his gaze over to the man in the bed then shook his head. "I'll be damned."

The murmur in the room rose into a crescendo of shock. The Councilman jumped to his feet and raced over. Serus stepped in front protectively.

"It's all right, Dad, he's just concerned about his son."

And with that, his son gave a low rumbling groan as if a mountain was awakening from deep inside. And he opened his eyes.

❧ ❧

GORAN ALMOST DANCED in place as the Nordic Councilman collapsed on his son's bed, tears rolling unashamedly down his face. He knew just how he felt. He'd been to hell and back over Tyson and if anything happened to Cody, he'd kill everyone involved. He couldn't imagine losing that boy. And the look on everyone's face when they'd seen Tessa pull off the stunt of the century. Like wow!

The first time, there'd only been kids watching. No one would take their stories seriously. Now the Nordic Councilman, well, everyone listened to him. His size alone commanded attention. If you added his presence, ancient bloodlines, and his position, everyone listened.

Now Tessa would get the respect she deserved.

Serus was going to go nuts trying to keep her out of trouble. As for Cody, he was going to go nuts trying to keep the men away. Tessa had just become one hell of a hot commodity.

She'd been interesting before, but she'd just transcended that now. He wouldn't be surprised if some of the clans didn't offer the joining of the two clans by asking for Tessa's hand in marriage. It was a hell of an honor should that happen. He chuckled. A couple of the young pups looked his way. His grin widened. The pups switched their attention back to the action.

The young Nordic boy was sitting up, looking a bit green, but he was holding solid. Damn, Tessa was good. He wondered how fast she had to get to a vamp after he'd died in order to save him. They'd been in the morgue with over a dozen dead vamps and she hadn't made a move to help them. Had she known she could? Or were they too far gone? She was a fascinating woman – okay child – woman–child. Or child–like woman. Whatever. He shrugged his shoulders and grinned wider. She was a hell of a girl, and she was going to give his son the runaround.

And that was a good thing. Cody would appreciate what he had to work for.

As he watched, Tessa tried to withdraw from the room, from the limelight. Cody tried to clear her path so she could get away. It wasn't working so well. Everyone surrounded Tessa and ignored Cody.

"What are you grinning about?" Serus growled from right in front of him.

"Damn, I didn't even see you." Goran laughed at his disgruntled look.

"I'm trying to get Tessa out of here," Serus said, "She's tired and needs some air."

Goran looked around, saw nothing but black suits and big men, and called out in the Councilman's language. "Councilman Njordvik – Tessa needs space to leave the room, and she needs fresh air to recuperate."

A spate of Norwegian soared across the room.

Instantly a channel between the men freed up, allowing Cody and Tessa, with Serus on their heels and Goran taking up last place, back out into the hallway.

"Oh, thank heavens, I wasn't sure how to get out of there," Tessa said weakly, her hand trembling as she pushed a few tendrils of hair back.

"It was crazy, but you can rest out here." Cody motioned to the long corridor ahead.

"Ha. It's a hallway. Any chance of a place to sit down and rest – in private?"

"Except this is a hospital," Serus said. "It's not our home."

"Too bad," she muttered. She hopped up on the wide window ledge and leaned back, closing her eyes. "Damn, I'm tired."

"How long until you recuperate?" Goran asked, studying her pale features and the bruises under her eyes.

"I don't know," she smiled wanly. "Hopefully soon."

Her father reached out and patted her shoulder. "Call on those vampire genes, girl. You should get fired up in no time."

That surprised a laugh out of her. But obediently, she leaned her head back and followed his instructions. Goran spoke quietly with Serus and Cody but kept an eye on her progress. When the flush of pink returned to her cheeks and she gave a heavy deep sigh, he realized she was back. Good thing. There were other vamps who needed her help. Not ones that had died, at least he hoped not, but there were others that were barely staying ahead of death. He could only hope she had enough reserves to finish this.

Then again, considering the number of vamps on the other floors, he realized this was likely too big a job for anyone. Considering it was a young girl who wasn't sure yet exactly how this worked, she wasn't going to be able to train anyone else to help her. Besides, they'd need someone who could see the same energy stuff that she did.

He'd lived centuries, and Tessa was the only one he knew. He hadn't even heard such a thing was possible.

Hell, she'd taught him so much in the last couple of weeks, he couldn't imagine what she'd teach them all in the next century.

For the first time in a long time, he was looking forward to his future.

∽ ∾

RHIA WATCHED WENDY and Sian search for license plates, drivers, and patients. She wanted to help, but they were adamant. She needed to rest.

There was nothing she wanted to do less.

She'd been lying here for hours, maybe days. Who could tell anymore? She was lost...and found. But the voice in her mind haunted her. She heard him. She knew him, but didn't. He was distant. Foggy. She tried to get closer to him, to speak with him. It was important.

He was important.

To her daughter. She just didn't know why. Or if it was

her imagination? It was so hard to know what was real and was not.

In the background, she heard Wendy mutter, "There's no record of that patient anywhere. Not even in that home."

"What?" Sian walked closer and read the monitor screen.

"No, there's no record of him arriving at the home. No record of him leaving."

Sian leaned back. "Which means no one knew either way. He became an asset they could do anything they wanted to."

"So he wasn't sick?" Wendy asked, starting to look sick herself. "Or rather he wasn't sick originally?"

The two women stared at each other. The shock was mirrored on their faces.

Rhia spoke up, "He's their guinea pig."

The other two spun, having forgotten she was there. Sian's face twisted in revulsion. "I thought there couldn't be anything worse than the blood farms, but this...to think that Tobias was ill and recovering, then sick again, at their whim...it's gross."

"Are we really thinking that they made him sick?"

"Or kept him sick and made him sicker." Rhia swung her legs over the couch and sat up. "The home and hospital made great cover for all of this."

"But that's the vamp hospital. Tobias is involved in the human medical system. Not ours."

At Wendy's words, the two women turned to look at her – neither said a word.

"Oh no." She sagged in her chair. "Please don't tell me there are traitors at the human's hospital."

"There must be," Sian said in defeat. "I'm not sure any place is safe."

"Neither is anyone," Rhia muttered. "You must protect

Taz."

Sian gasped. She spun away and pulled out her phone.

The look on her face when she heard Taz's voice was heart–wrenching to Rhia.

"I'm sorry about your memories," Wendy said in a quiet voice. "Is there nothing you can do to help them along?"

"I've been trying," Rhia said sadly. "It's not working."

Wendy smiled. "Somehow I feel like Tessa would tell you that you're going about this all wrong."

At the mention of her daughter, Rhia smiled. "Would she? In that case, what would her advice be?"

"To forget about trying," Wendy grinned, "And instruct your genes to work double time."

"Oh my God." Rhia sat down heavily. "Could it be that simple?"

CHAPTER 17

S HE LOST TRACK of the time, but Tessa figured she'd been at this energy business for several hours. If not longer. The only good thing about the last few hours' work was that her energy was holding. It was thanks to Cody's assistance and his constant reminder to call on her genetics. The issue only got worse the more tired she became. She kept moving forward as it all seemed like too much to sort out, so she just dumped it from her mind.

When she had time, she'd stop and figure it out.

After they'd finished going through the top two floors of the hospital without being challenged by any hospital staff, it made her wonder if they'd gone into hiding.

She mentioned that concept to her father.

He shook his head. "No. There have been several attempts to get to this floor, but Goran has the entrances covered. The top floors are ours. Take your time and do what needs to be done."

She nodded. She understood that his voice was flushed with success, but she didn't understand how holding the top floors of anywhere was a help.

Don't worry about it, Cody murmured. *You need to shut down.*

I do, she whispered, hating to hear the fatigue in her own voice. *Is there a place where I could lie down and just close my eyes for a few moments?*

Cody led her out into the hallway and over to her father. "Serus, Tessa needs to lie down. So we need to have a room clear for her."

"She can come over here," called out one of the many young males that had followed her from room to room, a group that was getting bigger with every stop.

Cody led her forward and motioned to the clean, non–creased bed. She looked at it gratefully but was loathe to lay down.

What's the matter? he whispered. *Go lie down.* She glanced around the room at the men she'd helped still slowly healing and the rest that just watched her.

I'll lie down if you sit beside me and watch over me, she muttered.

There was a gentle silence. *You know I will. No one will touch you while I'm here.*

She gazed into his eyes and realized he wasn't mocking her and would do his best to watch over her while she slept. And his best was pretty damn good.

Thanks, he murmured on a laughing note.

Don't make fun of me, she whispered. *I can't think straight. I'm so tired.*

She fell more than sat down then rolled over to face the wall. She lay tense, waiting for him to sit down beside her. When she felt his reassuring weight beside her, she closed her eyes.

Just before she drifted off, she murmured, *Thank you.*

CODY WATCHED THE gentle rise and fall of Tessa's chest and

listened to the sound of her breath leaving her body. She was exhausted. Once again having called on herself to do too much – and like always – to help others. She'd been unable to stand on her own for the last ten minutes, and he doubted that she even understood that he'd been half supporting her.

He shifted slightly to block her from view. Over a dozen men lounged around protectively. He wished he could take her away from here. At least for a little while. Help her to rejuvenate. And get her away from so many people, the curiosity, the prying eyes. She'd pulled off major magic in the mines, but there'd been no one to see. Now there was no way to stop the masses from seeing and hearing about what she'd done and continued to do.

"Cody my boy," Goran boomed from the doorway.

"Shh, Tessa's asleep."

"Then come here so we can talk."

"I promised her I'd sit here and watch over her until she woke."

Goran winced. "Yeah, she has good reason for asking that." He moved closer, dropped a bag of supplies at Cody's feet, and squatted down in front of Cody. Serus followed him in. "Okay, here's the scoop. There are more vehicles arriving. We've had attacks from the roof and the lower floors, but so far they are piddly attempts. I'm sure bigger and stronger are coming."

Serus said, "We need to regain the roof."

Goran grinned fiercely. "We already have. Now I've got a couple of fliers up there so they can do aerial combat if needed."

"Nice." Cody smiled. "So what's next?"

"I say we should go down a floor and take it over. Then go down one more. Eventually we'll be able to push them out completely and we'll have complete control over the hospital."

Serus straightened. "Have you got men picked out?"

"Picked out, and Motre is already leading the pack on the next floor. I'm going to head down to give him a hand. I'll keep in touch."

Serus nodded. "That works."

"And remember – no survivors." Goran grinned at the men.

The look on his father's face made Cody's heart freeze for a long moment before he realized he was safe as Goran's son.

Goran added in a very satisfied voice, "Not a problem. There haven't been any survivors yet." He twirled and walked back out to the hallway. From a distance, Goran could be heard asking the men gathered around outside the room, "Anyone here looking for a little payback?"

The resounding cries made Cody proud. They might not have known the assholes existed, but now that everyone had felt their first bite – the bloodbath was about to begin.

⁂

"IF YOU'RE OKAY here," Serus glanced down at his daughter, sleeping heavy and still, then over at Cody. "I'll go up to the roof level and make sure all is well."

Cody nodded. "We're fine." He hesitated then added, "Shouldn't you and Goran be exchanging places?"

"Yeah, we should," Serus admitted, "But your dad is stubborn. He won't want to be stuck on the roof now that it is secure if all the action is below."

At his words, Cody grimaced. "I hear you, but not sure it's secure given the equipment the people seem to have available and given the narrow staircases, I don't trust the assholes not to find a way to get onto a floor and come in from behind to get Dad."

Serus stopped. "Is that idle thinking, or do you know some way for the men to get onto the floors that we don't?"

"Not really." Cody shrugged. "But do we know that every elevator and every staircase is closed off?"

Serus nodded. "Yes, they are."

"Okay, then…" But Cody didn't appear convinced.

Crack. The huge sound was followed by the crash and tinkle of broken glass. A window?

Serus stared at Cody, Cody stared back, both minds twisting and churning with this newest event.

"If they have fliers…"

"And they know the layout and can crash through the windows in the stairwells where your father is…"

And like that, Serus bolted down the hallway, calling out. "The worst would be if there was gas bombs dropped on the men. There'd be no one left to save." He reached the stairwell and pulled the door open wide.

It was empty. Below, he thought he smelled something but couldn't be sure. He raced down to the next floor and again found the landing empty. He looked in on the floor, but other than a few vamps lounging around and trying to recover, there was no sign of any distress. Had Goran already gone down a floor?

Damn right we did. Also caught the flier who thought he could bring up some friends and toss them through the window. Luckily we saw them just as they hit the windows so we were on them before they'd regained their feet. They're gone now.

But none of your guys were hurt? Serus asked.

No. Now we have guards stationed at both ends on the look-out for another flight display if they decide to try it again.

I'm coming down to your floor.

I thought you were going to the roof level? Goran asked. *I guess you figure this is where the action is going to be.*

Yeah, it's always around you, Goran. Whatever happened to that damn peaceful life we wanted?

Ha. No retirement for us. Hurry up and get here. Looks like we have a few good skirmishes coming up.

Serus perked up. *So I haven't missed all the fun.*

Nope, not yet, but if you're not here in less than one minute, you will—

And Goran's voice went dead.

As his voice went quiet, Rhia's voice slipped through his mind, *Serus? Is that you?*

ༀ ༁

JARED RAN UP to Taz. "Sorry, I actually don't know your formal name. Tessa only ever referred to you as Taz."

Taz's lean, chiseled features split into a wide grin. "Hey, Jared." He studied him closely. "You look like you're doing pretty well."

"I am. At least physically."

Taz's gaze sharpened. "You're in trouble?"

"I don't know." He kicked at an imaginary rock on the floor. "Yeah, I guess." And his story poured out – from the dead men he found in the home, to his aunt and uncle, then the kid being carried out of the home.

Taz let him talk until he ran down. He took a deep breath and let out a heavy sigh. "Well. I guess that's a lot of trouble."

"Yeah, I'm going to have to go into foster care if I can't find some reputable place to stay for a few months." He threw up his hands. "And then there is the problem with the deeds to my aunt's house and my inheritance."

"Whew," Taz said. "You need a lawyer for that."

"Ha. I need an honest lawyer," Jared said. "Do they exist?"

Taz laughed. "They do. They do. But we have to make sure we also find one not connected to the blood farm mess. You've been sold once; I'd like to keep you off those meat hooks."

Jared groaned. "Me too."

He glanced behind him at Clarissa at the front desk. She appeared to be arguing with the receptionist. "I think the immediate problem is Tobias, who was taken out of the home last night. He was carried over the guy's shoulder like a sack of potatoes. No stretcher."

"You're sure about what you saw?"

"Yes," Jared answered. "I also climbed into the ambulance and checked to make sure the kid was still alive."

He nodded at Taz's sharp glance. "Yes, there was a pulse. But the guys were arguing, so I slipped out the other side and hid in the bushes."

"You and Tessa. You're both trouble magnets."

Clarissa walked over. "Jared, are you sure about what you saw? They said they have no record of Tobias arriving here."

Jared nodded, his features grim. "I know what I saw." He turned to Taz. "I have the license plate number. Is it possible to track those? I did send the information asking if Sian could help, but I haven't heard back."

"She's swamped." Taz nodded toward a series of small rooms up ahead. "Let's go to my office. I'll call someone and have them check the numbers."

He led the way to the back of the ER and into a small office. There he gave Jared a small notepad and a pencil.

"Write the number down."

He quickly jotted the sequence down and handed the paper over to the doctor. "That's what I remember." He watched as Taz dialed the number. Clarissa slipped her hand into his. He squeezed her fingers reassuringly, giving her a big smile. "Taz is one of the good guys. He'll do what he can."

And what he was doing was talking to someone involved with the ambulance service. He waited while Taz read off the numbers. He pulled his own phone out and winced at the time, realized he was missing his Calculus class, and checked for messages. They were a couple. David had texted. Said he was back at Council Hall with Jewel and Ian and Wendy. How was he doing? Tessa had told him about the bodies, and he wanted to know if any more had shown up. Jared snorted at that. And started the long text explanation similar to the one he'd given to Taz. He ended up giving him the license plate of the ambulance as well. At this point, he figured everyone must have it being he already sent the information to Sian.

It took time. But then, Taz was busy doing his calls and hadn't looked his way. So he continued to work his own phone. When he glanced over at Clarissa, it was to see her texting her friends as well.

He laughed. "Look at us. What would we do without our technology?"

"I'd die," she said with a tiny smile. "No one so far knows what happened to Tobias. No one heard from him last night after we left. As far as they know, he was sleeping well and was still supposed to be there this morning."

"And he should, but I know he's not."

"Which means we're back to thinking he might have been returned without anyone else knowing?" She groaned. "If that's the case, why take him in the first place?"

Jared couldn't even begin to think.

Taz got off the phone and turned to face Jared. "I don't know what's going on. That license plate is valid, but it's not for an ambulance in their fleet."

"So then…" Jared hated not getting answers. There should be answers. There wasn't going to be one in this case. And that was really starting to piss him off.

"So then what?" Clarissa asked.

Jared wrapped an arm around her shoulders and tugged her close. He hated the sheen of wetness in her eyes. He didn't know how close she and Tobias were, but it was obvious that she cared about him. He could understand that. "I don't know. We'll have to figure it out."

Inside, he was afraid he already knew.

He glanced over at Taz. "He's been taken somewhere private, hasn't he?"

Clarissa looked up in question. "Where? A private hospital? He has no money and has always lived with his grandparents. They have no money for private care either."

"I don't know what to say." Taz ran a tired hand down over his face. "I haven't spoken with Sian yet this morning, I'll check with her and see if she's found any reference to the boy."

"I'm wondering if you have a connection to find out what ambulances are doing the vampire hospital runs," Jared asked.

And watched as dismay filled Taz's eyes. "Oh, please no. Not again."

"I'm afraid so."

CHAPTER 18

TESSA WOKE AS if from a long deep sleep. She felt like she'd had eight solid hours of sleep. She stretched and would have rolled over but realized there was a large warm body stopping her. Cody.

She pushed herself up on one arm and said, "Hey."

He twisted, studied her face carefully and as if liking what he saw, responded, "Hey back."

She smiled and leaned back down on the bed. It wasn't much in the way of comfort, but she'd been so needing a chance to rest it had felt like a bed for a queen.

"How are you feeling?"

"Terrific," she murmured. "I really needed that."

There were no aches and pains, nothing but a sense of relief. She swung her legs over the side and sat up. "Now food would be helpful."

Cody smiled. "You and your food."

"It's not like you go days without needing sustenance." She grinned. "Do you want yours from here?"

"My dad brought back a bag of supplies from Council Hall for us." He motioned to the bag on the ground beside her. With a long look at him, she reached over and rummaged through the bag.

"Blood, blood, and more blood. Great." At least it didn't revolt her as much as it would have a few days ago. She understood the need to eat for her strength.

"Check the outside pockets," Cody said.

She opened one of the flaps and laughed. Tucked inside were a half dozen granola bars.

She snatched up the closest one, ripped it open, and took a big bite. "Your dad is a good man."

"Yeah, only he's gone down with a team to overtake the eighth floor."

She stopped, looked at him, and then at the granola bar. "So this is to keep my strength up in case I'm needed again?"

"Something like that."

He laughed as she shrugged and demolished the rest of the bar while reaching for a second one. "Then so be it. I might as well make sure I don't get hungry anytime soon."

He shook his head, watching as she polished the second bar off too. Then she hopped to her feet. "Okay, I'm ready."

"Ready for what?"

She turned to look back at him. "To go help. Surely we're not going to stay here safe and sound while our fathers are out there fighting – are we?"

He shook his head.

"Well, I didn't think so." She gave him a cheeky grin. "Good. Then let's go."

By the time they reached the eighth floor, the action was all over. The men were in the process of going from room to room and checking on the vampires inside. Tessa stood in the first doorway and surveyed the energy of the occupants. They were all going to be fine.

She moved through the floor checking, helping, healing, and releasing the occupants of a dozen more rooms.

She met up with her father at the other end of the hallway. "Hey, this system worked well."

He nodded. "They've already gone down to take over the seventh floor."

"Good, let's go."

She followed her father down the stairwell when her father stopped. He turned to look at Tessa. Then he frowned and averted his gaze, but he held his hand out to stop her from entering the floor.

"What is it?" Her heart sank.

"Goran says Deanna is here."

"What? Oh no. That means she was caught again." Tessa pulled the door open and ran inside. "Where is she?"

"Tessa, wait!"

But she'd already entered the first room, her father and Cody hard on her heels. Sure enough, there was Deanna, Hortran beside her. She rushed to the old woman's side. The tubes had been removed and were hanging drunkenly off the side of a big wall–mounted dispenser. Tessa eyed it balefully. The damn drugs again. These assholes had a lot to answer for.

She sat down at Deanna's bedside. "How is she?"

"She's gone," Hortran whispered, his voice hollow. Fading.

"Why didn't she call out to me?" Tessa asked, afraid that she'd missed hearing Deanna call her because she'd been sleeping, then remembered Deanna's call could wake anyone from Hell.

"There was no time. They knocked her out and got the drugs into her." Tessa started to frantically move the energy away from Deanna's heart.

"You're too late," Hortran said.

Tessa moved quickly to clean the blackness. She couldn't see any spark underneath. Panic set in. There was too much darkness. Not enough light. She poured energy into Deanna's system.

"You can't help her," Hortran said. "It's over."

Her hands still desperately worked to remove the heavy darkness. Tessa studied Hortran's face. A weird fire burned in his gaze, and he reached out a hand and placed it to the side of Deanna's head in a gentle gesture. Then he reached out with his other hand and cupped Tessa's head over her ear.

Instantly, she could hear Deanna's faint voice.

It's over, Tessa. My time has come. Even now my body is gone. This is the last of my energy. I said you were being tested. What I didn't say was that you passed all the tests with flying colors. And as much as I hate to dump this on you, someone needs to know. Someone needs to take my place. So far in all my travels, there have been none who cared as much as you. So I leave you all my worldly possessions and all knowledge. Be good, my child. Be wise. And her voice dissipated into a weird, faint echo until even that faint ringing stopped. And there was only silence. Empty vast silence. And confusion.

"Wait," Tessa cried. "Deanna, what are you talking about?"

"She means this," Hortran said, "You are the *One.*"

A bolt of lightning surged into Tessa's head. Her body contorted and danced, caught helpless in the grip of something she never knew could exist. Names, numbers, videos, and information that she'd never known before downloaded into her brain.

Hortran's voice chanted some mantra in the background. The noise overwhelmed her ability to sort through the information overload.

She couldn't hold on. She cried out, "It's too much."

There is no one else, Hortran said, *Only you. You must take it all. You have no choice. You are the One.*

Tessa's mind went into overload as she finally understood what was happening. She could hear Cody screaming at her in the background. Her father's voice. Maybe even Goran's. There were many others she didn't recognize. Hortran's voice never wavered. Instead, it gained in strength.

"I can't do this," she screamed. "I'm not strong enough."

"You are." Cody snapped. "I'm here. Hold on." And he grabbed her hand and squeezed. That helped her to stabilize, but she knew it wasn't going to be enough. She was going under. There was no escape this time.

"You're wrong," Cody roared. "You are the One. Use my energy. My father is here too. Use his energy."

She felt the surge of something old and powerful connect. Then another as her father reached out and grabbed her other hand. Suddenly, there were dozens of other energies swimming around her, pouring into her, giving her the strength. Fainter energy joined in, distant but connected.

"Hortran, what is happening?" she sobbed, her head exploding.

You have received the finest gift that was possible to give, he whispered in her head. *She has given you everything she had to give. Now use it wisely.*

He collapsed in front of her, his hand falling from her head. In front of her shocked eyes, maybe from the electrical force, maybe because it had been his time, or maybe he'd just lost the will to live, he dissolved into ancient ash and dusted the top of Deanna's dead body. Inside her head, there was a roaring sound. A building up of something huge. Something she had no idea how to control.

And something that suddenly got out of control.

She cried out, trying to tug her hands free, only to realize there were dozens of people all joined in one massive circle around her. Speaking, yelling, crying. A kaleidoscope of words fought for space in her consciousness. Yet she couldn't get any to take form in her mind. There were too many.

But like any universe under too much pressure – eventually it becomes too much to contain.

The pressure became too strong.

The heat too hot.

The pain too much.

The black fury in her head exploded.

She shrieked and her back arched before collapsing backwards off the bed to crumple on the floor.

In the background, she heard her father screaming for her. Inside her mind, she heard Cody screaming at her. But there was more. So much more.

As she drifted away, she heard Cody's cry resonate through her mind.

Tessa, don't leave me. Please. Tessa—

And she knew no more.

VAMPIRE IN CRISIS

BOOK #8 OF FAMILY BLOOD TIES

DALE MAYER

CHAPTER 1

"TESSA?"

Who was calling her? Why? She wanted to roll over and block out the noise.

"Tessa, wake up!"

"What's wrong with her?" cried a young male voice she didn't recognize. "Why won't she regain consciousness?"

"Shh, she will. She's just not ready."

That last voice sounded almost familiar. But it was thin. Distant.

Voices rattled through her consciousness in an endless sea of noise. The voices were there but remote, connected but not clearly.

Ready, my ass. You will wake up when you feel like it. Deanna's voice floated through her subconscious as the other conversations drifted in and out with no end. It was distracting and painful and deafening. She couldn't hear herself think.

Or sort out the voices. Were any of the messages important? Did she need to wake up? Or would she be better off just letting the words drift away unacknowledged? She wanted to ignore them and just keep on floating here forever. The air was peaceful. Gentle. She liked that. There'd been so much stress, so many shocks in the last few weeks. So much panic and pain and loss. This break felt right. It was good to be here. She could stay and enjoy. Let everyone else just drift away.

Maybe they'd disappear for good and she could just relax.

Not going to happen.

Tessa froze. Who said that?

Her mind flooded with memories of a thousand conversations and a thousand answers to who'd said something over the vastness of her experience. No, correction – the vastness of Deanna's experience.

With that, understanding slammed into her consciousness.

Deanna.

Hortran.

The One.

The one what? Oh, right, the only one to fit Deanna's list of requirements. Supposedly Tessa had been tested and passed without even knowing about it.

And without having given her permission for what followed.

Hortran's voice drifted through her mind on a faint whisper. She strained to hear, to make sense of the impression in her mind. Something about how she'd been given a gift like none other and to use it wisely.

Like an echo, the word triggered multiple associations in her head and conversation after conversation jumped to the forefront, all referencing the phrase "use her gift wisely." In a sepia-toned movie rolling through her mind, she saw Deanna speaking to young vamps, old vamps, council vamps, and strange vamps, either being cautioned to use something wisely or to tell someone else to use something wisely.

All the while, Tessa shuddered as her brain filled to capacity and battled past into overload. With a hard bang, her brain hit the end and she shuddered as her mind blanked out. Not sure what just happened, she lay there on whatever surface she was on, unaware of her surroundings as she tried to sort out the still reverberating recoil in her head. Just what had happened? Her body, her sense of place, had no beginning and no end.

"Deanna, couldn't you have at least left me an instruction manual? Something to show me how this works?" She felt more than saw a weird whisper through her mind. *Hortran?*

"Is that you, Hortran?"

No, it couldn't be. He was dead.

That whisper came again.

Or was he? She tried to remember what exactly had happened prior to the forced data transfer to her brain. Had he said something as to how to survive this? Hinted at a way out?

Instantly her mind was flooded again, the conversation as real as it had been the first time it played out in Technicolor with perfect audio pitch through her mind. And she realized there'd been no instruction possible. There'd been no time. It had been Hortran that had facilitated the exchange of Deanna's memories. Her knowledge. Her life. But…had he left a piece of himself behind in the process? Was that possible?

There was a tiny nudge of that same energy.

With an intuitive flash, she realized that Deanna might be gone and Hortran might have exploded into ash, but a piece of his energy…his consciousness had remained behind. The connection required to do what he'd done remained.

Somehow that was a huge relief. But she didn't know why.

It wasn't like she could communicate with it – with him – as if there was a person attached to it. It did, however, add significance to the meaning to his name – Deanna had called him a Ghost. Now he was in spirit form – more ghostly than ever.

Could he help her with this transition? Or better yet – reverse the process?

Instantly pain slammed into her temples. She groaned as sharp claws bit into her consciousness.

She focused on her breathing, trying to manage the on-slaught. After a moment, the weight in her chest eased.

She'd take that to mean reversing the process wasn't possible. Or maybe not desirable. After the trouble Deanna had gone through to find Tessa, it would make sense to learn to manage this new state.

Instantly, the air around her lightened, as if a silent pat of approval had smoothed over her head.

She sighed. "Hortran, can you hear me?" Stupid question, but she wanted to know for sure that it was him. The pat of approval came again.

Good.

"Can you talk to me?"

No pat.

"But you can communicate somewhat." Okay. She could work with that. Considering the option was no contact at all, it was a huge relief to know that he was there some of the time. "Any chance you can tell me what I'm supposed to do with this mess of information? I've barely got any memories of my own. To deal with hers is too much."

No response. Lost as she was inside, whatever space in her mind she'd ended up with, she sighed and said in a needy whisper, "Please, Hortran, tell me how to push this back into some kind of filing system so I can open it only when I want to and keep it safe in an archive of some kind the rest of the time. I can't live like this," she cried out. "It's her life. Not my life. Maybe I'll need her memories, but maybe not."

Instantly, a filing system popped up in her mind – by century. She stared in awe as the centuries opened to show decades, with the first of those opening to show years.

"Hey, that works. Now put all of those in a big folder called Deanna's Memories."

Instantly there was a folder with Deanna's name and, oh wow...a second folder appeared with Hortran's name on it.

"Hortran, do I have all your knowledge and memories as well?"

That warm whisper of energy slipped across her face this time.

"Why? Why would you do that too?" She was so confused. She had seen a lot of vamps die lately and none had a chance to pass on any information. Had they wanted to? Could any vamp do this?

Was it a common thing? A gift that each vamp could bestow as a gift on their loved ones? She didn't understand how that could be a good thing. And if it was so easy, how come she'd never heard of it?

Then she remembered the things Deanna had said about her prison and her partner. She shuddered at what information she could have access to. Instantly she threw up a mental shield and said, "Section off all intimate memories Deanna might have so I don't inadvertently see them."

There was a weird shuffling in the files. She stood in the center of the maelstrom as folders flew around her. When it was done, she could see a red folder off to one side for each century, decade, and year.

Good. It felt more respectful that way too. And much less like she was a voyeur into Deanna's personal life. It was a different story to have access to her business life and clan knowledge. There'd be any number of other bits and pieces in there she could use, but she didn't want to intrude on

Deanna's most private memories.

Who would?

Okay, anything else? Could she organize this in a better way? Maybe add a search function? It was hardly a computer, but it was a database. Then she realized all the folders were there, but they were empty.

Shit. She had to fill them.

⤳ ⤳

CODY'S FINGERS SPASMED with the effort of holding back from giving Tessa yet another hard shake to wake her up from the dead – or whatever unholy place she'd gone to. He *needed* her to respond – in some way – in any way to let them know she was okay. Her head lolled to one side. Her eyes closed and her mouth fell slightly open. The only reassuring thing was the steady rise and fall of her chest.

She was alive, and he had to believe she was fighting to stay that way.

He hated what Deanna had done. He didn't know why Tessa had been chosen or why Hortran would have helped facilitate what had just gone down, but just thinking about it made him angry all over again.

He bowed his head and once again called out to her, *Tessa. My love. Answer me, please.*

The blankness in his mind terrified him. He hadn't been able to mindspeak for very long but the absence – the sense of loss – by her silence shook him deeply. He wanted to reach in there – wherever *there* was – and grab her by the shoulders and shake her until she yelled at him to stop. He wanted to hear her voice snap at someone – even him, to say the real, the normal, the defiant Tessa he knew and loved so well was there.

And yes, the word was love. He was no longer afraid of it, of the feeling and definitely not the commitment. He'd like nothing better than to plan on being old and gray with her at his side.

He'd had no warning of how important she'd become to him, but he'd done well adjusting. Or at least he thought he had, but now this sense of grief at the thought of something finally being too much for her to handle – that realization that for all she'd done and managed to do, all she'd had thrown at her and had surmounted – she might have finally come up against something she couldn't deal with.

And that thought was going to kill him.

"Cody, lay her down so she can rest." Serus hovered in front of him.

"She is resting." Cody refused to do anything that would mean no longer having her in his arms. Sitting beside her wasn't good enough. He had to hold her.

"She could take hours recovering," Goran said quietly at his side.

Cody snapped his gaze towards his father. "This is Tessa."

A lopsided grin slipped out from his father's face. "I know. We don't know which way she is going to handle this. We have to assume it could take time. She is under a tremendous amount of pressure right now. She might need to adapt…"

There was a pregnant pause.

Cody leaned back against the wall, adjusted Tessa in his arms, and said, "She'll adapt just fine. She needs a little time, that's all."

He closed his eyes, determined to give her that time.

At least outwardly. Inside, he couldn't resist murmuring, *I'm here, Tessa. Tell me what I can do to help.*

For the first time, he thought he might have sensed a response. Staying still so as to not let anyone else know, he whispered in her mind, *Tessa? Sweetheart – is that you?*

And the whisper that came back brought tears to his eyes. *Cody? Where are you? I missed you.*

❧ ❦

SERUS WATCHED HIS daughter with a hawk's eye. She lay so pale and weak in Cody's arms. He couldn't have imagined what had just happened. The impact on Tessa. Damn Deanna. How could she do that to Tessa? His daughter. Not some nameless victim he could possibly ignore but his own daughter. He wished he could kill the witch himself. This time *before* she'd had a chance to grab onto his poor girl. There'd been rumors of particularly strong vamps downloading their memories in the past as in centuries ago, but he'd never known it to happen or seen it happen, and no one knew of it having happened. Hence, the myth that it was possible but not probable.

And now knowing the sheer power at Deanna's disposal and possibly with Hortran's help, he'd seen Tessa gifted with everything Deanna had to give.

What that would do for her – or against her, he couldn't imagine.

It was a huge burden and one he wouldn't wish on anyone, especially not his teenage daughter. She had enough challenges.

Cody's face twitched, his eyes moving under his lids. Serus leaned closer and whispered, "Can you hear her?"

Cody gave a jerky nod. "Barely."

Barely was enough. It meant she was in there – functioning at a level none of them could even guess at.

But to know she was responding already – well, his heart swelled with relief. She'd be okay then – maybe not in an hour or a day, but she'd cope – like she always had.

So she's waking up, is she? Goran's worried voice slid into Serus's mind. He'd only checked in every ten minutes since he walked away to find something useful to do.

His buddy had left rather than stay there and do nothing but hover over Tessa. Serus knew his friend hated to sit around and do nothing if there was something he could grab control of.

Cody says he's heard from her, so I'll take that as a good sign.

I will too then. Goran's voice beefed up. *I never doubted she'd handle this.*

Serus smiled. *Neither did I, old friend. Neither did I.*

STILL AT THE hospital, trying to find a comfortable way to sit on the hard seat, Jared stared at the list of names and license numbers. These were the potential drivers who were driving the ambulances yesterday when he saw Tobias taken away. None of the names were familiar. Then why would they be? He wasn't part of the medical world and knew few people outside of school friends. He lifted his head, his gaze falling on Clarissa, who'd curled up on the couch and fallen asleep. She'd been emotionally wrought since they realized what likely had happened to Tobias. Jared was afraid so much more might have happened to him but hated to speculate on the devious experiments the blood farm doctors might even now be doing.

"How do we narrow this list down?" Jared asked. "There

are too many here to follow up on."

"Sian is on it. She can access the tracking data for each of the ambulances and check out their routes. Might even be able to search for the address of the group home to see who was there." Taz stared off into space, as if contemplating what technology could do to make their job easier.

Jared didn't really care *what* could help as long as *something* did. And fast. He was fed up with sitting around and doing nothing. His future was up in the air too. He couldn't go back to the group home and they'd missed morning classes. Something he wasn't thrilled about, but priorities had to be set and this bloody nightmare had to come to an end sometime – surely.

As if reading his thoughts, Taz suddenly broke the silence.

"You two should go on to school. Leave this with me for the moment. If you want to, you can stop by after class and I'll let you know what we've found out."

Jared stared at Taz, his mind working. It was tempting. He just needed to finish this term and he'd be done. Failing was not an option. Neither was it for Tobias. But what could he do right now for the kid?

"Surely there's something we can do to help," Clarissa said in a sleepy voice. She sat up and yawned then rubbed her eyes.

"Not at the moment." Taz stood up. "Maybe by the time you get back I'll have something that we can move forward with."

Jared watched as Clarissa turned to him, a question in her gaze. He shrugged. "I don't know what else to do. Maybe we can find out something at school. There has to be someone there who knows something."

Her gaze warmed and she smiled. "True. School it is

then."

As they walked out of Taz's office, he called from behind them, "Be careful that you don't go asking the wrong questions of the wrong people."

A good warning to keep in mind – but how were they supposed to know what were the right questions and who were the wrong people?

RHIA SAT UP slowly and stared around the empty Council Hall room. Had she fallen asleep yet again? All she did now was sleep and lie here. She felt so out of it. So useless. She'd heard a gnarled rendition of something involving Deanna and her daughter, but the accounting could barely be believed. Could it? Surely Deanna hadn't gifted Tessa with all her knowledge. Rhia had heard of such things from other elders, but it was a hugely dangerous process with more failures than successes. She worried on the names that slid through her mind. She couldn't remember a single case where the recipient had actually lived through the process.

Supposedly Tessa was alive but unconscious. She was at the hospital – and what a joke that was. A hospital was supposed to be a place of healing. A place of helping those in need of care. A place to get help. Not this war zone it had become.

And of course all she held dear was caught in the middle.
Again.

Her mind froze. Not all – not Seth. No one had found out anything about Seth. Maybe that was something she could work on.

If she could only remember what she'd already done.

CHAPTER 2

THE WARMTH HIT Tessa first. Then cold followed by waves of cozy heat as if she was going through a myriad of different climates one after another. She didn't understand and could only sway as she was buffeted by the discordant sensations. In the back of her mind, she could sense something holding her in place. Something stalwart. Something enduring. Something she could trust.

There was a deep rumbling under her feet, sending more shockwaves up her lean frame. She closed her eyes and let her body, her mind, her spirit sink into the process. Go with whatever was happening to her. Surrender. Fighting was useless – worse, it would kill her. With a deep sigh, she released the last of her resistance and watched the filing system once again float around her as the centuries of Deanna's life flew into their correct spots. The relationships slid into another section. Her eyes opened in wonder as she caught bits and pieces of the truths that the old vampire knew. The trials and challenges she'd been through. There was an odd popping sound, then another and another. She watched as files closed one after another and disappeared – presumably into her own memory banks.

As each closed, the pressure she'd barely been aware of with so much going on eased back. The pops came faster and faster to the point that it was as if popcorn was popping in her mind.

It built to a massive crescendo of noise and then – stopped.

As in stark complete silence.

The air cleared around her, and the sensation of her head being too large to hold up eased. She shuddered. A freeing, relieved type of motion.

"Wow. That feels so much better."

Instantly, a small caring pat whispered across her head.

Then a murmur so faint, so soft and carried on a warm breath of air – so caring she wondered if she'd imagined it. *You did good.*

And the breath faded away, the sensation drifting off like a boat whose mooring had been untied.

"Wait," she cried out. "Are you coming back?"

This time the answer was slightly crisper around the edges, enough for her to hear the response.

Always.

And he – Hortran, the Ghost – was gone.

Tessa opened her eyes and slammed them shut just as quickly. A shocked gasp escaped. That couldn't be. She peeked out from under her lashes at the world gone brilliant. The space around her was alive with color – but not just any color. Luminescent greens and blues and purples spun and twisted in front of her. But not calm quiet movements as if blowing in the wind; more distressed, agitated, and the colors were packed tight into the same space, twisting and coiling in on themselves and each other.

She took a deep breath and let it out slowly. She wished the colors weren't so bright, so in her face. It was making her eyes hurt.

As if by her thoughts alone, the colors instantly muted.

She blinked and mentally thought to change it back – and sure enough, everything around her brightened up again.

Not possible.

Everything is possible. You are the One. She shuddered as Hortran's ghostly voice whispered through her mind again.

"I thought you'd died and disappeared forever." That he hadn't filled her with immense relief but brought his name up again and made her wonder.

No. I'm dead. But I live on in spirit. In energy. In you.

She swallowed hard at the last part. "In me? Like forever?"

You can access my energy anytime, anyplace, and if I can, I will come.

He made it sound like she'd be placing a telephone call and if the connection was decent, the timing convenient or something similar, then he'd come. Bizarre. She frowned. Then nothing about him or this situation worked normally.

As she went to ask him what was with the colors, she could sense his energy fading away again. Why? Because he was tired? Or because the question wasn't so important as to need him to give an answer? Or had she waited too long and he thought he wasn't needed?

She shook her head, trying to sort out the impressions running through her mind. Before there'd have been no need to sort, but now her head was stuffed and she couldn't think. It was getting worse every minute.

"Stop," she snapped. "Clear out. I want my thoughts and mine alone."

There was a slight snicker in her mind.

She lit up.

Cody!

Hey sweetheart, are you done rambling through that mess in there? Have you sorted yourself out?

His warm caring tone slipped down the path of her thoughts, brightening her world.

She laughed in delight. *I wasn't to begin with, but I think I'm slowly understanding how it works.* She quickly explained the little bit she had figured out. From the odd silence, she knew he didn't quite get it.

It's okay. I know it all sounds crazy, but it's improving, she said comfortably.

If you say so. He hesitated then asked in a low voice, *Are you ready to come back?*

Come back?

She didn't understand the question. *What do you mean? I haven't gone anywhere.*

No, but you're unconscious and there are some very worried people out here.

Unconscious. She digested that. *Then how come I can communicate with you?*

I don't know, but I'm glad you can.

Me too. She paused, thinking about all she'd seen. *Did you see my eyes open up a while ago?*

Yes, he said in surprise. *I called you, but you closed your eyes and drifted off again. It was weird, like you were caught in some strange half-awake, half-asleep state.*

When I first opened my eyes, there was just a crazy kaleidoscope of color. It was hard to look so I slammed them shut again.

Ah, and now?

The concern in his voice made her wonder how long she'd been out.

I'll try again, she said.

Yes, please. Your father is here and he's very worried.

Oh no. She hadn't considered that other people might be there waiting for her to surface. How horrible it must seem for those waiting.

Sorry, she whispered. *I didn't mean to stay away for so long. No worries, but we'd love to have you come back.*

Tessa let out a deep heavy sigh that seemed to come from a long ways inside – and released it.

As she let the last of the air out, she opened her eyes.

The color was still there. The vibrancy was still there but it was softer, less obnoxious – prettier.

Still different than what she was used to, but better in a way.

Then she caught sight of faces mixed into the colors. One in particular – her father.

Then she understood – the colors came from the individual people around her.

She could see them clearer than ever and the colors were more distinct than before, but they were still just the energy of the people around her.

Her father.

And Cody.

She tilted her head upward, smiled at his worried face, and said, "Hey."

ॐ ॐ

OH THANK HEAVENS. She was awake.

Not caring that Serus hovered at their side, Cody murmured, "Hey back."

Then he lowered his head and kissed her. A warm, caring, a-little-too-hard kiss that was a mixture of *Hey, I missed you* and *damn good thing you finally decided to wake up.*

Dimly through the emotions running through him, he could hear cheers and shouts resounding throughout the room. He lifted his head and realized they'd all seen that Tessa had woken up. The cheers were for her.

He dropped his gaze to stare down at the bemused woman in his arms.

"That greeting, Tessa, is for you."

She smiled gently. "Glad to know I was missed."

Serus leaned over and awkwardly wrapped his arms around her and held her close.

Cody was loath to let her go, but he could hardly tug her back out from her father's arms. Serus straightened with Tessa held firm against his chest and turned so the others could see her.

Immediately the cheers resounded louder.

She moaned.

"I'm so very grateful you survived that," Serus said. Cody was close enough to hear the tears clogging the ancient's voice. Damn if his own eyes didn't start burning.

How many damn times was this special woman going to hit the wall that would have killed anyone else – and climb over it?

She'd survived so much, and yet fear still snaked through him that she was skirting death all the time. One day Death was going to get pissed off at always being cheated out of his prize and he'd snatch her up and take her away.

And Cody would go after them and steal her back.

He was caught up in the moment, relief and fear mixing together when he heard her in his head, *I'm not going anywhere. At least not for a while.*

Good thing.

Cody watched as Serus and Tessa cuddled together. Serus had come a long way since not wanting to acknowledge Tessa's inability to attend the Council meetings because of her mixed heritage. As she carried the memories of one of the most powerful vampire ancients the world had ever known, they could hardly deny her entrance now.

Hell, they probably should give her a damn seat on the Council!

Right. Like that would ever happen.

"Cody?"

Startled, Cody turned to face Serus and reached out automatically to accept Tessa back into his arms. He shifted her weight and smiled down at her. "How are you feeling?"

"Fine, just a little off balance."

"In what way?" he asked curiously, knowing Serus was listening in.

"As if I'm too full and have to move carefully so I don't topple." Her smile was wry when she added, "I know that sounds silly, but it's as if I'm juggling two people in here."

"Two people?" Serus said in alarm. "She's not in there with you, is she?"

What a horrible thought. Cody couldn't imagine.

Tessa shook her head. "No, but all her memories are stored in here and Hortran's are maybe here, too."

"What?" Cody and Serus's voices blended into a low roar.

She shuddered. "Shh. Everything is super sensitive. Please keep your voices down."

"What did you say about Hortran?" asked Serus in a muted growl that fooled no one.

Cody watched her closely. "He's not in there, is he? He was dead."

"But he's a Ghost, remember?" she answered, a smile on her face. "And no, I don't know what that means."

"But he's there? As in you are in contact with him?"

"I think so. But not sure if he's all here or I'm speaking to residual energy."

Cody glanced over at Serus, relieved to see confusion on his face that matched Cody's. Like *what the hell?* It used to be that dead was dead. He was no longer so sure.

It was as if Tessa had connected one side to the other.

Unfreakin' believable.

Just then David burst into the room. His gaze beelined to Tessa, and such love and relief washed over his face at seeing his sister alive and well that Cody could feel himself choking up again. Damn, he was turning into a bloody waterworks factory. Still, there was such caring in Tessa's family, and Cody had just lost his own brother. They'd never been as close, maybe never would have either, but now that he was gone there was no chance of that happening, Cody had to wonder at the missed opportunities. He was blessed to be as close as he was with his father. And speaking of which... where was he?

※ ※

GORAN WALKED INTO the next room. He was on the second floor. With Tessa collapsed upstairs, the morale of the group he led had alternated from brutal anger to defeat and back again. They needed a good battle to get their blood up and some fight back into them. Now that she was awake and appeared to be recovering, they wanted to go see her. He did too, but they had a job to do. And he couldn't let them forget she was in the shape she was because these assholes had taken out Deanna. That old witch could have lived another century. Long enough for her to find someone else to dump her shit on.

And leave Tessa out of this. For once.

He stood in the doorway and stared around at the mirror room to every other room he'd been in here. He groaned. More people hooked up to tubes. He was sick of this. He couldn't tell the good from the bad – the victims from the volunteers. For all he knew, they'd been releasing vipers into their midst who'd turn on them in a second.

But he'd set on a course and he had to finish it.

He bent down to pull the tube out of the man on the bed in front of him. And stopped.

The tube was only taped in place. It wasn't actually inserted into the man's arm.

"Shit," he whispered under his breath.

He went to back up a step and realized he'd made a monumental mistake. He hadn't started at the front to work his way around the room, he'd walked into the middle.

He was surrounded.

Pretending he didn't notice anything different, he ripped off the tape and moved to go to the second man.

Inside his head, he screamed at Serus. *Second floor. Trap.*

And he backed up one step. Two steps. As he went to take a third, he was grabbed from behind and the room exploded with men jumping out of the beds and attacking.

Ah hell.

WENDY LIFTED HER head and rubbed her temple. The headache that had started a good half hour ago was getting worse instead of better. She'd been running these numbers and names for several hours, trying to sort through the database. She had the laptop they'd recovered from the blood farm comparing data against the information on Gloria's laptop that Councilman Adamson had handed over. She was looking to identify the victims the army had recovered after the mountain blew up and the victims that would remain buried forever. They needed to try and identify who these poor people were and how many had been kidnapped to hang up in the supply line.

"Tired, Wendy? Why don't you take a break?" Sian suggested from beside her.

"Why don't you?" Wendy retorted in frustration. This was the fifth or sixth time Sian had asked, but the woman herself wouldn't stop. And she was pregnant. "You're the one that needs rest."

Sian gave a light, trilling laugh that made Wendy smile. Sian was a hoot. "How about we both take one?"

She hated to admit that the older woman in her condition could outwork Wendy, but worrying about Ian had taken the stuffing out of her and she was…tired. Ian was sleeping and damn, she wanted to be sleeping beside him. It was the only way she could make sure he didn't get into trouble again.

"Let's check on Rhia. If she's doing well, we can go close our eyes for an hour or two."

At that moment, Rhia walked into the room. "Sian, I just spoke to Serus. Tessa is awake and talking. She appears to be tired and confused but healing."

"Oh wow, that's awesome," Wendy said. "She's so strong."

"She's very special," Sian agreed. "Hopefully they can get her out of there and bring her here to rest up."

Rhia let out a tiny snort. "I wish, but I doubt she'd come. She's not the same girl I knew a few weeks ago."

"No," Wendy said, "she's better. She's more confident. She knows who she is more and she's gained many friends and followers. She's always been 'different' – only now that difference is a good thing." She grinned. "Actually, it's more a case of everyone wants to be her."

"I'm glad to hear that," Rhia said quietly. "She didn't have it easy growing up."

"She'll not find it easy now either," Sian said. "Only the challenges will be different." She stood up and stretched. "I suggest we set the computers up to do some cross checking and then go lie down."

"I'll stay here and keep track of the results."

Wendy was torn. She was tired, and the thought of lying down and closing her eyes for an hour was irresistible. But she wasn't sure she could trust Rhia. From Sian's sudden stillness, she knew she was considering the same issue. Sian walked over to the computer and clicked on a few buttons. Wendy tried to see what she was doing without being too obvious but couldn't see what programs she'd brought up.

Rhia stood at Wendy's side, watching, waiting.

Finally, Sian stood up and said, "Naptime."

She smiled at Rhia as she walked toward the door. "They should be good to go, but there might be some questions on the filters."

"No problem," Rhia said, watching them. "I'll keep an eye on it."

Wendy opened the door and waited for Sian to walk into the hallway. She deliberately left the door open and never said a word until they were well out of earshot, then whispered, "Do you trust her?"

"With the drugs she's been given and the brainwashing…- absolutely not."

JEWEL WOKE UP with her body twisting in pain, the weight of the covers too much for her beleaguered system to bear. She kicked off the light cotton, almost crying out with the effort required.

She whimpered as the cool air brushed over her bare skin. She knew she wore something for clothing because she could feel the material binding her as she moved. The breeze, oh, it felt so good. She tugged at the confining material, wanting it off her heated skin.

"Easy, Jewel." A calm female voice spoke from beside her. Firm hands pulled her own up to lay them along her side.

"It's the drugs affecting you. Just rest. Sleep so your body can deal with the withdrawal from them."

"Can't," she cried out brokenly, hating the weakness coursing through her veins, making her want to weep and cry out to be held. To have someone who loved her at her side and tell her she'd be okay. That this would be over soon.

This nameless voice wasn't one she knew. She was too terrified to open her eyes or ask questions in case her greatest fears had come to pass.

Was she at the blood farm? Still in the hospital, a stage before the blood farm, or was she safe?

"It's all right. You're safe now." The words she'd so wanted to hear rolled over her on a sea of doubt. Was she safe? Or was the woman just saying that?

"David," Jewel whispered. "I want to see David."

"Well, I don't know anyone by that name, but I'll check and see. You just take it easy now."

Jewel whimpered. Her mind refused to listen to anyone. Where was David? Why was David not here?

If he wasn't with her – where was he?

❧ ❦

DAVID RACED DOWN the stairs toward Goran, his father at his heels. The cry of help from someone who rarely called for any was terrifying. They'd barely held Tessa and Cody back from racing down here with them. But Tessa wasn't up to it, and Cody needed to stay and look after her whether either of them liked that or not. Besides, there were a dozen young vamps behind them looking for a good dustup.

For once, Cody and Tessa needed to stay back and let others take care of them. Since taking Jewel back to the Council Hall and returning as fast as he could, David had been looking for a chance to get a little revenge himself.

No one should get away with what these assholes were doing.

Jewel was exhausted and terrified. Who knew what they'd done to her? Anything was too much.

He burst through the door to the floor and came to a staggering stop. In front of him, a dozen vamps surrounded Goran. One particularly mega-size model stood behind him, his hand on the back of Goran's neck. In his other hand he held a small weird weapon. Shit. Cody had mentioned something about those. UV lights or something. And he was in its direct line of sight.

Just then, the big man lifted his hand and pointed the gun right at David.

He dove to the left in front of his father and they both tumbled into the group behind them.

The big man laughed as the group struggled to right themselves.

David caught a glimpse of Goran's eye roll.

Not the best entrance he'd ever made. David hopped to

his feet, facing the giant. Out of the corner of his eye, he caught sight of Serus slipping off to the side. What was he up to?

"You guys are the rescue party? What a joke. No wonder they wanted us to take your place at the front of the line. Useless, the whole lot of you."

"Take our place?" David asked. "What do you mean?"

"The clan leaders. We're taking them over. All of them."

Goran snorted. "Like hell."

The big vamp clenched his arm tighter across Goran's throat, his bicep bulging. Goran choked and gasped for air. The vamp released him slightly. "Yes, we are. And obviously we're needed. You're all useless. Old. Used up. We are bigger, better, smarter."

David shook his head. "You're enhanced. You've been given drugs and DNA that wasn't yours to try and improve on our ancient bloodlines."

"And?" the vamp challenged. "What's wrong with that? It's not as if you are doing a good job running this place. Look at it. The damn livestock are running all over the place acting like they own the world. Like they have the right to live here free." He snickered. "As if."

"So that's what this is all about? The blood farms?"

The big man shrugged. "Not only that. But obviously that is the way to feed the growing number of vamps. Of course weeding out the old, the weak, and the useless helps too."

David took several casual steps forward, noticing that no one seemed to care. As if he wasn't enough of a threat for them to be bothered about. Hell, he'd show them.

He took another step. Several vamps straightened. He deliberately slipped and fell down, and as they chortled with laughter he twisted, landed on his feet, and flipped over, lashing out and kicking the UV weapon out of the asshole's hand.

He straightened, spun, and went to kick only to find Goran had already attacked.

Chaos broke out.

David jumped on the back of the big vamp as he fought off Goran. Goran might have been surrounded and allowed himself to have been taken before, but no longer. He wanted a little payback of his own. While David kept the big vamp from being able to move easily, Goran jumped and kicked the big man in the chest then spun, lashing out a powerful fist and hitting the big man in the jaw. He barely swayed.

Goran landed on his feet and bent over slightly, his chest heaving.

"Crap," he said, "Why are you guys always so damn big?"

"Because we're kickass," the big man boasted.

Goran snorted, reached into his pocket, and slashed.

David caught sight of the silver and jumped free as the big man blew up into a nasty pile of sour-smelling ash in his face.

"Oh, gross."

Serus came up along the side and smacked Goran on the shoulder. "Glad to see you're up to your old tricks."

"Always. Where the hell did you sneak off to? It's not like you to leave a good fight."

Serus grinned. "I found something. Come see."

CHAPTER 3

STANDING ON HER feet for the first time, and to the sound of resounding cheers, Tessa took one step. With a small grin, she took an equally shaky second one. The room swayed as if too big to comprehend. The absolute size and mass of the energy swarming around her, even though pale and not intrusive, was still startling. She could see the energy of the walls. The energy of the beds. Waves of color floated up from the floor, making her unsure of where to place her foot.

She understood the human lesson in physics. One of their famous scientists, Einstein, supposedly said, *Energy cannot be created or destroyed, it can only be changed from one form to another.* Now there was no doubt about it; she could see everything. A fact that was both disturbing and fantastic.

But confusing for her to sort through. She could see people as ghostly images behind the colors whereas she'd rather see the colors as ghostly images. Instantly, her vision shifted and morphed to her seeing it the way she wanted to.

"Oh Lord," she whispered.

Cody, ever at her side, asked, "What's the matter?"

She shook her head, not sure how to even begin. She'd seen so much before that she hadn't understood; what could she say about this now?

"I'm fine," she said in a low voice. "Things just look... different."

He shot her a long careful glance. "Good different or bad different?" he asked cautiously.

She smiled. "Good, as soon as I figure out how to make sense of it all. I saw a lot before, but now I can see a whole lot more."

"More?" He shook his head. "I can't imagine."

"I couldn't have before either." She stopped to study the group of males standing alert in front of her. They completely surrounded her. She had no idea why. "What's with the bodyguards?"

"You were injured," he said, laughter flooding through his voice, adding, "They are all trying to keep you safe." His voice was understandably humorous.

"From what?" And what did they think they could do for her that she couldn't do herself?

"Remember you were unconscious for a long time."

True. She had been. And apparently some people had been worried about her. Wait. She twisted ever so slowly and took a look back at the group that was leaning and standing around her, still on guard but relaxed, knowing there was no immediate danger.

Or was there?

She looked from one to the other and studied their energy. Only there was no need to study anything. Two of the men stood out so clear and so dark that there was no missing the blackness of their energy, and in this case she highly suspected for their soul. Had they infiltrated the group here at the hospital or had they been given the drugs unwillingly while captive? Or was it something else altogether?

She lowered her gaze and called out to Cody. *The two young men on the left, their systems are chock full of black.*

What? Are you sure?

Yes, she said softly, *but I'm not sure how or why. I haven't seen anything like this before.*

Maybe and maybe not. You were tired and had a lot going on. You could have missed it. Or not recognized what you were seeing.

True. Or the drugs were in their system and we unhooked them too late to stop it from taking them over. She pondered the issue. *Do you think it could be something else? We were so sure these men were all on our side.*

And they might be. It's possible the darkness is working its way through them and they know nothing about it.

Then how do we find out if they are victims? How do we save them?

Can you see more now? Is that why you are seeing this new energy? Cody asked.

Tessa had to stop and consider. Was she seeing things differently now? Definitely. Was it allowing her to see more energy? Hell yes, but was it showing her more of what she needed to see or was all this just background noise? Would she have seen these guys' black energy before? She'd have thought so. But maybe not.

She turned slowly to stare at the energy she could make out from where she stood. With seeing so much now, was what she was looking at the same darkness as before? Or was she seeing something different? Something on a different level? It made no sense. Why put energy into healthy males to make them look like they were diseased? To make them look like they were guilty – unless you *wanted* to have them appear that way?

If you wanted to get rid of them. She wondered just how tricky the assholes were getting. Enough to have them kill each other?

"Do you know them?" she murmured to Cody.

"Slightly. Not as friends though."

"I'm going to try something." Aware of his intent gaze watching her, she bowed her head and closed her eyes. Calling to her vampire heritage, she was almost blasted backwards with the force of the response.

"Whoa." Cody grabbed her and held her steady.

"I'm okay," she whispered. "It just surprised me."

"It?" he murmured. "Whatever *it* was, it damn near sent you flying."

"I was calling up my vampire heritage to help me." A tiny laugh escaped. "I'm guessing Deanna's energy has affected everything I do. I'll have to remember that."

"Or better yet, learn to control it."

"Hmmm. Easier said than done."

She took a deep breath and slowly opened her eyes. Instantly, the same vivid hues she'd seen the first time she opened her eyes took over, almost blinding her. She gasped, a shudder taking over her body. *Tone it down, please. I can't see.*

Instantly the force of the energy muted down. Still shuddering in reaction but in better control, she took a slow look at the two men. All the men were standing and staring in her direction, confusion and worry on their faces. She tried to smile back at everyone but wasn't sure it worked when their expressions didn't change. Sighing and knowing her oddness was growing in a legendary way, she focused on the two young men with the black energy weaving through their systems. She wished she understood where it was coming from. Maybe then she might understand how it got to that place. It was on the surface of their systems, but maybe not inside? She couldn't tell from here. Was everyone affected or only these two? If so, why?

With more questions tumbling around her head than answers, she walked slowly forward, the others moving away from the two men who now stood up and looked at her nervously.

"Hey, Cody, what gives?" one of them asked.

"Not sure. She's found something…odd."

"With us?" asked the second man in alarm. "What the hell? We didn't do anything."

"She's not saying you did – relax. But since the Deanna thing she sees…more."

"More? Crap. She already saw so much. What else is there to be found?"

"That's what she's trying to sort out."

Tessa froze, half her awareness on the conversation going on around her and half on the twisting strands of black. A superficial black. Almost a dusting *over* them – not through them like she'd originally assumed. The black looked darker, thicker because she also saw the dusting from behind them, too.

Odd. She took a step to the right, then a second one, keeping an eye on the dispersion of the energy. Looking for where it might have come from. And damn if the black didn't snake off to the right and zip out the door.

No way. She understood the blackness to be drugs, injected chemicals with an energy signature that affected the individual person, but there was no way it should be capable of leaving their energy space and travelling down the pathway unless they'd walked that direction themselves – as in that was their energy signature.

Instead, these two men had been sitting here for a long time. The energy pooled around them showed that. They had other colors twisting with them, but nothing dark like that very specific strand. As it raced out the door and down the hallway, she ran out after it. She didn't know where it had come from, but she needed to track it backwards. She almost laughed at the thought. It was the first time she'd tracked anything that way. Normally she caught sight of the energy and tracked it to the person. Not this time.

The energy, still black and strongly defined but in a waist high cloud, raced away in front of her. Clearly seen, and that in itself was odd. She hit the double doors at the end of the hallway, but they opened just before she made contact. Weird, but she didn't let it slow her down. She chased the black energy down the stairs, dimly realizing a herd followed her. She'd been so focused she hadn't noticed the group from the room was hot on her heels. She raced down flight after flight, determined to find the source of the energy affecting the men.

And then she hit a wall. Literally.

She bounced backwards and was picked up before she had a chance to regain her balance. She was lifted and set gently back down on her feet.

For all the shock of being lifted and straightened up there was no sense of danger. No fear. No dislike from the man – and yeah, it was a young man – who'd helped her.

In fact…she gasped and laughed. "You look so much better than the last time I saw you."

The man beamed. He said, "Xclkileens don."

Cody, slightly out of breath, stepped up beside her and said, "What the hell?"

Tessa laughed. "It's one of the Nordic guards."

"Okay, I can see that given his size, but what the heck did he say?"

Tessa smiled and responded in the same language the young mammoth had spoken. "I'm glad you are feeling better."

The man's face lit up, and a spate of gibberish streamed from his mouth.

Only it took just seconds for the words to reform into English. She beamed at his kind words of thanks for saving the life of his friend. And his apology for standing in her way.

He stepped to one side and gave a slight bow. As big as he was, the bow barely lowered his head to her level.

"Thank you," she said in his language and walked through the door.

"Ah, Tessa? Since when do you speak a second language?"

"I don't. Deanna did. Several, in fact."

With the stunned silence of his mind like a low hum inside her own, she continued at the slower pace, studying the hallway in front of her for signs of the same darkness. It was here, but fuzzier around the edges. It wasn't as contained or as powerful. Dispersed with time. As if older. Somewhere between the hallway and the staircase, it had lost much of its force.

Why?

She spun around and realized going back was not an option – at least not without some difficulty. More than thirty men stood in front of her, including the big Nordic man.

She turned to stare out the window, lost in thought, when it hit her. She was staring at a pool of black. That was where the energy stream stopped.

The window was the answer. Whoever or whatever had been part of that energy had come and gone through the window. She turned to study the large casement. It was surrounded in blackness. Dark, twisting, fresh black, but as she peered at it closer, the darkness was on the outside.

This wasn't the older dissipating stuff heading down the

hallway. This was fresh.

She stepped up to the window, studying the latch. It had not only been opened recently, it was still open.

She gave a hard push back.

There was a startled shriek, then sounds of heavy wings followed by harsh cries of panic.

With everyone crowding behind her, she watched as the two vamps who'd been waiting in position, weird cans in their hand, were burnt up by the sun's rays.

Cody shot her a sharp look. "Seriously? How did you recognize those vamps were here?"

"The energy," she said simply. "It's changed. It's still what I saw earlier, but now it's…different."

"It's different," Cody asked shrewdly. "Or are you different?"

❧ ❦

TESSA'S SHOCKED GAZE was clear and direct as he stared into her eyes. He'd followed her mad flight out of the room and down to the floor below, wondering what she was up to and just hoping that she had some clue.

Deanna's energy was a massive shift for her. To have all the memories, all the knowledge from the oldest vampire should have caused Tessa a fair bit of trouble sorting out the new reality she was living. Except with her typical aplomb, she'd shrugged herself into this new life, gave a wiggle or two to help things settle in place, and she was off and running into who knew what trouble yet again.

He felt like he did nothing but follow along behind. He wished he knew what kind of changes Deanna had made to her psyche.

None, she snapped. *Deanna's memories are filed away in my memory banks. They haven't changed me.*

Yet you spoke to that Nordic vamp in his own language. He barely held his surprise back at her tone of voice.

That was Deanna's ability, she said. And stopped. Frowned.

Exactly. It was because of Deanna that you could speak to him. So if she'd enabled you to do that much, what else has she done?

Nothing. It's not like that. I can open her memories when I need to but her energy, or maybe Hortran's, has somehow enhanced my own energy reading abilities.

Cody kept an eye on Tessa, hating the suspicious nature that made him second guess her actions, but he couldn't help but wonder if Tessa was Tessa or if that bitch had done something to her. Then again, a couple of weeks ago the shit Tessa was doing before the Deanna scenario was way out there too.

Still, in those couple of weeks, he couldn't remember one time when she'd snapped at him.

She stood in front of him, her profile clear and crisp and…beautiful. She was stronger, more capable, and more beautiful than ever – and he'd never been so concerned.

"I'm fine, you know," she said in a low voice.

"Are you? You've never used that tone of voice on anyone before."

She winced ever so slightly. If he hadn't been looking at her, he'd have missed it. As it was, he was glad to see it.

"I'm stressed," she said in a low voice. "I guess I'm not quite the same. Things don't look the same, they don't feel the same. My system has been placed under a huge load. It feels heavier when I take a step. It's harder to judge distances when I reach out and my voice…" she shrugged. "It doesn't modulate as easy as before."

He watched her, hearing the tunes of the old Tessa woven into the fabric of her voice. It was her. Just a Tessa that had once again been asked to do so much without any preparation and training, and like the same Tessa she was doing the best she could.

Instantly he felt ashamed. Who was he to criticize her? She'd been through so much. If she wanted to snap at him, she had every right to.

No, I don't. I don't want to ever have that right. I'm also so very tired – and yet energized as if my system hasn't adjusted to the changes so different parts of me are running at different speeds.

That sounds horrible.

She laughed. *It's definitely odd.*

He slid an arm across her shoulders and tugged her up close.

She nestled in. He smiled. She was still his Tessa.

The rest? Well, he'd find out as time went along. As long as she was still here with him in heart and mind, he'd learn to deal with the rest.

Yes, you will, she said inside his mind. *You won't get rid of me that easily.*

He smiled. Now *that* was his Tessa.

প্র ঙ্গ

SERUS SAID, "SEE? What did I tell you?" He laughed at the look of amazement on his son's face. David stood at his side, studying his find in silence. He'd led them to the back of the room where Goran had been attacked and where he'd found this gem.

Goran's reaction was much stronger. "What the hell is this?"

"I'm thinking it's a way in and out of this place that most people don't know about." Serus almost rubbed his hands together with glee. "Of course I don't know if the thing works or not."

He studied the big old metal elevator and the ancient panel that held the button to summon it to their floor. The whole thing was hidden inside a cupboard. Maybe a closet was a better description, but it was damn small and only held this big elevator. He couldn't resist. He reached out and pushed the button.

Instantly the double doors opened.

"Ah hell," Goran said, raising a hand to rub the top of his chin. "Did we let someone in on this floor without even knowing it? Is that how the guys who just attacked me got in?"

"It's possible, isn't it, Dad?" David stepped into the elevator and looked at the floors available. "It goes right to the roof. From the lower garage to the roof. One of the few elevators that gives the riders full access to the hospital."

"And hidden like it is, we'd have never known. The new arrivals could have mingled with the ones we released, and who'd be the wiser? The only vamps here were ones on our team or ones we rescued. We'd have assumed that every vamp we saw would be one of ours."

"You mean the only ones that we *knew* about. This changes everything."

"And what do we do about it now?"

"Set up a guard to keep an eye on the place."

"Sure, but we don't want anyone to know we found it, so

whoever is guarding it has to do it in such a way as to not raise suspicions."

"Ha. Put them in a bed in the room outside the closet here and make it look like they are in a bad way and might not make it," Goran suggested. "Then someone won't care if they are seen or not."

"Or they might be tempted to take the guard out permanently."

"And won't they get a surprise."

The three men looked at each other, big grins on their faces. "Let's do it."

∿ ∝

RHIA WAITED FOR Wendy and Sian to leave the room. They were both exhausted and needed to lie down. She was exhausted too but couldn't possibly sleep. Her mind churned with the events of the last few days. Her husband and their shaky mindspeak connection, her youngest son who she'd not seen since waking from her drugged stupor, her daughter who'd grown up while she wasn't looking, and then there was her firstborn and the reason she was going to work now. She had supposedly sent him off somewhere. It was the *where* that really bothered her. That she could have done such a thing in the first place was horrific. To think she'd done something to help those bastards at the blood farm was something else again.

She had to get Seth back. The longer he was with them, the more entrenched into their way of life he'd become. She refused to believe that her son had willingly joined that group. He'd been raised right. He knew exactly where the family stood on such a major issue, and he'd been right there with them. That meant, like her, he'd been under the influence of their brainwashing and drugs.

She was the only one straddling the line between that experience and the one she should be experiencing. She was the only one that could understand what he was going through. She had to help him. Failure was not an option.

And that meant finding out what she'd done to him.

The only way she'd come up with so far was dangerous.

And so far from 'right' that she knew no one else would help her. But as she couldn't remember what she'd done while under the influence of the drugs, there was only one way to return to the state where she could access the memories.

Therefore, she had to get hold of the drugs and take a small dose – hopefully putting her half in and half out of the state that she could remember what she needed to remember in order to save Seth.

And hope the others around her would understand.

But she doubted it.

Rhia? Serus snapped inside her mind. *I can hear you worrying. Don't do anything dangerous. There is always another way.*

No, she whispered. *There isn't.*

And she gently closed the door between her and her best friend and first and only love.

She'd never felt so alone. But it was the only way to right the wrongs she'd committed.

JARED STOPPED AT the front entrance way to the school, Clarissa at his side. The parking lot was full of cars. There wasn't a soul around.

She continued to walk past him, lost in thought. Several

steps on, she turned and looked back at him. "Are you coming?"

He really didn't want to be here. Finally, he nodded and said, "Yeah, it just feels…odd to be here."

"If you didn't skip as much, it wouldn't." She laughed. "Come on, we're late enough already."

He didn't think such a thing was possible, but he did want to finish his year and get out of here for good. He joined her at the bottom of the front steps. "I'll see you after last class then?"

"Absolutely." At the top of the stairs, she opened the front doors and entered. He stepped in behind her. She walked straight down the hallway, calling back, "Find me if Taz gets back to you with news."

"Will do." He stood and watched her walk away. She was nice. Friendly and caring but not flirty. He liked that. In fact, he liked her.

With a happy smile, he turned to the left hallway and headed to his class. He should be just in time for his lab.

The bell rang as he walked, confirming his assumption. Now if only the day would go by fast. He pulled out his phone to check if there was a message from Taz. None. And neither was there anything from anyone else.

Damn.

❧ ❦

IAN WOKE WITH a start. He froze in place, listening for something off. Something that would tell him where he was and what was going on. Something had changed in his world, but he didn't know what. And he was so damn tired he knew he was in a dangerous state. Anyone could have snuck up on him.

Looking around, he recognized one of the Council Hall rooms. He should be safe here.

Then again...none of them were safe anymore.

A movement rustled beside him. His breath caught in the back of his throat. He slowly turned his head.

Wendy lay curled up at his side. Sound asleep. Astonished, he could only watch in wonder as she snuffled, a tiny endearing sound that made his heart ache.

When had she returned to bed? They'd spent several hours together earlier then Sian had knocked, asking for a few moments of Wendy's time, and he'd fallen asleep while they spoke at the doorway. From the dark shadows under her eyes, he suspected she hadn't had much rest. Then again, given the time that he could see on the opposite wall, it was daylight and well past her bedtime.

They were safe and survived some horrific times already; that they were here together right now was precious. He slid down and wrapped his arms around her. She snuggled in close.

He closed his eyes and fell back asleep.

$\sim$ $\sim$

JEWEL OPENED HER eyes, gasped, and slammed them closed. Same bed. Same room. Same place. But what place?

She held still, waiting for the horrible memories to drain away. She'd slept, but not well. She knew she was alone in the bed as she could feel the edge on both sides. So a cot then. And damn if that didn't remind her of the hospital room she'd been in. But David had found her and rescued her. Brought her back to Council Hall. She should still be there. She opened her eyes enough to peek under her lashes. It looked like a hospital room, but the Council Hall had similar rooms. She'd seen them years ago and often wondered why they'd be needed when vamps could heal themselves, but she'd been chastised for questioning the wisdom of the elders.

Now she hoped it was the same room. She didn't want to be anywhere else. She rolled over slowly as if still asleep and peered out.

She was alone.

Thank heavens for that.

The room, small and sparsely furnished, was barely big enough for her needs. Not that she planned on staying. On a small table to side sat a pile of folded clothes. Her own clothes, now washed and dried and ready for her.

She sat up slowly, aware of a booming headache going on at the base of her skull. She had no idea why but had to consider an injury or worse, drugs.

She shoved back the sheet and swung her legs off the bed.

"Whoa," she whispered as the room spun. When gravity reasserted itself, she slid to the floor and used the bed for support.

Why was she so weak? Then again, when had she fed last? Surely her body just needed sustenance. She walked slowly over to the small room at the side, relieved to find a bathroom. There were also toiletries. A further search found a small shower.

She smiled. Wouldn't that feel perfect right now? Her smile fell away. Except she was weak. She didn't want to fall and have to call for help to get out.

But the hot water would feel so good on her aching muscles. She studied the shower and realized that there were bars and supports as if intended for patients or the elderly. She couldn't think of one vamp that had ever been so weak as to need such things, but it made her feel better to think she might not be alone.

There were towels in a cupboard in the bedroom. She grabbed three. Was she the only female to use so many? She had one to stand on, one to wrap up her wet hair, and one to dry off with. She shrugged. So what? There were obviously laundry facilities here.

Standing under the hot water, she let the heat soak through her wings. They'd been so useless for weeks it almost felt normal to not move them, but she wanted that sense of freedom back. She needed it. If she'd had the full use of her wings a long time ago, she imagined she'd have been able to get herself out of trouble before this. Now with more drugs…

Tears clogged her eyes and throat at the fear that was sitting just inside. Always there, warring with hope that her wings would heal again. She hated being injured. Always had. But this was different. A break she could watch heal. A scratch or bruise took minutes to return to normal. Drugs though, they wrecked her body and played with her mind. She didn't even want to think about what they did to her emotions. She wished David had stayed with her. She really didn't want to be alone now.

Through the misery in her mind, she thought she heard a voice calling. She froze, staring at the door. Had she locked it?

She could feel herself readying for a fight to come. Pretty pathetic. A young sick female standing soaking wet and nude – what was she going to do, throw water in their eyes?

Then – her heart gasping in shock all the while her mind struggled to believe – she felt her wings unfurl. And damn if one, at her instinctive command, didn't wrap around to hide her slender form.

CHAPTER 4

TESSA WALKED BACK along the hallway, a quiet audience behind her. She had no idea how the black energy was being transferred amongst the young men she'd saved. If she couldn't figure it out soon, the system could be repeated. She'd quickly lose control of who was on which side.

She spun around and looked back at the open window. There was a pooling of mixed energy sitting right there. Made sense. Anyone who needed a breath of fresh air would have been tempted to stand there.

Had the men been on the other side waiting for an unsuspecting dupe? If so, how had they administered the drugs? The canisters they'd held? If their canisters could be retrieved, the contents could be checked. She studied the turbulent mix of energies and realized the darkness, the original darkness, was thin and light and surrounded a much wider area than she'd suspected. From the looks of things, it had been turned into a deadly gas and sprayed on or around the men as they stood there – much like perfume would have been.

The men likely never knew anything was wrong. An odd smell perhaps, but likely nothing more than that. So how many had been affected and how could she tell for sure?

Plus she needed to save the two affected men. If she could.

And why administer the drugs this way? Or was the enemy trying new methods to regain control of the hospital? Still, this would be an incredibly slow method. Just one or two men at a time. "Of course," she muttered, her gaze going to the large group still following her. "As a core sample, it's a hell of a way to figure out whether this form of administration was effective or not."

"Administration of what?" Cody asked beside her.

"Drugs," she said succinctly. "In a gas form. Sprayed into the air in front of us. We walk through it and inhale a hefty dose." She looked back to see the two men and called them closer. The sea of men parted to let them through. She swept the black cloudiness from the first man's energy, noticing how much straighter he stood.

There was silence around her, watching her every moment.

"Surely that wouldn't make sense. It's a poor delivery system," Cody said while she worked.

"Maybe, but not as a trial."

"And if it works? Then what?" someone asked behind her.

"How would they deliver something like that on a massive scale?" Cody said, shifting his position so he could see what she was doing.

Murmurs around her had men crowding around in anger. She quickly cleared the second man's system. At the raised voices, she held up her hand.

"Think, everyone. What could they use to deliver a massive dose of drugs to everyone here?"

"Shit."

Cody's heartfelt whisper had her turning to him. She made a clipped movement with her head. "Exactly."

"What?" cried the young man she'd been working on.

"What are they planning?" the other men cried.

"The ventilation system would make the most sense. They

have a massive duct highway running through the hospital. If they wanted to, they could release the lethal gas into the vents and it would filter through the entire building. We'd all be affected." She stared at them grimly. "It would happen so fast we wouldn't have time to react. Hell," she said, shifting her gaze. "We might not even notice when it happens."

Silence.

"That would ruin the building for themselves as well, right?"

Several of the men looked around uneasily.

Tessa shook her head. "Not if the drug had a limited time of effectiveness. They could drug us all and come in later today, for example, and either kill us off or inject us with other drugs – if we hadn't already converted to their cause."

She shrugged, her mind thinking madly of all the other applications for such a delivery system. "Think about them going to schools and gaining hundreds of potential blood farm victims in one stretch. They'd never be short of supply again."

Shocked gasps filled the air.

"You have one twisted mind," said someone quietly from the back of the crowd. "You know that?"

"Good thing that's only speculation," one male said, but he eyed the ventilation shafts above his head uneasily.

"Do you *know* that's what's happening, Tessa, or are you guessing?" Cody asked.

"Both," she said in an equally low voice. "Deanna's memories are telling me that such a delivery system was worked on a few decades ago. The concept had been brought back up again recently."

"Ah hell," said someone behind her. "If we aren't safe here, where can we go?"

Just then, a weird hissing sound crept through the walls.

Horrified cries filled the hallway as everyone scattered in all directions.

Everyone but Tessa and Cody.

She watched them all stand back and staring at her. "We need to evacuate the building."

"And how do you suggest we do that?"

"The same way the others left maybe?" She shrugged. "I don't know. I am not up on where we are for numbers of vamps still in the hospital."

"Well, maybe I do." David, a huge grin on his face, came around the corner, walking directly to them. "I think we've found a way out. It will take time and some methodical action on our part, but if you're right, we could have an answer." He quickly told them about the elevator Serus had found.

Tessa opened her eyes wide as the information filtered to the back of her mind and joined with information she had already stored there. Deanna's memories.

"Deanna knew about the elevator. She'd used it before."

"Where does it go?" David asked.

She sorted through the files in her mind, the folders flicking faster and faster as she moved through the information. Suddenly, it all stopped and the information she needed stood in front of her.

"Oh, interesting."

"What? Tell us already, Tessa."

"It leads to the main headquarters."

CODY STUDIED HER features. "What headquarters?"

"The blood farm headquarters. It was in the basement of the hospital for decades. It might be still there."

"Or they might have cleaned it out when we took over the building," David said. "How would we know? We just found the elevator."

"Does it give access to every floor?" Cody asked. At David's nod, he frowned. "And more floors than we know of?"

"I can't say. It goes to the morgue and the two garage levels."

"Remember, Cody, there was the other elevator at the morgue level. That one goes below." Tessa's face got an arrested look on it. "I think the bottom button has a label that is misleading."

"Bottom label?"

Cody got it. "There is no second garage level to this place. That's where it is."

David spun around. "You two stay here. I'll go check it out."

"Not alone," Tessa warned. "You won't necessarily know what you're looking for. I got the impression the headquarters was well hidden."

David paused. "How are you feeling, by the way? You had quite the trip."

"Yeah." She snorted. "A Deanna trip."

Cody grinned, loving her sense of humor.

"I want to go with you downstairs," she said.

That wiped the grin off Cody's face. "Like hell."

She turned to glare at him. "Why not?"

"For one, you don't have your strength back. If we're attacked, you will be vulnerable. Two, you're the one that brought up this gas stuff. We need to be on that first. We can't have everyone running scared now."

"The elevator is basically the same issue for both problems. We need to get organized and get the men moving downstairs. I'll go with David and the first group to make sure it's safe."

"Not a good idea."

She stepped toward him, the look in her eyes damn near making his heart ache even more. She'd sent him around the bend for weeks already, and she could still do it with just one look.

"I need to do something," she pleaded. "I need to move, to find a way to integrate the new energy into my system. I feel…full. No, overfull. Maybe moving around and doing something will help."

"Then you can do that here," he said calmly, refusing to let her go back into the danger zone.

She smiled. In his head, she whispered, *And I love that about you. But we need to be there to keep the others safe.*

We? At her look of astonishment, he felt better. *You didn't mean to leave me here?*

She shook her head vehemently. "No. You have to come with me."

He paused. "Have to? Why?"

Confusion peeked through her lashes as he tried to read the look in her eyes. She looked as baffled as he felt. "Yes, have to. But I don't know why."

"That is so weird to have you guys speak half out loud and half in your heads," David groaned. "And the why doesn't matter. If he has to, he has to. Let's make sure we follow it. There's too much shit going on for us to screw up on something like this. Besides, it's not like Cody has left your side willingly yet," he said. "He's not likely to now either."

True enough. But there'd been a warning in Tessa's voice. Something premonition-like. And that scared the crap out of him. He didn't dare leave her alone now.

"Give us a chance to organize the exodus. We need to make sure we take care of our own first," he said. "Then we'll go. All of us – together."

"Like always." she smiled. "Thank you."

He shrugged. "David's right. I wouldn't have let you go anyway."

A light, tinkling laugh escaped. "I know. You've been a wonderful protector."

"Okay, enough, you two. The rest of us would like to get to the end of this damn war so we can be with our honeys too." David growled out the last words, reminding Cody that Jewel was at the Council Hall along with many other people.

"How is she, David?" Tessa asked quietly, instinctively understanding that her brother was hurting.

"She's asleep. So are Ian and Wendy apparently. Hell, nice for them. I'd like to get this done so I can join them."

Tessa nodded. "Let's go then."

☙ ❧

SERUS WAITED AT the top of the elevator. "David should be back by now," he said, chafing at the wait.

"Ha," Goran replied. "It probably took all this time just to get through the crowd hanging around Tessa."

"Don't remind me. Got to admit I'm kind of glad Cody is in the picture right now. Helps to keep the young cubs off her."

"Even he won't hold them off for long, you know that. They'll wait for an opening and stomp him into the ground to get to her."

"Only if she lets them." Serus grinned at his old friend. "And it looks to me like that's not going to happen anytime soon."

"Good. She needs to look out for him as much as he needs to look out for her."

Just then running footsteps raced toward them. Should be the guard they'd sent for, but just in case, both men stood side by side to face the newcomers. It was two of the young men that had been rescued earlier. "Oh good. Two of them are better than one."

"As long as these two are on our side," Goran muttered. "I don't trust anyone anymore."

Serus gave his instructions to the eager vamps, then set them up in beds along the far wall. "Remember to look injured and sick. We don't want anyone to know what we're doing here."

"Got it," they both called out.

"Good, then keep it down. We'll be leaving soon and will check out where this leads. You keep an eye on the elevator and report any activity to Motre." He glared at them. "No heroics. If something happens, call Motre."

❧ ❦

DAVID BARRELED AROUND the corner to find the ancients waiting impatiently. "What did you do, go to the Council to find her?" Goran asked in disgust. "We could have put an end to the war by now."

David laughed. "No such luck. Tessa and Cody are pulling a team together to organize the evacuation through this elevator. She wants to come down with us to the lower level. She says that Deanna's memories identify the second garage as the headquarters to the blood farm."

Serus bounded forward. "What?"

"Yes. They should be here any moment."

"They'd better be here now or we'll leave them behind," Goran said.

"Whoa. No, you're not," Tessa cried, running down the hallway toward them.

"Tessa!" Serus opened his arms to close around her as she jumped toward him. After a quick peck on her cheek, he grinned at Goran and said, "Now we're ready to go."

"Sir." Cody stood at Goran's side. "I think we've got a few minutes to get down, but if we don't go now, then we are going to be inundated with vamps trying to leave."

"Now then," Goran growled, stepping into the elevator. "Are you coming or am I going alone?"

It was Tessa's laughter that bounced around the elevator as she stepped up beside Goran. "I missed you too," she said with a big grin on her face.

In a very uncharacteristic sign of affection, she reached up and kissed Goran on the cheek.

And damn, Serus watched in amusement as color washed up his best friend's cheek. It was a good thing she'd done. Goran would never admit it, but he was as hooked on her as everyone else was.

He snickered.

Goran pressed the close door button with more force than necessary. And ignored Serus. But as Serus glanced over, he caught Goran glancing back at Tessa, an affectionate look in his eye.

Damn, his girl was good. She'd tamed the worst of the growly bears.

WENDY WOKE UP and stretched. Her body groaned as she straightened her back. Too many hours on the computer. She sat up and looked around. Ian slept soundly, his back to her. She wouldn't mind a few more hours herself. Snuggling back down, she closed her eyes…and they popped open instantly. There was something wrong. Something she needed to do. Or check on.

She frowned, letting her mind roll over the actions she'd taken before her nap. Sian had set up the computers to do something while they'd slept.

And they'd left Rhia alone with the computers.

As she lay there, unease snaked around inside. She couldn't do it. She couldn't go back to sleep. She had to go and check on Rhia and the computer search. See if there'd been any results yet.

And most of all, to see if Rhia was doing okay.

She slipped out of the room, careful to not disturb Ian. He needed his rest. So did Sian. Wendy walked down to the computer room. The hallway appeared deserted, her footsteps giving off an odd clipped echo as she walked toward the computer room. She stopped at the doorway, but there was no sign of either Sian or Rhia. Wendy could hope that Rhia had followed their lead and lay down to get some rest as well.

She walked into the empty room to find the computers asleep. She brought the main two up so she could check out the searches Sian had set up before she left.

The machine blinked the results. Interesting. Wendy sat down and quickly became immersed in the names of those reported missing or dead and those with no report, then cross-referenced them to those numbers assigned to the victims found hanging. There were over a thousand victims and less than three hundred reports of missing people. Another fifty were reported deceased. She had to wonder if bodies had been found to match the reports. Or were they fake reports to cover kidnappings for the blood farm?

Goosebumps rose on her arms. How could people do this to each other? She understood it was her people who'd set this up and were the ones buying, accepting the victims, probably actively soliciting more victims – but what made the humans buy and sell their own people? Sell off a parent, a brother, a daughter? How could they? This wasn't about sibling rivalry or distant relations; this was about hate. You'd have to hate someone to sign them up for this. Or want what they had and be in a position to take it. She pondered the quirks of human nature as she saved the information.

They had survivors from the blood farm in the hospital but as most hadn't come out with numbers attached, they hadn't all been identified. Some had. But no names had been released until the police figured out how the people had ended up in the farm in the first place. If the people didn't regain consciousness, then that would be a long process as well. Several had died already.

She sighed and leaned back to stare out the window. It was getting dark. The day was almost starting.

The door opened beside her, letting in a sleepy Sian. "Hey, did you have a good rest?"

"I did. Not long enough, but that seems to be par for the course these days." She covered a yawn as she looked around. "Where's Rhia?" she asked abruptly, a frown creasing her beautiful face.

"No idea. I haven't seen her yet."

Sian walked to the computers, saw the search results on the screen, and smiled. "Glad to see we got something to work with here."

"We did. Hopefully enough so the humans can identify the survivors."

"And figure out who was responsible for them getting strung up there in the first place."

She plunked down on the second computer and stared at the normal desktop screen. She frowned and slowly went to the history on the computer, her spare hand gently massaging her baby bump.

Wendy watched her closely, hating to see Sian's frown deepen. "What's the matter?"

"Maybe nothing." She shrugged. "But I feel like I need to check what Rhia did while she was here alone. I can't quite forget the heavy drugs she's been given."

"Are you thinking they are still affecting her? As in she might do something to sabotage us?" As much as she tried not to, her voice rose at the end.

Sian shook her head slowly. "I hope not. Normally I'd trust her with my life. But she's not herself and not necessarily thinking straight."

"True." Curious, Wendy rolled her chair closer and watched as Sian checked out what Rhia had being doing.

She caught sight of the pages at the same time Sian did. She leaned closer, trying to understand what it meant.

"Oh no," Sian cried. "Why is she looking for the drug storehouse?"

Sian pushed her chair back and raced to the door, leaving Wendy staring behind her.

ے ک

JARED STOOD OUTSIDE the school, tired and confused. He hadn't heard from Taz all day and the several texts he'd sent hadn't been answered.

Where did he go from here? It was late by the time he'd gone to each of his teachers and caught up on what assignments were missing. He was heading into midterms soon too. Midterms on what? He'd barely had a chance to look the work over as he'd missed so much.

He rubbed his temple. This wasn't the way today was supposed to go. He thought to have answers and a place to stay. He'd planned to ask Taz if he could stay with him, but while talking to the good doctor, it had seemed like a huge imposition. And he'd held back. He also hadn't seen Clarissa all day. That worried him too.

But not as much as her not answering his texts. His phone *was* working. He'd checked several times, however, something in his life was definitely not working.

And he didn't know what to do. Forlornly, he walked down the hallway to the front entrance. It was almost five. The group home and dinner was damn appealing, and yet he knew there was no way he could go back. He walked out the door into the late afternoon sun. It was gloomy and gray outside.

With few options left, he walked in the direction of his aunt's house, half wondering about moving in there. He'd considered it several times but hadn't really come up with a decision. It was empty. It belonged to his father. So maybe to him then in a few months. If he was lucky. But she'd hung around with some unsavory guys, and who could forget that she'd been murdered?

Would he be safe there?

In a way, his uncle's house would be better as he was known around there, having lived there most of his life. The neighbors wouldn't be surprised to see him. It was also a more unsavory neighborhood then over at his aunt's place. Chances were good that no neighbors would call in his presence for any reason. More likely they'd keep to themselves and hope no one turned *them* in. But he had to remember that his uncle had been murdered as well.

His aunt's house was closer.

Maybe she had food. He could hole up there for a day or two. There was money available. He could salvage what he might need.

At least until he'd had a chance to come up with a plan.

The house was only a couple of blocks away. He crossed the distance in less than ten minutes and, acting as if he belonged there, he walked around to the back door and let himself in.

It appeared the same.

He walked over to where he'd stashed her purse and found it in the same place. A quick search found the money still in the wallet. "Well, thank heavens for that." Helping himself to fifty bucks and adding it the bit he still had, he hid the rest away again. He could order a pizza now. Or save it in case of emergencies and find something else to eat.

Making sure he was alone first, he did a quick search of the property and smiled happily. Not only was he alone, but it looked undisturbed since he'd been there last. He walked into the spare bedroom and dumped his bag. He could sleep here. He could make this work. He checked out the bathroom, turning on taps to make sure there was running water. There was – and even better – it was hot.

Feeling relieved, he headed back down to the kitchen to rummage for food. The fridge was half full, but considering how long his aunt had been gone, he couldn't be sure anything was still good to eat. He grabbed a garbage bag from the drawer and started tossing anything that looked dubious. By the time he was done, there wasn't much left. A couple of apples, a tomato, and several bottles of sauces.

He turned to the freezer and was delighted to see it fully stocked. It had everything from pork chops, veggies, fruit, and ice cream. A real feast. He couldn't resist. With a big grin, he grabbed the carton of chocolate ice cream and a spoon. Between spoonfuls, he continued to check out the food. There were cans too. He could make something for dinner for himself. It might not be as good as what he'd get from the home but as long as he didn't burn it, it should be fine. He'd done some cooking at his uncle's house, enough that he could look after himself.

He laughed, the sound odd and comforting in the kitchen. "I never thought I'd be grateful to that old bastard for anything."

But he was.

An hour later, he was feeling pretty decent. He'd eaten, had a hot shower, had his clothes going through the laundry, and had cash in his pocket. Damn, it was the best life had been in a long time. He grabbed his phone and checked for messages.

Clarissa.

His face splitting into a big grin, he clicked on it. Instantly his smile was wiped off. The message was only two words. *Help me.*

CHAPTER 5

A S THE ELEVATOR door closed in front of her, Tessa caught sight of the two men in the beds. She frowned, surprised that she'd missed them. She tried to peer through the space before it closed, but she was at the wrong angle to see them clearly.

"What's wrong with them?" she asked. She hadn't been able to see how badly hurt they were, but it wasn't like the ancients to leave injured men alone – especially not given the number of times she'd been called in to help lately.

"Nothing," Serus said. "They are only pretending to be ill. They are going to watch for anyone coming up this elevator."

"Except no one will go up if we have it full of people coming down all the time."

"True," Goran conceded. "But if we have someone watching what's going on, then they might see a stranger arrive that we might have otherwise missed. It's definitely a problem right now. We don't want to have anyone infiltrate our organization through a doorway we didn't know about."

"Too late," Tessa said dryly. She didn't think those two men would make a bit of difference.

"We can hope not." Serus stepped in front of her. "How are you?"

Tessa smiled. "I'm okay. A little more tired than I'd like and still not sure of how to handle all this, but I'm working on it."

"Good. Keep working."

She nodded, her mind caught on his earlier words. She frowned and said, "Sorry, did you say those two men *aren't* sick?"

"No. We just wanted a couple of men to stand guard in case anyone from the other side used this elevator. Seemed like a good idea for them to appear sick. That's all."

"Why, Tessa?" Cody asked quietly.

She turned to look at Cody when David groaned. "They looked sick to you, didn't they?"

"Sorry, yeah, their systems had both gray and black," she said.

"What?" roared Serus. "We just grabbed the first two men we saw."

He glared at Goran as if this was entirely his fault.

Goran groaned. "What if they'd just arrived and that's why they were the closest?"

Tessa snickered. Her father spun and glared at her. "If you knew, why didn't you say so?"

"I only caught sight of them as I entered the elevator. I didn't know for sure," she replied. "And I don't honestly know how black. I'm finding out that black is different now."

"Harrumph." He turned and glared at Goran again. Goran grinned back at him. "Too bad she took so long to join us. She could have told us what we were doing wrong."

Stiff, Serus turned his back on all of them.

Holding back a giggle at the ancients' antics, Tessa watched the elevator lights flash as the machine descended to the lowest floor.

Cody slid an arm around her waist, tugging her backwards against his chest. She loved these moments. They didn't happen often or last long enough. They were stolen bits of time. Special time. She grabbed his hand and laced her fingers with his. She squeezed gently, loving the instant response.

Too soon the double doors opened. Goran and Serus immediately slid out of the elevator, each taking a different side and crouching low, ready for anything.

Tessa assessed the weird energy, with nothing feeling right anymore since Deanna, and strode out. Ten feet ahead, she stopped and studied the vast empty area. It had a familiar look to it – but was that familiar to Deanna or to Tessa? She opened her vision wider when the colors slammed into her head; she cut that back by half. The place had a gray cast to it. Lots of energy having come and gone in years past, but much less recently. But there'd been some activity on the right.

She pointed in the direction of the energy trails. "The energy disappears in that direction." She did a slow circle to make sure she didn't miss anything. Satisfied, she walked toward the energy trails. "A dozen or so slightly older energies, likely the ones Goran met up with and a half dozen that are fresher. Like an advanced party arriving."

"Well, the new arrivals…they won't be given a chance to warn the others, that's for sure," Goran snapped, pulling out his phone. "And these two men at the top need to be sequestered until we know for sure which side they are on."

Tessa, realizing he'd be calling Motre up above, turned to make sure all the new energies had actually gone into the elevator and not come out as the older ones had. It took her a moment to sort the colors before she realized. "Six arrived as a single group. One came here and went back the same way. Five went up the elevator."

"Shit."

David shook his head and kept moving forward. "Let's

make sure no more are coming. The others upstairs can deal with the trojans in their midst."

"Can they, though?" Cody wondered out loud. "Or is it going to take Tessa to see who is good and bad again?"

"If so, then she needs to go back up and find the traitors," Serus snapped. "We will follow this direction and find out where they came from."

Tessa hated to be sent back but if she didn't go, could the others find the right men? If they didn't, how much damage could the men do on their own? Her footsteps slowed. And those two 'guards' needed to be checked over. But given the potential drug issue through the vents, it was dangerous. Too dangerous. Especially for those she loved.

"Damn it."

Cody stopped a step ahead of her and turned, his gaze piercing. "What's the matter?"

"We need to get those men out of there. What if there are other elevators here like this one? Or hidden staircases or something," she cried out in frustration. "Our people won't know until it's too late."

"Are you wanting to go back upstairs?" he asked.

"I don't want to leave my family alone to face whatever is around the corner," she said.

Serus tossed back, "We'll be fine. Go find those sneaky bastards."

Crap. She could see the energy trails in the distance but had no idea what lay off in the shadows beyond.

As if sensing her uncertainty, Goran stopped and faced her and said, "We've been fighting wars like this for a long time. Don't worry. Go get the others separated so they can't do more damage to the place."

"I'm more concerned about the gas," she admitted, "than

the actual vampires."

Everyone stopped.

Her father turned his hard gaze on her. "Gas? What are you talking about?"

"I told you about that when I first saw you at the top of the elevator. Some of the men that were clear now have drugs in their system." She frowned at the confusion on both Goran and Serus's face. "Remember I was afraid that they'd be using the ventilation system to spread gas throughout and poison all of us." When anger started to light their gazes, she cried out, "I told you about it – that's why the mass exodus."

Goran shook his head. "You told us about everyone leaving via the elevator but not why."

Sure she had, hadn't she? Confused, Tessa tried to remember what she'd said to whom and realized she couldn't. She closed her eyes and groaned. "I swear I did."

"It's too late to worry. Give it to us now," her father demanded.

Quickly she explained about the two men and the black trail leading to the window and the vamps hiding outside who'd then been burnt in the sun.

The anger in the men's faces turned darker. "Little buggers. A gas like that is likely to affect everyone."

"Exactly. That's why I thought everyone should leave."

"You do realize that as we've all come down here, we won't know if the gas has been administered already or not. We could go back up there to find out we lost the war already and didn't even know it," David spoke up impatiently.

"Therefore Tessa needs to get back upstairs so she can let us know what the energies look like and find the assholes that snuck in on us." Serus said. "We'll go track down the base these guys are using and hopefully find out their plans for this gas. The heating system should be housed in the mechanical room, likely on this floor. We can scope it out and make sure no one is there."

"We'll go there first," Cody nodded. "Make sure our people are safe from attack."

"That no one is coming down yet also concerns me." She turned and glanced back at the elevators. "The first group should be here by now. I'm going to go up and send a group down to help you." She looked back to see Goran with his phone out again. "I suggest we get word out to Sian and Councilman Adamson. If the attack happens and many of our people are drugged, they could be taken in no time. With spikes, our friends and family could be gone in seconds – permanently."

And she needed to go alone. It was too dangerous for them. Plus this way, she could communicate through mind-speak and Cody could keep the rest of the group apprised of what was going on. Keep them all safe.

She picked up the pace and ran to the elevator. The double doors stood open.

Inside, she pushed the button to close the door. Cody raced toward her.

"Wait for me, damn it," he roared.

"I can't. The drugs aren't likely to work on me, but they will on you." She smiled sadly at him as the doors snapped shut in his face. "I have to keep you safe." She screamed back into the empty room, "Help the ancients."

She didn't know if he heard her, but she didn't dare have him become a victim too. All her friends and family at the hospital were down on this level. If they stayed there, they'd likely be safe.

At least as safe as anyone could be now.

ॐ ॐ

CODY KICKED THE elevator doors, then kicked them again. "Goddamit, Tessa."

"Easy, Cody. Wait until the elevator stops, then go up," Goran called. "You know she's just trying to keep you safe."

Cody turned to glare at his father, anger speeding through him. "I don't want to be kept safe. I'm trying to keep *her* safe."

"Ha, good luck with that one. She's a spitfire, that girl."

Cody watched as the ancients strode ahead almost out of sight, David trailing behind them. Did he go with them and help keep Tessa's family safe like she wanted him to or go back up and try to look for that little witch? How effective was that going to be if she tried ditching him at every turn?

And why the hell had she done that this time?

The drugs. I don't want you to get drugged.

He spun to stare at the elevator as her voice sounded through his mind.

Damn it, Tessa. You aren't immune to the drugs any more than I am.

No, maybe not, but with any luck I'll see them coming. In your case, I won't be able to warn you in time.

Hell, you won't be able to do anything yourself in time either. You have to stay alive, Tessa. Stop thinking you are indestructible just because you've got Deanna's energy.

No, I don't think that. If anything, her memories, her information, all that wisdom are a burden that makes me realize I need to stay alive so I can pass it on to others.

So use it to figure out how to stop this war instead.

I have to help the others upstairs. I'll keep you updated.

And how are you going to do that? he demanded.

I don't know yet. She added, *You'll have to shut down the heating system.*

No, let David do that. He's good with that type of thing. You go find the traitors. Leave that system to us.

She smiled in his head. *Okay.*

But her acceptance was a little too fast. A little too easy. Then he realized what he said. *Damn it. You did that on purpose.*

She laughed. *We all have a job to do in this war.*

And my place is at your side. You're the one who refuses to understand that, he snarled, pissed at her for the manipulation. *This isn't something Tessa pre-Deanna would have done. She'd have explained her reasoning, understood that I had a right to the truth and could deal with being sent off in one direction or another without games. Don't start the games, Tessa,* he warned. *You aren't going to like the outcome.*

At the instant silence in his mind, he wondered if he'd gone too far. Shit. He closed his eyes. This woman was going to be the death of him.

That's exactly what I'm trying to avoid.

He heard her take a deep breath before she said in a small voice, *And I'm sorry. I'm not sure who I am anymore.*

You're Tessa. Just stay true to her and keep that damn Deanna bitch locked away.

Is that what I am doing wrong? Is she changing me?

I don't know if she had something to do with it or not but there's no doubt you're changing.

In a bad way? she asked, her voice shaking, making him feel horrible instantly.

No. He sighed. *Not in a bad way. Just don't play games,* he pleaded. *Please don't ever play mind games.*

Okay, I promise.

And that was the best he could hope for. If she did get into that mode, he'd know it was Deanna's influence and he'd have to haul her back. He couldn't imagine her struggles right now, but it was important to stop her from becoming Deanna #2.

He couldn't imagine anything worse.

DAVID HURRIED BEHIND his father. Both ancients had already moved well ahead of him. He didn't know what Cody was planning on doing, but he wanted to go and shut down the heating system. That made the most sense to him. But the ancients didn't work off logic as much as instinct and they were looking for a fight. It would be hard to steer them in any other direction. They'd been duped and wanted to get their own back.

He could understand that, but he wanted this damn war over. He hadn't heard from Jewel yet, and that worried him, too. She'd been in the doctor's care at the Council Hall but after so much espionage and so many traitors in their midst, how did he know who to trust? Jewel had been through enough already. She needed rest and to know she was safe. That couldn't happen yet.

But neither had he thought to roust out a phone for her to use. She'd lost hers earlier. He chastised himself for not considering it. Hopefully she was still sleeping. Although if he could grab a moment, he would ask Sian or Wendy to see if they could get one to her.

"What the hell is taking you so long, son?"

David shook his head. His father was maybe ten feet ahead of him. Hardly far enough to worry. "We need to get to the heating system first. Especially if you're looking for a fight."

The two men came to a dead stop and spun around to look at him. "Why is that?"

"If they are planning to do something like Tessa suggested, then they have to guard the delivery system."

"Humph. Maybe." Serus stared at the door ahead. "Let's find out what's on the other side of the door then go to the mechanical room."

David groaned. Herding ancients was like herding cats – each had a mind of its own and knew exactly what to do – and it never matched up with the others.

ॐ ॐ

WENDY WAS OUT the door and running down the hallway seconds behind Sian. She'd seen what was on Sian's monitor briefly, but not enough to comprehend the significance. Even now, her mind was trying to sort through the information. Something about the database of drugs and the location of a small stockpile of drugs. Surely Rhia would know most of the drugs anyway. Besides, as she'd been injected herself, it was common sense to research the drugs she'd been given. Wendy would. How else would you know what to expect if she'd been drugged?

Being younger and not pregnant should have made it easy to catch up with Sian, but instead the woman was running down the hallway at a rate that was making Wendy panic.

Just as she geared up for another burst of energy to catch up, Sian turned left. Wendy couldn't hit the brakes fast enough; she bolted past before managing to stop and retrace her steps and go down the correct hallway. Sian was nowhere to be found. Wendy approached the doors – three of them – carefully. She didn't know anything about the Council Hall or who and what could be behind these doors. Did she just open them and ask for Sian if she couldn't find her?

The first door was locked. Wendy moved to the second one and tried that knob. It turned and the door opened easily. She stepped inside to find a lab room full of refrigerated coolers.

She frowned, staring at all the glass walls containing small vials of liquids. Her gaze carried along the wall and found Sian standing in front of one, her fingers punching numbers on some kind of mini computerized lock system guarding the door.

Wendy walked over cautiously, not sure she wanted to know what was going on, but she knew it concerned Rhia somehow.

"Sian?" she asked carefully, "What's the matter?"

Sian dropped her forehead to the glass door and closed her eyes. "Someone has been inside the drug vault. We keep samples of each of the drugs we've found and work to make an antidote."

"Someone?" Wendy still wasn't sure what this meant. "As in Rhia?"

She nodded. "I'm afraid so."

"But why?" Wendy didn't get it. Rhia had been through so much. She wouldn't want more drugs – why would she? She laid a hand on Sian's shoulder, her gaze locked on the mini screen that said the lock had been released; the door had been opened approximately two hours earlier. That matched the time frame that they'd left Rhia alone. "What reason could she possibly have for taking out some of the same drugs that had been used on her?"

The term junkie come to mind and Wendy knew that was always a possibility, but given Rhia's strong constitution, it wasn't likely. Still, she'd been injected many times. Another dose might kill her.

Surely she knew that.

"I don't know. But it appears to be what she's done."

"Do you think she injected herself with it?"

Sian glanced at Wendy, then turned to look around the room. She pointed wordlessly at the empty syringe package lying on the counter. "Under normal circumstances, that would never be left lying around. I think it's from her."

Uh no. Wendy walked over to study the package. Unless...

"Could someone have forced her down here to let them in to grab drugs they wanted?" Wendy motioned around the cool room full of stainless steel and glass. "There are drugs of all kinds here – why would that one be of any value?" Wendy struggled to make sense of this.

"She might have been weak, but Rhia is a formidable fighter even at the worst of times. Someone looking to take her out would not find it easy to do so. If they'd wanted these drugs and she wouldn't comply, then they'd have to have major leverage to face her."

Wendy groaned, "You mean like holding one of her kids hostage, for example." What a horrible thought, but given the mess of nastiness she'd already seen, that didn't seem too far out of line.

Sian's gaze flew up to lock on Wendy's as she added, "Or to help one of her kids."

Sian turned her attention back to the missing vial and said, "What if she couldn't remember anything important – like where she'd sent Seth? You know how much that bothered her. She'd do anything she could to retrieve that information."

"Find it how? She couldn't remember anything she'd done."

"Exactly. And she needs to. So what better way than to give herself a little bit of the same drug and hope that she could straddle both worlds to find out what she'd done with Seth, yet not have so much of the drugs in her system that she lost herself again?"

"She knows how dangerous that world is. One of these times she's not going to wake up." Wendy shook her head. "Besides, she'd never risk losing Tessa, David, or Serus. She just wouldn't."

Sian looked at Wendy, the sadness in her expression bringing a stinging to Wendy's eyes. She shivered and, not able to help herself, she reached out to stroke the other woman's shoulder.

"That's true," Sian said, her voice heavy, "But she's a mother and she feels guilty. She won't abandon her child. Especially not when she's responsible for his current plight. And as I'm learning, we'd do anything to save our child – even sacrifice ourselves."

~ ❧

IAN WOKE UP, rolled over, and fell back asleep. When he woke up the second time, there was still a heaviness to his mind, making it hard to be aware enough to stay awake. He didn't have an explanation for why he was so tired, but he was. Just rolling over made him groan. Hell, the ancients would laugh like crazy if they could see him now.

How the hell could they keep going when all he wanted to

do was lie down and die? Keeping up with those two was killer. Motre was no better. He hoped he aged as well as the others did because it seemed like youth wasn't a gift. He was weaker, tired more easily, and didn't have their endurance.

Oh well. He sat up, biting back a groan as his muscles engaged. Why the hell was he so sore? Sure, he'd been in a fight or two, been knocked around a few times – okay, more than a few times.

The room was empty. He glanced around, searching for signs of where Wendy had gone. He knew she'd been working with Sian to help identify the survivors and had also been involved in trying to track down the ambulance carrying away Jared's friend. Likely Taz was involved then.

With Taz working at the human hospital and both councils involved, everything was getting mixed up. He'd heard something about the humans wanting Tessa to go and identify the bad guys in their ranks like she'd done once before, but Ian didn't think she'd be the right person for the job. In many ways she was a complete pushover. A smart one, but still a big softie.

And then there was Wendy. He really respected the woman she was becoming. This blood farm mess had truly brought out the best – and the worst – in many of his friends. He thought back to Jacob who'd died weeks ago. Who knew he'd be someone to hate his people and the humans so much as to want to destroy all of them?

Ian certainly hadn't.

He yawned and thought about lying back down when the door burst open.

Wendy flew in. "We need help. We can't find Rhia."

JARED SNUCK OUT of the house and raced down the street toward Clarissa's home. He knew vaguely where it was but didn't know the exact address, and he couldn't confirm that's where she was. Her message hadn't exactly been full of details. He'd texted her back but hadn't heard anything. Still, it was a place to start.

The police weren't an option either. Not with his history. Now if Clarissa called them, they'd likely help. Still, her call for help hadn't given him any way of locating her or knowing what the problem was.

His cell phone buzzed again. He pulled it out and checked the message. Clarissa. *I'm caught.*

Jesus.

He quickly answered, *Caught how, by whom, and where are you? I'm on the way to your house.*

No. Don't go there. That's where I was. I woke up in a van.

Shit.

Are you okay? Have they hurt you?

I'm fine, but I'm really scared. What if they heard I was asking about Tobias? Jared. Help me.

He answered. *I am. Stay calm. Can you see where they are taking you?*

No answer.

He waited a little longer then sent another one. *Clarissa, any idea where you are or what direction you are travelling?*

Then he got a reply back that made him want to scream.

Sorry, Clarissa is no longer able to answer you. But hi Jared. We miss you. Just know we'll be coming for you soon.

Chapter 6

TESSA RODE THE elevator up the floors, her mind churning in confusion. The conversation going on in her head made no sense.

Leave him behind. Stay strong. Be you. Be the new you.

No, I am *Tessa. That wasn't fair what he said, but it's true. I'm not letting Deanna influence me.*

No, it wasn't. And you aren't.

Yes, it was. And I am

She shuddered.

"What the hell is wrong with me?" she whispered to the empty interior. Was anything wrong? No, of course not. Everything was fine. Everything was always fine.

She frowned. No, everything wasn't always fine. Things hadn't been fine for a long time. They'd only been fine on a few levels recently. And she didn't want to do anything to screw that up. She didn't have the security of years of confidence to draw upon. Life had gotten tough and she'd fought her way through it, so why did she think she was sliding backwards – or maybe losing some of that hard-won self-confidence?

You're not, said her subconscious.

She sighed as relief swept through her. No, she wasn't. She was good.

Of course you are.

She froze. That last line was a bit too much for her to swallow. She'd always had self-confidence issues. She'd never been cocky or arrogant like some women she'd known. So where was this coming from now? It so wasn't her.

If she didn't know better, she'd think she sounded more like Deanna every moment. Cody's words trickled through her as the elevator door opened in front of her, but she didn't move.

Had Deanna's energy integrated into her psyche to the point that she was becoming *like* Deanna?

Had that been what Deanna wanted? And did it matter what Deanna wanted? Hell no. That woman had a thousand-plus years to do what she wanted to do. She wasn't going to be yanking Tessa's chain from the grave.

Except…she already had.

Tessa closed her eyes and groaned. *This is not what I signed up for. I want to be me. Not Deanna and not a cross between her and I. Hortran, can you hear me?*

There was a ghostly whisper, like a breeze blowing through her mind.

Tessa would take that as a yes. *Is this what Deanna wants – to take over my mind and make me more like her?*

There was a quietness in her thoughts, her spinning myriad of questions stilling, becoming a pool of peacefulness in her mind.

Remember to use this information. Her wisdom, her knowledge is yours to use as you deem appropriate. But it is you who are making these decisions.

Me?

Yes, you. She is gone. Her time has passed. You can feel her, sense her, be like her if you wish, but it is you doing so then, not her. Her will is no longer here. The force of her will, being as strong as it was, lingers.

There was a long pause.

You are you. Do you stay that way or do you morph into something else? Your choice. Your will. Your life.

And then a shorter pause.

You have only one to live.

And with that prophetic message, the essence of Hortran slipped away.

So what the hell had she done then? Allowed Deanna's knowledge to affect Tessa into thinking it was her own knowledge? That Tessa had been the one to learn all Deanna had learned as if it were her own information, knowledge, and experiences?

She smirked. As if. If she'd learned it all in her short years, then she likely *would* be cocky and arrogant – but she hadn't. This wasn't her experience and it wasn't her achievement.

She sighed and rubbed her head.

Hortran, I need a way to stop me from unconsciously absorbing Deanna's attitudes, her thoughts, her emotions.

There was an underlying rumble through the space in her mind. She frowned, trying to understand.

I mean it. I don't want to become Deanna. I don't want to take on any aspects of her personality. I am happy to carry her information, her knowledge and wisdom. I will honor her for who she was. But I don't want to become a Deanna clone. And I appear to be doing just that. So please, help me. Zap me, poke me, and scream at me – something to stop me when I start.

And damn if a light laugh didn't ripple through her mind. Surely that wasn't Hortran – was it?

Cody?

Deanna?

No response. Shit. Confused and pissed, she took a step

toward the still open elevator doors.

The tiny room was empty. She took a cautious step forward into the outer room. It was empty too. Why? They should be lining up the vamps to go downstairs. Of course she hadn't been gone but a few minutes, so maybe they hadn't had time?

Then where were the two guards Goran and Serus had left?

❧ ❧

CODY TRIED TO contact Tessa mentally. There was a pathway but it was cloudy, as if there was static instead of a clear audio path. Like the speakers weren't plugged in. He hated it. *Tessa, can you hear me?*

A garbled response slid his way, but it wasn't distinctly her voice. That really worried him. Deanna better keep her distance. He wasn't sure if he was crazy or what but considering how powerful that woman had been in life, he wouldn't put it past her to have a long-reaching influence in death.

And what about Hortran? He remembered Tessa speaking about Hortran and some kind of telepathic highway. And he was a Ghost. Whatever that meant while he was alive didn't mean the name didn't take on a different meaning after death.

He had seen things these last few weeks that he wouldn't have believed before. To have that same belief system pushed back yet again also wasn't a hard thing to imagine. He could see Tessa learning to do more and more.

Were her capabilities actually due to her Leant heritage? Was that why Deanna had managed to do what she'd done because they were both Leant? He wished he understood more. It would make it easier to watch out for her.

At the moment, he wanted to turn her over his knee and beat some sense into her.

Hell, she'd likely send him flying for even thinking of doing something like that. He almost wished she would. It would make him feel better to know the same girl was in there.

"Cody, are you coming with us or going after her?" David called from across the huge garage.

"I'm going after her." That's when he realized he'd crossed the room to the halfway mark and had stopped. For a reason. It was wrong to let her go alone.

"I'll see you later," he called out. "Check out those damn ventilation systems."

"Good enough." David raced behind their fathers. Cody stood in the room and watched as the three of them jockeyed for position to get through the door first.

And then he was alone.

Shaking his head, he returned to the elevator and pushed the button – several times.

Damn woman.

She'd better be there when he arrived.

And she'd better be ready to listen.

Because he was tired of her trying to save him.

It was time for him to save *her*.

❧ ❧

SERUS PULLED THE door open and charged through. Goran almost slid past him to take the lead. Not a chance. He shoved an arm in front of his friend and snuck ahead. Hearing the growl in his wake, he burst out laughing.

There was nothing on the other side of the door.

Damn right. They probably saw them coming.

He grinned, feeling more alive than he had in a long time. His family was safe, even Tessa after all she'd been through. Even his beloved wife Rhia was doing so much better – in many ways. Then he remembered their last conversation.

At that thought, he called out to her. *Rhia? How are you?*

Silence was his answer.

Good, maybe she was sleeping.

Then he heard her voice. And her words… oh no…

Serus, I know you won't understand why I'm doing this, but please know I'm doing it to save our son.

And the voice cut off.

He froze in place. *Rhia – what have you done?*

Remember, I love you, Serus. But I can't live with my actions – I have to save him.

And his mind went blank.

She was gone.

❧ ❦

RHIA CURLED UP on the floor in the deserted Council room. She should be safe here.

Do it.

No. I don't want to.

Too bad. You started down this path.

I need to save my son.

And what about your other son? Your daughter? Your best friend and husband? Do you betray those three to save one?

No. I'm not betraying them. I need just enough of the drug to remember.

How much is enough? Face it, you're addicted. You need another shot. It's already working. Look at you. On the run from everyone who cares about you.

No. I'm not on the run. I'm going to go to the last address I saw that I could remember having made any sense. But not yet.

No. You're going to the source. You want more. Need more...

"No," she cried out to the insistent voice in her head. "I don't. I just want to know what I did with my son."

And how are you going to figure that out?

"By going back to the scene of the crime – where I sent him away. I can access those computers. They will have the information."

So then where is that?

"The hospital. I'm going back to the hospital."

You know they are trying to kill your family, but you're going to go to their stronghold why? Who are you deluding? The only thing you're going to do is give them the power to control you and hold that over your husband's head to get him to do what they want him to do.

"No, he'd never do that."

He would in a heartbeat, scoffed her conscience. *You know he'd do anything for you. Including sacrificing himself.*

"That's why I have to save his son. I have to do this – even if I sacrifice myself."

So be it then. But if you fail, Serus will be the one that takes the brunt of your behavior.

"He's strong. He will survive."

The reason he's so strong is he's had you at his side. What do you think he'll do when he finds out the others have you in their clutches again?

She shuddered at the thought. Serus would go crazy, and he'd destroy them all if anything happened to her. "I'll have to be smarter than them. I have to win. The stakes are too high to fail."

But are you strong enough to withstand the drugs coursing through your veins?

"I have to be. There's no other option."

JEWEL STOOD TALL and proud – at least on the inside. Outside she looked ridiculous, wrapped up in her own wings, but oh, the joy of having her wings follow her command once again was priceless.

"What are you doing?" a nurse stood at the bathroom doorway, shock and concern on her face. "Come back to bed. You shouldn't be up, and you definitely shouldn't be walking around. I sure hope you didn't have a shower as well," she clucked as she walked toward Jewel and before she knew what had happened, Jewel had been coerced gently but implacably toward the bed.

As she collapsed back down, Jewel realized how much the shower had zapped her strength. That and the shock of having someone walk in on her.

She still didn't understand where she was or if this woman was there to help her or hurt her, but Jewel had to accept the ministrations.

She was as weak as an infant.

There was no way she could escape.

At least not yet.

Damn it, Tessa. Why hadn't you shown the rest of us how to tell our vampire genes to kick in and power up when we need it?

Instantly, she felt a weird stirring inside. She straightened, her gaze widening in shock, then closed her eyes and lay down again. The last thing she wanted to do was let this woman or anyone know that she was going to heal a lot faster now.

But she knew, and that's all that mattered.

JARED RAN TO the hospital, cursing that he couldn't find the keys to his aunt's car. It still sat in the driveway, but he'd been unsuccessful in finding the keys. And he'd wasted precious time to go back and look after getting the last horrific messages. Damn. He turned the corner and peeled down the street, hating the panic coursing through his blood. He was a good sprinter, but now it was as if his feet had wings. He couldn't stop the thoughts of what the doctors might be doing to Clarissa right now. Hopefully they'd not taken her to the final destination. He remembered the time it took for the blood to be taken, sorted, and tested. He'd had at least one day in there where he was safe from their drugs. He couldn't remember any clearer than that.

It was dark out now, and he watched the skies as carefully as he watched the traffic. He didn't dare get caught by any vampires out hunting. So few people understood what he was going through. So few people he could trust. And he knew more vampires than humans in both categories at this point.

How sad was that?

He turned another corner, feeling the power and need driving him forward. It helped to have the blood pulse through his veins, reminding him why he was doing this. Why the vamps were doing this. They were higher up the food chain. They could do this, so they did. It was people like Tessa and her family who would be able to stop this massacre – with his help.

Hopefully before they got their damn needles into Clarissa. He didn't know her well, but he sure liked what he did know and he couldn't let any more humans be sacrificed to that damn farm.

He should have asked her if she had family – friends. Maybe a better question was if she had any enemies. Although chances were good that given the timing, her questions about Tobias had triggered some alarm and the assholes decided she'd become a troublemaker and needed to be taken out of the picture.

As he'd been labeled the same.

He didn't care if they did come after him. Let them. He was more than willing to have a chance at payback. Especially since he realized Tessa and her family would come after him again.

If she knew about this.

Which was a very good point.

Pursing his lips, he thought about who to tell and why. With his breath harsh and raspy, he realized he needed to tell Tessa – just to be sure. He hadn't heard from her in a long while, and that bothered him. But he also had no idea if she was even awake.

If he found Clarissa safe and sound, then no problem, but if something happened to him in the process…well, he'd like someone to know. Someone who'd do something about the travesty. That meant Tessa.

He could only hope she'd ditched the arrogant Cody, but he doubted such a thing would be easy.

Cody looked like he went where he wanted regardless of anyone else's wishes. Right now Jared figured Cody would be busy thrashing Jared for getting into trouble again. And blaming him for Clarissa's disappearance. Which maybe he was responsible for. He hated the thought, but it couldn't be avoided. If he hadn't told Clarissa what he'd seen that night, then she wouldn't have ended up at the hospital looking for Tobias.

And wouldn't have found Taz.

So how had someone found out about what they were doing? Had they been overheard at the hospital? Were the phone lines bugged? Or had someone seen her asking unwanted questions? Or had she asked the wrong person at school? He wouldn't put it past her to have told damn near every student and teacher there about Tobias. That widened the suspect pool to almost everyone as those she'd spoken to initially were likely to have spoken to one or two friends. Especially by now. Gossip travelled fast.

That's how misinformation and gossip turned the corner from being harmless to being a big problem.

He didn't need more problems, but he needed to find Tobias. He'd seen the condition he'd been in as he was hauled out of the group home. Not a pretty sight.

He reached the hospital and came to an abrupt halt. It wouldn't do to go in there in a panic. It was the emergency room. Likely they'd have him flat on a stretcher and undergoing an examination before he could tell them what he was doing there.

With his breath under control, he wiped his sweaty hands on his jeans and entered.

Ignoring the front desk, he headed to Taz's office. When he reached the last corner and went to duck around it, someone called out, "Can I help you?"

He turned and gave the green uniformed woman a headshake. "No, I'm fine, thanks. I'm just looking for Taz."

"He's not here," she said, glaring at him. "He's gone home for the night."

As if seeing a protest about to burst forth, she said in a waspish tone, "What did you expect? That he lived here? No, he's gone home for some well-deserved rest."

Meekly, he walked away, but inside he was trying to figure out how to get a hold of Taz. Then he realized he could text him. Stupid.

He sent a short message to both Taz and Sian and waited for a response. In the meantime, he sent Clarissa's message to Tessa in the hope that she might have some idea of how to hunt his friend down. He then added several more by way of explanation.

When he was done, there was still no response from Taz. He couldn't go home when he'd done nothing yet for Clarissa, so he sat on the closest bench and waited for the good doctor to get back to him.

It wasn't long and the message made him smile. It was the doctor's address and a terse message. *Come.*

He grinned, feeling reconnected. He responded with, *Okay, Taz, I'm on the way.*

"Let's hope you have some magic left in your world to pull out yet another trick to help Clarissa. Hell," he said aloud, "How about a way to stop this whole damn issue?"

With a look at the map, he turned in the direction of the doctor's house and started to run – again.

CHAPTER 7

TESSA WALKED FORWARD slowly into the empty room. Had the two vamps they'd left behind been taken out? Or had they gone to take other vamps out? Her gaze spun from side to side looking for anything out of the ordinary. If the assholes had actually managed to do a mass drugging, she could be in deep trouble. She had to avoid that at all costs. But how did one do that when she was in the same building? She sniffed the air experimentally, ready to bolt back to the elevator.

The air smelled normal. She frowned. Would she know the difference? Maybe not by odor, but she would by color. She shifted her gaze slightly to look at the air, searching for the black effect of the drugs, and found nothing unusual.

She opened the door to the hallway and snuck out. The long white hospital corridor stretched endlessly in front of her.

The look made her skin crawl. She'd seen a similar sight way too often in her life and would like to never see it again. That this was the hospital and not the blood farm made her pause – because they were just too much alike. Especially considering the number of bad guys she'd met at both places. The connection made her cringe.

Still, she had a lot of people in here that needed her help. She'd do that between the two locations regardless of the look to the place. Besides, it might keep her focused. Help her remember why she was here and what could happen again if she screwed up. Something she had no intention of doing.

Hopefully with Deanna's help, they could put a stop to this once and for all.

Except Deanna hadn't done anything about this blood farm before, and she wasn't exactly going to be of much help now. But she knew things. And some of those things Tessa needed to know. As she walked silently toward the room she'd left with Cody, she opened the pathway to Deanna's memories she'd filed away. *Need information on the hospital. Who built it, why and when?*

Ninety-two years ago by the Council currently in place, to hold vamps in the event humans caused a major catastrophe.

She came to a stuttering stop. *Really? Were they so bad to have you worried about such a possibility?*

Chemical warfare, bombs, nuclear energy, war and more war that continued to escalate. There wasn't so much an answer to her questions as the information streamed through her mind in a series of text. No emotion or judgment passing with it. Odd and yet fantastic at the same time. Nice to get some background on the place.

And speaking of background, how long have the blood farms been running?

In one form or another, for centuries. They come up as an animal husbandry option. The early ones went under due to mass die-offs. Infection and disease were big issues, but each new farm is technologically more advanced than the last one with the latest human weaknesses addressed.

Were you ever a part of them?

The answer was confusing. *Not really.*

Tessa stopped at one of the doorways and realized the first three rooms were completely empty. Interesting. So where the hell was everyone?

She kept walking.

What about your partner?

Yes, Mikko was a great believer in keeping the blood supply flowing. I wasn't of the same opinion.

Hmmm. Tessa wasn't sure how much she believed the answers. In terms of Deanna's memories, this information was coming across more like a tape recording, not necessarily the encyclopedic information Tessa had seen earlier. How did that work?

Shoving the problem to the back of her mind and the niggling suspicion that she couldn't trust everything that was coming up as truth, Tessa asked about the other blood farms. *Do you know where they are located?*

No.

Damn. Why couldn't Deanna know something useful? And didn't that contradict what she'd said to Tessa when they'd first met her? She'd intimated that she knew where the blood farms were back then. She tried again. *Do you know anything useful in this situation?*

Silence.

Feeling slightly off, Tessa gave up on the questioning and continued to walk down the hallway, then realized she should let Cody know that something was going on. He could keep the ancients apprised of what was happening.

Cody, the entire floor is deserted. The good news is that there are no piles of ash floating around. As good news went, that came in at the top.

A startled sound came though her mind. *Are you sure?*

Yes.

Maybe they are already moving down and out of the hospital. That fast? I doubt it.

There could be more exits.

Maybe, she said doubtfully. *There were a lot of men here. And the two guards our fathers left behind aren't here either.*

Now that's not good. Stay where you are, I'll meet you there.

No. You have to tell the others.

Uh...I can't.

Why not? she asked in exasperation. *They are right there with you.*

Silence. And she knew. She groaned. *You are on your way up, aren't you?*

Not quite, he said in a quietly humorous voice. A very close voice. She turned to see him enter the hallway behind her. She glared at him.

"Don't bother," he said mildly. "I don't take orders from you or that Deanna bitch. I'm here to keep an eye on you. If you don't like it, too bad."

She opened her mouth then realized she had nothing to say that would make him change his mind so she closed it, turned, and carried on down the hallway.

He raced behind her. Just as he was about to catch up to her, her arm was grabbed, she was spun around, and the world shifted as she was pulled into his arms.

And he kissed her.

Heat enveloped her. Him. The two of them were wrapped in caring energy. She sighed against his lips. This was Cody. Her Cody. And her world slipped back into position again.

Damn right, he said.

She smiled, but then she couldn't do anything as he deepened the kiss until all resistance was gone. He lifted his head, smiled down into her eyes, and held her close.

She lay against his chest, her whole body trembling with need.

Now that's more like it.

What is? she whispered, desperately trying to clear her head.

This is the response I know, he said, *and love...* And lowered his head again.

☙ ❧

CODY DIDN'T WANT to stop. The touch of her lips, the gentle tentative strokes of her tongue – it was ambrosia to a starving man. Lord, he wanted her. But he wanted to have time with her, all night, several nights. He'd take what he could get, but there was no way he'd take her in this scenario. He was just torturing himself doing this all the time. The more he kissed her, the more he wanted to kiss her. She was like a drug he couldn't get enough of. He broke away and tugged her hard against his body. She should be able to hear his heart pounding inside his chest. The need coursing through his loins. He shuddered, trying to think of something else, anything else before he lowered her to the floor right here.

Then she did something that completely disarmed him. She giggled.

He rested his chin on top of her head and smiled. "What is so funny?"

She twisted in his arms so she could look up at him. "The timing is always terrible. I wish we were anywhere else but here."

He closed his eyes, her words undoing all his hard-won control. He asked incredulously, "And that's funny?"

Her shoulders shook as a laugh broke free. Frustrated and confused but as always charmed by her natural freedom, he watched her laugh at his expense.

"It's not that it's funny, but…"

He glared at her, but there was no heat in his expression. "Meaning you're laughing at the state I'm in. Well, thanks a lot."

She gave him a lopsided grin. "I'm not much better if that helps."

Cody brightened. It did help. He'd hate to think he was alone with his frustration. She'd been with him every step of the way. Thank God.

She turned around to look down the long hallway. "Now that another ten minutes have gone by and no one is here, where do you think they are – and why?"

"No idea." He dropped his arms and walked in front of her. "I see the cameras are still functioning."

"Hmmm." She narrowed her gaze at the red blinking light where the wall met the ceiling ten feet ahead. "Maybe we should find the security room and look at the cameras. They should have recorded what happened to the others. Maybe it will also help to sort out who's on which side."

"The security room is in the basement," he said absently. Then stopped. "At least I think it is."

"Deanna's memories say they are too." Tessa gave a long hard look at the empty hallway. "Rather than going floor by floor, I suggest we go and take the security room. Those video feeds should be able to tell us all sorts of things."

Cody rolled his eyes. At least they were going in the right direction now. Maybe they could catch up with their fathers after all.

"We need to contact Motre, too."

They walked back to the elevator, both holding their cell phones in their hands and looking for messages from any of the missing people, when Tessa's phone beeped. Thinking it was from Motre or one of the family members, he read the text over her shoulder. A message from Jared.

Damn if he didn't want to kill the pipsqueak. Especially when Tessa's face went all soft and glowing. Like what the hell? How had Jared gotten into her psyche so easily? That was just wrong.

She laughed. "It's from Jared."

She scrolled through the long message, her footsteps slowing before finally halting altogether. "He's in trouble. Or rather, a friend of his is. Two of them," she said in slight confusion. "At least I think so. He's fine but... he's been threatened."

Horrified, she gasped and looked up at him in shock. "Why would anyone do that?" she cried. "Hasn't he been through enough already?"

Cody could think of a half dozen reasons why, but getting to Tessa via Jared was the first and primary reason. Cody liked Jared. He seemed to be a decent human being. But he didn't like his interest in Tessa.

She was his.

"Oh my. Someone kidnapped this boy from the home where he stayed, then he met this same girl he'd met on the way to the blood farm rescue. They joined forces to help the kid that had been taken away on the ambulance, only now she's been kidnapped too." She looked up at Cody, sadness in her eyes. "This is terrible, Cody."

Part of it was terrible. Still...another girl. Perfect. Jared was starting to be a nicer person already.

GORAN SPUN AROUND, saw the stricken look on Serus's face,

and raced toward him. "What's the matter?"

"It's Rhia. She's done something."

"Something? What something?"

Serus shook his head. "I don't know, but it has to do with Seth. She said she had to do this but didn't explain what. Something about she can't live with having done something that might hurt him."

Uh oh. "You can't sense what she's up to?" He worried about Serus. Rhia hadn't been herself in a long time. Not that it was her fault, but her actions were now suspect. What the hell could she be doing?

David raced over to them. "Okay, Cody has gone up to join Tessa."

"Like she'll let him," Goran scoffed.

"Maybe she will. Cody seemed pretty determined."

Goran nodded, his gaze switching back to Serus, who was still trying to pull himself together. Likely to avoid alarming David.

Too late.

"Dad," David said, leaning in, worry crinkling his face, "What's wrong?"

"Nothing." Serus's attempts at a smile failed. He tried to walk past them.

Goran winced as David's features set with determination.

David stepped in his father's path. "What's wrong?"

Serus glanced over at Goran. Inside he said, *What do I tell the boy?*

The truth. He's not a youngster anymore, and he's been through too much lately to hide the truth. Who knows, maybe he can help.

"Dad. Stop talking to Goran in mindspeak. Tell me what's going on," David urged, adding, "Please."

Running a tired hand over the back of his head, Serus said, "It's your mother. She basically said goodbye and that she was doing something she had to do. No other explanation except for that fact that it has something to do with your brother."

"When?" David's voice was all business. He had his phone out in his hand. Before Goran even understood who he'd called, he was speaking to someone.

"Hi, Wendy, it's David. Can you give me an update on my mother?"

Goran watched as David spun sideways to stare into his father's worried eyes.

Over the years, he'd watched Serus and his close-knit family with envy. For all his efforts, Goran hadn't managed to find one woman to stay with. Whether the fault was his or the timing or maybe he was never meant to be monogamous, he'd always been jealous of the relationship Serus had with his wife and kids. Goran had lost track of his oldest son Tyson, and look what had happened there. He'd had many partners over the centuries, but not so many that he'd lost track of them. He did well for fifty years, even seventy years or so, then they all seemed to hit the rocks. Typical.

Still, right now watching the pain of what Serus was going through...what he'd gone through...it was horrible.

He hated to see his buddy suffer like this.

He loved Rhia like a sister, but damn, what the hell was she up to?

He turned to David, seeing the little bit of color washing from his face as he listened to Wendy's tale.

This was not going to be good.

JARED CAME TO a shuddering stop outside the tall Victorian-looking house with black window coverings. He had to once again consider the complications of a human and vampire co-existing. Like how the hell did they work through the very basic issues of just the night and daytime shifts? Except with Taz being a doctor, chances were good he worked a lot of night shifts. That would be ideal. Jared pulled out his cell phone to check the address against the numbers showing on the front of the house by the mailbox. This was it.

He glanced around the affluent neighborhood, the large properties, seeing the major upscale houses versus the area where he'd been raised. Must be nice to have money. Then again, he'd seen firsthand how hard the doctor worked. Any money he had, he deserved. The same for Sian; she'd done a lot for the human/vampire communications and treaties.

Besides, he didn't understand how assets and money worked in the vamp world. It might be completely different from the human system.

Hesitantly, he approached the front door. There didn't appear to be any activity at the house or on the block. It was late, but not so late as to make him uncomfortable.

At the double front doors, he took a deep breath, trying to regain his composure, then knocked.

The sound echoed gently. He rapped a second time, searching for the doorbell. But there didn't appear to be one. His gaze landed on a long pull attached to a chain. He grinned and gave it a hard yank.

Bells tolled heavily in the dusky light.

"Whoa." He took several steps backward as the noise rolled and rolled and rolled.

He spun to look around him. Seeing nothing, he turned back to the front door and stumbled back with a startled cry.

Taz stood on the front steps. "Jared?"

"Sorry, Taz, I didn't mean for the bell to sound like that." And he felt like an idiot for making the neighborhood ring.

"No problem. That's a typical vampire doorbell. Helps to wake them when they're asleep."

"Yeah, I'd say so." Jared took a second deep breath, hating that he was still shaking, his voice thin. He held out his phone with Clarissa's texts. "I got this."

Taz's genial air disappeared. He shot Jared a hard look and grabbed the phone out of his hand. He read the series of texts, his features darkening. With a narrowed gaze, he looked at Jared. "Who have you contacted about this?"

"Only Tessa. I just came back from the hospital." Jared gave him a lopsided grin. "For some reason I figured you'd be there."

"I mostly am." Taz smiled. "Come in." He pushed the door open and backed inside, his attention once again on the cell phone. "What is going on here?"

"I don't know. But they know me. And they've got Clarissa."

Taz nodded. "And we can guess why they've got her and what they are likely to do with her, but where? That's the question. If we could find her, we'd also likely find yet another of their blood farms."

"I don't care about the other blood farms," Jared burst out. "I have to find Clarissa. She's in trouble because of me."

"How do you figure?" Taz stopped to look at him.

"I told her about Tobias."

The look on Taz's face was enough to make Jared wince. "She was looking for him. I didn't know who to tell. Then we came to you. Now look what happened. The only way they'd know who was looking for Tobias is if they'd overheard us at the hospital or maybe the school."

"You think there are humans at the hospital involved?" But there was no note of incredulity in his tone.

"You already suspect that, don't you?" Jared accused, his gaze narrowing. "You've seen something. Someone."

"Not anything specific. But there was always that possibility and since the survivors were brought into the hospital, my suspicions have been aroused."

"Why?" Jared didn't get it. "What do these people have to gain at this point?"

"I think there is one person, maybe more, making sure that specific individuals aren't identified. And if they are...that they don't survive long enough for any legal issues to arise."

"What? You're saying that those poor survivors haven't been through enough?" Jared said in shock. "Someone is hurting them now?"

"No, they are being murdered – again."

❧ ❧

IAN HURRIED DOWN the hallway, Sian and Wendy on his heels. He had no idea why he was heading to Rhia's room first; it was an instinctive move on his part. The others appeared to be willing to follow his lead.

At the door of the ancient's temporary room, he pushed the door open, expecting to see Rhia reclined on the couch like he'd imagined she'd be.

It was empty. He frowned. Walking forward, he searched for anything that would tell him where she'd gone.

From the doorway, Wendy said, "She's not here. We already checked."

"I didn't expect her to come back," Sian said, sadness filling her voice. "She might have left to join the others."

Ian cast a dark look at Sian. "She wouldn't join the others. She's only doing this for her son's sake."

"Oh, I do understand what she's doing and why," Sian said in a gentle voice. "Still, how can she find out if she isn't with them? If she doesn't have access to their information?"

Wendy gasped. "What if she had access to their computers?"

Ian spun to look at her, hating to see the fatigue showing on her face. She looked damn tired. "What are you thinking?"

"Gloria's laptop," she whispered, excitement threading her voice. "She'd know about Gloria's laptop."

Sian bolted. She was there one moment and gone the next. Wendy turned to follow.

"Wait," Ian said urgently. "Are there other laptops here? Other equipment from the blood farm that she might go to? Let's not all focus on the one place. Rhia is a smart lady – she knows about Gloria's laptop, wouldn't she expect you guys to have guessed that's where she'd go to search?"

Wendy chewed on her bottom lip, thinking about his words. "Many computers were seized in the raids. Potentially any of them could provide her with the information she needs or at least give her a place to start." She turned and walked out to the hallway. "Let's go to the tech room. Sian mentioned there are men working on deciphering the data we found."

"Good. We'll start there. Let Sian know where we're going and she can meet up with us."

Wendy already had her phone out and was texting.

"Did anyone try texting Rhia?" he asked. "Maybe she's not completely turned to the other side. Maybe she's looking, hoping for someone to stop her from doing this. Maybe it's the mind control." At Wendy's horrified gasp and worried gaze, he shrugged.

"Anything is possible now."

RHIA LEANED AGAINST the back wall of the small room she'd locked herself in, tears in her eyes. Oh Lord, please let her be doing the right thing. She had to save her son. Life wasn't worth living if she was responsible for his death. She couldn't have that be the end result. Seth was a good kid, becoming an honorable man. She didn't know who was ultimately to blame for what happened to him, but she steadfastly believed in his innocence.

She was a prime example of what happened when those bastards got their drugs into someone. And that wasn't her fault, and neither was it his. The things he'd done while under their control also weren't his fault, but she'd never be able to prove it to anyone when she'd done some horrible things too. Thankfully she hadn't been under the drug's influence for very long. She'd already done major damage in that little while. Imagine if that was years like what Seth had been through. She partly blamed Tyson for this. He'd been the one to get his claws into her son. But in truth, they were all to blame for this sickening situation. She still struggled with not having noticed a change in her son's behavior.

As his mother, she should have seen it.

Another failure on her part.

They were starting to rack up.

Now what she was doing was going to be considered traitorous by so many. But what choice did she have? She had to help him.

She stared down at the half-full needle in her hand, shuddered once, then squared off her chin. She had no choice.

And she shoved the needle into her arm and pressed down the plunger.

CHAPTER 8

ONCE OUT OF the elevator, Tessa let Cody lead the way to the security room. The air showed no sign of new energies having arrived or left recently. Weird. Where had everyone gone? They'd sent out several messages asking multiple questions but so far, there'd been no answers.

Cody sidled up to the corner ahead, his hand telling her to stay back. She smiled. She could see energy billowing around the corner up ahead but it was older, stale.

Cody peered around the corner and pulled back. She shifted closer.

Anyone there?

Yes. Approaching.

The feral tone of his voice had her looking at him. *Remember, not everyone here is an enemy.*

And not everyone here is a friend.

He jumped forward in front of the newcomer. He pulled a fist back… and damn if a strangled squawk didn't escape.

"Cody?"

She raced around the corner, worried at what he'd be facing – and stopped.

She stared.

She giggled.

Then she burst out laughing. In between her giggles, she managed to say, "Hi, Bart. I wondered where you got to."

And damn if the tubby vampire didn't turn white like the tiles surrounding him. His jaw dropped and he looked frantically around as if searching for a way to escape.

So not happening.

Cody stepped to the side of him, effectively boxing the vamp up against the wall. Tessa brightened her smile. "So tell us, Bart, what are you doing here? And how does this place fit into the blood farms?"

"No, oh no. Not you again." Bart finally found his voice. He shook his head like a lumbering bear. "Hell no. You have a death wish. I don't want to be anywhere around you." He turned to look behind him, but there was a hint of something there…fear, maybe.

What would make Bart afraid? Curious, and feeling it was important, she studied Bart, looking for his reaction intently as she said, "What are you scared of?"

His eyes rounded before he started to shake his head. "Nothing. I'm not scared of anything." He glared at her. "Except maybe the trouble you bring. A damn trouble magnet you are. Worse – you go looking for it."

He suddenly stopped talking and leaned forward as if his eyes didn't understand what they were seeing. "You're different." His gaze narrowed. "What happened?"

As soon as the words left his mouth, he shook his head rapidly and backed up. "Never mind, I don't want to know." He took another step back and Cody stepped in the way, caging him in again. Bart glared at him. "You're just as bad if you're with her. I don't want nuttin' to do with either of you."

Tessa laughed. He was a beauty. She'd never met anyone before or since like him. Now if only she knew which side he was on. She asked him.

He just glared at her.

She narrowed her gaze at him this time. "I asked you a question," she said. "One I've asked you before. As I recall, you didn't answer then either."

"I don't know what I might have answered back then, but it wouldn't have been any different than now," he said. "I'm not on anyone's side. I want to be left alone. You go off and live your death wish. The others can go and kill each other. I don't give a damn. Me...I want to live a life of peace and quiet."

"Then you don't mind showing us the security room, do you?" said Cody.

Bart glared at him. "What part of wanting to be left alone don't you understand?"

The grin on Cody's face had Bart backing up again.

"It's just around the corner," he blustered. "Go find it yourself."

"And you?" Tessa asked. "What are you going to do?"

"Me?" He tried to inch past her. "I'm going back to the damn caves where I'll be alone."

"If that's the case, why are you here?" Cody's voice vibrated in exasperation. "You're in a hospital that is run by the same people who ran the blood farms."

"What?" Bart cried out in a shocked whisper. "I am not. I was brought here to look at the heating pipes."

Tessa's antenna perked up. "What about the duct work, Bart?" she asked in a soft voice.

Her tone had him backing up again.

"Hey now. No threats. I ain't harming anyone." He glared at her. "They got a problem – so I'm helping fix it. Done it lots of times before."

"Maybe not, but if you are part of their plans for the ventilation system, then you are definitely hurting others."

"Whoa, what plans?" His gaze widened to huge orbs. "I don't know anything about their plans."

"If that's the case, then you don't mind telling me what you were fixing with the system, will you?" Cody snapped.

Bart glared at them but remained silent.

"Tell us," Tessa urged. "Please. This is very important."

"To you it is." Bart shifted his big belly. "It isn't to me. I go where I'm told to go."

"Told by whom?" Tessa gave him a cold smile. "Bart, give."

"Oh, whatever. My buddy said they needed the system fixed for some reason." He shrugged. "So I came and made a coupling so they could attach some damn canisters."

Tessa's skin ran cold. She glanced over at Cody. He looked ready to tear Bart to shreds. "And have they attached their canisters to the system?"

He shrugged. "They were working on it when I left."

And then she knew. "You left without them knowing, didn't you? You figured out what they were up to so you took off, didn't you?" She snorted in disgust.

"Hey, I did not. But they couldn't be doing anything good, and I didn't figure they'd leave me around to tell any tales so I made sure I did the job well and disappeared."

He shoved his chin forward, his gaze pugnacious. "I don't like to get involved."

"And you like living...?"

"Yeah," he eyed Cody nervously. "I do like living. So?"

"So if you want to continue to do so, you're going to help us stop them."

CODY WANTED TO laugh at the look of chagrin on the old fart's face. Just what the hell was he doing here anyway? Cody never trusted the guy in the first place and now that he was here…well, once again…it was suspicious. He might have let him go last time as a bad coincidence, but to come back again…that was two strikes and likely not forgivable the second time. First time was ignorance. The second time, however…

"I got nothing to say."

"Good. Then I'll make sure you can say nothing," Tessa said, calmly lifting her hand as if to slash across his chest.

Cody knew what was coming next. "Whoa, what are you doing?"

She stayed her hand, her gaze never leaving the cringing vamp.

"Yeah, what are you doing?" Bart stuttered. "Jesus, you are weird."

Tessa lowered her arm, much to Cody's relief, and glared at Bart. "I was going to make sure that you didn't cross us."

"Hey, let me go and I'll be happy to disappear."

Tendrils of loose hair flew everywhere as Tessa shook her head. "Not happening, Bart. You can't walk the middle road anymore. Give us something helpful to stop these guys from drugging everyone in this hospital or I'll take you out now."

"Man, you need to take anger management courses or something." He reached up and gave his old ratty shirt collar a snap. "Boy."

He turned his attention to Cody then froze. Horror slowly whispered across his face. He slowly turned back to face her. "Did you say drugs? Drug everyone in the hospital?" His voice rose to a squeak at the end like the mouse he was.

Cody wanted to reach out and give him a good shake.

"Surely you understand what's going on. There's no way you couldn't."

Bart's eyes bulged as he processed the information Tessa had threatened him with. "Whoa, I don't have anything to do with drugs." He spun to face Tessa. "You know that."

"Really? And yet by your own words you just said you fixed the system so they could hook up their new canisters."

"Yeah, but they weren't drugs," he protested. "If they were, I didn't know." He spun around and stared behind him, a stricken look on his face. "We have to stop them," he cried, and he bolted back the way he'd come.

Cody hadn't even had a chance to register that the old vamp had moved; then he was struck by how fast the bugger was scuttling away.

With Tessa was racing behind him.

Shit. Cody took off after the other two.

"Tessa, I wouldn't trust him. He could be leading us into a trap."

"Yep, he could be," she called back. "But I don't see that we have much choice."

Damn. Neither did he.

JARED STOOD IN Taz's home office nervously shifting from side to side. He was desperate to do something to help Clarissa. There'd been no further communication from her or her kidnappers. Just the thought of those bastards made his blood run cold. He didn't want to think of Clarissa in their hands. That they would consider coming after him – that they knew him, where to find him – yeah, he might never sleep again. He looked around the brightly lit room, dark curtains still protectively covering the windows – even though it was dark outside – and wondered if they'd find him here. They could associate him with his uncle and aunt's places, but would they find a connection to Taz?

He glanced sideways at Taz tapping away on his keyboard. Would Taz let him stay here? Surely they'd never think he'd hide out in a vampire hideaway.

Then again, this was only a half of one, with Taz being as human as Jared. Interesting times. He shifted restlessly.

"Pull up a chair, Jared." Taz motioned to the far side of the room without taking his eyes off the monitor. "I'm going to be a while."

Taking that suggestion to heart, Jared grabbed what looked like a Victorian-style kitchen chair and turned it around and sat down backwards facing Taz and the computer system. A very elaborate system. He wondered at that.

"That's a lot of computer equipment," he said casually.

"It is, and some came from the blood farm. I'm trying to decipher all the codes used for the victims we found hanging."

"What codes?" He leaned forward. If this was related to his father, he wanted to know everything he could. Maybe he could help somehow.

"Drugs they were given and why. If they ever awoke. The drug doses. Health issues found."

"Oh." He tried to make his voice sound normal, but the thought of someone treating his father as a number to be analyzed hurt more than he thought.

His pain must have trickled through into his voice. Taz turned abruptly to look at him, his gaze foggy, lost in his thoughts. His expression cleared suddenly and he closed his eyes. "Lord, I am so sorry, Jared. I forgot about your father."

"It's okay." Jared shrugged, wishing saying that would

make it so. "At least it's getting easier."

"Good, but this has to be hard."

"It is, but it also helps keep me focused on catching these bastards. Clarissa did nothing to them. They shouldn't have taken her."

"And Tessa would have said the same thing about you."

Jared sat back. "That's a perspective I hadn't thought about. Tessa really started something when she came after me." He hated that so far he hadn't been able to do anything to help Clarissa. At least it seemed like nothing. Look at the war Tessa had brought on in her fight to save him. He felt like a nobody. A failure. He hadn't managed to stir anyone to action. It was driving him crazy. He dropped his head on his arms over the back of the chair. "I'm really lucky that Tessa took up the fight to save me."

Taz looked over at him, a crooked smile on his face. "If you had any idea how and what that girl went through well…" Taz shook his head and returned to his monitor.

"Maybe that's why I'm so stricken now," Jared admitted. "Someone saved me. I think it's time for me to save someone else. I couldn't save my father – I have to save Clarissa."

"And we will. We will."

❧ ❦

BART RACED TO the mechanical room and those bastards who were trying to drug everyone in the hospital. He damn near worked for nothing now to keep Lacy safe. They weren't going to go back on their word and take her out with gas. Like hell. If need be, he'd carry her out himself.

He cast a glance behind him. They were still following. Gaining even. Not good. He hitched his pants up and tucked in his energy and sped forward. He might not be a warmonger like most of his clan, but he'd certainly picked up a trick or two in his time.

And he knew how to disappear. Escaping was his thing. From trouble. From battle happy vamps. From teenage girls who had a death wish.

Hell, they wouldn't catch him easily.

Hopefully they wouldn't catch him at all. He needed to talk to the guys he'd help install the canister for. Find out what was in it. Find out what the plan was for the contents. They made him a promise a long time ago.

And he planned on making sure they kept it.

THE NURSE CLUCKED around Jewel like she'd been missing for hours. This was the nurse's third trip to check on Jewel in just over an hour. All she'd done was have a hot shower. Who knew she wasn't supposed to do such a thing so fast? She felt good physically. Maybe even mentally, but emotionally – yeah, not so well. David hadn't shown up. She had no cell phone to text him with and the nurse had no idea where or who he was.

She also hadn't explained where Jewel was either.

And her wings no longer appeared to be working. How depressing. At least they had worked once so she knew it could happen again. Healing was in progress.

And that made her more determined than ever to not let the nurse know how quickly she was recovering. At least until she knew if she could trust her.

"Now no more showers. Rest. Your body has been through a lot of trauma. It needs time to heal."

"What trauma?" she asked curiously.

"Drugs, of course." The nurse smiled. "What else could it be?" Her clear gaze suddenly intensified, as if thinking Jewel had hidden some kind of injury from her.

Not likely and certainly not after being found in the shower. A little hard to hide much that way.

"Now I'll just be outside. You eat and rest."

And the woman walked out.

Jewel looked at the blood slushies the nurse had left for her. She was so very hungry. Was it safe? Or were there more drugs hidden in her drink?

The door closed behind the nurse, leaving Jewel alone with her thoughts – and her dinner.

CHAPTER 9

TESSA WATCHED BART disappear around yet another corner. For a chubby guy, he could sure move. If he was upset about the concept of drugging the whole hospital, did that mean he was on their side? At least maybe he wasn't on the bad guys' side. He had to have some conscience in there.

She opened her vision to study the figure in front of her. His energy was fast, energized, and definitely not black.

In fact, she couldn't see anything like that on him. So he'd not been taking or been given any of the blood farm drugs as far as she could see. Feeling better, she quickly shared her findings with Cody.

"Do you trust him?" Cody asked.

"To try and disappear as soon as he can? To find a way to stay out of trouble? To avoid getting into trouble? Yes to all three." She picked up the speed as he raced ahead. *How is he going so fast?* That's not like anything she'd seen before...except Hortran. *Nah, Bart is as far from being a Ghost as I am.*

Why? It's not like we've seen more than one Ghost to be able to make assumptions about them all.

I think he'd have said something or been something special if he were a Ghost.

He is special. Just not the way you might think. The snigger in Cody's voice made her laugh.

It felt good to be back on track with him. In spite of Bart's presence, or maybe because of it, she felt better. More normal.

Anything that helped her feel more grounded in this energy vortex she was living in was a good thing.

Bart slowed to a halt then took one half step forward, his head tilted to the side as if listening for something.

She tuned in her hearing, feeling more energy pulses there than she'd ever felt before. She toned it down and then tweaked the colors playing around beside her. Instantly, her hearing sharpened and the voices sounded clear as a bell in her ears.

Only she didn't understand a word they were saying.

She turned to Cody, who'd snuck up beside her. "I can hear them, but I don't understand the language."

He looked at her oddly. "Doesn't Deanna know it?"

Tessa shook her head. She'd have to wonder that later. "No. I'm not getting any indication that she did."

Cody nodded then nudged her shoulder. "Looks like Bart might."

Bart spun back to look at her; he mouthed something but she didn't understand. She sidled closer, not wanting to alert the others to their presence. When she was beside him, she asked him to repeat what he'd said.

"They are looking for me. They can't get the second canister connected."

"They have two?" Shit.

"Go join them as if someone sent you to help them out," she whispered. "And we'll come around and take them from behind."

He glared at her. "No way. I brought you here. That's all I'm going to do." He gave a silent snort. "You're the one with the death wish, not me."

"But if you stay here in the hospital, that death wish is going to be yours, remember? That gas will fill the whole building and no one will be safe."

"Precisely why I'm not sticking around."

"Going to run away again, Bart?" Cody asked. "How is it you can run so fast?" He watched Bart's face turn belligerent, his puffy jowls filling up in a huff.

"Good question," Tessa interjected smoothly. "I've only ever seen a Ghost move like that."

At the word ghost, Bart spun around to look behind her. "Ghost? Did you say you saw a Ghost?"

Only there was no fear in his voice. More surprise. Puzzlement maybe, as if he didn't think there was such a thing. At least not any longer.

"Yes, a Ghost." Cody went to brush past Bart and look around the corner when Tessa added, "Hortran."

Bart grabbed Cody's arm. "As in Deanna and Hortran?" Now his voice vibrated with some unnamed emotion, but it sounded suspiciously like fear...mixed with a big dose of rage.

Tessa nodded. "Did you know Deanna?"

"Everyone knows Deanna," Bart said harshly. "She's a mean old bitch and can't be trusted."

Tessa winced. "She *was* a mean old bitch. She's dead now."

He gazed at her in shock. Then his head shook like a wet dog. "No. You are mistaken. She can't be dead."

"Why?" Awareness kicked in. What did Bart know that Tessa didn't? She narrowed her gaze, waiting for him to answer.

"If she'd dead, there's been a major shift in power. She'd not have died easily either."

"She died here," Cody said, his voice harsh. "At the hospital."

Bart continued to shake his head in that lumbering bear way of his. "It can't be. It can't be."

He looked so stricken that Tessa wanted to reach out and pat him on the shoulder, offer comfort even though it wasn't going to be wanted.

"Why not? Was she special to you?"

Instead of answering, Bart turned back to where the men stood talking, his shoulders slumped as if he didn't quite understand how his world had changed.

She could sympathize, but she still wanted to know how he knew Deanna and what their connection had been. He wasn't anywhere near as old as Deanna had been and there hadn't been any type of similarity in their features, so she wasn't sure just what kind of question to ask, but she knew she needed to know what was going on. It might be personal, but the time for privacy issues to rear their ugly head was long past.

As she listened to the men's voices getting louder and louder, she grabbed Bart's shoulder, forcing him to pay attention to her. "Bart. Tell me. What was Deanna to you?"

He shrugged off her hand. "Not going to tell you."

She frowned. She could make him, maybe. But was it worth the effort? Maybe not considering that the bad guys were almost upon them.

Tessa? What are you doing?

Yeah, I know, but I really want to know why he's so stricken at Deanna's death.

It's his business.

So? Since when does that matter now? she said crossly. *This concerns Deanna, and I need to know.*

There was a funny silence in her mind. Trying to pay attention to the men coming around the corner, she turned to glare at Cody. *What?*

If it's about Deanna, Cody asked gently, *why don't you check your – her – memory banks to see what the relationship was and how their last meeting took place?*

Just then the men caught sight of Bart. "There you are. We need you to fix the hatch on pipe seven. The new canister won't seal properly."

Tessa wanted to laugh at that. It *might* be a design flaw or the higher ups' way of getting rid of those men who were doing the gassing. This way, dead men could tell no lies.

If the gas was just going to knock the people in the hospital unconscious, then she didn't know what these men's role would end up being. And maybe she didn't want to know.

She sighed and stepped out from behind Bart.

It was a testament to his size that it took them a moment to register her presence.

"Hey, who are you?"

She smiled. "I'm Tessa. Bart's buddy."

Bart stiffened beside her. He shot her a resentful look but stepped forward to help the men. "Show me," he said. "I'll have to check the coupling on it. Maybe it just needs tightening."

"I hope so," the first man said, worry etched on his face. "We came a little early to make sure this worked, but now that cushion is narrowing and we're going to be in trouble if we don't have this up and running soon."

"I'll get it going." He walked ahead slowly in that shambling way of his when Tessa caught sight of his hand and fingers pointing to the man on the left. What the hell did that mean? Go in that direction or take out the guy that was in that direction? Or was that guy important?

Then Bart stabbed the finger impatiently at the man closest to Tessa. Fine. Whatever.

She reached out and grabbed the stranger in the sweet spot on the neck, slapping her other hand over his mouth so no one could hear his cry. As it was, the other two men were deep in conversation with Bart over the pathway this heating vent travelled.

Bart wasn't giving them too much information. According to him, he didn't know anything about the vent system in place as he hadn't spent much time here. He hated hospitals. The others laughed.

One said, "Me too. Especially after tonight. I'll probably never come back to the place."

Tessa barely heard his words, but as they filtered through her consciousness she heard an *oomph* as if the man had taken a light punch to the gut. She frowned but couldn't see as she was attempting to maneuver the unconscious vamp off to the side when she suddenly tossed the man casually into a corner. Surprised by the easy strength of her actions, she studied the crumpled position and wondered. She'd meant to only drag him like she'd normally have done, but apparently she'd used more force than she'd understood. The man was dead.

Weird.

She turned her attention back to Cody, who held out his hand for her. *Come on,* he urged. *We don't want them getting too far ahead.*

They caught up to the others as one man collapsed to the ground, writhing in pain. Leaving Cody back a few steps, she raced forward to see what was wrong. The man gave one, two hard jolts then went still.

She dropped to her knees onto the floor. "What happened

to him?" she cried.

"Me," Bart said, and the second man dropped to the ground. "Leave them alone and pass me the canister. I'll get it out of here."

She looked up to find Bart pointing out a dark gray metal tin that was the size of a good-sized backpack. Cody snagged it up, his own arms dropping with the weight. "Are you sure this is it?"

Bart sent him a disgusted look and grabbed it easily in one meaty paw. "Of course. We were trying to attach it earlier."

"What are you going to do if anyone comes looking for these two men?" Tessa asked.

"No problem. I'll make sure they disappear, then I'll disappear after them." His smile was something to see. Cold and feral, it sent chills down her spine. This was no longer the unkempt Bart. In his place was this tubby ninja. She wanted to laugh but figured it would not be a good idea.

"And the second canister?" she asked quietly. "What about that one?"

"The system needs both shafts closed off for the system to be operational. So they can't use the other canister anyway. Now," he wagged a finger at her. "Go. Kill yourself off if you feel the need, but don't involve me in your plans."

"I won't," Tessa said cheerfully. "At least I know where to find you."

"No. You *knew* where to find me. After this, you won't find me again."

There was no give in that glare of his, but she didn't think he was as big a hard ass as he wanted her to believe. She'd met hard asses. Generally they didn't look or act like Bart. "Before you go, why won't you tell me what Deanna meant to you?"

He laughed, but there was nothing humorous about it.

"Why do you care? The bitch is gone and who and what she was, the things she's done, well... they'll die with her."

"Not necessarily," Tessa said. "Did you have a grievance with her?"

He glared at her. "With what she'd done. The poison she set into action...that was no grievance. That was Deanna being Deanna all over again. She saw. She liked. She took. No matter what it was or who had it."

Tessa hated hearing such things but knew there was likely a lot more to come. Deanna hadn't lived an innocent life, and as much as Tessa wanted her to be the big purist she'd thought her to be, Deanna had done many things over her long life that hurt a lot of people. And those she didn't hurt, she pissed off. But should she tell Bart about the parts of Deanna she carried? How much did he hate her? Would he see Tessa as a surrogate target?

His venom rolled over her.

"I've spent years hating that witch. I'd have done anything to see her turn to ash, preferably by my hand," he snapped. "That I didn't get a chance to kill her is sad, but that is life. As long as someone did the job, then I'm good. If there is proof of her demise – so there can be no doubt – then I'm even better." He grinned for the first time, his cartoon-like features twisting with glee. But then Tessa heard his words, and his funny face ceased to matter.

Uh oh. "You wanted what? Revenge?"

"Exactly."

"And again, I have to ask you – why? What did she ever do to you?"

"I hated her."

"I got that." Tessa understood, but there had to be a powerful reason for that much hate, to wait so long for revenge.

He had to have a major reason.

But getting it out of him wasn't going to be easy.

"She must have hurt you badly."

The fire in his eyes would have told another person to back off. Tessa didn't listen. She had to know the connection to Deanna. With the men lying prone at their feet and time wasting, knowing Cody didn't understand why she pushed again, guessing, "She hurt someone close to you."

Bart narrowed his gaze at her, his jaw locking then pulsing. He wanted to speak. He wanted to let it all out.

"No, she didn't," he snapped. "It's none of your business."

"And yet it is. I have to do something for her," Tessa explained. "I can't do my job if I don't know what I'm up against."

"She got to you, did she?" Bart snarled. "Well then, you're going to get your death wish after all. That bitch killed my daughter. All I had in this world. She killed her, and my girl was only trying to help."

That didn't sound right. Tessa said, "I'm so sorry for you and your girl. What happened?"

"Some bullshit story about needing an apprentice to pass all her knowledge onto after her death."

Tessa gasped, but Bart wasn't listening. "One day after an elaborate ceremony, they did this mind thing and Deanna was supposed to pass over big chunks of her knowledge, her wisdom, but it didn't work out that way. Instead of my daughter waking with all the new information, Deanna killed her."

He glared at Tessa. "One minute my baby was there with me and laughing like she always did, and the next thing I know she was screaming for help as her brain overloaded –

and she died in my arms."

SERUS TRIED TO focus as he followed his son and Goran through the bowels of the hospital in search of the mechanical room. He'd held them back long enough trying to raise the alarms about Rhia both mentally and via Sian. Everyone already knew she'd taken off, but no one had found his beloved. She'd hidden and if she'd taken the drugs again as Sian suspected, she'd know the best places to hide. Had she turned? Had she become so addicted to the drugs she had to go back for more?

He hoped not. He had visions of spiriting her away to an old hideaway where he could keep her locked up and safe until the addiction, the horrible craving, passed.

Not fun. For either of them. But he'd do it if necessary.

Then again, he also wanted to race after her and give her a heavy shaking. Or a damn good kick in the backside. How dare she take off alone? She could trust him to help, whatever it was she was trying to do. And he'd understand. He might not like it. He might have tried to stop her, hell, he would definitely have tried to stop her – at least he would have spent the whole time trying to talk her out of it – but that wouldn't mean he wouldn't have also looked for a different solution to help her.

He pulled back slightly as Goran slipped into his mind, berating him. *Damn it, Serus, get back into the game. There are bad guys here.*

Hell, there are always bad guys lately, he grumbled.

What? Goran was racing ahead. *We're almost at the heating system and someone beat us to it.* He paused then laughed. *How the hell did she do that?*

She?

Serus caught up to the others and peered around Goran's shoulder to see Tessa and Cody ahead of them. "Tessa? How did you get here so fast?"

His daughter's face lit up at the sight of him, making him smile inside. Damn, she'd turned out well. He wished Rhia could see her. Hell, he wished Rhia was here.

"I am not sure, actually. We took the elevator back down to find the security camera feed to see what happened upstairs when we found Bart here." She tugged a fat vampire out from the center of the group and damn it if he didn't recognize him from the blood farm.

"Bart – hey, we were afraid you died when the mountain came down."

Bart shrugged. "I escaped out one of the shafts. She's a walking disaster." He glared at Tessa.

Tessa gave a sheepish shrug. "Hey, I'm getting better."

Goran snorted. "So not true."

"See, even he agrees with me," Bart snickered. "I barely escaped with my skin."

"You're lucky you got out," Goran reminded him. "Thousands didn't."

"Yeah, lot of good it did me when you consider that I'm sitting here with her again."

This time Tessa glared at him. "You're the one that helped them hook up the canisters full of drugs. Sounds like you don't deserve to escape again."

"Ha. I just took those guys down too." He hitched his belly up and hooked his thumbs under the straps to his overalls.

Serus wanted to laugh, but a smirk slid out instead.

Goran stepped forward. "And did those drugs get into the vents? Is that why you are down here again? Is everyone upstairs dead? Drugged?"

"No." Cody spoke up. "We never found anyone, but once Tessa realized the guards you left watching the elevator were gone, she was afraid there was a trap up ahead. She wanted to come down and search the video feed first. Instead, we found Bart here trying to sneak away after helping them set up the new drug delivery system."

Goran's phone rang. He stepped off to one side and answered it.

"Hey, I didn't know what was inside those damn things. I wouldn't have helped if I'd known. There are a lot of vamps in this hospital."

"Versus a lot of humans, I suppose." Tessa shook her head, all the while managing to glare at Bart. Serus had to wonder at their relationship. It appeared they knew each other quite well.

"We're wasting time," David snapped. "We have to stop them."

Bart snarled right back at him. "We are doing something. We just took out these couple assholes and got the canister back. The system won't work if there is only one canister. They'd need to seal off this half of it first."

David stared at Bart in surprise. Serus admitted he was a little surprised himself. All he'd seen of that vamp had been a sleepy disinterest. Now he was agitated...and angry.

Serus wished he understood what was behind it.

And apparently Tessa didn't either as she studied Bart intently. "What's the matter, Bart?"

"You," he snapped. "All of you. You cause so much trouble."

"It's not me," Tessa said in surprise. "We're trying to fix the problem."

"And the problem just keeps getting bigger. If you'd left well enough alone, we'd all be living our normal lives."

Sadness whispered across Tessa's face. Serus's heart tugged at what she'd been through.

"That wasn't possible," Tessa said quietly. "People were getting hurt. It had to stop."

"And now vamps are getting hurt because of it. When do our people not count?" There was so much bitterness in his voice that no one appeared to know what to say.

"It's true that trying to help my friends brought on more problems than we could have ever understood ahead of time, but that didn't mean I could let them be hurt and do nothing about it."

"Whatever." Bart turned away. "The hospital was doing a lot of good here too, you know. They were trying to help some vamps. It was a medical facility. A treatment center." He headed to the door. "Now it's just a disaster zone."

And he walked through the doorway, canister in hand, leaving the others to stare behind him in wonder.

Goran walked forward, closing his phone. "What happened to him? The last time I saw him he was completely disinterested in the war going on around us. In fact, I think he was hoping it would pass by and not disturb his sleep."

"He was."

Serus, a glimmer of understanding trickling into his conscience, suggested, "Maybe the war has struck too close to home. While it was at the blood farms, as long as he didn't take part in the consumption of the blood and had no caring for the humans involved, he wasn't involved. But now that it's here…"

"Where the hospital was doing testing and treatments." Tessa added, "He does care."

"And that would give rise to the assumption that he has someone here that he cares about who is being adversely affected."

"Then again," David said, "We all are. If he'd helped out early on, this stage might have been prevented. It's not like Jewel or Wendy wanted to be drugged. Or Mom. Or how about Darren? He was one of the few vamps hanging up in the blood farm – it's not like he asked for this. We're all suffering. Bart has to decide which side he's on."

"I think he already did," Serus said, following after Goran. "He left, didn't he?"

"He said he was going after the second canister, but whether he does or not…" Cody said.

"Speaking of side," Goran said, "Motre just filled me in. They were attacked trying to get to the elevator. They broke off and raced down the stairs. The fight was bad enough that they lost a few men before they managed to hole up on the second floor. They are safe but pinned down. He says the men need some time to recover, so don't race to their rescue just yet."

"Good. We'll straighten this out then go to him."

"Jared?"

The voice wove through his dreams. Tessa? Clarissa? No…Sian. He woke with a jolt and bolted upward, knocking out the chair from under him and falling backwards. Catching himself, he shuddered with shock as he stood frozen in place, trying to figure out where he was.

"Easy, Jared." Sian stood in front of him, worry creasing her beautiful face. "You're fine here."

"Sorry." He shook his head to loosen up the cobwebs. "I guess I fell asleep."

"No wonder. You and Taz," she turned her head to another man Jared only just now realized had crashed on the couch opposite him, "are working so hard."

Taz opened his eyes and gazed at his beautiful wife. The look in his eyes made Jared wish for things he'd never had. Someone to love him. Someone to love.

The two people were so well suited to each other; he couldn't imagine a better couple. And Taz was human. "You guys are great together," Jared said warmly. "You're very lucky."

Sian laughed, her light caring voice rippling through the room. "Thank you. So many people would not agree with you."

"And they'd be wrong." In a smooth muscled movement, Taz came off the couch to stretch his arms to the ceiling. He walked the two steps over to his wife and gave her a loving kiss. "Did you get any rest?" he asked, staring down at her, his gaze studying her features.

Jared turned away from the intimate look into the relationship between two people he barely knew. Behind him, he heard the gentle murmurings but deliberately tuned it out. He walked to the window and stared out into the dark of night. God, he hoped Clarissa was safe and sound and tucked into bed somewhere warm. He couldn't stand the thought of her lying in one of those horrible cells he'd lived in while they checked his blood out.

She was innocent and fragile. She had a loving family – and he hadn't contacted them. Shit.

He spun around to look at the couple still talking quietly behind him. "I never contacted Clarissa's parents."

Sian nodded. "We tried but haven't connected yet. We'll keep trying."

Jared pulled out his cell phone on the faint hope that Clarissa might have contacted him while he'd slept. But there were no messages. He immediately sent her one even though he knew the assholes had her phone. He just couldn't help himself.

As soon as he hit send, he panicked. "I just sent another message to Clarissa. What was I thinking?" he exclaimed. "What if they can track it? What if they know I'm here now? They will come after me. And find you."

Oh no, what had he done? He hadn't meant to but hadn't thought his actions through. He'd reacted, and not in a good way.

He raised his stricken gaze upward to stare at the other two.

"If that's possible, which it likely is, then we'll have to take your phone somewhere to lead them away from here," Taz said calmly. "And you'll end up losing yet another phone."

Another phone? Jared stared at Taz in dismay. "But I just got this one."

Sian laughed. "And we'll help you get another one. The bottom line is if they can find you, they can kidnap you yet again. Once was enough, don't you think?"

She held out her hand. With a sigh of disgust, he placed the phone in her hand then snatched it back up again. "Wait, I need to grab the numbers off of here."

While the others waited, he wrote down all the contacts he'd worked so hard to regain these last few days. He didn't want to lose those numbers. He ripped off the piece of paper from the pad that Sian had provided and folded it. Pulling out his wallet, he tucked it inside.

Immediately he felt better. Still connected. Sadly, he watched as Sian took the phone and tucked it into her purse.

"Uh, that's not a good idea."

She turned to look at him, a question in her eyes.

"If they come looking for that phone, they are going to find you instead. That's not a decent alternative to finding me."

"No, it's not." Taz walked over and fished it out of his wife's purse. "We need someone on the Council to come and pick this up."

Sian shrugged. "I could have taken on anyone they sent," she muttered.

He chuckled softly, one arm reaching out to stroke her rounded belly. "I'm sure you could, but Junior needs his Amazonian mother."

She blushed prettily. Jared sighed happily. This was another thing he missed in his life. A family.

Maybe he'd be lucky enough to have one someday.

RHIA HATED THE woozy feeling in her brain. The drugs coursed through her blood, making her weak. God, what had she done? Surely there'd been another way. She'd only given herself a half dose – hoping to keep some of herself along with enough drugs to access some of the memories and knowledge she'd picked up while under the influence. A faint hope maybe, but she had no idea what else to do. The information she needed was inside her head. And maybe inside the computer equipment she'd help seize from the raids. She just needed a safe place to hole up while the drugs did their thing. She stared around the small room. It had a bathroom and a table and a bed. Surely that would be enough for her needs.

Then she looked at the locked door. No one else could get in if she didn't want them to. The problem was if the drugs took over so strongly that she chose to unlock the door and leave the Council Hall. If that was the case, the drugs and whatever brainwashing had been done would be in control and she could cause untold damage to those she loved.

How to stop herself from doing that?

She couldn't lock herself in.

She needed someone else to do that.

Wracking her brain for a solution, she sat still, letting her mind work. Letting her mind access the information. She had a computer in front of her. One taken from the blood farm and one from their own servers here at the Council. Surely that would provide the necessary tools she needed to sort this out.

Except for the damn door.

What was she going to do about that? She heard voices outside. She tensed, then forced herself to relax. No one could get in. It wouldn't matter if someone was out there.

She watched, her nerves pulsing as the footsteps and voices came closer and closer. There were many locked doors in the Center. She didn't even know what was behind many of the doors. She swallowed hard, hearing the noises right at her door. The knob turned.

Shit.

Then a key was inserted. Instead of the door being unlocked and the door opened, the lock clicked several times before a hard snap cracked. She bolted to her feet. What the hell happened?

The footsteps on the other side moved on down the hallway. Her throat clenching, Rhia raced to the door. Her hand out, she reached for the knob. It had to be the drugs making her tremble. She grasped the knob and, ready to peer around the edge, she turned it.

And pulled.

It didn't budge. Frowning, she threw the bolt on the top of the door and turned the knob again.

It still didn't move.

Panicking now, she flipped the bolt back and forth several times, trying anything she could to open the door.

Everything failed.

Knowingly or unknowingly – she'd been locked inside.

CHAPTER 10

TESSA FOLLOWED THE group chasing after Bart – only slower. If nothing else, they needed to know where the second canister was going to be attached and save it – and to make sure Bart did what he said he was going to do. A part of her felt they should go rescue Motre but as he said, they were safe for the moment. She understood the males were hoping to meet up with more bad guys, but she was still caught up in Bart's words.

And the odd sense of betrayal that had taken over her consciousness. So she wasn't the One? She was just Deanna's last choice? A choice made in panic when Deanna found herself at the end of the road with no other place to go. How the hell did that make any sense?

"Are you okay?" Cody placed a hand on her shoulder and squeezed gently.

Slowing down, she gave him a wan look, noticing in spite of her own turmoil that he looked tired. Down. "Hey, I'm fine. Just processing."

"You're doing a lot of that lately," he muttered. "It's not the way things were supposed to go."

"A lot of my life hasn't gone the way I'd thought it would go." She almost laughed given that a few short weeks ago, she'd been lovesick over a chance to sit beside Jared at the movies. God, she'd been young. And stupid. Who knew what she'd go through after that? And the impact on her life.

She felt old now. Tired.

Tired, yes. Old, no. That's Deanna talking, Cody said calmly in her head. *It's not you.*

Tessa stopped in her tracks. *Give me a minute*, she muttered.

She closed her eyes and checked the stupid filing system she'd put into place. The cabinet was there. The filing drawers were closed and didn't appear to be bleeding energy. So where the hell was that Deanna influence coming from? Because she didn't doubt it was mixed with her energy now that Cody had pointed it out.

You're welcome.

His voice, warm and caring, brought unexpected stinging to her eyes. Her response. Not Deanna.

"I don't know what I'd do without you," she whispered, hating the fatigue now singing through her. Was it hers or Deanna's? *She was so tired of trying to sort this out. She hadn't found much good in Deanna's legacy. Just a confusing burden to carry.*

"Sometimes legacies are just that," he said, reaching out a gentle hand to rub her shoulder. "Kick her out if you don't want it all. You don't owe her anything."

"Don't I?" she asked sadly. "I can't say that I agree at this point. Although I might get there eventually. I'm still shocked by Bart's revelation. And the thought of Deanna having tried this with at least one other person. A person who didn't survive. Had she done this before that? Had she killed other women – maybe ones who were willing and maybe ones who weren't? It's not like she gave me a choice. Did she give this other woman a choice before she died screaming from the chaos in her brain while her father watched yet unable to help her?"

"Deanna had a lot of power. According to what we've heard, she wasn't a nice person, so I highly doubt she used all that power to help people. Maybe sometimes, but I think she wanted to live or at least have her heritage not go to waste."

"So she dumped it all on me?" Tessa shook her head. "I'm not sure I want it. In fact, I'm pretty damn sure I don't."

"You need to stuff her inside into a sealed locked space so she doesn't impact you as much as she's doing. Wrap her up in your energy or something to keep her in her place."

She could hear the worry in his voice, a worry her own mind was repeating. Surely there was something she could do. "I'm going to need to figure this out."

"Do it now. The others can go fight the battles. Tessa, you need to fight the one going on inside of yourself. This is too important to put off."

"I thought I had a warning system in place to let me know when her energy is influencing mine."

"Then it's not working," Cody said patiently. "Or she has a work-around."

Was that possible? Or was someone else involved in sabotaging her plans? Or maybe she'd just screwed up herself? That was so possible. She looked around. "I think I'd like to lie down and go inside. See if I can figure this out."

"No problem," he said. "I will watch over you."

She smiled mistily. "I don't know what I'd do without you."

"Remember that when Deanna and I go up against each other," he said in exasperation. "You're Tessa, not a Deanna clone, and you need to show her energy who is boss." He studied her face intently, as if looking to see who was peeking out of her eyes. "Can you do that for me?"

Her lips quirked. "I thought I had."

"Not enough. Or you missed something. Time to go and do this right." He looked around the long hallway, shrugged and said, "Here is as good a place as any."

"It's an odd place," she said, lowering herself to the bare floor. "But short of taking time to go back upstairs to all the beds, this will do."

"We're not talking that kind of time." Cody squatted down and leaned against the wall. "You've got fifteen minutes. Start when you're ready."

A laugh escaped. In his own way, Cody was as indomitable as his father. And just as stubborn.

Obediently she lay down on the floor along the wall so he could get up and walk around her if need be. "Don't let me be out for too long." She closed her eyes.

"I won't. So stop wasting your precious minutes."

She grinned. Trust him. She'd been given an order. Go in and fix this. Then get back to him. Fast.

She felt comforted thanks to his grounding presence and his straightforward and practical personality. She could do no less than give him her best.

And luckily enough, so far her best had been good enough.

She took a deep breath and sank into her consciousness. *Deanna, here I come, ready or not.*

❧ ❦

GORAN STOPPED SO suddenly, David slammed into his back.

"Damn it. What's wrong?" David peered over his shoulder then looked around behind him. "We have to hurry or we'll never catch up with Bart."

"Not sure catching up to him matters," Goran muttered. Something else was wrong.

But what? He shook his head to clear his thoughts, then turned back to face Serus. His friend looked old and traumatized. Damn Rhia for doing this to him. Unfortunately, it didn't look like he'd have time to recover. Not with this odd feeling rolling around inside him. "Serus, do you sense anything wrong with Tessa?"

Serus glanced up at him in surprise. "No." He spun around. "Where are they?"

"I don't know. I just got this weird feeling. I figured it was maybe Cody. Then I realized they weren't coming after us."

"Oh, what the hell," David groaned. "Why is it so hard to stick together?"

"Maybe they are just slow," Serus said his voice slow, uneasy. "But you're right, something…feels off."

"Have the drugs been put into the system after all?" David asked, pulling out his cell phone. He sent Cody a text. *Where are you?*

The response came back within minutes. *Watching over Tessa. She's working on the energy stuff in her own system, trying to corral Deanna's energy so it doesn't impact her as badly.*

"Now? Couldn't she have waited?" he said out loud, repeating the message to the elders. He texted the same response back to Cody.

No. She couldn't, came the message back.

"Damn. So now what do you want to do? Go back to them and watch over her as well or keep chasing Bart?"

"I want to keep an eye on Bart. I don't trust him with this canister stuff and now that I know he hated Deanna and blames her for his daughter's death, I'm not sure what he'll do if he finds out that Tessa was the second choice for Deanna and that she survived the process." Goran snorted. "Or that parts of Deanna may have survived as well. More than survived if what Cody is saying now is true. Apparently Deanna's energy has more will to live than I'd thought possible."

"No one thought any of this was possible," Serus said. "That means there is much that could still happen that we couldn't imagine as well."

"She was only supposed to download the information Deanna had. How the hell did that turn into energy?" Goran growled. "And how does 'energy' become parts of her personality – her will?"

"Information is energy. Energy is in everything," David said, trying to hold onto his patience. "It seems like Deanna's energy is almost as big a force with her being dead as she was when she was alive."

"And that's not good. Deanna was a bitch," Goran snapped. "If she figured out a way to exist beyond the life span of her body, then that's bad news for Tessa."

"Did Deanna pick her or was Tessa just convenient?" David asked. "She'd need to have someone who she was capable of doing this to – does that mean weak? Open to suggestion? I don't know."

"Or compassionate, caring? Tessa hated to think of Deanna's suffering. She'd have done anything she could to help." Serus ran his hand over his face. "She didn't get the option here. And now she's paying the consequences."

"And what about Bart?"

Goran frowned and looked at the floor, then back up at the others. "Given what he's lost, his potential need for revenge, we'd better make sure he never finds out."

◈ ◈

TOO DAMN LATE. He'd just found out. Bart glared at the open double doors and the men who were just around the corner and out of sight. The sound of their voices whistled straight toward him through the hallway. They didn't know he was there. He'd stayed ahead of them and stopped to take a break when he'd heard them talking.

What the hell had Tessa done? He didn't hold anything against her; she was just a young naive kid who'd been taken advantage of by Deanna. Of course he'd seen himself that she had a death wish. He could put that down to her age and compassion. She'd just wanted to save the world. Like that would happen given the fine state of affairs. His anger trembled with painful memories.

She was just like Lacy. His beautiful precious daughter. She'd been gone for a long time and it didn't matter. It seemed like it was just yesterday. Moisture stung his eyes. Shit. He scrubbed his face.

He'd been lost ever since. Living a life in the shadows and avoiding everyone on both sides of the damn system. He did his work, had a few drinking buddies, and that was good enough. After all, he'd lost the most precious thing in his life. What else mattered – except hating Deanna? He'd hoped to be able to do something about her, but he wasn't a skilled killer. Nor was he as powerful or as cruel as Deanna was. His options were limited. Hating his inability to fight her and not knowing what to do to avenge his daughter, he'd done nothing but sink deeper into apathy.

Until Tessa came along and blew up the status quo.

He'd had no idea a few weeks ago that he'd suddenly have a way to avenge his daughter. Be pitted against someone more his level of power. Tessa was just a kid and hadn't grown into her full abilities. Some would say she'd be more powerful than Deanna if she lived that long.

But that didn't change the element of truth to her current life. She housed energy from that bitch. He didn't know exactly what that meant. But he'd find out.

Then he'd rip it out of her and make sure it was destroyed. One way or another.

Deanna wasn't allowed to live – in any form.

If that meant Tessa had to die – then so be it.

"I'M GOING BACK." Abrupt and hard, Serus surprised himself with his decision.

"Going back?" David asked, a blank look on his face. "Where?"

But Goran knew. "Good idea. I was just thinking to do the same."

"No, you two carry on. I'll go check up on her."

David stood in front of Serus. "Go where?" he cried out in frustration. "What am I missing?"

"Something isn't quite right about your sister. I have to go make sure she's safe," Serus said.

"Do you want all of us to come?" Goran stood at his side, like always. Ready to fight in any war as long as the cause was just and belonged to a friend.

Serus smiled at his best friend. "No. I got this. You go chase after that damn Bart and collect both canisters. We need to take them back to the Council Hall for testing. Make sure we come up with an antidote and fast. Just in case they decide to try this on a large scale somewhere else."

"Not a happy thought," David said. He turned to carry on down the hallway. "I think Tessa can probably handle anything life throws at her these days, but if you're worried about her, go. We'll find Bart."

Serus nodded, his gaze going to Goran.

"Go," Goran urged. "There's something wrong there. I can feel it."

So could Serus.

"Regular updates though so we know for sure you're okay."

Already heading back toward his daughter, Serus nodded. "Will do."

JARED CLUNG TO the passenger door handle as Taz careened around the corner in his sports car. Fantastic car. Crazy driver. Taz treated the night roads like they were a raceway. Jared moved from delight to dismay in seconds and rolled back just as fast.

As they got to the hospital and parked in a reserved spot, he gave a happy sigh of relief. "Nice car." He unlocked the door and hopped out. Taz's laughter rolled freely around him. He turned to face the other man, who was already striding toward the entrance. "You were never in any danger, Jared."

"Hey, I never thought I was," he protested, racing to catch up with Taz. The older man was moving so fast he struggled to keep up.

"Sure you didn't," Taz called back as he entered the quiet of the building.

Jared stopped to marvel at the difference when one entered the hospital. The low hum in the background, the silence…the smell.

"Come on, Jared. Don't be so slow."

He picked up the pace and caught up to Taz as he turned the corner toward his office. "Do you ever worry about the hospital itself being attacked?"

Taz turned and shot him a narrow look. "Is that an idle question? Or do you know something specific?"

"No. It's just the smell is so distinctive here it made me wonder."

Only Taz wasn't happy with that explanation. "Wonder what?"

He shouldn't have started this conversation. "I didn't mean anything, but I've seen some of the nasty stuff these guys do and wondered if they'd ever attacked the hospital before."

"No. They haven't," Taz said shortly. "But thanks for giving me something new to worry about."

❧ ❧

GORAN FOUND IT hard to keep up with Bart. How that vamp could scuttle through the lower hallways and tunnels blew him away. He'd heard David panting behind him. Stupid scary.

"How can he be doing this?" David groaned. "I'd like to stop the little idiot myself."

"If he's got something to show us, then he needs to run right to it."

"Do you think he knows what we're up to?"

Goran shrugged. "I'd like to think not, but who knows? He's running awfully fast if not."

Goran pulled the double doors in front of him open and

stopped. David slammed into the back of him and bounced off. Silly kid.

"What the hell, Goran?" David groaned as he scrambled to his feet.

"Oh sorry. He's not here. The hallway is damn long and there are no doorways anywhere. Where did he go?"

"If there's no choice, then the only choice is the one that must be," David said with a silly grin on his face.

"What the hell does that even mean?" Goran snapped. These young punks made no sense at the best of times. Now that he was goofing around, he really made no sense. What the hell was he supposed to do with this?

"It means there's only one place he could have gone, and that's straight ahead of us," David said patiently. "So that's the only place we can go after him."

Goran glared down at the long white hallway then back at David's grinning face. "So why didn't you say so?"

David snuck by him, grinned, and bolted ahead. "Take a rest if you need it, old man."

∾ ∿

JEWEL WAITED UNTIL the door closed after the nurse's latest check-in. Crossing the room, she listened for the receding footsteps. Jewel had to consider if that was standard for everyone or if Jewel was getting special attention. It seemed about right, but her suspicious mind wouldn't let go of the possibility that she was getting a little extra care than needed.

There was another blood slushie for her. She'd drunk the last one after taking a sip then waiting a half hour. When she'd experienced no side effects, she'd downed it quickly.

She needed energy to get out of here.

The door was closed but she hadn't heard a click to say it had been locked. She was anxious to open it and sneak out but knew it could be an irrevocable step. She was warm and cared for here. Out there...who knew what she'd find? She really wanted a cell phone to call David. That she hadn't seen him in all her time there scared her.

Would they try to stop him from seeing her? Every time she'd asked, the nurse said she hadn't seen anyone by that name.

If that was true and that was a big if – then David was busy doing something important. He wouldn't have left her to fend for herself alone like this. He'd have checked in.

There's no way he wouldn't.

He would also have his cell phone on him. All she needed to do was borrow a phone. Or find one. How hard could that be?

Not knowing when she'd get more, she tossed back the slushie and walked across the room to the door.

Placing an ear against the wood, she listened again. Hearing only silence on the other side, she opened the door and quietly slipped out.

❧ ❦

IAN FOLLOWED WENDY down to where the other computer equipment was stored. They'd spent hours searching for the material taken from the blood farm offices. They'd found lots of information but as Wendy had pointed out, much of it – the most critical – was missing. And she wanted to know why. She'd sent a text to Sian asking her but hadn't heard back yet. She knew Sian had needed to leave, to go home to see her husband. Wendy was lucky enough to have Ian right there but they had families too…only they couldn't…make that *shouldn't* leave.

It was too dangerous. They were targets, and contacting their families could put them in danger.

But Sian had left with Wendy's blessing; after all, Jared was there and someone needed to find out what was going on with him. And his missing friend. She hated the blood farms. It was inherently wrong.

"Wendy, what's behind this door?" Ian turned the knob on one door that was the fourth in the long line of similar doors. She shrugged. "Who knows? There could be any number of things inside." She paused, thinking of the room Rhia had been recuperating in. "And people. I think the ancients or at least the Council members all have their own quarters here."

Ian looked at her. "Really? Why?"

"I don't know. Maybe for when there are problems and they aren't allowed to leave. A society is only as good as the government who can keep everything running." She laughed. "Wasn't that one of the lessons we were taught in school?"

He snorted. "Was it? I never paid attention to politics."

"Maybe you should have," she teased. "There's lots of intrigue going on in that department right now."

"Too much. With all the foreign diplomats assembled here in the Council Hall now after being rescued from the hospital? It's big time and big time bad news."

"We have to find out what's going on there, too." Sighing heavily, Wendy added, "One thing at a time."

She moved to the next door and went to knock. The door opened as she was about to touch the wood.

"Yes?" A massive male opened the door. Not super huge, but wide. Not fat – muscle.

She swallowed hard, trying to remember why she'd knocked. She wasn't looking for living quarters. She was looking for the IT people or the IT equipment.

And realized chances were good it was with men like this. Men who worked the equipment in private, coaxing it to give up its secrets.

They so weren't going to want to let her know anything about it.

"Sorry, I'm in the wrong area."

"No problem, come in."

She shook her head. "No, thanks."

Ian placed a warm reassuring hand on the small of her back. She straightened, bolstered by his presence. "I've gotten lost and was looking for Sian."

The man, his black eyes sharp and assessing, smiled. "No problem. But this Sian of yours, he's not here." And he closed the door. In her face.

She swallowed hard, shock reverberating inside. They didn't know Sian? How was that possible?

"Please tell me that wasn't a wall of computer monitors in there."

"It was," Ian said grimly. "And I have no idea why."

They walked quietly down the hallway, both silent, both wanting to put some distance between them. At the end of the hallway, Wendy pulled out her cell phone and dialed Sian. No answer. Crap. She sent her a text anyway. Normally Sian was always reachable. *Why does the fourth room on the left of floor six of the Council Hall have a room full of computers and monitors? Are they on our side?*

She reached the double doors and pushed them open.

They wouldn't budge.

Ian lent his weight. The doors still wouldn't move. Puzzled, Wendy turned to look behind them at the long hallway. All the doors were closed as they'd been as they walked past. All the doors but one.

The one where the computer center had been.

They watched as the same huge man stepped out into the hallway, a second one right behind him. Side by side they walked down the hallway toward Wendy and Ian.

Only there wasn't a smile on their faces. In fact, they looked downright scary.

She mustered a smile. "Hey, this door is locked. Do you know how to open it?"

"If you don't have a code, you can't get through there."

The second man said, "No one goes in there."

"Why not?" Ian asked, stepping forward to slightly shelter Wendy. The way the men were looking at them made her want to hide. But there were two of them and only one Ian. Besides, he was tired and worn out too. He wasn't up to fighting both of these assholes.

"Okay then. We'll go back the way we came." Wendy plastered a bright smile on her face and went to walk forward. Instead of moving out of her way, the men shifted, a subtle movement that allowed them to cover the full width of the hallway. In other words, they weren't going to allow her to pass.

"Crap," she whispered.

Ian reached out and grabbed her hand and tugged her backwards slightly. She resisted, then accepted his lead. From a slightly more sheltered position, she watched as the two big men approached.

"What are we going to do?" she whispered.

"Get the hell out of here," he answered slowly. "I'm getting a little tired of being knocked around, drugged, and getting my ass kicked. It's time for a little payback."

The two men must have heard him as they stopped and looked at the two of them a little uncertainly. But they didn't say anything.

Wendy grinned. "Good. I'm really glad to hear that." She straightened and stepped up next to him. "Because I'm a little tired of you going through all of that, too. It's been a hell of a week. I'll be happy to go home and rest. What about it, guys? Are you going to let us pass?"

The first man laughed. "If you can get past us, you can leave."

The second man snorted. "Look at the two of them. They're just kids."

"Oh, absolutely, we're young compared to you. But we also have friends in high places and you are so crossing the line right now." She felt justified in warning them, but a part of her hoped they ignored it. She almost wanted a fight.

What the hell was wrong with her?

"It must be Tessa's influence," she muttered under her breath.

Ian heard her, and then as if understanding, he grinned at her. "Hey, don't feel bad, we're all changing with that girl around to show us the way."

"I'm all about picking the fight you want to win," Wendy said comfortably. "And making sure you can win the fights you start."

The two men snickered. "What fight is that? What the hell kind of fight do you think you can give us? And who the hell is Tessa?"

Ian's shocked laugh burst free. "You don't know Councilman Serus and Rhia, and you don't know their daughter Tessa?"

"That retarded girl? What's she got to do with anything?"

"Oh, nothing," Wendy said, hating that Tessa was viewed in that light. "She's just responsible for bringing down Moltere's Mountain, shutting down the blood farm, taking the hospital – and that's just the start."

The look on the men's faces was comical. Ian didn't wait for them to process the information. He up and kicked the first one in the jaw, then lunged forward and slammed his fist into the nose of the second man.

Both went down screaming.

CHAPTER 11

TESSA SANK DEEPER into the maze in her mind. On her left was the door to the highway Hortran had showed her. She needed to go down there – sometime – but not right now. She had to stay focused. And get Deanna into her place. Whatever that meant.

It was so weird to consider this concept. A few days ago she'd have laughed her head off. Now she was struggling to navigate the impossible mess in her mind. How was anyone supposed to do that?

This wasn't normal.

But she had to find a way. She turned so the highway access was at her back and surveyed the vast emptiness in front of her. The all-encompassing darkness. Nothing moved. No light shone to highlight objects or to cast shadows.

What was she to do with that?

With a deep breath, she called out, "Show yourself, Deanna."

Nothing moved.

"Damn it," she said. "Stop playing games. This is my body. My mind. You are a guest. Welcome only as long as you behave."

A ripple of laughter shifted through her consciousness.

Damn.

She frowned. Cody said deal with this and she wanted to,

but she was at a loss as to how. She considered the things she'd learned to do so far. Trial by fire, so to speak. Maybe she only learned under duress. When it really counted.

"No, that would be silly. Everyone would prefer to learn while they had time – not when the only option was learn or die."

Yes, her growth these last weeks had formed a pattern. But in truth, the pattern had been set by circumstances, not by choice. Now she was trying to settle this early before it became a life or death situation.

Too late, came a tiny whisper.

She froze.

Who said that?

"Deanna," she called out. "Is that you?"

Being inside her mind, it could have been her own inner thinking. No, that didn't make sense. She'd spoken to Hortran, Deanna, and Cody this way, but no one else. So her options were limited.

"Deanna, what are you doing?"

No answer.

She turned in a slow circle but couldn't see anyone. Then she stopped. What was she expecting to see? Deanna in person? Deanna in energy form? A ball of seething color? She didn't see much in her own mind at any time. Why was she giving Deanna a form when she no longer had one?

She closed her eyes and waited. She didn't know for what. There was a tiny brush. Then a longer stroke. She waited. It came again. Was it Deanna? She peeked through her lashes. A color wiped across her vision. She gasped. What was that?

Energy, of course. But whose? She watched it come back again then dance around her. A different color moved in then out. A blue color. She smiled. That was Cody's energy. She had no way to know how she knew that, but she did. As she identified one color, several others popped through her mind. Her father. Her mother. David. Seth.

"Seth?" She gasped in joy. Could it be? "Oh my, Seth. Is that you? Are you okay?" She fired off the questions, hoping for an answer. There wasn't one.

But his energy swarmed around, at a slower speed and alone, as if not quite there. She couldn't explain it. Cody's energy swirled around her in peaceful waves. Other energy darted and danced. Slowly she identified a few more. Her friends from school, Wendy and Jewel were there as well. Ian.

In fact, it appeared that every person she'd met recently appeared to be here.

How did that work?

As if the information was already there, the answer floated to the top. When she worked energy, she picked up energy from those she worked with. Sometimes they reached out for her energy hoping she'd save them, and sometimes they'd reach out for her energy looking to attack her.

In other words, she was carrying around bits and pieces of everyone she'd ever had contact with, and that meant a lot of energy given the healing work she'd done lately. There was a bright shiny energy that twisted and curled to the side. It looked different. She studied it for a long moment – then laughed. Jared.

"Hey, Jared." The energy froze.

She gasped. Leaning forward, she whispered, "Jared, can you hear me?"

The creamy yellow line wiggled. She laughed incredulously. Surely not. But maybe…

She glanced down to see Cody's energy. She reached out and stroked it. "Cody, can you feel that?"

There was no answer, but the wave of blue undulated as if he did. Like a huge panther waiting to be stroked.

She giggled and did it again. The energy moved under her hand as if the panther reared his head and butted her fingers looking for more.

She sighed happily. She didn't know what this place in her mind was, but it was special. Her brother was here. She knew that meant he was still alive. For that, she was grateful. Her relationship with him had definitely taken a hit last time. She hoped they could save him. He'd been drugged, was likely still drugged.

A second energy hung around him. She studied the orange rust-colored energy and realized it wasn't so much dark and murky as it was slow, sluggish, as if not in full health. She studied the other energies around it. Most were spritely. Dancing or moving with spirit. Except that one. It had the same sluggish movements of her brother. Her heart sank and sadness crept through her heart. That was her beautiful caring mother.

She'd turned into a dragon with those damn drugs. Did the sluggish movement now mean that the drugs were still coursing through her mother's system or did it mean energy, at the time it had come from her mother, had been drugged? Surely that was it.

The alternative was unacceptable. She kept a careful eye on her mother and brother, wishing they'd stick together. Instantly the two energies slammed up against each other.

"Oops," she whispered. "Did I do that?"

The energies stayed locked together. She couldn't decide if that was a good thing or not. Could the two communicate? If they could, was that a good thing?

There were too many unknowns.

She looked over at Jared. If he could hear her and Cody could sense her, was she able to communicate with everyone here? Was this like a major communication hub?

And if so, how could she use that?

Was Deanna here? Did Tessa have access to all the energies of those people she'd communicated with? She hoped not. That would be way too much energy.

Besides, she downloaded Deanna's memories and information. Surely she didn't download Deanna's *everything*?

She groaned. *There has to be a way to make this all go away.*

Instantly her mind went blank. The colors were gone in a nanosecond.

The enormity of the shift left her shaking. Where had her friends and family gone?

Please return those that I just sent away.

And immediately her world filled with color.

She curled up in a small ball, letting shudders ripple down her spine. And damn if Cody's energy didn't wrap around her. Tears came to her eyes. What would she do without him? She hoped to never find out.

Suddenly afraid of her new ability to have thoughts create a world in her mind on command, she knew that she'd have to control her thoughts or could easily lose something special – someone special. She was afraid that even thinking like that was the same thing. She peeked from under her lashes and stared around. It looked the same. So she hadn't damaged anything.

This time.

Good. Feeling slightly better, she straightened her shoulders. "Look, I don't mind having all of you around as long as you don't interfere in my world more than I want you to. So if you do what I allow you to do then fine, you can stay. If not, you'll have to leave."

The energy enmasse twisted in agitation. She sighed. "Damn. That's not what I wanted." And she realized something else. If the energy was here, it was here because she'd allowed it. They also likely couldn't leave on their own. She'd have to send them packing herself. But she didn't want to send them all away. That made no sense.

"Sorry, forget I said that."

Instantly, all the energy calmed down.

"Deanna, come here."

A red – a deep, dark blood red – slowly, sinuously swayed in front of her. How appropriate. "Deanna, I need you to stay in your place. I need you to stop interfering or trying to take over. Even if you aren't trying to do that, it seems like you are. Like your energy, your opinions, your thoughts…they are not my thoughts."

The same red energy twisted in front of her. It was silent, but there was a mocking appearance to the movements now. How that could be she didn't know, but there it was.

And damn if that didn't piss Tessa off more. "This isn't a game. You are not in control here. By my generosity, by my hand, you are allowed to stay. Behave yourself or I'll trash you."

The energy quivered before its form started to bend with angry movements.

"That's right. This is my body, my psyche." Tessa stopped. Then, in a hard voice, she continued, "You had yours forever. This is mine. Now stop, or I'll stop you."

And Deanna, laughing like a crazy loon, launched herself at Tessa.

CODY WATCHED TESSA'S body lying peacefully at his side. The hard floor had to be uncomfortable, but she didn't appear to notice. He had no idea what was going on, but it was as if he was a part of it, too. He sensed when she was disturbed. Knew when she was in trouble. He'd stretched a hand out and covered hers with it. It had seemed to help. How he didn't know, but maybe it was enough for her to know he was here. Her hands clenched as he watched. That could not be good. A puzzled Tessa was one thing; a thinking Tessa was a beautiful thing as she got that wild and wonderful mind of hers focused in a specific direction. An angry Tessa – not something anyone wanted to see.

He waited. There'd been no more texts from anyone else. He hoped they'd solve the problem of drugs being fed through the duct system or find the camera and security room to determine what had happened to the others. He glanced at his phone. He re-read the text that he'd gotten earlier from Ian, but it really made no sense. It was long and cumbersome with reference to Rhia and more drugs, to Jewel at the hospital, and to two men attacking them. They'd gotten the first shot in though so all was well. Even Ian and Wendy were in the middle of things. Why would anyone at the Council do that to them? A case of mistaken identity? Or something more sinister?

Apparently Sian hadn't shown up yet either. But they weren't worried. Cody might be though. There were any number of reasons for her to be missing, and none of them were good.

Tessa stiffened at his side, her foot jolting out and kicking him. He reached down a steadying hand. Her skin was cold, clammy even. He hated to see that. Tessa had one of the prettiest complexions he'd ever seen.

But right now there was a gray pallor to her skin, and she looked...old. As in seriously old. He shifted to peer closer at her face, and sure enough it appeared to have taken on a hint of Deanna's features.

The face twisted in anger, then horror, and was yanked away.

Jesus. She really was in the midst of a fight.

"Come on, Tessa. You can do it. Don't let Deanna do this to you. You're way more powerful than you know." Cody reached over and clamped her hand between his. "Damn it, Tessa." He watched her face, his heart pounding, his hand clutching hers tight. "Fight her off. Beat her at her own game."

Tessa's features scrunched up in a ball, then they relaxed. He watched carefully. Was that Tessa in there or Deanna? Another set of features slipped across her face. Jesus. What the hell was going on in there? He sat back on his haunches, his own belief system once again in shock.

"Damn it, Tessa, stop this. Kick those assholes out of there and come back to me."

Her face twisted again as if in pain.

"Stop it," he shouted. "Don't make me come in there and stop this for you."

An idle threat. He hoped. He had no way of going inside her mind and doing anything.

Except talking to her.

He frowned, noting the slack skin tone and loose jaw. Whatever the hell was happening wasn't easy on her.

That damned Deanna. She should never have picked Tessa. He thought about Bart and his daughter having gone through what Tessa had and not surviving. That had been brutal for a father to witness. If his daughter hadn't been prepared, hadn't been strong enough to handle that down-loaded information, then of course she'd have died. He had been afraid of Tessa doing just that.

He didn't understand how Deanna's force of will could still be in effect. The damn woman was dead – wasn't she? It was Hortran who'd been the ghost. If he'd been the one to download all that knowledge and then hung around, maybe it would make sense.

He thought about the bond between those two people. Was it possible that Hortran was helping Deanna survive past her "best by" date? If so, that would mean that Hortran really was a Ghost.

Wait, what the hell was he saying? That was crazy talk. Hortran was only part of the Ghost species. He wasn't actually dead and still here in ghostly form.

Right? Cody couldn't help look around the room to make sure he was alone. When the back of his neck broke out in goose bumps, he damn near bolted to his feet and spun around to face a new enemy. Of course the hallway was empty. It had been before, too.

What the hell was going on? He glanced down at Tessa again. She looked… He crouched down and studied her beautiful features – she looked normal now.

❧ ❦

"WHAT DID I just see?" Serus dropped to his knees at Tessa's side. He'd been watching her face as he arrived, seeing something…not right. "Surely that wasn't another face on Tessa's features, was it? Please tell me my eyes were playing tricks."

He knew it was a stupid question, but as he looked up at

Cody and watched that super slow shake saying he hadn't imagined it, he had to wonder what kind of nightmare was going on inside her body.

That damn bitch.

"Deanna, you get the hell out of my daughter," he snapped down at Tessa. "Just walk away and leave her alone."

"Sir, do you think that's a possibility at this point?" Cody asked.

"I wish, but if she can find a way to survive death and live on inside Tessa's memory banks, then that greedy bitch would do it in a heartbeat. She really doesn't care about anyone other than herself." Serus studied Tessa. "God, I hope she pulls through this."

"She will." Cody's voice was hard, but sure.

Serus looked at him, appreciating the confidence Cody had for Tessa. He'd proven to be a wonderful protector. "Thanks for looking after her so well."

Cody lifted his gaze. "I had no choice. She snuck into my heart and left me no option."

"I know how that feels."

"Is there a cure?" Cody asked curiously. "Not that I'm looking for one…but I'm wondering if this is a life sentence."

"Yes," Serus grinned, seeing the lovelorn look in the young man's eyes, "If you are lucky…"

☙ ❧

SIAN DROVE THE last block to the Council Hall. She was still tired. Maybe she shouldn't have tried to make it home to spend a little time with Taz. It seemed all they did was talk on the phone these days since that damn blood farm mess came to light. To find out Jared was at her home had personalized the issue for her. Both of the men sitting together in the office made her realize both were survivors of the same system. Both had been hung in blood farms and both had endured long enough to be rescued.

She wished there'd been more opportunity to get to know Jared. The more she got to know the humans, the more she realized the similarities between the species. That didn't mean she wanted to have more to do with the Human Council though. Lord, they were stubborn. They still sent regular requests for Tessa to come and help them. Some of those requests were demands couched in softer words and others were downright pleas. They were trying to clean up their house but didn't appear to have many tools to do so. They also weren't a harsh enough people to make good on their threats of punishment should people not want to talk. Vampires had no problem applying torture tactics to get what they wanted.

Humans were wusses in that department. But they took action whereas vamps sat around and discussed options for decades. But she still didn't want Tessa making the decision of who got to live and who got to die. She was a kid to the vampire clans. She wouldn't want her to lose her innocence until she was over fifty years old – preferably a century.

That Tessa was the only one to see the poison in each person – human or vamp – was disturbing, but it was also difficult in that no one else could help her out. Cody and Goran were happy to sort the people into each group, but only after Tessa gave the command as to which group.

The traffic light stopped her one block away from her destination. Damn. She'd gotten some very garbled texts from Wendy and Ian earlier. She'd set them aside to deal with Taz and Jared but now needed to figure out what the hell was going on at the Council. There shouldn't be problems there.

Sian pulled up to the next stop and yawned. She wondered if she'd ever feel rested. The baby was adding to her fatigue as well. She dropped a hand to lovingly caress her rounded belly. She was so happy. Of course this bullshit going on around her was a different story altogether. She just wanted it all over with and her family safe at home. If she could, she planned on taking Taz away alone for a bit. Just the two of them. There were a few vampire hideaways she'd like to show him. That he was going to die well before her was concerning, but she had hopes she might find a solution to that down the road. She knew he'd never agree to become a turned vampire and it was against her rules to do such a thing, but there was something she knew about him now that made her wonder about his biology. He wasn't aging at the same rate as the other humans. When she'd brought it up, he'd just laughed and said she was imagining things and besides, men who were happy were known to age slower.

She'd left it, but the thought of spending centuries alone…

The light changed in front of her. She waited for the car in front of her to move, only it appeared to be stalled. She groaned and looked out the windows to see if she could drive around him. Another vehicle was in the second lane and she had no shoulder.

Damn. She settled back to wait when a third vehicle, exactly the same color and model as the second one, came up behind her – too close behind her.

She grabbed her cell phone and sent a warning to Taz and gave him her location, and then she repeated the message out to her friends. She had no idea what was going on, but there was no room for error here. Not when she was carrying her precious baby.

And this baby was half vamp and half human. Something that many on both sides of that genetic marker might not like.

The driver's door on the car in front of her opened and a huge vamp got out. She smiled, a feral sound coming from deep inside the back of her throat.

Let them come. They hadn't met a wild Amazon vampire until they turned on a pregnant one. There were few pregnant vampires ever, and most hid away until the term was up. Not Sian. She'd done the same as Rhia. She'd walked around proudly. Screw her critics.

Now these assholes would see what happened when they threatened a baby vamp while the momma was still around to avenge the insult.

A second man got out of the truck in front on the other side. Then two men stepped out from the vehicle behind her. Her grin turned lethal.

"You'd better have sent more men than that or I'm going to be very insulted." She glanced to the other vehicle parked beside her. Sure enough, there were two more men getting out of each vehicle.

Her cell phone beeped. She glanced down to see a text from Taz. *We could use them alive to find out about Clarissa and Tobias.*

Damn.

She frowned. Then a second one came in from him. *They are after your DNA and that of the baby. Watch out for the drugs. I'm on the way.*

Drugs. Her blood froze then shattered into icicles. That would hurt her child. And she'd kill both of them before she'd let them have her baby – or her baby's DNA. She wasn't sure how yet, but she knew this was likely the end of the line for her. She closed her eyes. Damn. She thought she'd have more time.

She quickly texted Taz. Just in case – *I love you.*

❧ ❦

JARED WAITED IMPATIENTLY for Taz to get off the damn phone and point them in a direction to move.

He stared out the window. Then heard *shit.*

He spun around, for the first time seeing the doctor's face go sheer white and panic setting in. Instead of bolting out the door, he called someone else and immediately yelled into the phone, "Sian is a block away from the Council Hall. She's been surrounded. Get help now."

He'd hung up, but he was already halfway to the car. Jared raced to catch up, his own stomach churning. Jesus, was there no end to what these guys would do to one of their own? Sian was pregnant, for God's sake. And then he considered how they'd view her baby in their eyes. As an abomination or a curiosity.

Taz jumped into the car. Jared threw himself into the passenger seat and was almost thrown out again as the powerful sports car took off. With his door flying open, Jared clicked the buckle in place. The door slammed shut as Taz ripped around the next corner.

His knuckles turned white as he clutched the seatbelt to his chest. He thought Taz had driven like a crazy man on the way to the hospital. Now he realized that had been Taz impersonating a senior on a Sunday sightseeing tour.

He swallowed as they screamed past a line of cars on the sidewalk.

"Holy shit," he whispered, then he started a quiet prayer

in his head.

Before he'd finished it, Taz had run two red lights, jumped the sidewalk again to pass someone going too slow, and came to an earsplitting stop in the middle of the road.

He was also out of the vehicle, his tracks a blank whirr of moving energy. Shaking and so damn glad to be alive, Jared forced his fingers to unlock their grip on the one safety line he'd been able to grab – his seatbelt. Still shaky, he made it out of the car, realizing more and more vehicles were screaming around them. Great, he was surrounded by vamps again. Shit. The only place he felt safe was with Taz. He didn't know any of these vampires. And worse, it was nighttime. Nothing quite like it to make one feel more vulnerable.

He managed to make his way to the center of the vehicles and stopped.

Sian, the most ferocious look on her face, completely covered in blood, stood, spinning in a slow circle as if looking for more enemies. Jesus. Vamps were down and disabled around her, some dead and some still moving sluggishly.

Taz's voice cut through the night, a caring, soothing sound that Jared had never heard. "Sian, it's me, Taz. Take it easy, sweetheart. You're safe. The baby is safe. Easy."

A howl slid out of the back of Sian's throat. Jared caught the blind look in her eyes. She didn't know where she was or who was here. She'd gone into some animalistic mode and wasn't hearing or seeing anything but danger.

Taz kept up the same soothing tone as he talked to her calmly and lovingly. As he walked toward his wife, Jared had to wonder how he could trust her in this space. From the heap of vamps – dead ones, maybe – he knew she'd been on a killing spree.

He'd known she was capable, but to see this kind of evidence in bloody clarity…yeah, that was a visual he'd be a long time forgetting.

"Sian," Taz said, his tone sharper now, "It's over. Come down from battle mode. Please."

As if she'd been dipped in ice water and pulled back out, the shift in her demeanor was as startling as the shift in her circumstances. She dropped her head and closed her eyes. The crowd around him all sighed and the tension in the air cut back. It was over.

She was going to be okay.

"Taz," Sian's trembling voice said. "They wanted our baby to do experiments on."

An angry murmur whistled through the place, and tension immediately spiked as everyone understood what this had been about.

"Maybe," Taz said, his voice hard, edgy. "And they might have just said that to torment you."

She shuddered, a long, bone-wracking movement that left her slumped in place. Taz immediately walked through the blood and took her into his arms. He held her close.

Cheers erupted around them.

❧ ❧

THE NOISE DIRECTED Wendy to the scene. Ian's hand in hers, they'd raced out as soon as they realized something major had happened. With all the yelling back and forth, they'd gotten the gist of the situation. Now as cheers rang loudly around them, they realized that something good must have happened too, but what?

They squeezed through the black-thronged crowd until they got to the center.

"Jesus," Wendy whispered in shock. Sian, held tenderly in Taz's arms, was covered in blood, and so was the scene around them. The cars, the cement, everything was dotted with the stuff. And the vamps on the ground were in one large heap. A couple still moaned as they were tugged free of the pile. Good. She hoped the bastards paid for what they'd tried to do.

Then she realized something. "Hey, everyone, one more thing."

Ian at her side looked at her in surprise. "Huh, Wendy?"

"No," she said in a loud voice, "this is important."

The other vamps ignored her.

She put her fingers to her mouth and blew a hard, loud whistle. Everyone stopped talking and looked at her.

"Not only were they after Sian and possibly her baby, but they were also after her DNA. This entire area is covered in blood. I realize," she said, raising her voice, "that most of it is going to come from these sorry ass vamps, but Sian likely left some of hers behind as well. It needs to be cleaned up. These vehicles need to be impounded and decontaminated. Those assholes have enough of our heritage. They. Don't. Get. More."

She glared at the shocked surprise in everyone's faces. At the same time, there was an understanding and a growing respect.

In a louder voice, she continued. "Our numbers are dwindling. Theirs are growing through artificial means using our genetics. They don't get any of hers today."

She waited a beat, then added in a harsh voice, "Understood?"

There were loud shouts of agreements as everyone got to work.

"Wow," Ian said. "I didn't know you had that in you."

"I didn't either," she said with a sigh. "But when a cause is worth it…"

"Well, I for one am grateful to you for thinking of that, Wendy." Taz half-supported an exhausted Sian in front of them.

"So am I," Sian said in a faint voice, "But if you'll excuse me, I think I need to go lie down."

"And stay down this time," Ian said in exasperation, coaxing a laugh out of all of them.

Her smile wan but valiant, she said, "I plan to, but one of the men said something before…" She stopped and swallowed heavily. Several of the vamps cleaning up around them stopped and gathered around.

In a heavy voice, she said, "He said something about a secret weapon within that would destroy us all. And he couldn't wait." A dark rumble filtered through the crowd. "I didn't give him the satisfaction of staying around that long."

And damn if that look on her face didn't make Wendy want to back up. She was seriously scary.

"But he never said what that weapon was?" asked Taz, his face creasing with worry.

She shook her head. "No. Just that we wouldn't know until it was too late and that one of the ancient lines was now bad news." She shuddered. "The laugh he gave was horrible. He knew something but wasn't prepared to share."

"There are a few men left alive. We'll get it out of them."

With a nod and a grateful smile, she started limping toward her car. "I could use a chance to rest."

As Wendy and Ian walked over with, Wendy watched as Sian looked around furtively. Realizing they were alone, Sian said, "I'm afraid it's either Rhia or Jewel, considering they've both been drugged."

CHAPTER 12

THAT LAUGHTER WAS something Tessa didn't think she'd forget ever in her life – presuming she had a chance to live again past this point. Snaky and sly and freakin' scary, so not a reassuring sound. And from Deanna, in the situation they were both in, not confidence building.

But that blast of energy as it slammed into her body had her gasping in fear. For the first time, she realized she just might be up against something she couldn't handle.

"Damn right you are."

Shit. Another blast came out from nowhere and picked Tessa up, slamming her to ground. She groaned, rolled over, and got hit again.

Okay, this was enough of this shit. She mentally placed a buffer around herself in this weird space. She could make them all disappear – except for Deanna, apparently.

From the center of that buffer, she dragged her body upward, watching warily as bolt after bolt hit the protective layer. Like what the hell? This was her mind. Not Deanna's. It was Tessa's world, and Deanna could take a hike. And given all that, why could she not make Deanna disappear like she could all the others?

"Because I'm stronger than you." Deanna's voice reverberated through the safe hollow Tessa had created for herself. "Besides, you invited me in."

"In that case," Tessa shouted, "consider yourself uninvited." At the silence around her, she wondered if Deanna had left.

Then that nasty cackle came again. She was playing with Tessa.

"Deanna, this is my body. You behave or I'm going to kick you out of here."

That same laughter warbled free, the sound echoing throughout the hollow cavern in her mind. Wait, what? What cavern? Tessa spun around in a fast twirling motion. She was alone, standing in the center of some kind of arena.

She was in a huge cave with a ceiling so high she couldn't tell where it started or stopped. The floor was rock and the place was dark. Empty.

She shifted her vision, wondering that it made no difference. Then she understood that in her mind there was no difference because she could already see everything she needed to see.

She could also switch this up. If this was Deanna playing games, Tessa didn't have to play with her.

This was Tessa's mind. Her playground. She made the rules.

Deanna was the guest. And a shitty one at that.

She hated that sense of superiority Deanna wore whenever she brushed up against Tessa. As if she knew so much and Tessa would never get there. Yet Tessa owned all of Deanna's memories, so in theory, she could absorb it at will, and that made her the superior one.

"Never." The whisper was low and dark and purred forth on a growl.

Tessa's back came up and she crouched down, ready for that insidious attack. She didn't know if it was coming or not, but the sense of being hunted was inescapable. The predator and the prey. She hated it. She'd been there before and hadn't planned to be there ever again, yet here she was. And worse, it was in the very core of her own soul.

How the hell did that work? And if Tessa worked energy, why was she feeling threatened?

Because Deanna worked energy too. And in a bigger, better way.

Bullshit.

That same laughter rippled around the cavern, scaring the crap out of Tessa, and that was half the problem. As long as Deanna had her on the run, she was winning this fight before it even started.

She need to put Deanna into defensive mode and get a little of her own back.

"Not going to happen, child." The old voice was hard, brittle.

"There is no fight here, Deanna," Tessa said as calmly as she could. "This is my space. You are about to get an eviction notice."

She stepped out of her safe bubble.

A blast of white slammed into the side of Tessa's body, picking her up and throwing her down several feet away. Sore but more pissed than hurt, Tessa bounded to her feet. She knew this was ridiculous. That damn bitch Deanna was attacking *her* in her own damn mind. How the hell could she? She still had so much power. Even though it was only residual energy, it had way more power when narrowed into a tightly focused stream than Tessa could ever hope to have.

Stop it, she screamed at herself. *You're thinking just the way she wants you to think. Don't get sucked into that crap.*

Besides, Deanna's energy was in a limited amount and if

she was too strong now, then Tessa could drain some of it.

Tessa didn't know why she didn't just turf Deanna out on her butt; maybe she cared about her vampire heritage more than she realized. And maybe she was terrified to discover she couldn't turf the bitch out. Because really, how was she supposed to do that? Surely if that was easy it would have already happened. It wasn't like Deanna disappeared when the others did.

Besides, there was information in there that was worth protecting. At least until she could download it onto something else.

Someone else.

That thought scared the crap out of her. Do to someone else what Deanna had done to her – no way. Not happening. She couldn't physically or emotionally or ethically do that.

But there had to be a way to deal with Deanna. She raised the light inside the cavern. Instantly she could see the corners all around her. Deanna instantly lowered the lighting. Tessa grinned. That had to take up energy, too. Good. She raised the light again.

"We can do this all day if you want to," Deanna smirked from the shadows.

Damn, really? She so hadn't signed on for this. "What's it going to take to have you disappear, Deanna?"

"Nothing you've got to give."

Or did she?

How many times had she been put to the test and figured out the contest wasn't about strength, or power even…but about inner strength, and as Tessa had found out – she had lots of that. And cunning. And a different way of looking at things. All things.

So if she couldn't turf Deanna – and no, she didn't know

that she couldn't – but it wasn't her prime choice, but Deanna need to be stopped somehow. The filing system worked before for all Deanna's knowledge, so maybe Deanna should have her own damn filing cabinet. A box all of her own. Made out of something she couldn't open or use power to put Tessa into her own damn box – one that Tessa could open if and when she cared to.

Would that work?

Hell yes it would. If she could create anything, then she wanted a prison to cage Deanna so she'd be there if Tessa needed her. Other than that, she'd be incapacitated.

Tessa built a steel box inside her mind, making it thick and strong and able to withstand Deanna's blasts, and she kept it tucked out of sight in the back shadows of the cavern. Now if only she could coax Deanna inside and lock her up forever. Forget about coaxing her – that damn woman needed to be wrapped up in a tornado of Tessa and tossed inside.

As soon as she thought of it, a huge hurricane of energy whirled around her. Damn, that was good. She directed it toward Deanna, like a vacuum on steroids, and it sucked out everything in the cavern. Making sure it was a sealed unit, she proceeded to slam the vortex into the container and slammed the door shut.

She waited and listened. Nothing. Just lightness and a breath of fresh air. She grinned. It hadn't been that bad. It just went to prove that Deanna was only a shadow of her former self and although her energy might still by feisty, she had little power to back up that attitude.

That should take care of the old bitch – forever.

GORAN WALKED QUIETLY through the hallways, realizing that these corridors were narrow and dark, resembling more of a passageway meant only for the maintenance guys who worked on the equipment rather than for actual patients or medical staff to navigate along. That gave him hope that Bart truly was heading for the other canister.

They needed both canisters. They should be able to test the contents at the Council Hall. And if he could ever catch a break and be able to slow down, he'd be able to send out a few text messages to catch up on some information.

Serus had already gone back to Cody and Tessa and had given regular updates as he made his way. The last thing anyone needed at this point was to get captured.

Now he was there – alive but busy. Or something like that. These last few weeks, there'd been more instances like that than anything he'd ever experienced before. It was like Serus had put him on hold.

He sent out a call. *Serus, any update on Rhia?*

Serus's response was immediate. *No, none.*

Tessa? Or anyone else?

Serus filled him in on the attack on Sian.

He stopped in his tracks. "What the hell?"

Goran didn't know what to say. That was beyond bad news. And it wasn't going to get any better if they couldn't put a stop to this bullshit. And now. Damn it. He started running again.

With David racing behind him, Goran came up to a large machinery room and doors that reached way up into the ceiling high above. The doors were open slightly. He snuck up close. There were several vamps talking in a group off to one side. Bart was not one of them.

There was no way to get past these men so…he shrugged

and stepped forward nonchalantly.

"Hey, who the hell are you?" one of the men asked, a frown on his face. "You don't belong here."

"Maybe and maybe not," Goran said. He motioned at David behind him. "But maybe we should be here and you guys shouldn't. We heard you lost one of the canisters."

Fear whispered through the group as if some kind of major threat loomed. And it did, just not the one they were afraid of.

"We had nothing to do with that. That entire group was taken out."

David snorted. Standing beside him, Goran could hear his labored breathing, but he stood tall and strong. "Like we believe that. Where is your canister then?"

"It's attached." The men pointed down the long wall of equipment. "It's just being hooked up now. It will be ready to go in minutes."

Goran smiled, but the men cringed backwards. So much for making them feel better. "Good then. You guys aren't needed anymore." And he jumped them.

David roared and knocked down the first one, his silver spike reducing the first man into ash. Goran cheerfully spun a few times, loving the feeling of getting his own back, then decided they didn't have time to play anymore and stepped back to watch David dispatch the last of them.

"Good – now to get Bart and that damn canister!"

LIKE HELL.

Bart needed to grab the canister and get back to where he belonged. Without the canisters, he had no leverage. And he needed leverage. He had an agreement with the doctors. This damn blood farm business was screwing up his life.

He'd been good with everyone going about taking care of their own business. It left him in good shape to take care of what was important in his.

Not now.

Now everything was different. That damn kid Tessa. She started this mess.

Well, Bart might finally have to take a stand and finish it, too.

He had plans. Plans that needed to be carried out. But in order for that to happen, he needed time. The doctors needed time.

They couldn't fail.

He wouldn't let them.

So he had to do his part. Therefore, he'd do what he needed to do to keep them on track.

And that meant giving them more time.

In whatever way he could.

∂◦ ◦∽

IAN AND WENDY made it back to the computer room without meeting anyone else. They had no idea who the two men were or why they'd threatened Wendy and Ian. They hadn't stuck around to find out. When the men had gone down, the two of them had bolted.

Looking back, he realized none of it made any sense. Nothing in this place did. That room full of computers didn't either.

They stared at each other. Ian was scared to verbalize some of the thoughts running through his head in case Wendy thought he was crazy.

He desperately wanted to talk to the ancients. Any one of them would be helpful.

"We could ask Councilman Adamson," Wendy said quietly. "Or just wait until Sian returns."

"I vote we wait for Sian," Ian muttered. "I can't imagine what Adamson would say if we end up being in the wrong here."

Wendy winced. "True."

"Any idea when Sian is going to come back?"

Wendy shook her head. "No. She's resting after her attack. But honestly she's been working so hard, one of these times I'm expecting her to drop and sleep for hours and hours."

"Let's hope it's not today." Ian stared at his cell phone, wondering if he should text the others. Then he remembered. "What about Jewel? Is she okay? I haven't even seen her since we came back. Would she know? We could use her help right now."

"I don't know," Wendy said.

He frowned. "David wanted us to find her a cell phone. Is she awake, aware enough to use it?"

"She was in tough shape, and I know the doctors have her under observation."

"Fine, but where? Maybe we could find her and see that she's okay for ourselves."

"I like that idea. We've been so focused on this stuff and Rhia that we forgot." The chagrin on her face made Ian feel guilty too.

"So let's go. Maybe she can shed some light on what's going on."

He stood up and reached out a hand. Wendy put hers

into his and he tugged her into his arms. He held her close, loving the security of the two of them together, safe.

At least for the moment.

RHIA CURLED INTO the corner, her body wracked by shivers. She'd been drugged before, but this time her body was struggling with the injection. Had she given herself the wrong one? Too much? Not enough? Her mind spun and twisted, looking for answers. Answers that weren't coming. Her brain wasn't working. She was conscious but not conscious. Aware but not.

She'd wanted to be half and half but hadn't realized what she was asking for. She'd hoped to straddle the line between drugged and not. Instead, she appeared to be bouncing in a limbo of neither. "Not good," she whispered, rocking back and forth. "So not good."

And the pain – in her head, in her bones, even. Who'd have thought drugs would make her marrow cry?

Groaning, she lay down on her back, curling back into a fetal position. What had she done?

Through her gray haze, she heard footsteps come down the hallway. Oh thank heavens. Stumbling to her feet, crying out against the agony of moving, she stumbled to the door.

The footsteps sounded louder and louder.

Tears rolling down her cheeks, she pounded on the door, and pounded and pounded.

"Help me, please," she cried. "I'm locked in."

She leaned against the door, sobs ripping from her burning chest.

"Help," she whispered again still crying her fists giving

one last feeble pound before she slid to the floor.

JEWEL PEERED AROUND her door and looked outside. It was a normal looking hallway from the Council Hall. She almost laughed with relief. So she was safe. She grinned. After peering down the hallway in both directions, dressed in her normal clothes, she headed off to the right. She had no idea where all her friends were. But David had to be somewhere.

At the very least, she should be able to find a cell phone and call him. How hard could it be?

There was no one around for ages. She kept going in a straight line for ten minutes and saw no one. Finally, she passed several huge men moving monitors from one room to another. They glared at her. She smiled brightly, snuck past, and kept on walking. She didn't look back. She didn't want them to remember her face if anyone came looking for her. And they certainly didn't look approachable. So no cell phone there.

She might be safe here, but until she was with her friends or family, she wasn't going to feel safe – anywhere.

Surely Ian or Rhia…maybe Sian was here somewhere.

There was an odd sound coming from one door up ahead. She automatically slowed her footsteps. At the door, she stopped. A woman was sobbing. She frowned. It sounded familiar. Rhia maybe? She hesitated. Should she knock?

She hated to. The poor woman had been through so much; if she needed a few moments to collect herself, then she deserved it.

Resolutely, Jewel kept walking.

CHAPTER 13

TESSA LAY QUIET, her body aching in places she couldn't identify. Her mind floated in the aftermath of exhaustion. It felt like she'd fought a hard battle.

Had she won?

There was no response from the inside. Did that mean yes then? She shuddered, a long aching sigh working down her spine, bones, and legs. She swore even her toes shook. Needing to move – maybe to feel connected – she stretched out her legs, her arms, even her feet. She almost laughed. She could feel her body inside, her ownership, a hundred percent ownership, in every tiny molecule. Satisfied, she opened her eyes and smiled up at the two worried faces above her.

"Hi," she said, her voice low, sleepy, as if waking up from a long nap. "Did I make it in the proper time frame?"

"Almost." Cody crouched down beside her, his gaze assessing, searching into the very soul of her. She couldn't blame him.

She smiled. "It's me."

"Is it?" His tone was still doubtful, his gaze more penetrating than ever.

She let him look. She knew who she was. Maybe for the first time since the Deanna incident.

She felt like Tessa now. From this renewed feeling, she could see how confused and conflicted she'd been before.

How she'd been struggling to find normal in a world gone wrong.

"I'm fine. In fact, I'm feeling better than fine."

"And Deanna?" Cody asked cautiously. He reached out a hand. She grabbed it, and he straightened and pulled her upwards with him in a smooth movement.

She laughed, feeling young again, happy again.

No longer oppressed. Maybe not oppressed...how about no longer fettered by centuries of emotions and feelings, and knowledge of her actions, the actions of others.

Clean. Fresh. Innocent.

She knew she'd lose that over time, but it was precious. She wanted to experience this, a time of passage, her right as a young female to have this time. She'd get to Deanna's stage sometime along the way – maybe. She could see how Deanna's choices had made her who she was. And Tessa didn't know the details. But as if on a large canvas, she'd seen the roadmap of Deanna's energy and how the colors still weighed her down. How her actions played on her, affected her next decision.

She imagined it would be the same for everyone. After centuries, there wasn't much else one could do about it.

And if there was, she'd have to find a way. At least she had a sense of the end result; she'd do her damnedest to make choices along the way to give her a different ending.

Remembering might be a different issue.

Her father stepped forward, his gaze warm, and damn if it wasn't over bright. She couldn't check as she was suddenly engulfed in a bear hug. He buried his face in her hair. Tears came to her eyes and she cuddled in closer. She'd spent most of her teen years at odds with him, and all she wanted now was to stay here with him soaking up his love.

But she was no longer a little girl. And given what she'd been through recently, that little girl was now a distant memory.

Cody's voice whispered through her mind. *Are you okay?*

She clutched her father hard, sniffling a couple of times before stepping back. With a big smile, she said, "I'm fine."

He dropped a kiss on her forehead. "You are more than fine."

Her smile turned misty. "You are the best dad, you know that?"

"Damn right I am." He turned, wrapping an arm around her shoulders to face Cody.

"So now that I've waged war on the inside, it's time to wage war on the outside," Tessa said, a grin on her face.

With that, she strode between them and headed down the hallway. She laughed the first truly free laugh since she'd woken up after battling with Deanna. She couldn't be sure that Deanna didn't have more tricks up her sleeve, but she could hope so.

It had been the weirdest battle ever. How could she even explain? She couldn't, so she just shoved the details to the back of her mind until she had time to study them longer.

When she was alone.

If that time ever came.

Then there was Hortran. She had no idea what he was up to, if anything. He'd been noticeably absent in that go around. But he'd lurked in the background. Or something reminded her of him was there. But was his personality as obvious as Deanna's when he wanted to be? And if it was, could she access it? She had yet to have time to try. None of this seemed real. And that sense of being so far off the reality ledge kept her isolated more than she wanted to be. She needed to find a way to share some of this with Cody. He might struggle with it like she was, but then at least she wouldn't be struggling alone.

He'd met Deanna and Hortran. He understood the weird relationship between the two. Maybe Hortran had plans of his own in this mess. But if he did, if he knew more about Deanna and what she was at this point, he wasn't talking. Maybe energy always fought for supremacy, or maybe it was just that Deanna's energy couldn't stand that she'd been reduced to being the one not in control.

Either way, there could be only one. And as Deanna had said, Tessa was it.

❧ ❦

CODY GRINNED. TESSA was back. After worrying how much was Deanna and how much was Tessa, he couldn't believe it – she was here. Damn well about time. They were so far past late.

"We need to hurry," he said.

"Oh, why?"

"Motre is preparing against another attack."

She spun around, shock widening her eyes. "What? Why didn't you say so?"

"Because you were busy fighting your own war," he said patiently.

"Let's go, let's go," Serus said patiently. "He's got a large group of our people secured at the second floor. But they have been attacked several times. Many of his group are weak. They needed recovery time."

"We should have gone there earlier," Tessa fretted, running in front of him now. "He's going to feel like we deserted him."

"Well, he might, but Motre would know there had to be a damn good reason."

She seemed to ignore that. Then her heart was so damn big she wanted to make sure everyone was okay all the time. So far life hadn't worked that way.

They came to the elevator. She went to push the button then stopped. She turned. "Did we ever get hold of the second canister?"

Silence.

"I have no idea." Honestly, he hadn't even considered it.

In a low tone, she added, "And Bart?"

"He's gone. Just booked it."

"He's good at that," she said with a smirk. "I wonder if he's gone after the second canister."

"I wouldn't count on it."

"No," she said slowly, "but if the system can't work without both canisters, then maybe that's not our priority."

"Getting our people out is," Cody added. "I agree."

She bolted toward the elevator.

He groaned. "Damn her."

Serus laughed. "Get used to it, boy. She won't change much."

"That is not what I need to hear."

"Maybe not, but her mother is just like that."

"What? Stubborn, headstrong?"

Serus went quiet, then in a low sad voice, he said, "Yes, exactly that."

SERUS TRIED ONCE again to talk to Rhia. He wished she'd

never closed the door between them. His beloved was indeed stubborn and headstrong, but she was also compassionate and caring and filled with remorse. She was doing what she felt she had to do. He could understand that.

But it sucked big time.

He'd still couldn't believe the attack on Sian.

Everyone needed to understand what lengths these people would go to. That they'd tried for Sian, thinking to keep the child, brought a level of disgust and fear he hadn't experienced in a long time. It was morally and ethically wrong and made his stomach churn to think of other innocent and vulnerable women caught in their clutches. Sian was Amazonian. That she'd survived the attack was awesome, but a lesser female wouldn't have made it.

Still, she had survived and even now she was sleeping, healing. At least she was supposed to be. He could see her wanting to throw off her rescuers and make a run for it. Not like Bart, looking for an escape, but like Rhia hunting for her attackers.

Damn women. God, he loved them. Both were so different and yet wired the exact same way. And stunning in their loyalty. Hard to argue with. He walked the hallway, every doorway open and every room empty. He frowned. They should be here somewhere. At least one or two of them. Where could they have kept dozens of vamps? Could they have all escaped? At least most of them? If they hadn't, as long as they were conscious, he could get them out of here. If they weren't, then saving them all would be close to impossible.

Still, like his daughter and his wife, he had to keep putting one foot in front of the other and walk in the right direction.

Too bad all he wanted to do was snag up Rhia and take

her away. Reconnect with her on a level he hadn't been able to for a long time.

Instead, he was following their daughter once again back through the hospital hallways.

And why the hell was he following *her*?

Somewhere along the line, he'd lost control of the shy insecure daughter he once knew. And likely forever.

Thank heavens.

SIAN LAY BACK, eyes closed, on the couch. She knew she needed to rest, but at the same time she couldn't stand that Rhia was still missing and that they were no closer to finding out more about her own attackers. She was fine. A little bruised, a little cut. A lot sore. But she was healing. Another few minutes and maybe she could leave.

"No." Taz's warm caring voice washed over her.

Her eyes flew open. "Now what?"

"No, you aren't chasing after them," he said.

She frowned at him but lay back down willingly. Maybe she could use a little more rest. Then again, she had good reason to be tired. She'd been working long hours and taking no breaks for days. Make that weeks. If this mess didn't finish soon, it might finish her.

Before that happened, she was going to make sure a lot of nasty vamps suffered. Now if only she could figure out how.

"Did you find Rhia?"

Taz shook his head. "No. She hasn't shown up anywhere. In the Council Hall or out."

"I don't think she'd have left."

"Why?"

"She wasn't trying to go to the enemy, she was trying to save her son. She needed information, and the best place for that would be the computers that were seized."

"That would be the room Wendy and Ian told us about."

"Yes." She sat up eagerly. "It would. We should find out who those men were. Maybe they are trojans here made to look like our computer crew who were working on sorting through the databases for anything incriminating."

"Maybe, and maybe they attacked Wendy and Ian for a different reason. No point in guessing. We'll find out soon."

"And why is that?" she asked in a plaintive voice. "I'm fine. I can go back to work now. I'm not a baby."

"No. There are a lot of other people here. Let them help. A team is searching floor by floor. Ian has gone with them."

"How long ago? They should be back by now." She hopped to her feet. "I should go look."

"No. You are fine right where you are. If they were done, then they'd be home but if not, they won't be. Give the men time to do their job," he said in exasperation. "Rest."

Obediently, she lowered herself on the couch again. "I am resting."

"Rest more. Think about the baby."

"I am thinking about the baby," she snapped. "I'm trying to make sure she lives a long life without anyone attempting to kill her."

Silence.

Slowly, he lifted his head and stared at her. "Her?" he asked delicately. "A slip of the tongue, or are you trying to tell me something?"

She stared at him, her mind consumed with her words. Did she mean what she'd said, or...

"Sian?" He leaned closer, his gaze warm, searching, hoping…

"You want a daughter," she said in surprise. "Don't you?"

"I want a healthy baby and I'd love a son, too," he said with a small laugh. "You know it doesn't matter to me."

"But…"

He shrugged. "I'd love to have a baby girl to call my own."

She smiled. Inside, she could feel a centering. A sense of rightness. "Well, in that case, you're in luck." Her smile deepened with the inner joy blasting through her. "We're having a girl."

❧ ❦

IAN WALKED UP to the door where the men had been the last time he'd seen them. "It's this one," he said, motioning to it. He was sure it was the right door. He'd already taken them to the wrong door once and had felt like a fool.

"Here?" The first of the four-man team knocked on the door at Ian's nod. "That's what you said last time."

There was no answer from inside the room.

Ian shrugged. "Who knew all the doors looked alike?"

No answer. He knocked again. Still no answer. With a second questioning look at Ian, he raised his eyebrows and asked, "Are you sure?"

Ian nodded. "They were in there with multiple computer monitors all linked together."

The men glanced at each other then back at the door.

One of the men in the back stepped forward and said, "Let me."

The others backed away. He came forward with a funky tool and played with the lock. Ian wasn't sure if it was a master key or some kind of lock pick. If it were the latter, he wished he'd had a chance to try Tessa's credit card trick. But he had no cards of his own. Still, it would be nice if he could be the hero one day. Tessa made it look so easy.

There was a loud click and the door opened. The man pushed the door wide and studied the interior. It was completely empty.

Ian's stomach sank. Shit. They'd booked it, and these guys were going to assume Ian and Wendy had made it all up.

"This is the door and they were here." He followed the first man inside. "Surely they'd have left something behind to prove it."

He walked the large empty space and realized one thing. "It's *too* empty. As if they had no idea what belonged here originally and so they took everything."

The others looked at Ian, then at each other. "That's possible but hardly likely. They'd have been seen."

"Or they took the other furniture out over time so no one would know, and all they had to take this time was their stuff."

The room had bits of garbage on the wooden floor, but there were no chairs or tables, no desks, and definitely no computer equipment. They'd stripped it clean. He turned and walked back to the hallway, wondering if he could have possibly made a mistake. No. It couldn't be. He was sure this was the room. He walked back inside and closed the door. Then stopped. Something white was on the back of the door.

He reached up to snatch it off then stopped. "They forgot something."

The others turned to look then crowded around. "It's some kind of calendar."

Ian caught just a glimpse of the lines on the paper before

it was ripped off and they pored over it. But the lines, the dates, times… "It's not a calendar. It's a schedule."

They froze, stared at him, and then glanced back at the writing on the sheet. "I think he's right."

"But a schedule for what?" muttered one of the others.

"An attack? A delivery system? Supplies?"

"Ugh." Ian hated to think of anything from the Council having to do with the whole blood farm mess. Then he remembered the international members they'd rescued at the hospital. "Or meetings."

One of the men snorted. "Why would they keep track of those? It's not like they would be attending any if they were here to sabotage us."

"Unless," the man who'd unlocked the door spoke up, "unless he's planning to attend the meetings in another way. Those European delegates had been snatched from some-where."

"We need to check these times against any possible op-tions, but let's start with the concept of meetings. We've had more than enough of our delegates kidnapped. Enough is enough."

The speaker glanced around the empty room. "Let's get the lab techs in here to go over the room and make sure we didn't miss something else. I'll take this over to the Council and see if we can match the times and dates up."

He walked to the door, waited until the others all trooped outside, and as Ian walked through the door, he gave him a rough slap. "Good job, Ian. We'll take it from here."

The door was relocked before the four men turned and walked back the way they came –a straight line of silence.

Feeling left out and not liking it, Ian raced to catch up. It had been his idea. He wanted to help bring these assholes down. Maybe they'd let him stay involved. He'd do anything he could to take these bastards out before they came after him and his friends again.

JARED SAT BESIDE Wendy in the vamp Council Hall. Just being here made his teeth ache, he was clenching them so hard. He was waiting for Taz and trying not to fall asleep. His people were all asleep at this hour, but he wasn't with his people. Keeping his head low, he glanced around the quiet dark room. It looked the same as most offices he'd been in. Except for the windows. The curtains were open and the moonlight shone in – not that there was much. More clouds and darkness than light. Just the way the vamps liked it, he presumed. Once the Council had realized Jared was in the Hall, Wendy had been designated as his babysitter and he'd been given orders to not leave her side.

He had no plans to.

This was one scary place.

But Wendy was super nice.

And she was looking for the ambulance that had taken Tobias away. He could get on board with that.

"Got it!" she crowed beside him. "It did have a GPS installed on it."

He pivoted. "What? What has a GPS?"

"That old ambulance. At least I think it's that old one." She pounded the keys some more. "I found a couple of old ambulances that were retired and sold out of the hospital system. Three, actually. The serial numbers look like they were altered at the point of sale and were duplicates of ambulances in the system but out of service as they supposedly needed repairs. However, I found old documents that have different serial numbers, and those numbers are no longer in the system." She turned a triumphant smile on him. "Now I can track them."

"Wow, that's awesome hunting." He leaned forward, watching as Wendy clicked through screens and entered a password then a serial number. And damn if a crazy ass map didn't show up on the screen with a zillion colored lines crossing and intersecting the map.

"What are all of those?" he asked, trying to find a legend to explain what he was seeing.

"Let me change the filters." She clicked a drop down box and changed numbers on the screen. After she entered the new data, the map cleared to just one single squiggly line.

"What did you do?"

"I changed the GPS to show the ambulance's tracks for just today." She sat back, her gaze narrowed with concentration. "If we can see what this ambulance was doing all day, we should be able to figure out why."

"Can you put the street names on the map?" He'd been trying to figure out where the tracks led, but there'd been no names or numbers.

"Sure." She clicked a couple more keys and sure enough, now he could see the street names.

"Scroll in."

She did.

He leaned forward and gasped then jabbed his finger at the monitor. "That ambulance was at the home where I watched Tobias being removed."

"Really? Are you sure?" She clicked on something then tapped a few more buttons. "I'm just printing off this screen." She got up and walked over to the printer while Jared studied the screen some more. Then he saw something else. "Wendy, this may not be the right ambulance we're looking for."

"Oh? Why's that?"

"It was at the real hospital twice today." He tapped the screen. "That would be totally normal."

Taz walked into the room right that minute. "Sorry, Jared, what did you say about the hospital?"

Wendy and Jared quickly explained. Taz held out his hand for the printed sheet and pursed his lips as he studied the map. "Interesting. You're right, Jared, it was at the hospital twice today, but any of the normal ambulances would likely have done more trips than two each." He tilted his head and stared off in space. Placing the paper down, he added, "Sometimes they can only get a couple of trips in. Wendy, can you get a time of day for each of these stops? I could then double check the patients that were admitted, transferred, or released during that time frame."

"Sure."

Fascinated, Jared stayed in the background as Taz logged into his administrator account at the hospital and checked the times over. When they both sat silent, staring at the screen, Jared burst out with, "Well?"

He moved to stand in front of them. "Is it the one we are looking for?"

Taz and Wendy looked at each other, then at Jared.

With big grins on their faces, they both said, "Yes, it looks like it."

CHAPTER 14

TESSA SLIPPED ONTO the hallway of the second floor where Motre had holed up with the last group – and found it empty. Good. Or not. She had no idea where things were on the war front. It felt like she'd been out of the loop a little too much. Damn Deanna and her machinations. But Tessa was fine now, and that's what counted.

She walked faster and turned a corner. There was a group of men ahead. Their energy was all glossy blue and green. She smiled at them. "Any vamps I need to look at?"

They all straightened and shook their heads. "It doesn't look like it."

"Is that Tessa?"

A huge voice boomed out of the room.

Motre. She laughed delightedly. "Hey, stranger."

"Stranger?" He grinned. "Only because you're so damn slow getting here."

Tessa winced. She could well imagine. She'd been fighting her own problems. "Sorry. I was a little busy."

He nodded, already greeting the men with her. "Hey, Serus. Glad to see you in fighting form as usual. Hi, Cody, still on guard duty, I see."

Tessa tuned out the men as she turned to stare at the room full, and she meant full, of vamps. Some were in better shape than the others. But she noted with relief that there was no blackness coming off of any of them. That was indeed good news.

She spun around. "So are we ready to leave then?"

Motre nodded. "We tried to do that not too long ago but hit a fighting party, forcing us back. So—" He shrugged. "We backed off. But I'd say my group is raring to give it another try."

One young man slouched against a wall in the back piped up insolently, "Except that we were waiting for reinforcements. They are hardly reinforcements. A woman, an old man, and a kid. Like what the hell, Motre? We need an army."

Serus, his hackles visibly rising, opened his mouth when Tessa jumped in first. "I don't doubt *you* do," she said with emphasis. "We, however, don't. You're free to stand back and wait for another group to rescue you." Her gaze swept past the others. "Any of you can." She shrugged. "But your best bet is with us. Don't believe us? No problem." She gave him a feral smile. "Feel free to stay."

Motre jumped in front of her as she spun, ready to stalk back out of the room.

"So we have a plan?" he asked, eagerness in his voice.

She nodded. "We do."

"Glad to hear it," Serus muttered. "Cause if we don't, how about I just throw men out the window in a heap and when it's big enough, those left still standing can climb out."

Tessa laughed. "Wouldn't that be fun? No, we're going to go down the stairs just like you did before."

Motre studied her. "And what's going to be different about this attempt versus the last attempt?" He glanced back at the group listening in and lowered his voice, adding, "Some of them are pretty weak. The last battle wasn't pretty."

The others crowded around to hear her answer. She smiled. "You'll see."

And she left.

Cody hurried to catch up. "Um, Tessa, could you let me in on this plan of yours, please?"

Serus, from behind, called forward. "I want to know what's up your sleeve too, young lady."

"Especially since nothing has changed out there," Motre said.

"Sure it has," she said cheerfully. "I'm back in fighting form and could use a good dustup." At her words, she chuckled. "Speaking of which, where's Goran?"

She spun around to look at Motre. "I thought he'd come here with David to help out."

"Nope, no sign of them here." Motre glanced back at the mess of young injured and weak vamps mixed among those that had recovered. "Sure could use them though."

She nodded. "Dad?"

"I'm asking him – so far he's not answering."

"He went after Bart, didn't he?" She spun to look at her father. "You knew?"

"Sure. It wasn't a secret." He shrugged. "That guy is a loose cannon."

She thought about it and realized that it was a good idea. At least this way someone was going to run down the canister. So that worked. She still hadn't looked at the camera shots either. "We were going to go to the security room and check the video feed of what happened here."

"Don't bother," Motre said, "We took them down a long time ago."

She glanced at him in surprise. "Oh, so much for that idea. I'd hoped they'd tell us who was still on the enemy's side."

"Everyone who's not here," he snapped. "At least that's how we're going to handle them."

Tessa stopped and glanced back at the men following. She couldn't see any of the foreign delegates. "Did all the men and dignitaries get out safely?"

"Everyone is out except what you see here. We were only a little ways behind the last group, but it was just enough for them to move into position." Motre shrugged. "In theory, they should have well-shored up defenses by now making them dangerous as hell, but I've seen you do some pretty interesting things these few weeks. If you say we can go this way and handle whatever is out there, then I'm willing to follow you."

She laughed. "Smart choice."

"What choice?" muttered someone behind her. "Kill or be killed. What happened to my nice university life?"

"I'd say you got caught up in the blood farm roundup." Cody snorted. "You're not the only one. Lots of guys here did, too."

Motre spoke to Serus behind her. "Do you think they have another place to hide out if we can get this place cleared?"

Serus growled. "They do. We're still seeing way too many of them for them to be hurting for men or supplies, and that means they have places to go to restock. Grab reinforcements."

"How do we find and kill all those bastards?" the same kid piped up. "I'd kinda like to go back to school."

"We're working on it," Cody said. "The more places like this one that we can clean out, the more we can hurt them in a big way. You guys were all the next batch of recruits. Count yourself lucky that you're not further in their process to becoming enhanced."

To Motre, she asked. "Are you sure this is the last group?"

He nodded. "Yes. We've gone from the top down. We did a sweep on the lower floors earlier but didn't find much."

She nodded. That confirmed their findings, except that there were always rooms on these floors where people could hide. She knew Goran and David were down in the lower floors and if they were, then there would be others. "What about the nursing staff? Anyone see any of them?"

"No, we haven't seen any staff here."

"Good. Then we don't have to worry about them."

"What are you going to do to keep them from moving back into this place – if you can actually get it cleared out?"

"No idea," she answered cheerfully. "Not my problem."

Cody laughed. "It might become your problem."

"No," she said calmly. "Someone else needs to take that on."

"So delegate," he said. "They listen to you. You can set up a team and set them on it."

"They won't like me making those decisions."

"So? You're in a special position now. You hold Deanna's information. In theory, you're the one with the most information. The vast wisdom of the elders."

"Ha. Not sure how wise Deanna was. She made some shitty choices."

"So have we, Tessa. So have we."

She glanced at him. "Well, the one decision I want to finalize right now is the one that lets me leave this hospital. I'm starting to hate anything that stops me from doing or going where I want."

Behind her, she overheard Motre and Serus discussing the

attack on Sian. She couldn't believe they'd been so brazen and had attacked Sian so close to the Council Hall. And what about Taz and Jared? She still struggled with the concept of Jared in the Council Hall. And she hadn't even heard it firsthand from him. No, Ian had texted Cody. Like who'd have thought that a human would be allowed?

Things must be changing for him to be there. Then again, it was also overflowing with the intruders and foreign visitors. She'd like to be there herself. What to do with an empty building wasn't her priority. Getting out was.

Motre had said he had the last of the injured vamps, but she couldn't trust the enemy.

She pushed open the double doors leading to the first floor and walked through. The others followed. Ahead was a large group of vamps. A cry rose in front of her and they raced toward her.

The hallway was narrow here. There'd only be a skirmish up front, and no one else would be able to get into the action.

The group behind her groaned, and she could hear the collective back straightening and shoulder squaring as the fight approached. They might be injured and drugged and weak, but they were game. She could respect that. But they didn't have to fight.

In fact, no one did.

She'd take them out before the first punch was thrown.

Just one of the benefits of having fought Deanna and won. She understood so much more.

In fact…she drew on Hortran's bit of energy, wrapped it around her, and walked faster. Keeping ahead of the rest of her group, she added more wattage to Hortran's old bits and felt herself power up. She almost laughed. The system he'd used to kill was so easy a child could do it. In fact, she'd been using a form like that to do her healing work.

The lesson always was energy couldn't disappear. It could only change form. In this case, it was the energy of his enemies that kept Hortran alive.

And likely Deanna, too. Memories bounced inside her head. Of Hortran teaching Deanna. Of her practice runs that hadn't gone so well. And her successful attempts.

Later, much later, she'd have to analyze how she felt about Deanna's methodology for having such a long life, but at the moment she realized the trick was damn good.

Cody, stay back.

Like hell.

You need to. You'll get caught in the backlash.

❧ ❦

HIS FOOTSTEPS FALTERED.

Good. Keep the others back too.

He instinctively threw out both arms to stop Serus and Motre from following too close.

Neither man appreciated it, sending him dark looks.

"Let us follow, Cody," Serus said impatiently.

"You can't seriously expect her to face them alone," protested Motre.

Only Cody wasn't listening. Instead, he was watching as the men approached Tessa and fell, dead or dying at her feet. She never paused or slowed down. She kept walking in a straight line, and the men peeled off on both sides and everyone – as if they hit a wall of energy as she approached – everyone at the right time – collapsed dead.

She walked to the end of the crowd, a sea of bodies at her feet, and turned. She had a big grin on her face as she said,

"What's taking you so long?"

With that, she spun around and carried on down the hall.

Damn, she was good.

Such class. He knew he looked like an idiot standing there with a foolish grin on his face, but it was hard to shake off the moment.

The others had no such problem.

"What did she just do?"

"Holy crap."

"How did she do that?"

And from Motre: "Damn, that was fine."

Cody laughed. "Hey, Tessa!"

She turned, a smirk on her face. "Yes."

"You wouldn't want to teach all of us to do that, would you?"

She laughed. "Sure. As soon as you can see energy, I can easily teach you this." She waved her hands at the pile of dead vamps in front of her. "No problem."

"You did that with energy."

"Yep, now that I understand how Hortran did it."

Then Cody understood. They'd been told a Ghost could kill by just walking past someone. "Are they dead?" He was in the middle of the row, walking slowly as he tried to see just how they'd been left. He nudged one, but there was no corresponding groan. In fact, there was nothing.

"I believe so. We should probably check, but we don't really have time." She shrugged. "Let's get moving. Our men need some help."

And she proceeded to lead the way, the group slowly picking a pathway through the debris she'd left behind her.

SERUS HAD SEEN a lot of things in his life, but he'd never seen anything like what his daughter had just done. It was…scary. As if the men just brushed up against something lethal and never had a chance. He followed behind Cody, studying the pale faces around him on the floor. They didn't look like they'd been burned or died in pain, but more like they were so tired they didn't have the energy to live anymore.

Energy.

Had she stolen their energy from them?

Made them die because of it?

It was an odd feeling. He almost felt sorry for them. And he almost felt afraid of his daughter. He knew Hortran had somehow shown her how to do this, but she was becoming something he barely recognized.

He thought he'd hidden his confusion well, but Motre leaned over and asked, "What the hell just happened?"

Serus shrugged and explained what Motre had missed out on. The Hortran and Deanna mystery and what had happened to Tessa. Although he'd heard about that part through the grapevine, he hadn't gotten all the details. The telling took quite a while, with Cody interjecting at various parts.

The group following behind listened in as their shock quickly turned to curiosity, demanding answers.

"Wow, I wish I'd met him. I'd heard about Ghosts but never actually thought to see one."

"And chances are you won't now either. I think Hortran was the last of his kind."

"And you think he taught Tessa his tricks?" Motre asked. "Because that was seriously wild."

"It was. She must have learned from him, although I don't know how."

Serus frowned. "How do we stop it from getting worse?"

Serus muttered. Was this a problem, or was she capable of handling this Deanna mess? It was not what he'd hoped for his little girl. Then again, he hoped she'd just managed to have a somewhat normal life, knowing that being different had already cost her a lot.

He'd never considered a future like this. It worried him. Carrying Deanna's knowledge was something others were going to covet. They'd want the information from her if they couldn't get it any other way.

JEWEL KEPT WALKING through the hallways. She was beyond lost. The damn Council Hall was a maze as soon as you got away from the main meeting area and Council chambers.

She'd taken a wrong turn and ended up at a dead end, and somehow in the retracing of her steps, she'd gotten even more lost. All the while the crying woman was in her head, something she couldn't forget. If she could go back now, she would. And damn if she could find her way.

She stopped at the next hallway intersecting her path. Where the hell was she?

And why hadn't she managed to find a phone yet? She could send out a call for help. If she'd had a phone, she'd likely have never left her room; she'd have waited for someone to rescue her. Now she seemed to be actually going deeper into the damn building.

Why did the Council Hall have to be so big?

Her curiosity piqued, looking behind because she really didn't want to retrace her steps, she forged on. The hallway coming up looked promising. She peered around the corner, hating that she was so nervous but given what she'd been through, maybe that was normal.

The hallway was empty. More doors, but they were a darker color. Maybe older.

As she wondered what to do, one of the doors close to her opened.

She gasped and quickly pulled back behind the wall.

Had they seen her?

Shit. Her mind immediately asked, *Why should it matter?* She was lost. Not hurting anything.

Her heart pounded, her hands clenched, all the while her mind wondered if the newcomers could help her find her way back to the main floor. Or should they be avoided at all costs?

When no one barreled around the corner into her, she took a cautious peek. Two men strode down the hallway in the opposite direction. Two men so wide in the shoulders they almost touched the walls as they walked away.

She glanced at the door where they'd come from. It was slightly ajar.

Damn it.

Should she open it and look?

Nah. That would invade their privacy. So not a good idea. Yet…

RHIA SWALLOWED, HER throat dry and hard. She'd been locked in and had yet to find a way out. She thought she'd brought her cell phone with her. She never went anywhere without it – yet it wasn't here. She had to wonder if someone had come while she'd been out cold and taken it.

She'd woken up on the floor, sore, stiff, and physically exhausted. She'd also woken with a clear head. Just not sure which side she was on.

That she questioned that mental state at all said that she should be herself. Information and questions swirled through her head. Seth. Could she find out anything about her son? Had she shipped him out of town? Was he safe?

It took a long moment, then the answers started coming. The order to ship Seth out of the country. Germany. Reciprocal agreement.

Chaos.

Shouting.

Hitting send.

More arguing. Her frantic glance to see if the order had gone through.

Seeing the bar paused almost at the end… still going, going…

And the power going off.

She groaned. "Oh my heavens. Seth's orders to move him never went through."

The thoughts continued to control her mind as she considered the issue from every aspect.

It was all too possible that because of the power outage, her son was still here. Still a patient somewhere in enemy hands.

And it was all too possible that when the power did come back, that page might still be there. It wouldn't continue to send, but someone else might have seen the order and completed the process.

Or not.

Either way, she now had hope. He could still be here. She'd hold onto that and she'd track him down.

First off, she had to get out of this room.

Renewed hope had her genes pouring energy through her

blood, powering her muscles, and for the first time, stability to her emotions.

She could yet save her son.

"WE NEED TO follow that damn ambulance now," Jared shouted. He ran his fingers through his hair, struggling to hang on to some semblance of control. They appeared to know the culprit vehicle. They had the damn GPS number to track it and they knew where it currently was. Why the hell weren't they already there?

Because so many vampires liked to talk and talk and talk before actually doing something. He didn't know how Taz could stand it. He glanced over at the older man to see him, head resting on his crossed arms, eyes closed.

"Is he really sleeping?" he asked incredulously.

"Don't forget he works all day and it's his sleeping hours right now," Sian scolded. "And he's used to us."

It was on the tip of his tongue to say that was impossible; no one could get used to this.

He slumped back in his chair and closed his eyes. There had to be a way to get to the ambulance. He could drive. Did Wendy have a vehicle? He cast a sideways look her way.

She was staring at him.

He lifted his eyebrows in question.

She motioned to the doorway.

He glanced around the room, but no one was paying any attention to him. He got up and casually walked out to the hallway.

Wendy joined him. Glancing behind as if afraid they'd been followed, she whispered, "I just heard from Ian. He thinks he's found the men from the monitor room."

Jared's eyes widened. "What?"

He looked around. Had Ian been out searching the whole time Jared had been stuck here at Wendy's side in this damn meeting? And even if he had, what did that have to do with the ambulance he needed to find? Clarissa's time was running out.

"Where is it?" he asked in a low voice.

"Downstairs. Like way downstairs."

He shot her a long look. "I had no idea that there was as much downstairs as there is to this place." Torn, he admitted, "I was just thinking about borrowing a vehicle and chasing that damn ambulance down myself."

She grinned. "I figured as much. Come with me to Ian and we'll check this out. If it turns out that we are wrong, then we'll go with you to check out the ambulance trail. Ian has wheels we can use."

He brightened, then his mood dimmed as he thought of something else. "Wait, what if we find the room with the monitors?"

"Not sure." She shrugged. "If it looks dodgy, then we'll turn it over to security and let them deal with it." She added, "Then we'll go find the ambulance."

Jared took a final look at the room full of conversationalists and realized this was likely the best offer he was going to get all night.

"Let's go."

CHAPTER 15

TESSA HEARD THE mutterings behind her. She didn't know what to tell them. Things were easier for her now. And bigger. That didn't make them better.

She didn't want anyone to see her as any odder than she already was, but it was likely too late for that stage.

Especially after this.

Still, it had been totally cool to see Hortran's trick in action.

Trying to shuffle off the sense of being looked at differently, she strode ahead. The men had been clustered around this end of the hallway. And she wanted to know why.

There were several doorways up ahead.

She stopped at the first one.

Interesting. It was empty. She went to the second one. Also empty.

The windows on the left showed the dark night dotted with heavy gray clouds. The moonlight peeked through. The hallway itself was gloomy.

The atmosphere strained.

Too bad. She sighed and settled a mantle of indifference on her shoulders. She couldn't help being who she was.

And you shouldn't have to.

Cody's voice, as always, brushed through her mind like a warm hug.

Thanks. I guess that last display pushed them over the edge.

Just some of them. The others are still trying to figure out how to get you to teach them. And you just shot up off their respect meter.

Really? She laughed. *Good to know. I always wonder when it's too much and I go from something cool to something ugly again.*

Never.

She glanced behind her to see him rapidly catching up. She held out her hand, loving the strong secure grasp as he connected. He tugged her backward into the circle of his arms.

From against his chest, she motioned to the closed door in front of them and said, "This is the last room that they were either protecting or just accidentally standing around."

"I doubt they do anything accidentally."

Stepping back slightly, she pushed the door open. And damn if Bart didn't bolt to his feet.

"What are you doing here?" Cody snapped from behind her. "I thought you were after the other canister and the assholes that were part of that delivery team."

Bart's face turned ugly. He pointed at the almost empty bed on the side of the room holding the two canisters. "Both are here."

Tessa heard them arguing, but her gaze had landed on the beautiful, delicate-looking vamp female on the bed.

"She's so pretty," she exclaimed, walking closer.

"She is." Bart stepped forward, stopping her forward motion.

Tessa studied Bart. This wasn't the same who-cares-what-the-world-is-doing Bart she'd first met. Neither was this the one that she'd seen get irate over the drug canisters. This was a different side to his personality altogether.

She puzzled on it, her gaze going from his surly but ready to do battle look to the young woman in the bed.

And she knew.

With a heavy sigh, she asked, "Is this your daughter?"

Bart's glare deepened, but he never volunteered an answer.

"Can't be," Cody said. "Bart said his daughter died after that encounter with Deanna."

Tessa nodded quietly. She could sense the sadness inside the big man. The pain. "She did die – in a way, didn't she, Bart?" She nodded to the woman. "Has she been like this since that incident?"

As if understanding Tessa wasn't there to cause more damage, and maybe the compassion in her voice was enough to soften his stance, he nodded. "She never woke up again."

Tessa could hear her father's shocked gasp beside her. The men in the back crowded around, wondering what was going on. From the murmurs deep behind her, she realized some people were filling the others in on the story.

So sad.

"Was she not strong enough?"

"The doctors never had an answer."

"So she's been like this since then?" Cody asked incredulously. "That's a horrible way to live."

Bart took a step toward him, his fists clenched and his hard voice snapping, "It's the only life she's got to live."

Her father's voice at her side asked, "Tessa, can you help?"

"I don't know," she said honestly. And she didn't. This wasn't anything she'd seen before. There was energy, but it wasn't black. It wasn't old and gray and used up. It was just so very thin. And almost pure white.

She had no idea what she was seeing.

But she wanted to. She took a step forward. Bart growled at her side. She stopped and shot him a look. "I've helped a lot of vampires these last few weeks. I don't know if I can help your daughter or not." She deliberately took another step toward the comatose woman. "But I'm going to take a look and see."

"Like hell you are." Bart lowered his head and lumbered toward her.

"What if she can save her?" Cody asked quietly. "She's already not here in so much of the sense that we understand life to be," Cody continued, emotion threading his own voice as he worked to convince Bart to not try and stop Tessa. "If she *can* help, what have you got to lose?"

"No one can help. That bitch Deanna did her job well." Bart glared at Tessa. "I might not have been able to take Deanna out while she was alive, but I'll be damned if I let her live on through you."

Without warning, he launched toward her, silver spikes in one hand and some kind of weird gun in the other. There was an odd flash, a pop, and a bolt shot forward so fast no one seemed to recognize what was happening.

"No." Serus knocked Tessa over at the last moment. She fell slightly. Just enough out of the way.

The bolt zapped into her father's side, knocking him to the floor.

He roared.

Cody raced to tackle Bart.

Tessa screamed and raced to her father's aid. The wound ripped into his side.

She shoved her hand into her father's open wound, pouring as much healing energy as she could and with a weird chant, almost a hum in her head and uncaring of those around, pulled the bolt from his body. There was a mix of color in the wound. His, hers, more than she expected, and a tinge of Bart's, and then the damaging energy of the silver bullet.

But her father hadn't gone up in ash – he should have – but he was still here.

Except…was that a hint of smoke?

"No." She plunged as much bright blue energy as she could manage and shoved it deep into the hole, surrounding the open edges, stopping the burning from getting to the point of blowing up. The bolt had taken a piece of leather from his jacket in with it, protecting his skin. The rest? She could only imagine that some of her energy had been sitting in the space as he jumped into her place. The bolt would have taken a little more inside as well.

She poured more and more energy into him, wrapping the silver in a tightly confined ball before slowly raising it.

Once out, she lowered it to the floor beside him, watching as the blood gushed clean from her father.

She smiled. He'd make it now.

"If you're smiling, I'd like to think that means I'm going to live," he growled on a short gasp of pain. "That obviously wasn't silver."

"Oh, it was," she said with a big grin, "but it also took a chunk of your leather jacket in with it. That and my energy appear to have stopped the silver from letting you explode."

He leaned back and closed his eyes, but she knew. Relief was coursing through him that they'd get to live another day.

She was feeling pretty much the same. Still, he'd need time to heal, and this wasn't the place for it.

"He has to go back to the Council Hall," she ordered.

"Like hell," he snapped. "Give me a minute and I'll be fine."

"Like hell," she snapped right back. Rather than argue with him, she waved her hand and knocked him out.

Looking over at Motre, she nodded down at her father. "Take him and the others out of here. It should be safe now."

He shook his head. "What about Bart?" he protested. "I'm not leaving you with him here."

She gave him a smile that had him backing up.

"Don't worry about Bart," she said in a low, hard voice. "I'll take care of him."

❧ ❦

WENDY AND JARED raced down the hallway toward Ian. With Ian's instructions, they'd gone deeper into the Council Hall.

There he was. Wendy laughed and waved as she ran the last few feet to his side. He stood outside the doorway, a big grin on his face.

"This is great," Wendy cried. "I've never been down here."

"Hey, it's better than sitting there and listening to those crazies talk themselves in circles," Jared grumbled.

Wendy smirked. "Jared is struggling with the Council."

"Who isn't?" Ian snorted. "They are all idiots." He motioned to the room. "Come look at what I found."

The three entered the room. Jared made it a few steps inside then stopped and stared at the wall of monitors. From where he stood, he recognized the meeting going on in one of the screens. In another, Sian slept. So not good. Did these people know they were being watched? "Wow, what do they need with all of these?"

There was an odd sound behind him. He twisted around to look at Wendy and Ian.

And damn if the door didn't snick closed and lock behind all three of them.

Ian spun and took a blow up the side of the head.

Wendy, hissing, lashed out and kicked the man who'd taken out Ian, but another vamp grabbed her from behind, a huge vamp, making the fight short and sweet and before anyone had realized it, she was down and out cold. The fight was over before it ever started.

Jared stared at the two huge vamp males facing him. If Wendy and Ian, both vamps, hadn't been able to do anything against these guys, what could he do? He held his hands out in front of him. "Hey, this isn't my fight. I don't know what you guys want, but I don't have it."

"It's all right, Jared. We've got exactly what we want."

A third man gave a cold raucous laugh. "Yeah. We want you."

☙ ❧

WHERE THE HELL had he lost that damn Bart? Seriously? He and David had been going around in circles, but the evidence was clear – Bart had booked it again. He stopped and glared down the hallway. "What the hell, David? Where did the bugger go?"

"I don't know," David answered, gasping for breath. "He has to know passageways we missed."

Goran growled. "Where are we?"

David snorted. "Somewhere in the damn hospital." He pointed to where the wall changed up ahead. "I bet that's the stairs and elevator."

They walked toward the area and sure enough, it was the exit. As they walked closer, the elevator doors opened and a large group of vamps exited and turned toward them.

Motre. Relaxing slightly, Goran grinned, happy to see his friend. Until he recognized the burden he carried.

"Serus!" he roared and raced toward him, reaching his side in seconds.

"What happened?" he demanded harshly, his worried gaze going from Motre to Serus and back. That Serus was slowly waking up was reassuring, but that he'd fallen in the first place was too shocking to contemplate.

I'm fine, Goran.

Like hell, he snapped. *Who did this to you? Are they still alive?*

For the moment, but I don't give them long. Serus groaned slightly, his body twisting with pain. He gasped out, *Tessa saved me, Goran.*

How? Goran glared at Motre. He switched to speaking out loud. "Who did this?"

"Bart. He shot him with a silver bolt of some kind." Motre stopped walking to talk to him. "Tessa snatched the bolt out and did something to stop the silver from affecting his system." He shook his head. "I never would have thought such a thing was possible. One minute Serus here was smoking, then next he wasn't."

"Tessa did that?" Goran exclaimed. "Really?"

Serus and Motre and the men surrounding him all nodded. Goran shook his head in disbelief.

"And Bart? Where is he now?" He quickly searched the group, but neither Tessa nor his son was there. "Tessa and Cody are up there still?"

Motre answered him. He shifted Serus in his arms, reminding Goran that he'd been adding to the man's work. Goran stopped forward and collected Serus. "I'll take him."

"Good. I don't want to leave Tessa and Cody alone."

Goran was already marching down the hallway as the vamps behind him slowed. He turned and pinned Motre in place. "Why not?"

Motre, already walking back toward the elevator, said, "Because there was something odd about that scenario." He shook his head. "I don't know, but I'm not sure anyone is safe anymore."

Serus struggled to gain his footing. "Let me down, Goran."

"Whoa, you're not going anywhere." Goran glared at him and looped him back up into his arms. "Silver is nothing to fool around with."

"It's Tessa. If she's in danger…"

"Ha, there is nothing that girl can't handle."

Serus stopped struggling. He stared at Goran. Then with the color bleaching from his skin, his muscles turned lax and he sagged back. *I hate to say it, old friend, but I'm not feeling very good.*

"Hold on. I'm getting you some help."

He glared down at Serus, who glared back until his eyes rolled to the back of his head and he collapsed.

Shit. He started running. "Motre, grab Tessa. We need her." He waited, then added to make sure the message got across, "Now."

All he heard after that were panicked shouts and running feet.

JEWEL COULDN'T RESIST. She sidled to the open door and gave a long look down the corridor. What if they came back while she was looking?

Really, she should just walk past.

It was none of her business what they were doing.

Except everything was kind of her business now. At least if it was suspicious.

She'd never been to this level of the Hall and she couldn't stop the worry inside that it was a different area altogether, one that no one knew about.

Still, it was the Council Hall. She should be safe. She needed to be safe.

Resolutely, she dropped her hand.

She could note the door and tell someone else to come check it out. That was the right thing to do. There was enough going on without her getting into more trouble. She looked down the hallway and realized there were no markings anywhere. She had no way to know what door this was.

One step. Two steps. She went to take a third step away…and stopped.

She couldn't do it. Spinning around, Jewel walked back to the door.

Casting another look around to make sure she was alone, she pushed the door open.

FEELING INVIGORATED LIKE she hadn't felt in a long time, Rhia walked to the locked door. She tried the handle first. No change. She was locked in.

She shrugged, pulled out her a hair clip from her pocket, and in seconds had the door open.

Her daughter should learn that trick. Or maybe she should keep some things to herself. Although why she hadn't remembered that trick earlier, she had no idea.

Boldly, she walked out of the small room and looked around. There were closed doors all along the hallway. The ones she wanted were down below.

Way down below.

Where no one knew what was going on.

But she did.

Now.

Her gaze narrowed, shifted, assessed. She needed to go right to go where she was needed.

With one last glance to the left, she turned right and strode quickly to the staircase.

∂♥ ♥∂

CODY HADN'T SEEN that look in Tessa's eyes before. Then again, this was a new improved super version and he wasn't sure what she was capable of. He'd seen so much that each step pushed her abilities a little further, but this...

He needed to know that she wasn't going so far and do something she couldn't come back from.

Having someone attack and injure her father was bad enough; to know she'd been the target had *him* wanting to rip apart Bart's throat.

But Tessa had been the one to say that killing in war was one thing. To kill cold-bloodedly was something the ancients could do without a qualm, but Cody wasn't so sure that Tessa could.

Or should.

That might take her someplace dark – and would she return to the light afterward?

"Tessa?" he said quietly. "Think about what you're doing."

She smiled, but there was nothing reassuring about that smile.

"I'm thinking about what I'm going to do," she answered calmly. Too calmly.

"Your father is going to be okay, remember that." Cody couldn't help trying to talk her down. He knew Bart was living his last moments. But he didn't want Tessa to be living her last moments the way she wanted her life to be, too.

"Let her come," snapped Bart. "There's nothing good left in my life. Why would I want to live like this for hundreds of years more?"

"Because your daughter isn't dead," snarled Cody, trying to stay focused on Tessa. "And how is she going to feel when she wakes up to find out what you did?"

"What?" Bart exclaimed, then scoffed. "Wake up? Right. Do you think I'm stupid?" He hitched his pants up over his belly. "There's nothing to be done for her. They've tried for decades."

"Except no one had Tessa. And no, she might not be able to help, but you can bet she no longer wants to try."

Bart stared uncertainly at Tessa and then Cody. "She's just a kid."

"And has some very serious skills that no one else has ever seen. She's been saving everyone around you for days, just like she saved Serus from a silver bolt right before your eyes. Now when you actually have someone who might be able to give you daughter a fighting chance, you try to kill her father." Cody was roaring by the time he finished.

Tessa was silent at his side, but waves of anger washed off

her back. And waves of something else.

Anticipation?

He studied her closely. "Tessa?"

"I'm fine," she said calmly. "But Bart won't be."

"Maybe take a look at his daughter while there is still time." He looked for a softening of her countenance. When there was none, he added, "There might not be anything you can do but...maybe there is. You should find out first."

"Why?" Her tone was so reasonable and cold, he was at a loss for words.

"In case you can help her."

"Matters not to Bart's future."

Then he got cagey. "Maybe it will. You want him to suffer? Well, what if you save her but kill him, knowing that he'd lost his future with her?"

She shrugged, her hooded, unblinking gaze locked on Bart. A nervous, suddenly worried Bart.

"Can you really help her?" he asked in a low voice.

Cody shrugged. "She won't know until she tries, and as you can see, she's not leaning toward trying anything."

It was painful to watch Bart look for a reverse gear. Now that the possibility had arisen, that his daughter might actually have a chance, he didn't know how to make it happen.

"Then do it for her sake and not mine," he said in a deep voice, having dropped all the hatred from his tone. "It was Deanna that did this."

Silence.

Bart slowly disintegrated. Cody hated to watch it. He understood Tessa's stance and knew he'd be the same way if it had been his father. The fact that she hadn't taken Bart out already gave him hope that she could be reached.

The big man, now visibly shaken from being on the verge

of being destroyed from the inside out, finally burst out with, "Please. I don't care what you do to me, but help her."

Suddenly, as if a switch had been thrown, Tessa walked over to the bed where the young woman lay in a stasis state. She had an IV connected with blood running into one arm, keeping her sustained. From a blood farm most likely. Cody still hated to see it. To see one of his own people like this – it hurt. To know that Deanna had caused this – that was even worse.

He still didn't trust that bitch but as she wasn't here to face her actions, he could only hope one of her victims could help the other.

Tessa never did anything for a long moment. Bart shifted uneasily at her side.

"Deanna put her hands on either side of her face and said 'You are the One. You are the vessel I need right now.' And she started doing something to my Lacy. Lacy cried out and told her to stop. She was in such pain and crying out that it hurt too much and to stop. Only Deanna wouldn't. She said it's the way it had to be. She'd left it too long. There was stuff that needed to be done. Rulers needed to rule."

Bart frowned when he finished quoting Deanna, and the anger had returned to his voice. "What ruler? Deanna was no ruler then, and my Lacy is no ruler now. What does any of this have to do with ruling?"

Tessa sighed. In front of them, she reached out and placed a hand on Lacy's abdomen and lowered her head.

Cody stepped up, wondering what she was doing. Bart crouched beside her.

After a long moment, Bart asked, "Can you help her?"

Tessa slowly shook her head. "No, I don't think so. In fact, I'm pretty sure this is exactly how Deanna expected her to be."

Cody started.

"What?"

Bart stepped closer to Lacy's head. "What do you mean?" he cried. "It was an accident, she said."

Tessa shook her head. "No, this was no accident. This was a setup right from the start."

"A setup?" Cody felt stupid, but he didn't get it. "What are you talking about, Tessa?"

She shook her head and reached out a second hand, which she placed on Lacy's forehead.

There was a weird static in the air. Enough that the tiny strands of hair around Tessa's face actually lifted up.

"What's happening?" Bart cried out behind her as he leaned closer.

"Nothing you need to worry about," Tessa said. She tilted her head back, her face to the ceiling, and closed her eyes.

Cody could see something happening, but he was lost as to an explanation.

Lacy suddenly arched her back as if a string was pulling her up from her belly.

"Lacy!" Bart reached out to touch her when the invisible cord attached to her snapped and she dropped back to the bed.

She gave a great gulping sound that rattled all the way up her chest then her chest sank down, down, and down.

It never rose again.

"No." Bart dropped to the floor, sobbing. "Lacy."

Still shocked at seeing Tessa fail at something – if she'd failed – Cody didn't know what to say.

Bart looked up, anger and hate back in his eyes.

"You killed her," he cried. A meaty fist reached out to hit

her and came up against something she held in her hand.

The silver bolt she'd pulled from her father's body.

Bart blew to ash right in front of him.

"What the hell, Tessa?" snapped Cody stepping back and waving his arms from the explosion in front of him. "What happened?"

Tessa looked up, her gaze going from Bart's floating remains then back to Cody.

"See, that's your first misunderstanding."

"What?" Lord, he felt like something major had just happened, but he didn't know what. And damn it, he wanted to. He needed to understand.

What the hell was going on here?

"I'm not Tessa."

Vampire in Control

Book #9 of Family Blood Ties

Dale Mayer

CHAPTER 1

C ODY STARED AT Tessa/Deanna in horror.

She sniggered. "Yes, it's me, Cody. Surprise!"

No, not a surprise. Getting an unexpected visitor at your front door was a surprise. Finding an ex-lover unexpectedly in the mall was a surprise. Having a test come back with a perfect score – those were all surprises. This...this was a nightmare of gigantic proportions.

"I guess you figured your little girl could handle anything, right?" Deanna's voice, half-modified into Tessa's voice, rolled over Cody in a wave of sickly sweetness.

He couldn't answer. There was no answer to this. He wanted to leave. Hell, he wanted to puke.

"Well, she can't. She might be strong, powerful in her own way, but she is not me. And she never will be as strong or as cunning as I am." And Deanna laughed, that same horrific sound he remembered from before.

Dear God. Where the hell was Tessa? She couldn't be gone. No, it wasn't possible. She was too...too what? Innocent? Trusting? Naive? Yes, she'd been all of those things, and look where that got her.

He wasn't any of those things. And he'd be damned if he let Deanna live while Tessa died.

While Deanna's laughter mocked him, he reached for the spike he carried in his back pocket.

If it wasn't his Tessa, it wasn't going to be anyone.

"Oh, I don't think so, lover boy." Deanna lifted her hand and flicked her fingers.

Cody was lifted off his feet and flung back against the wall and held there for a second before being released to do a long slow slide to the floor.

"In case you get any ideas, I suggest you remember that Tessa is still in here. So if you kill me – you kill her."

Stunned by what had happened, overwhelmed by the ease of how she did it, he could only stare as the door burst open and men raced in, Motre leading the pack.

"Tessa, we need you. Now. Your father…something's wrong."

Shit. "Everyone out," he roared. Motre stood his ground. The others backed away. Cody bolted to his feet and raced in front of Deanna. "Stop. This isn't Tessa. It's Deanna."

The men milled around uncertainly. Motre stepped forward. "What? How can you be sure? We need Tessa. Her father needs her."

"I hear you, but it's not that easy." Cody spun to glare at Deanna. "Give us Tessa back."

She snorted. "Like he—"

Only to freeze, her eyes going wild, her face twisting into a mad contortion. She tried to move and couldn't. She tried to move her mouth to say something, but her lips shifted, stopped, wrinkled, and froze.

Cody's heart flared to life in panic – then in hope.

"Tessa!" he cried. "Yes, fight it. Fight her. Come back to me."

And not knowing how or why, but understanding she needed something from him, he stepped forward and placed his hand on her forehead and called out to her, "Grab onto me. Use me. Take my hand and come back."

A weird rent ripped through the air and as if unseen balls were bouncing through the small space into the confines of the room, the air shifted, bounced, turned dark – as if a war was being fought on the inside.

A war he couldn't see.

But a war he could feel.

Motre whispered at his side. "What the hell…"

"Yeah, my life with Tessa. It gets weirder by the moment." But he was grinning because he knew Tessa was fighting back. "Come on, Tessa, beat that bitch," he urged. "Come back to me."

ꝏ ꝏ

THAT BITCH!

Tessa struggled to move but couldn't… She struggled to force the walls of her sudden prison back and couldn't… She tried to talk to her jailer…and couldn't.

Shocked, she slumped in place, her mind reeling over what just happened.

Deanna happened.

Yeah, she understood that. But why? How? And what the hell was Tessa going to do about it?

A tiny fearful part of her mind snaked through her consciousness asking, *What can you do about it?* She'd been imprisoned by an older, more powerful vampire who'd played a game where she was the only one who knew the rules.

No, Tessa corrected. She's older, yes. Stronger? Hell no. And neither was she the only one who knew the rules. Sure, she'd created this game, perfected it even. Made the rules up to suit her, but she wasn't the only one in the know.

Hortran, I need you.

Silence.

Tessa shook her head. No. He wasn't going to do this to her.

Hortran. Where are you? You promised you'd be here. And I need your help right now.

"I wouldn't worry about Hortran, child," Deanna said in a mocking voice. "He is not going to help you."

Tessa stumbled over hearing Deanna's voice. She'd heard Tessa calling for Hortran? How did that work? Hortran had said he was there for Tessa. In what way was he actually here? And for who? Tessa or Deanna? Surely, as a ghost, his alliance shouldn't be just for the person who was doing wrong. That Deanna had been plotting to take over someone younger and prettier in order to live for another thousand years was something Tessa couldn't quite comprehend yet. She under-stood wanting to live forever, but what about Lacy then? Why had she needed her? Or had that been part of the smoke hiding Deanna's true purpose? Or did she need the younger Lacy's energy for this transfer?

Lacy had been consumed by Deanna's actions. Had Deanna no compassion, no heart?

Or was she all about revenge? Was this to get revenge on her husband's killer and everyone else connected to it?

In which case Seth, Tessa's brother, was in danger. Still, no one knew where he was. If Deanna did...Tessa needed to know what she knew before Tessa shut her up. How, she didn't know, but she wasn't going to live like this. Although if this was going to come down to a last man standing type of fight, killing Deanna might very well kill Tessa herself.

Or by killing Deanna, Tessa could end up in control of everything. And if she lost...well. No, it had to end in a good way. Tessa couldn't live like this. And neither would Cody.

Cody would kill Deanna if Tessa didn't return.

So not going to happen.

Tessa ignored Deanna's warning. But how to stop her?

You might as well give it up. I'm in control.

And Deanna laughed.

In fact, I always have been.

Like a chess game, Deanna had been moving the pieces of Tessa's life in order to win the prize, Tessa's body.

Tessa sat silent as her mind worked furiously on the problem. Except she was still thinking about all the moves that had put her in this position. Looking for a pattern. A weakness.

Her mind reflected on everything that had happened since meeting Deanna. She'd always believed in Deanna's good side. Cody hadn't believed the woman had one. It had been Tessa who'd so staunchly defended the older vamp.

Where did that leave Tessa now, a prisoner? Until when? Till Deanna extracted her revenge? Forever? What was Deanna's end game? Was it something dynamic or static? Was she out for blood or for the fountain of youth?

And now that she sat in the power position, how likely was she to step down?

Instinctively, Tessa figured that anything Deanna gained, she'd fight to keep. So the first step was to knock this bitch off the perch she sat on and lock her back into place.

Tessa had no idea how to get rid of her permanently at this point. She could hardly kill her. Tessa would have to kill herself for that to be permanent—right? Except Tessa had existed fine without Deanna. And returning to that state sounded perfect right now.

Dying wasn't in the cards.

Tessa hadn't worked so hard to live that she was ready to

be blindsided by this bitch. No, Deanna might have looked long and hard to find a victim she thought would be perfect for her to take over, but she hadn't seen who Tessa really was inside. Because she was not the same as anyone else, and she'd be damned if she'd become Deanna's little pet.

This was her body, her mind, her soul, or whatever the hell people called this consciousness. And she was not going to lose all she'd gained.

She tilted her head back, feeling a rage she'd never experienced before roll through her.

It started at her toes and rolled up in a continuous wave of dark emotion. Her parents had often warned her to not lose her temper, and she'd laughed at them. She didn't have one. Everyone knew that. She was the mildest-mannered person in the family.

Until now. She could feel the power inside her. She could feel the emotions as it rolled upward in a tsunami of red. Red like she'd never seen before.

It was the anger of righteousness. The anger of injustice. The anger of knowing she'd been shafted even though she'd done everything right.

A rage that once started, unleashed a powerful backlog of emotion from her lifetime...and knowing she could, she tapped the same indignation and injustice in Deanna's life. As soon as she unlocked that pain, that fear, that hatred of being treated badly, the tsunami increased tenfold to the point she didn't know where she was or who she was anymore. Images and sounds raged through her as she built up the force. A force she was struggling to contain...and she needed to. She needed to control this. She needed to wield this fury...this energy...that she had such an affinity for and wield it like the pro to take out her opponent and regain what was rightfully hers.

The herculean wash of energy built and built and built as the thousand years of Deanna's memories poured into Tessa's psyche. There was no way to resist the pull of this power, more power than she'd ever imagined. There was no way to stop what she'd started.

All she could do was ride the bullish rage and direct it at the one target in her mind.

Deanna.

But where was Deanna?

Inside Tessa. Inside Tessa's own psyche. But outside of whatever barrier Deanna had erected to keep her inside. Only the barrier no longer existed, the building energy having dissolved that minuscule defense system without even noticing the blip on the screen. Like the tsunami it was, it picked up all things in its path as it moved ever forward.

Relentless.

Unstoppable.

Closing her eyes, Tessa held Deanna in her mind's eye and concentrated. That bitch might be in here with Tessa, but – in Deanna's own words – there could be only one.

And she released the final hold restraining the fury and like an arrow pulled back taut, she let loose the rage on her enemy.

And collapsed.

GORAN COULDN'T WAIT for Tessa. She'd arrive as fast as she could to help her father. He knew that. That she wasn't already here meant she'd found trouble of her own. And that girl could find trouble. How, he didn't know. He raced down the stairs. Was it safe to go out the front door? Was it even nighttime? Could he fly? He was so twisted around and upset he wasn't even sure what to do. As long as Serus lived, he'd be fine. But he had to make sure that happened. "Serus old boy, you've sure done it this time."

To his delighted shock, a thin laugh swept through his mind.

I'm going to live. I don't feel so well at the moment, but I'm sure it's temporary.

"If you say so." Goran wasn't so sure. But the two of them had been through so much and had been close to death several times before. They'd survived then, and they'd survive now.

"Besides, I have to find Rhia." Serus whispered.

Goran had completely forgotten his friend who was on a quest to save her son. Save Serus's son. Goran was in doubt about the success of that venture already. It's not like the boy had been coerced into doing all the shit he'd done. Yet he had been drugged then mind-controlled, so maybe... And what about Goran's own son? If he could forgive Seth, Serus's boy, could he forgive his own? Especially now that he was dead and gone?

Tyson had brought pain to a lot of people. Pain with no way to forgive or forget. But he hoped with a little time they could all move forward.

Except Serus needed help first. *I'm trying to get Tessa to come and heal you.*

"She already did, my friend. She actually pulled silver from my body and stopped the rot at the point of entry."

Goran shook his head. *How is that even possible?*

I don't know. She said something about a mix of energies and that the bullet took some of the leather from my jacket. That plus her abilities seemed to make the difference.

You need rest and time to heal. She's nuts, but you're still going to the hospital.

Hate hospitals.

Right, well, that was a slip of a tongue. It won't be a hospital. I'll take you to the Council Hall, let the doctors there take a look at you. You can reconnect with Rhia and Sian.

Good, he whispered. *I need to find Rhia.*

Yeah, Goran winced. *Sorry.*

I'll find her. At least there I should be able to track her mentally. I'm no good to my daughter at the moment, so maybe I can help my wife.

Goran glanced out the windows along the long hallway. It was dark enough to fly. That was good. *Hang on. We're going now.*

He pushed open the exit door, took a quick look around, then took to the air, easily carrying Serus. They had been surrounded by the enemy earlier but as far as he knew, the skies were free. He only needed a few minutes to get to the Council Hall this way. With any luck, they'd make it without being seen.

Now to get Serus where he could be helped. He glanced down at his old friend, hating to see the gray color seeping into his skin. Using as much power as he could, he sent the two of them on a hard and fast flight to safety.

THERE WAS SOMETHING about this room. Shit. Knowing it was stupid but unable to help herself, Jewel pushed open the door and looked inside. At first glance it appeared to be empty. But…she stood in the open doorway and perused the dark space. There was nothing here. She laughed, relief washing through her. So it *was* all her imagination.

Better that than the alternative. She went to close the door when she realized how small the room appeared when compared to every other room she'd seen in the Council Hall. The others were huge. This one appeared to be less than half the size. Or were there two rooms here? She pushed the door open wider and turned on the light. The room was empty. And tiny. She studied the far wall, wondering if there was a second door. She turned off the light. A small bar of light underneath a section of the wall at the far corner said there was another door. And that a light was on in the other room. Curious, she checked the hallway, but she was alone. Stepping inside, she closed the door behind her and walked to the inside door. She put her ear against the wall and listened. An odd hum sounded from the other side.

There were so many things at this Hall that she knew nothing about, but what if there was stuff going on here that *no one* knew about? That noise...it was almost familiar.

She frowned and reached out... and pushed.

RHIA STOOD SILENTLY in the empty landing, her back against the closed door. She didn't feel bad but she didn't feel...right. Yet she didn't feel wrong. Images and sounds whispered in and out of her consciousness. Like when she was looking for the right word to explain her thoughts but the word was just out of reach. Now there was so much more than a word missing. There were whole memories lingering on the edge of her mind. Too far to grab and haul in where she could see them better and too close that she couldn't forget or dismiss them altogether. She knew they were there. She knew they were important.

But...she couldn't reach them.

And they were about her son. About the orders to keep him safe. She'd sent him somewhere, or at least had tried to, right? Maybe? But had that order been changed, or had someone else sent him away anyway?

Losing Seth would be the end of her. The guilt of her own actions was a crushing weight she couldn't bear. The disappointment, letting the rest of her family down, their lack of trust in her every move...no, she couldn't live like that. She had to find him.

With a deep breath, she looked around. No one from the Council ever came down here to these levels. There was no point. These floors were empty and useless. There was no need of so much space. The Hall's attendance was way down. Why was that? Where had the vampires all gone? She remembered thinking that their numbers needed to be replaced but hadn't questioned why or what had happened to reduce their population.

She was so confused. And with her mind wandering from one direction to another, she had no idea if she was on the right track or not. But she had the vague idea of a plan in her head. An important plan. She pushed away from the door and headed to the exit. This was the first step.

JARED STARED AT the massive vamps in front of him. The words he was hearing weren't computing. He was in the vampire Council Hall. He was with vamp friends who had helped him. Big strong vamps who were there to protect him And should have been safe themselves. Who were these assholes? Why had they attacked his vampire friends?

Ian and Wendy were still unconscious on the floor.

"Come along, Jared. We have a hook waiting with your name on it."

His blood ran cold. He was not going back to the blood farm. He couldn't. Not again. He'd see these guys in hell first. He had to. Jared shook his head. "No, you can't."

"We can do anything we want. In fact, we have been for a long time." The massive vamp sniggered. "You are not going to stop us."

"This can't be happening," Jared whispered in shock as he watched several males pick up Wendy and Ian and after carefully checking the hallway to see if anyone was coming, carrying them out of the room and down the hall to the exit. He couldn't be taken prisoner. Who'd help Clarissa then? She'd been taken by those assholes and presumably to a blood farm too. And she'd been only trying to help. No, he couldn't abandon her.

He was nudged forward.

"Move it." The vamp nodded in the direction the others had gone.

Jared tried to pull back.

"Oh no you don't." The vampire snapped his arm forward. "You're not going anywhere but where I tell you."

"I don't want to go," Jared snapped. "I really hate you guys."

"Yeah, like I give a shit."

The large vamp grabbed Jared by his upper arm and dragged him forward. "You're going one place and one place only. Back to the blood farm."

"The blood farm is gone," Jared cried out. "There's nothing left."

"There is always something left. Did you really think there was only the one blood farm?"

He'd known there were more but he hadn't wanted to contemplate it. But maybe, just maybe, he could find out more. "How many are there?"

"Several. Enough for our needs, that's for sure. But maybe not for the growing population…"

"We've done a good job decimating those up and coming numbers, too," Jared sniggered.

"Yeah, you have," the vamp growled. "But we're building up more."

"Trying to take over the world?" Jared asked.

"Going to take over *your* world. Humans are food. Need to be farmed properly. Bloody disgusting the way they live and reproduce. Should be shot. Every last one of them."

Jared cringed inside. "They're no worse than you."

"Disgusting. We're kings compared to you."

"Kings?" he snapped. "Then why all the DNA modification if you're so damn perfect?"

"Why? How about because we can? Because the technology is available. Because it's at our fingertips, and who amongst us can resist the temptation to be bigger? To be more powerful. To be better in all ways."

Jared could understand that much, but that was no reason to kill off the little guys. And he was running out of options. The red exit sign was just ahead. There was no one around to help him. No one to call out to. In fact, this area seemed as deserted as a ghost town. How could this be?

The Council Hall was the hub of the vampire world. It should be teeming with life. Instead, all the lower levels appeared to be collecting dust. He didn't get it. There had to have been many more vampires here at one time. What happened to them all?

Then he didn't have time to worry about the vampire society as he had more than enough vampires to deal with now. There were a half dozen at least. Between carrying Wendy and Ian and herding him, there were several others carrying large boxes. He wanted to know what was in the boxes but at the same time, he didn't give a shit. He just wanted to find a way out of here. The man dragging him along like he was a two-year-old opened a vehicle and shoved him into the back of a van. He ended up on his knees on the floor beside Wendy and Ian, both still unconscious.

Gathering his wits, he spun around and shoved the door open. And met a fist head on.

It cracked against his nose and propelled him backwards into the van beside his friends.

"Now stay there."

And the door slammed shut. This time, he heard several clicks outside the van door. They were locked in.

CHAPTER 2

TESSA PEERED THROUGH her eyelashes. Was she back in control? She hurt everywhere, but inside there was a weird emptiness. As if she'd burnt to a crisp and been reborn. There was even a leftover smell of ash.

Including a weird smokiness to the space around her. Was that inside her head or outside? She barely knew what had happened in this room but could see the events as they'd played out in Deanna's hands. She'd killed Bart. Or had that been Tessa at that point? God, she'd been mad. Thinking in a red rage and not with her emotions under control. But she wasn't sure it had been her. She'd felt her hands doing the act, but she hadn't been able to stop herself from acting. Deanna? Maybe Tessa also hadn't had time to save Lacy. That was even more devastating. She'd been beautiful and so young to have gone through so much. Innocent, she'd only wanted to help Deanna.

A tragedy. And one that Tessa wasn't sure she understood yet.

It had been her intention to help, but somehow Deanna had taken over. And what exactly had Deanna done? It's not like there was any part of Lacy living inside her...was there? Stumped, she considered that question and realized that it was all too possible. There was energy all around her. Anyone she touched would have left her energy here, so why not Lacy?

If she'd been inside that young woman, then she should now have bits and pieces of Lacy within her. Except she couldn't feel anything. Was that after the purging fire? Or was it because there'd been nothing left of Lacy to absorb?

If that was the case, then Lacy had been just a shell and likely existing on Deanna's energy. A neat trick on Deanna's part. And not easy, but as Lacy was basically comatose, keeping her in that state wouldn't require much effort.

Only this had been going on for years.

Deanna was powerful, as she'd proven already, but keeping that young girl alive for all that time? Why? What did Deanna gain from it?

And if Tessa couldn't feel Lacy, could she still feel Deanna? Her eyes drifted close as she sent out feelers in all directions. She wanted to believe she was gone. Or at least been reduced so small in power to the point of no longer taking over, but she couldn't trust Deanna. She'd been so damn sneaky before. And besides, with all the fire going on, where was Hortran? Had he disintegrated in that fire? Or had he some way to survive as well? In which case, had he saved Deanna? Or maybe vice versa.

Not feeling quite right but so damn happy to be back, she raised her hand and touched her temple. She could feel skin, soft and supple. It felt...with a surge of relief, she realized it felt normal.

She opened her eyes and slammed them close again. The room was so white... So bright.

She was in the damn hospital. The burning she smelled was from the last attack. The ash belonged to Bart. She frowned. He'd attacked her father. Yet she understood. He'd believed that Deanna had hurt his daughter. He was so focused on revenge...like Deanna.

And maybe like Tessa. She'd wanted to bring the blood farms to the ground and get her brother back. Seth was in danger. These assholes had caused her and her family untold pain and heartache, and it wasn't over. The need to save her family, to put a stop to this nightmare, was overriding her judgement.

As Deanna's emotions had overrode her judgement, too.

Tessa let her head, heavy and unwieldy as she struggled to 'fit' back into her body, roll to the side, her gaze falling on a beloved face.

Cody held his head in his hands. His body slumped at the end of the bed.

Had he seen this fight? She could remember hearing him talk to Deanna...vaguely.

His dejected look had her heart warming. God, she loved this man. "Cody?" she whispered his name into the empty room. He froze then slowly raised his head to look at her.

She smiled at him, her lips actually moving in an upward motion. "Hey?"

He frowned.

Not the reaction she was hoping for.

He moved closer, his gaze narrow, assessing.

"It's me," she tried to reassure him. "Honest."

"Is it?" he said in a hard voice. "How can I tell?"

She frowned. "I gather you had a conversation or two with Deanna while she had me locked up?"

"You could say that. She caused a fair bit of damage in her little rampage."

He spoke the right words, but not in the right tone. It was irritating but understandable. Still, she needed him to believe her.

"Well, I'm not Deanna."

"You might not be right now, but that doesn't mean she's not lurking, ready to take over at any moment. She killed Lacy. Killed Bart…"

"I know. I could feel her actions, knew what she was doing, but couldn't control my body. Couldn't stop her." Tessa swung her legs over the side of the bed and sat up slowly.

"Prove it…"

She stared at him. "How?"

He stared at her. "Who was the human male we found when we were first looking for Jared?"

Instantly, the man's name popped into her mind. She'd never been able to forget him. "Wallace Carstairs."

He leaned back slightly, surprised at her answer.

"Believe me now?"

He frowned. "I'm not sure," he said grudgingly. "Maybe. You sound different."

"Different how?"

"Younger? Normal?" Cody studied her face. "But Deanna fooled me, too."

"Did she sound like me?" Tessa asked curiously. "Really?"

"Yeah," Cody frowned. "Well, maybe not." He leaned back. "Only maybe it was because of the confusion at the time. The utter chaos. There was no time to think. No time to figure out if there had been a different person speaking. I was expecting to hear you, so I heard you. Until I understood the words."

That made a weird kind of sense. She stood slowly, her body achy and slow to respond. But it was answering her commands, so that was all good. She took a few shaky steps, trying to avoid the pile of ash that had been Bart. The bed was covered with Lacy's remains, too. This whole place was a death trap. It was supposed to be a hospital, but instead it was a funeral home. It was all she'd seen since she'd been here. And she was so done with killing.

Except that didn't mean she could stop just yet. It wasn't possible until this war was over. In fact, there were several more traitors she had to take care of. She rotated her neck, turned, and faced the door. She needed her power back. That, along with Deanna, appeared to be long gone. And that was dangerous as hell.

She turned to face Cody, hating the distrust, the distance between them, and asked, "Ready?"

❧ ❧

CODY DIDN'T KNOW what to think. He'd watched Deanna take over Tessa in such a way that no one knew until it was too late. Tessa hadn't even known until Deanna had her locked up. Then just as quickly as it started, the air calmed as if a breeze had blown through the room and taken all the old stale air with it, leaving something fresh and renewed in its wake.

Now that she'd managed to wrestle control back – if she'd managed to regain control – and that was a big if at the moment – was Deanna going to do that all over again? Because he didn't know if he could trust Tessa again if that was the case.

And it was killing him. He didn't want to doubt her. He wanted to believe in her. He wanted to have the same relationship they'd had before.

Inside his head, she said, *And we can have that again. It's not something we've never not had. I could hear you in my head, but Deanna had taken over and I couldn't get into your head. The highway had become one way only.*

Highway? What the hell?

Yeah, I see the communication between us as doors and highways. It's easy to open and close, but sometimes there's a ton of traffic and I can't get through to you. While Deanna was in control, the traffic was like a super highway.

A super highway? She smiled at him as if he could understand. There was *no* understanding this.

When he didn't answer, she frowned and asked, "What is the mind-speak like? How is it for you?"

"I just hear your voice in my head speaking to me normally. No doors. No highway."

She nodded. "Right. Maybe the highway was due to Hortran. Remember, I opened that door and there was all kinds of road-looking waves where I could supposedly communicate with more people using that system. When I get better at it, I think I'll be able to communicate with other vamps."

"I can't imagine. It's enough that I hear you. I can't imagine trying to talk to a dozen people."

She kicked her legs out one at a time. He watched as she gave each arm a shake then a body wiggle. As much as he was enjoying the view, he had to wonder...

Then she strode to the open doorway. She spun back, stared at him briefly, and said, "Where are we at in this war?"

Her complete shift in topic left him standing behind her in shock. He raced to catch up. "My father took your dad back to Council Hall to recover there."

She froze. "Is he okay?"

Cody was grateful that Motre, who stood watch outside the door, had brought an update with him. No one else knew about the Deanna moments. He needed to keep it that way. And he needed to find a moment with Motre and let him know to keep an eye out for that witch, too.

His back pocket jingled with the silver spike he'd put away. He wasn't going to let Deanna win this fight. She'd die before he'd let her live in Tessa's body. Tessa was his. And he'd make that decision if she lived or died.

"You won't have to," Tessa called back to him, reading his mind as effortlessly as ever. "She's not going to take over my life again."

So she said, but he wasn't so sure.

∂ ❦

RHIA WALKED DOWN the hallway, her mind cataloging off the rooms as she went. She was on the wrong floor. And she didn't want to meet anyone on the way. She needed to be alone to do this. And she needed to do it fast. Her son could already be on his way out of the country. It was too horrible to contemplate.

"It's all too damn much." She reached the stairwell, took a quick glance around, and slipped through the doors. The exit she wanted was one floor down. Now to get there fast. She quickly raced down the stairs and outside. A large van was parked to one side. She studied it carefully but couldn't see anyone in the front. It appeared to be empty. The driver had to be in the Hall. Why? Spinning, she studied the doors behind her, realizing that the driver could be returning at any time.

Still, it was wheels, and she could use a set herself. There would be vehicles she could borrow up at the main parking lot, but she didn't want to risk being seen.

Walking closer to the van, she looked in the driver's side. There were no keys in the ignition. She'd have to find a way to start it. Or she could sneak into the back and catch a ride out. But if it was empty inside, then she'd be seen.

She peered in through the side window. There were blankets on the floor. Hearing sounds from the exit, she crouched down beside the passenger door to stay out of sight.

"They aren't going to be happy that we don't have it all."

"We do have it all. There weren't any other boxes to collect."

"They said ten boxes. But we only picked up eight."

"There weren't any others though, which means we've got it all." The speaker's frustration snapped his voice higher at the end. "Look, we've got two new vampire offerings. They will be happy with us. We also got the asshole Jared. So they will be doubly happy with us."

Rhea's breath caught in the back of her throat. They had Jared? She stopped to think. Was that a good thing? Jared had escaped before. She'd helped him rescue the other prisoners. So this wasn't a good thing. But somewhere in the back of her mind, she realized that *some* part of her thought it was a good thing. She shuddered as the conflicting information swept through her, followed by her reactions. *Help him.*

Don't help him.

What the hell was she supposed to do? If she opened the van door, she could pull Jared out. And what about the others that were in there? Who were they? If they were with Jared, she'd likely know them too. So...she should help them all. Except the part of her that was fighting this information was saying having them captive was a good thing. *They needed vampires for testing. They needed the DNA of a specific few. They needed new vampires for their army.*

Army? At that, the information slid back down the back of her mind to let the rest of her knowledge come front and center. These assholes were part of the blood farm. She needed to help *her* people. But more than that, she needed to save her son.

Just when she didn't think she'd be able to act, torn in two as she was, one of the men walked around the van and caught sight of her.

"Hey, what the hell are you doing here? You were in the blood farm last I saw you."

And that was the opportunity she needed to do both jobs.

"I was. I'm trying to get back there. Can you give me a lift, please?"

JARED HEARD THE van doors open again but he couldn't move for the pain reverberating down his spine. These assholes were strong. Super strong. They didn't know their own strength. The blow to his head could have killed him. He understood they considered humans expendable, but surely they needed everyone they could get right now. Unless they had rebuilt and restocked all the blood farms already. He thought that's why he'd been kidnapped in the first place.

And they'd been after him since he'd escaped.

They'd finally caught him. He opened his eyes a slit to see a beautiful woman get in and step over him and his friends to sit on several boxes stacked up toward the front.

His heart pounded in relief. That was Rhia. Tessa's mother. *Thank God.* Then he remembered all the bits and pieces he'd heard from the other vamps about her being drugged and brainwashed and how she'd gone missing. He held himself still as he tried to figure out what her presence here meant. Was she on the bad side? Had she ever left it? Had their brainwashing been so complete that she fought all her natural memories and was an enemy now? Hadn't Wendy said something about Rhia searching for more drugs? So that made her a junkie, right? He couldn't reconcile the beautiful women who'd helped him with the concept of her being a mindless junkie now. Surely she was made of sterner stuff.

Then he'd seen firsthand how the drugs worked and the damage they caused people who had actively fought against them. There were vamps who had willingly signed up for more, and then there were those who'd been injected as a sort of a live research test case. In each case, the drugs managed to overcome the person's natural instincts to be themselves.

Like Rhia.

So he had to assume that she wasn't here for a rescue. Unfortunately.

When the van started up and drove forward slightly, he knew they were out of time. It was now or never. He tried to lurch toward the double doors, but his legs weren't cooperating. Whatever blow he'd taken, it had partially paralyzed him. He lifted an arm, but it flopped down again almost immediately.

And landed on his hip and thigh. He clenched his fingers, and they closed around something odd. He realized that the men were so sure of their power over him that they hadn't searched for or removed his cell phone.

Excitement gave him strength. Now to send a message without being caught. As the van turned to go around a corner, rising up through the ranks of the underground parking lot, his body listed with the heavy movement. Good. Out of sight of the boxes. He pulled out his cell phone and managed to get it up in front of him. On the next heavy corner, he rolled over to face the side panel of the van and muted his phone.

He quickly texted everyone he knew who could help. He sent several texts in succession.

Help.

Caught by vamps.

Have Ian and Wendy too. Need help. Need to find Clarissa too.

Taken out of basement of Council Hall by van.

Heading to blood farm

Rhia's here too.

Please. HELP

His fingers stumbled through the letters and finally collapsed as his arm gave out and he realized something else. It wasn't a case of the injury causing a temporary paralysis and his body would slowly wake up. It was the reverse, the paralysis was slowly overtaking his body.

Soon he wouldn't be able to move at all.

In a last-ditch effort to keep his phone a secret, he managed to tuck it inside his jeans. The effort finished him. He couldn't move anymore, could only stare up at the ceiling of the van. But he could hear.

"How are the kids in the back of the van?" the driver asked.

Rhia's cool voice called back, "Looks fine. The human just succumbed."

"Good. That's the way we like them."

Jared closed his eyes as the weak anger that had kept him going drained out of him. His last thought as he lost consciousness was damn them all to hell.

And he was out.

❧ ❧

SERUS WOKE UP in a bed covered by a sheet. Not his bed. Not his sheet. He glanced around and didn't recognize anything. He felt better, but not perfect. And then he moved. And cried out. Shit. He collapsed back down as pain listed through his body. What the hell was that from? When he could breathe again, he lifted the sheet covering his chest and tried to take a look. The place where Tessa had removed the silver bolt had turned a horrific black and green color. But the hole was closed over. So he was healing, but damn slow.

Who knew a vampire body could sustain an injury from silver and still survive? Although from the puffiness, he was going to be another day or two getting back to where he needed to be. Maybe the damn war would hold off so he could heal this time before jumping back into the fray. He had to get back. But knowing what he knew, not likely. He shifted gently in bed to find a better position and shuddered as the waves of pain crashed over him again. So no movement at all in any direction – got it.

As he lay there waiting for the pain to subside, he could hear voices outside.

"You're not going in there. The patient needs rest. When he wakes up, you can talk to him."

"He's awake now," snapped Goran. "I'm going in there regardless of what you say, so move out of the damn way."

The nurse gave a frustrated shriek that brought a smile to Serus's face. Mentally, he said, *Still tormenting the medical staff, Goran?*

Hey, buddy! Goran stood in the doorway, a huge grin on his face. "So nice to see you awake."

"Yeah, I'm thinking that heading off to a cave for a few

years when this shit is over would be a good idea. I could use the rest."

"Ha." Goran smirked. "You're just getting old. Not cut out for the fighting life anymore."

"Bite your tongue," Serus growled. "I'm younger than you."

"Only by a few years," Goran said, his face splitting with a big knowing grin. "Besides, I'm me and you're you and we both know who is better."

Serus shook his head at his friend. "Ass."

Goran laughed. "I won't make fun of you until you're back on your feet."

"Too late." But Serus gave him a sideways grin. "It's good to see you. Wasn't sure I was going to make it this time."

"Neither was I," Goran admitted. "I should be back at the damn hospital even now. We've chased the bastards all underground again, but that's a problem as we don't know where."

"Under the hospital?"

"Yeah, but everywhere we've searched, we've found no sign. Lots of places where they *were*, and no doubt they have hidey holes where they are coming and going without us knowing, but...no lairs."

Serus leaned back against the pillow. He was tired...so damn tired of this shit. "If they've gone underground at this point, it's going to be hard to force them back up to the surface again."

"It is. But they haven't had much time to go far." Goran hesitated. "I almost hate to say anything, but if we could find Rhia, she might know more."

"Do we know where she is?" Serus cried out. "I can't sense her. I've called out to her but there's no answer," he added in frustration. "I've only recently noticed a low-level hum. I have no doubt that's her blocking me."

"Right." Goran walked closer. "Any chance you can track it?" He leaned forward. "Take a page out of your daughter's book and think outside the box. Track that noise back to her. You're getting a signal. Let's see if you can do something to make that helpful."

"I don't know," Serus said slowly, thinking on it. "Maybe if I got closer to her I'd be able to hear it better, but I can't say until I try."

"Exactly," Goran said. "So you need to try, then we'll know."

Serus rolled his eyes. "You're such an optimistic idiot."

"And you the perfect counterpart," Goran said cheerfully. "Besides, my life has taken a couple of rough hits. If I can find something to be cheerful about, let me have it." And with that, the lightness in his face disappeared behind a cloud of darkness. "I also heard from Motre. Bart is dead. His daughter is dead and worse," he took a deep breath and said, "Deanna took control of Tessa and killed Bart on her own."

Serus froze. He narrowed his gaze at his old friend and said in a low, barely leashed voice, "What did you just say?"

Goran flinched. "Now we're not sure if the situation is still the same or not as the verdict appears to be out on that at the moment, but..." He launched into the explanation of all Serus had missed after being injured. "According to Motre, Tessa is back in control and she feels quite confident that Deanna is locked into place again."

Serus slowly shook his head like a grizzly bear having tasted something that didn't appeal. Too bad he couldn't back up too because he'd love to have a running charge for when he went after Deanna.

"The thing to keep in mind is that Deanna isn't getting a free pass at this, and the stronger Tessa gets, the easier it will be for her to control the bitch," Goran reminded him.

"We have to remove her from Tessa's energy. There's no way that bitch should be able to do what she did."

"I know. Cody is pretty shaken up over it all. He says he believes that Tessa is back in control but is afraid he won't be able to tell when she isn't."

JEWEL OPENED THE second door to a bright overhead light and tons of smaller lights along the side walls. Outside of the counters full of bottles and test tubes filling every surface, she couldn't see anyone inside. But what the hell was all this stuff doing here? She had to let people know what she'd found. She pulled out her phone, snapped a couple of photos, and sent them to Ian and David and Cody. Who know where anyone was? As an afterthought, she sent the images to Sian and Serus as well. She didn't want to disturb Rhia, but this was important. At least she thought it was. She took another dozen photos then retreated, making sure to leave the room exactly as she'd seen it. Rushing out, she quickly went through the outside door and ran down the hallway. She didn't know what that nightmare of chemicals was all about but couldn't imagine it being anything other than something she wanted no part of. Even though she was in the Council Hall and should be safe. This level of the Hall appeared to be more empty than alive. Reaching the staircase at the far wall, she heard the ding of the elevator.

An elevator she hadn't realized existed. She dodged into the stairwell, ready to dart up the stairs. The last thing she wanted to do was run into anyone down here. But...her footsteps slowed...she did want to know who was here and what they might be doing.

Hiding behind the door, she waited until the elevator opened. Footsteps, a single person, male from the weighted hard clip, but she didn't recognize the stride. She peered carefully around the corner and saw a tall male striding away from her. Dressed in black.

Of course he was dressed in black. Every damn vampire wore black. She'd have to see his face, but she couldn't from here. He stopped suddenly and started to turn. With a shocked gasp, Jewel pulled back out of sight. Had he seen her? Please not.

She didn't dare risk a second glance. She'd caught a glimpse of his face and profile, but it had been fleeting. Still, she frowned. Could it be? He looked very familiar. As in *very* familiar.

What door had he gone in? She slid forward slightly and peered around the corner. There was no sign of him.

Could she figure out which door? It had to be one of two based on the distance. And one of those had been the door she'd been through.

Somehow she knew he'd gone into the room with the chemicals. Of course there was no reason to go into any other room. Everything else down here was empty. Right?

She frowned as she looked at all the doors. She hadn't opened more than the one, so that was a huge assumption to think all were empty. She looked at the door closest to her. Should she check it out? Making a fast decision, she turned the knob and pushed, but it was locked. She quickly went to the next one. Locked as well. She switched to the other side of the hallway and tried to open that door. Also locked. She raced back to the stairway. As she bolted to the doorway, she heard a voice call out, "Hey, who are you, and what are you doing there?"

CHAPTER 3

TESSA STRODE PAST Motre, her gaze catching the confused, wary look on his face, and ignored it. If people knew about Deanna's game play, then of course they wouldn't trust her. She'd just have to deal with it and prove to them that she was herself again. It might take time, but she had that again. Thankfully.

The hallway was empty. She had to pull her memories up to the front as she tried to refresh herself on the recent events. She was sorry about Bart, but given what he'd done to her father, she wasn't sad that he was dead. Enough was enough though. So much death, and there was no end in sight. Why? For the damn blood farms. Ones that should have been closed down a long time ago.

She ran a hand over her temple, wondering when she'd last fed. At the word, she paused. God, she was starting to sound like a vampire. She was one, but she hated to be associated with them. At least in that way. What she wouldn't do for a granola bar. Only there wouldn't be any here. Where in this war were they? Bart had taken the canisters. So where were those now? She came to a stop and spun around to face Cody and Motre. "What happened to the canisters?"

"They were taken back to the Council Hall for analysis," Cody responded. "No one has gotten back to us as to what was in them."

"Not enough time, I imagine." She kept walking forward. "And my father?"

"He's improving." This time it was Motre with the update. "Goran is with him. He's recovering slowly."

She nodded but kept moving forward. "And the war?"

"It's at a stall. The enemy appears to have retreated."

"Damn. The hospital is clear?"

"It is ours."

"Well, that's something. Do we know where the enemy is now?"

There was no immediate answer, and she knew she wasn't going to like what she was about to hear. She slowed and turned. "Motre?"

"No." He winced. "We lost them."

"What about the men from the mechanic room."

"None were left alive."

She groaned. "Of course there weren't, that was David and Goran I suppose." She smiled at the memory. "How is David doing?"

"He's fine." Cody said. "He's looking for Jewel."

"Jewel?" Tessa gasped. "What's wrong with her?"

"She was at the hospital but walked out."

"Right." She vaguely remembered hearing something about that.

Of course David was searching for Jewel. Tessa would be on it herself if she wasn't tied up here. But David was out there. If he ran into trouble, he'd ask for help. He was good at knowing his boundaries. Too bad she wasn't. She'd walked where angels feared to tread, and look at what it had gotten her. Just mistrust and suspicion from the others, and she had to admit to having doubts herself. She not only couldn't be sure about Deanna, she now had to wonder – where was

Hortran in all of this? Had her cataclysmic fire burnt him to ash too?

She hoped not. She liked Hortran. And if he was still alive, he had much he could teach her. And she'd like to learn everything he was willing to share. That highway system to communicate with others like them would be wonderful. She could only talk to Cody right now, and that was awesome—

Damn right, he growled in her head. *And that's the way it's going to stay.*

I got that. But there is more to learn. Hortran knew so much.

Knew? Past tense?

Maybe. But I can't tell for sure.

Can you sense him anymore?

No. Her answer was short, curt.

She felt more than saw his smile. He was walking on her left, Motre on her right. There were others around somewhere. Her reality had shifted so much she didn't even know what she was thinking or feeling. One dominant sensation was fatigue. Lord, she was tired. Why? Right. The fight with Deanna. The energy required for what she'd done had drained her. She needed to refresh her energy supplies. She could feel her vampire genes kicking up, but almost like a wet spark plug, as if they were there and willing but not capable of jumpstarting the engines. She needed food and rest. But not here.

"If everything here is fine, then I suggest we head back to Council Hall."

"Best idea yet." Motre laughed. "My men are in need of blood and some rest."

"Me too," she said, trying to keep her voice strong. She could hear the fatigue in it herself. "I don't suppose anyone has a granola bar on them, do they?"

Motre laughed. "Not likely."

"There are several cases at Council Hall," Cody said.

"Good, I'd like to be there. And catch up on the news. Not to mention to see everyone." She yawned. "I hope they are all okay. I really need to rest."

"Sian is fine," Cody answered. "Your mother is still missing, and who knows on Jewel? I'm presuming David has found her. If not, then he's still looking."

"Yeah, and Jared? Wendy? Ian?"

She frowned at the confused look on his face. "I have no idea."

Just then, Cody's cell phone rang with text messages, followed by Motre's phone going off.

She glanced from one to the other.

And heard Cody's whispered, "Shit."

"What's wrong?"

Then her phone went off. She pulled it out of her pocket. "Jared." She grinned. "Perfect timing." She read the message and gasped then cried. "Oh my God. My mother?"

Behind her, she heard Cody muttering about Ian and Wendy. She spun to look at the men. "How can we track them? We have to find them now before we lose all of them into the system. They'll be drugged and lost to us within hours."

Cody stared at her. "We have Jared's cell number now. We should be able track his phone and find them."

Motre frowned. "It was always Ian who could do that stuff."

"And my brother."

"I'm not as brilliant, but I can do this," Cody said defensively, already clicking on his cell phone. "We've been able to track several people this way through the tunnels."

She laughed, remembering. "We did indeed."

"And now we can use it again to track the others. One big rescue and we'll be able to scoop all of them up." Motre grinned. "I like it."

"We'll need backup." Cody said.

"No problem," Motre said, holding up his phone. "I've got lots of young men ready and willing to join the fight. We just need to know where to send them."

He turned to look at Cody. "How long is that going to take?"

"I'm on it. Give me a few more minutes..." Cody muttered, clicking away.

"We need to contact the others. Our fathers. Sian and Taz," Tessa said. "They need to be a part of this."

Motre nodded. "Call them. Bring them up to date. They need to hear from you too." And he walked a few steps away to make calls of his own.

She stared down at the phone in her hand. It was almost as if they were coming full circle. Jared had been kidnapped by rogue vamps and she was mounting an army to go after him. It was funny and sad at the same time.

She called Sian and filled her in. It took longer than she expected, and then she had to speak to her father and Goran too. They were all at the Council Hall, all of them ready and willing to come to the rescue.

God, she loved that about them. All of them. Not one questioned her sanity or identity. They all trusted her.

She glanced over at Cody and realized he'd been watching her for the last few moments.

Now if only he would trust her too.

CODY WATCHED TESSA walk out the exit. She looked normal. Sounded normal. Acted normal. Except Deanna was a time bomb waiting to happen. And he couldn't help feeling that having happened once, even though Tessa believed Deanna was no longer capable of such a thing, Deanna could just be waiting for another opportunity to strike. Or rather waiting for the time to move her agenda to the next level.

Somehow Tessa had to be convinced that she had a problem. And as much as he wanted to trust her, he wasn't sure that he could. At least until he knew that Deanna was gone. Or had so little control that she couldn't take over Tessa again.

I can only tell you that I can't feel her, Tessa said quietly. *Her memories are here, but there's no hint of anything else.*

Maybe she's just hiding.

There was an odd silence. *I don't think so,* she said.

Neither did you think so before, he snapped, his frustration boiling over. After a moment, he said, *I'm sorry, but it wasn't much fun to watch Deanna in action.*

No, she whispered. *It wasn't much fun for me either.*

He reached out and wrapped an arm around her shoulders and tugged her closer. When she leaned into him, he kissed her temple.

He hated that he wondered if Deanna was going to spring out and surprise him with a cutting remark. He'd love to kiss Tessa, but to know that Deanna…

"She's not here," she whispered.

"So you say, but you didn't see her in action…"

"No, I didn't," she said softly, her voice low so Motre, walking slightly ahead of them, couldn't hear. "But I could feel her. It was horrific not being able to get free of my prison."

"Prison?" He hated the thought of Deanna having that level of control. And to think of Tessa imprisoned inside her own mind, aware but incapable of doing anything about the situation, well, that was really hard to deal with. Let alone accept. He was so damn pissed at that old biddy he wanted to punch something, but it was Deanna he wanted to punch.

"What about a signal to say that it's me and not her?"

"A signal?" He studied her as she walked. "But if she's in there right now, wouldn't that signal be something she'd know, too?"

Tessa was quiet for a long moment then said, "Not if the key was something from your mind. She can force her way into anyone's mind, or rather she could, but she couldn't access *your* memories."

"And?" How was that going to help him?

"So she couldn't know about things you know."

"We could only use it once though, because as soon as she knows, then it's no longer a safe word to use."

Her feet slowing, Tessa nodded. "I'm not sure what access she has to my memories right now. I want to believe she's completely incapable of accessing anything..."

Cody snorted.

She nodded, "But I'm not a fool. She's tried to take over several times already, but not since this last dust up."

"Thank you for at least acknowledging she's potentially still a problem."

"Only for your sake. I'm sure she's not in there anymore." Tessa stopped and closed her eyes. After a moment, she shrugged her shoulders and said, "I can't feel her."

"Can you feel Hortran?" he asked curiously.

She closed her eyes then said, "No."

"So as nothing happened to him and you know he's in

there somewhere, then you know that she likely is, too."

"But there is only a tiny bit of Hortran left."

"Well, maybe after what you did, there's only a tiny bit of her left, too," he said in exasperation. "But I don't care how small, that women is a menace."

Motre stopped and turned back to face them. "Are you two done?" He motioned around them. "The vehicle is supposed to be here with a driver. Now there's a vehicle all right, not that you two noticed," he snapped. "But there is no one here."

Cody did a slow search of the car park. There were a few parked vehicles farther away, but there was no sign of anyone. The ministry van was in front of them, cold and empty.

"Then where is he?" Cody asked, his back going up. "Like we need more shit going on."

"There's no energy around it. This vehicle hasn't been driven in days."

She spun and waved her arm. "The same for the rest of these. There's been no one around here for a long time."

"Can you see *any* energy?" Motre asked. "Anywhere?"

In a sharp voice, Tessa said, "There's been no one in this lot in days. So I don't know where we are, but it's not the same place everyone else was."

✂ ✄

HELL, THE LAST thing he wanted to do was tell Serus about the text he just got from Jared. How the hell had that kid found his number in the first place?

Except considering how many of the kids had hooked up comparing notes, it shouldn't be that much of a surprise. The kids were running circles around him when it came to technology.

"What is it, Goran?" Serus asked.

Goran looked over at this friend. "I'm not sure I should tell you."

The skin on Serus's face tightened. "Tell me."

With a shrug, Goran handed over his cell phone. "Read it yourself. It's from Jared."

Serus snatched the phone out of his hand and read the message. His eyebrows shot up and the little color he'd had in his face completely drained away, leaving his skin a gray pasty color. "No, oh no. Not this shit again."

He scrolled up and down the phone then tossed it on the bed close to Goran. "Game plan?" he barked. "What's our first step?"

Goran studied his friend. "For you to get healthy."

Goran's phone buzzed. He checked the incoming message. "Jared apparently contacted everyone. Cody is working on tracking the cell phone and Motre is collecting an army," he crowed. "Yes. We're on it, Serus. You are going to stay here and heal."

There was a snort at the doorway. Goran looked up from the phone to see Serus out the door and striding down the hallway ahead of him.

"Hey, wait for me," Goran raced after him. "You shouldn't be doing this, you know."

"My wife is in trouble. My son is missing and my daughter is going after them both. Who the hell knows where David is, why hasn't he checked in?"

"No idea. He's searching for Jewel, who walked out of her hospital room."

"Smart girl." He shot Goran a ferocious grin. "If I'm going to die, it's going to be in a way that I take dozens of assholes with me."

"Ha." Goran poked him. "In the condition you're in now, you'd likely die in the first confrontation."

And with the two men wrangling like old times, they raced to the main elevator. And came to a complete stop at the wash of sunlight shining through the doors.

"God damn it. It's like the world is against us. Even Mother Nature won't let us catch a break."

"We need suits and bikes or a good vehicle."

"No bikes. I might be on my feet, but I'm not sure I could handle that right now. So a Council vehicle it is."

The two spun around and raced to the garage. There were always a half dozen vehicles available. And sure enough, Goran found several empty ones. Another drove up. Goran hopped into the driver's side as the driver got out. He looked like a doctor. He nodded at him then hopped in and slammed the door. He started up the vehicle and waited while Serus buckled up. "You sure you're up for this?"

"Just drive. There's no way in hell my family is going off to war without me."

"Can't wait to see what Tessa's going to say when she sees you."

"She's my daughter. She won't say a damn thing."

Goran roared with laughter as he hit reverse and drove the vehicle out into the sun. "Wanna bet?"

❧ ❦

DAVID RACED DOWN the hallway. It couldn't be her, could it? He'd just caught a glimpse of her profile as she darted around the corner, but it had been enough for him to race after her. "Jewel, is that you?"

Could it have been her? And if it was, what the hell was she doing here? He'd been searching for her for hours. He thought she'd be safe, but instead she'd walked out on her own. And why run from him? Unless she didn't know it was him? He stood undecided in the middle of the two sets of stairs. One up and one down. Which way had she gone? "Jewel, damn it, where are you?"

He heard a startled squeak and just had enough time to open his arms when she dropped over the railing above and into them.

She laughed and threw her arms around him. "Oh my God, I didn't know it was you. I wondered but figured it had to be someone else. I've been wandering lost in this place forever. How can it be so big? Why? Where the hell is everyone?"

There was only one way to stop the stream of questions. He lifted her chin, lowered his head, and kissed her. A kiss of relief. Of overwhelming joy. Of passion. She'd always been the only one for him. When she'd decided he was the one for her, he'd known he was blessed.

She threw her arms around his neck and kissed him back.

He'd have stayed there, even contemplated grabbing one of the many empty rooms on this floor, when his phone buzzed. And again. And again. Regretfully, he pulled back but kept her in the circle of his arms. He grinned when her wings wrapped around him, too. "Damn, it's good to see those working again."

She reached up and kissed him on the chin.

"I know. I was so relieved. Where did you come from?" she asked as he pulled his phone out to look at the mess of messages stacking up.

"I just came up the stairs from the floor below. Checking

out the room you found," he said, reading her message. "I'm pretty sure that was testing on the canister contents that Bart had," he answered in a distracted voice. "We've got trouble again."

"Again?" she exclaimed. "We've never yet *not* had trouble."

He showed her the texts. She gasped and turned pale as she read through them all. "Oh no. Poor Jared."

David shook his head. What was it about Jared that everyone felt so damn sorry for him? He understood Cody's problem with him but up until now, David hadn't been worried. Now Jewel's tone was anything but detached.

"Poor Ian and Wendy, you mean," he snapped. "Poor Jared, too. But damn it, that man is a trouble magnet."

"He might be, but he's our trouble magnet." Jewel glared up at him. "And we have to help him."

"I'm going to help," David said, his temper rising. "You are going to stay with Sian and man the fort here. Someone needs to be with her."

"I'm not hurt anymore. I'm fine now."

"Maybe, but we don't know what they've done to you. And we can't take the chance of you being drugged again. So helping Sian it is. No…" He held a finger to her lips. "No arguments. There are enough able-bodied males to handle this, and you are needed here. Sian and Taz need you. Do you have any idea how many sick vamps are here?"

"Then your sister should be here too, helping," Jewel argued. "Those are my friends too. And I want to help them."

"I know you do. And thank heavens for that. But the bottom line is, we need you to help upstairs." David was already leading her up the first flight of stairs. "Sian isn't recovering well after that last attack in the middle of the street. She's been holding it together but if you look at her carefully, you'll see the strain. She's terrified these assholes will try again for her and the baby's DNA. She has to look after herself for the baby's sake. Therefore, you need to help."

Her shoulders slumped, but he knew he'd made the right decision. She looked so much better than the last time he'd seen her, but the bottom line was she didn't have her full strength back.

"While you are with Sian, you will also feel safer."

She nodded. "I wasn't sure if I was safe in that medical room or not. It felt wrong...so when I could, I left."

"And maybe that was the right decision." David admitted. "I never did find the nurse who'd been looking after you. I don't know if she was a plant, or if she's dead, or if she just left to go home, but the doctor said he hasn't seen her either."

Jewel gasped, her hand going to her mouth as she studied his face. "So I was right?"

"I don't know," he admitted. "But let's make sure you are with friends and not strangers this time."

She smiled and reached up and kissed him. "Thank you."

☙ ❧

IAN OPENED HIS eyes to see Wendy lying beside him. He smiled. Damn, she looked fine. She was draped across his chest and he had his arms wrapped around her. He loved this woman so much, but he hadn't told her yet. Maybe today was the day. He lifted his head to see where he was when he realized they weren't alone. Jared was with them.

Crap. So he hadn't gone to bed snuggling with the most beautiful woman in the world. Then what the hell had he done? He glanced around everywhere and realized they were

DALE MAYER

in a single room. Two beds. Him and Wendy in one, and Jared in the other. Weird.

Then he remembered. The three of them had been looking at a room full of monitors when they'd been attacked. They'd been taken prisoner again. God damn it. He wanted to lash out at the world that was constantly against them. Why couldn't they catch a break? That's all they needed. One decent break. Was that too much to ask for?

He realized then that Wendy was lying in a too deep, too unnatural sleep. He bolted upright, his fingers checking to see if she was breathing. She was. Thank God. But there was blood on the back of her head. The bastards had hit her.

He'd kill them for that.

Now all he had to do was figure out where the hell they were. He rolled over and laid Wendy down beside him on the bed. Getting to his feet, he walked over to Jared and studied the slack face. Drugs or injury? He reached out and moved the man's head to the side, but there didn't appear to be any blood flowing. Yet there were black and blue marks on his neck and arms. He'd fought. Good on him, but completely useless against the vamps. As his gaze wandered down Jared's body, he realized there were no tubes in his arm.

That was a relief. The last thing any of the three of them needed was more drugs. He spun around and assessed the otherwise empty room. There were no other beds. No window, no cupboards, and only the one door. Most likely a locked door. The beds explained Wendy on his bed – maybe, but they could have just as easily dumped one of them on the floor.

He turned his attention to the ceiling. Tiles. He frowned and remembered the many rooms he'd seen, larger and holding more beds than this room, but the same colored walls and ceiling tiles. Were they really in another damn blood farm? And if they were, was this the missing one they'd been looking for? Surely there couldn't be more – right? Then again, if it was a blood farm, why was Jared here with him and Wendy? He'd be hanging up again. Poor guy. His lips thinned as he remembered the few vampires they'd found strung up, too. Not to mention the vamp guinea pigs forced to take enhancements.

Shitty way to live. So not going to happen to him. He glanced back at his unconscious friends and realized this time the rescue was up to him. He studied the door in front of him. No lock on the inside. Checking his pockets, he realized he still had his cell phone. Gleefully, he pulled it out and checked for a signal. None. Right, so they'd been allowed to keep their phones because they wouldn't work down here. He stopped and rolled the word 'down' around in his head. How was it he assumed they were down anywhere? Because it was cooler. The air thinner. The floor...stone?

Yeah. Blood farm. Instead of being afraid, he was fiercely glad. They'd bring this one down now, too.

RHIA WASN'T SURE how long she could do this. Her head was splitting with pain and the effects of fighting the drugs still pouring through her system. Her mind was split and fighting to think coherently. She had to keep this up for a little longer. She'd been assigned to work on the patients on the lower floors. Fine. She'd be under surveillance after her odd arrival. She knew that. She could handle that. But she had to find Seth. And that was in the moments when she was lucid. Then there were moments when she could feel and sense her body following orders, the drugs and brainwashing commanding in a way her mind couldn't fight.

Please let her not have taken too strong a dose that she couldn't recover from. She had no wish to be a part of this mess – ever. At least her lucid mind was saying that. Her drugged-out mind couldn't say please and thank you to these assholes fast enough. Rhia needed to save Seth and after that…well, she'd bring this nightmare down to the ground.

Her lucid mind smiled joyously. Her drugged mind hissed in fear. Then she remembered those she'd seen in the van. Jared, Wendy, Ian. Her children's poor friends.

Yes, they will make great additions to the blood farm and testing programs, her drugged mind said in a sartorial whisper. *Good luck saving them.*

CHAPTER 4

TESSA WANDERED THE parking lot. "We must have taken a wrong turn somewhere," she cried. "This isn't where the others were."

"Does it matter?" Motre called from the far side. "There is only the one door in and out of here. No one is here now and it's obviously not a well-used place."

"Right. But we won't get any answers here."

"No, but we have a vehicle available, so let's grab this one and go." Cody walked to the front of the Council vehicle and opened the door. "Of course keys would help."

"We can do without them if need be," Motre said, approaching rapidly from his quick search of the lot. "I'll hot wire it in two seconds."

He reached the two of them and opened the driver's side. He quickly opened the plastic under the dash and fiddled with a few wires. Less than a minute later, the engine fired up. He grinned and hopped into the driver's seat. "Ha, I'm driving."

Cody rolled his eyes and walked around to the passenger side and found Tessa grinning at him from the front seat. "You get to ride in the back."

"Right." He opened the side panel of the truck and let out a startled grunt. Tessa turned around to look in the back of the large vehicle. There were two dead men, eyes open and staring upward in the back. Motre turned on an inside light and twisted to look at the men. His voice grim and hard, he said, "We rescued these two men from the hospital. They were part of one of the foreign dignitaries group."

"Then why are they dead?" Cody asked, studying them. "Not disease, or energy shit. They look to be…"

"Frozen," Tessa said, her voice hushed in shock. "They look frozen."

Cody shot her a hard look and reached out to touch the men. "They are damn cold."

"From the morgue," she said. "They were in the drawers in the morgue. Not frozen, but so cold that they have very low body temperature."

"But they are dead, right?" Motre exclaimed. He got out of the van and came around to where Cody stood staring. "Tessa, are they dead?"

She was trying to figure that out. She'd seen some pretty strange things already and this was just one more. "I'm not sure," she whispered. "I can't see any energy lingering on their bodies that would normally say there's life here, but neither is there blackness of death or drugs. In fact, I'm not seeing anything at all."

Cody looked over at her. "And has anything changed in your ability to see?"

She looked over at him and shook her head. "Not that I know of." But she knew he could hear the doubt in her voice. Was she losing some of her newfound abilities? Had her confrontation with Deanna changed her abilities? Done anything to them in any way?

No. She couldn't have that. Still…she closed her eyes and said mentally, *Vampire genes, fire up please. I need to be able to read energy again.*

She could feel the heat from inside surge forward and

bathe her body in warm light, the sensation moving upward in a continuous wave. When it reached her neck then her face, she smiled. As it hit her eyes, she opened them and looked at the two men standing and staring at her. Men who were less physical and more energy than she'd ever seen before. She hadn't lost her abilities. She'd tucked them away, and now when she called them into play, they were there for her. She was more in control than ever.

She turned her gaze toward the two prone men in the back of the van and could see a faint blueness to their body. So slim as to not be there. But it was there. She scrambled over the center console and reached out a hand each toward them. She slammed a wave of hot color toward the two men, forcing it into the bodies to blend with the icy blue. She poured energy down into the hearts and willed them to beat. More and more energy rippled inside the two men, filling them.

Suddenly, the man on top gave a huge sigh then gulped for air. Again and again.

He groaned as the second man started to gulp for air. Then both men opened their eyes.

"What the…" The first man sat up slowly then grabbed for his head. "What did you guys do to us?"

"Nothing," Tessa said tartly. "We saved you. Now, who are you and what are you doing here?"

The first man looked over at the second. "We're from England. Came over for the conference. All I remember is our arrival and the panic for everyone to get organized for the meetings. We were just settling in when something happened." He looked around at the van in confusion. "I just woke up here."

"You came over for the Clan Summit?"

He nodded, still rubbing his head. "There were four of us." He glanced around at the back of the van. "Where are the others?"

"We don't know. We've only seen you two. But we found part of the Nordic party and some of the Germans."

He frowned. "There was a lot of arguing at the start. The Germans weren't happy about something. A change in venue if I'm not mistaken. They had a reason for us staying where we were, I believe, but the organizers had felt a change was necessarily. Something about a security breach."

"Well, there was that." Motre shook his head. "We need to ask Sian to check who attended that Clan Summit and cross check against the people we've found. For all we know, there might be dozens still missing."

"Missing? What happened?" The second man sat up gasping as his body struggled to function properly. "What the hell happened to us?"

"We can't say for sure, but what we do know is a group of rebel vampires appeared to have crashed the summit and taken everyone hostage. They are after your DNA for their experiments."

Both men paled and quickly checked their arms. Both showed signs of punctures. "Jesus. I can't believe this," the first man cried.

But the other man was shaking his head. "The Germans were yelling something about that. Saying that something had to happen as the vampire races were becoming diluted. I didn't hear all the conversation though."

"Yeah, I don't think there are many in the German delegation left. And the foreign dignitaries that we've managed to find and help haven't been too eager to join with the rebel group, hence the party crashing and mass kidnapping."

"What type of experiments?" the first man asked. "I'm Alexander of Cheshire. Our clan is one of the oldest in existence. The leader, Rothberg, was supposed to come, but there was a meeting and sudden change of plans and I was ordered to come in his place."

Tessa glanced over at Cody. "Sian needs to have a look at Rothberg." She turned her gaze back to Alexander. "I'm thinking he didn't like you – did he?"

Alexander shook his head. "No, but he was our leader and of course I respected him for that."

"But you didn't like his policies?" Cody asked shrewdly. "He wanted to return to the old ways. Bring back more fresh blood. Blood farms perhaps. And you...you wanted to keep the clans progressing forward."

Alexander stared at him in shock. "How do you know?"

"Because the people who kidnapped you have a massive blood production system with over four blood farms in operation, and we think they've gone international. We've rescued more than a few people with powerful enemies who found the blood farms an easy way to remove the competition."

"Oh my God," the second man cried. "Alexander was supposed to be leader, but he became so sick at the time of his rising, he couldn't attend so Rothberg, who was second-in-command, took over. He has yet to hand the leadership back to Alexander."

"Well, he wouldn't, would he? He's planned it so you don't ever go back." Motre was already talking on the phone. "Sian, we've got Alexander and..." he looked at the second vamp, who responded with Rupert. "And Rupert from the British clan. They were at the summit as well. They were dead in the back of a van we found on some deserted parking level."

He snorted. "Yeah, you heard me, dead."

The two men turned to stare at each other then back at Tessa. She shrugged and turned away to retake her seat. Like hell she was answering. Her fatigue levels were really rising now, and it didn't look like there was any rest in sight for her.

She could hear the men talking in low tones in the background. She didn't need to be part of that conversation to know what was being discussed. She could feel the shock waves from where she sat. She stared out the window and waited. They needed to hurry up and make a decision on their next move before she collapsed. To that end, she closed her eyes and tried to rest.

"THAT'S NOT POSSIBLE." Alexander shook his head in disbelief. "Besides, if she could do that, these assholes would want *her* DNA."

There was an awkward silence before Cody answered, his voice cold and harsh. "They've tried several times."

"And failed," Motre added. "Another reason we're going after them. They have gone after several of our Councilmen. Ancients."

"Shit," Rupert said. "This is messed up."

"You don't know the half of what we've been through, but this girl is the reason we're still alive. She's saved our asses more times than we can count."

"And she's learned to do more as well." Cody laughed. "Hell, this was a shy insecure girl when this mess started, and now she's one of the most powerful women in all the clans."

"Ha, the strongest woman I know is Deanna. That old witch is powerful."

Motre looked at Cody. Cody stared at him.

"What are we missing?" Alexander asked curiously.

"Deanna is dead. And she did transfer her knowledge to Tessa." Motre nodded to Tessa at the front seat. "Quiet."

Cody leaned forward and whispered in his mind, *Tessa?*

No answer, just a gentle hum.

He nodded. "Good. She is asleep." He glanced at the inside of the van, wondering about the blood supply. "She also needs food."

"We're dead short on time," Motre said. "But we're going to need to swing past Council Hall and drop these two off. We can grab what we need then."

"Whoa, I want to go home, not to Council Hall," Alexander said.

"And that's not a choice. You're alive because of Tessa, however, your full recovery could take a day or two. Besides, we haven't the time to fill you in on all the rest. You'll have to get up to speed to keep yourself safe from the head of your clan at home."

Alexander subsided in the back of the van, a gray cast to his skin. "Great. I'm not feeling so good now, and if he saw me, he'd finish me off in a heartbeat. Call me weak and a taint to the blood."

Motre snorted. "Sounds like a nice guy, but we have our own just like him. We're in a full-blown war here, and it's going global if we can't stop it in time."

Cody nodded. "It's already gone global by attacking all the foreign dignitaries. The Nordic group almost lost the son of the leader. So many died until Tessa managed to get them back."

There was an odd silence as Motre hopped into the driver's seat. Cody found a place to sit in the back.

"And how did she do that exactly?" Rupert asked delicately. "Don't get me wrong, I'm very grateful, but…"

"Yeah. No one really knows, but she sees energy, including the energy inside our bodies, and can tell by that amount if she were to add more to it if it would save us. She's helped all of us in many ways." Cody really didn't want to have this discussion, and worse, he knew Tessa was sleeping, but it was likely a light doze and he didn't want her to think they were talking about her. Or insulting her. People tended to speak their mind more if the person wasn't there or was sleeping.

"How is that possible?" Alexander said in shock. "There have always been people who see energy, not many, but one or two per generation I'd say, so that in itself is not unusual, but the rest… yeah, it is."

"Many of her friends were being killed, and she instinctively tried to stop it from happening. When she realized she could affect their energy—"

"Both positively and negatively," Motre interjected from the driver's seat.

"Right. She realized she was an effective weapon both ways."

Cody leaned back and tried to rest. They had a ten-minute trip to the Council Hall so they could regroup and get back into action – if someone had found where their friends were. He checked the GPS locator and realized they still hadn't moved. That meant they were likely being unloaded. He just had no idea where this place was. It was part of the valley to the left of Moltere's Mountain – or what remained of it.

"We have to hurry," he snapped, feeling panic rise at how long Ian and Wendy had already been gone. "The GPS signal isn't moving anymore."

"Almost there." Motre said, pulling the vehicle onto the main road.

The van pulled into the Council Hall lot where several vamps were waiting with stretchers. The two British vamps were unloaded and taken away to the medical side. The other vamps, as Cody found out, were reporting to Motre. He was damn glad that man had stepped up and proven to be such a great military leader. They needed more like him. They were running out of allies while the bad guys were just building more. They might have put a crimp in the process taking out hundreds that were in growth stages, but the enemy could replace the stock they'd lost.

They had to find a way to take the whole mess down and although they were well on the way to that, there were those places and leaders they needed to find and kill.

And they would. It wasn't an option not to.

"Ready?"

With a start, Cody realized Tessa was awake and studying him.

He smiled. "Ready for what?"

She gave him such a sad smile, his heart ached.

"War."

&ᴥ&

RHIA LOOKED AROUND the hastily-constructed offices and tried to remember if she'd ever been here before or not. She didn't think so, yet it could be any number of the same offices she'd been in the last few weeks from any of the blood farms. Still, this one might have access to the current information on Seth. Was he still here? She needed him to be. He was too good a kid to lose this way. And she couldn't bear to be the one responsible.

"Rhia, please take blood from the new arrivals so we can do a cross match and start testing as soon as possible."

Rhia nodded and walked to the sideboard where there were boxes of supplies. She had to play her part.

And ignore the part of her mind that said, *You're not playing. This is perfect. You're back where you need to be.*

God help her.

She just might be.

❧ ❧

IAN WAS STRONG and fit, so why the hell couldn't he get out of this damn room? Wendy and Jared were both still unconscious, and he didn't like that. But he hadn't been able to find a way to open the door. Neither could he carry both friends—at least not far. And they were running out of time. Someone would be coming soon. And he knew they'd be after blood and delivering drugs. Neither he nor Wendy could handle those. Jared had been through enough already, too.

Walking to the door, he put his head against it and listened. Voices in the distance. They were down the hallway, not outside the door. He didn't recognize words or the tones.

Then he heard a sound he recognized. Footsteps. Coming toward him. He stood behind the door and waited for it to open.

This was the one chance he had.

There was no way in hell these assholes were going to string him up like the others.

Surely a rescue was coming soon.

Right?

The footsteps stopped outside in the hallway. It didn't

have to mean someone was coming here, but he knew he didn't have much luck in this damn place.

His worst nightmare was if those footsteps did come here and it was Rhia. How could he tell if it was the good Rhia or the bad?

SIAN STUDIED THE information coming in endless streams from all corners as they tried to coordinate their next move. Time was of the essence, but this was going to be a horrific mess if not coordinated properly. They had one chance here to end this. And she hated to admit it, but for that reason, she'd kept the Human Council out of the arrangements. And she wasn't sure that was the right thing to do. They'd been coordinating well so far, but time was short and humans didn't move fast.

And they were vulnerable to vampires. She hated to think she was sending the military to their deaths, but so far both sides had sustained major losses. It's just the humans had been worse.

Still, she'd signed the Accord, and she'd be the one breaking it if she didn't notify them.

Just then, the phone on her desk rang.

She sighed when she recognized the caller as the new leader of the Human Council. They had several, but her particular liaison had changed after the Council had seen Tessa in action. This contact was more persistent.

"Victor, how are you?"

"Not good. Rumors are swirling that there might be another blood farm?"

She winced. "I wouldn't say that at the moment." Who

the hell had leaked that information? "We have a report of three people kidnapped and the GPS tracker has given us a location. So far, we don't know what is at this location. We're trying to pull together a team now."

"My men will be ready," he said in a harsh voice. "And I'll put the medical facilities on alert."

She gave in. "I'll let you know as soon as we're ready to move out."

They worked out a few more details before she hung up.

Just then Goran and Serus burst in. They rolled over her with questions. "What and why and how?"

She threw up her hands. "I'm glad you came to see me first instead of charging off."

"Ha," Goran growled. "I was hoping you could convince Serus to stay here."

Sian snorted. "If you couldn't, then there's no way I can. Besides, if Rhia is there, then we need him."

"What do you mean?"

Sian stared at him, sadness in her voice as she said, "We can't figure out whose side she is on. And too many vamps want to take her out just to be safe…"

❧ ❧

SHE WAS SO damn happy to be back in David's arms it was easy to forget all she'd been through. But one thing bothered her. "What happened to Rhia that she broke down so bad?"

David glanced down at her in surprise. "To Mom? I don't know. She went missing and no one has been able to find her."

"What?" Jewel shook her head. "I heard her earlier. Two hours ago tops. Maybe just over an hour even."

"Where," he said, his voice sharp, hard. "Can you show me?"

She gave him a startled look. "Maybe. It's back the way I came, close to the beginning. She was sobbing like her heart was breaking, but I didn't want to intrude so I kept walking." She shrugged. "I'm not even sure which door it was."

David nodded, but his gaze had turned inward. "If we can find her, it might help." He winced. "Although she's not there now according to Jared. She's in a van that was hauling him, Wendy, and Ian away."

"What? No, not again."

He nodded. "Everyone is afraid that Mom took drugs so she could go back and find out what happened to Seth."

"But how will she know when she's not in her right mind how to find the information she needs?" Jewel cried. "Poor Rhia."

David pulled his cell phone out and called Sian. "I found Jewel. She heard Rhia in one of the rooms on the lower levels, crying. She doesn't know which room, but we need to do a full-on search down here. If Mom was here, she might have left behind signs of what she'd done. And if she was down here, who the hell else was? With Jared and Wendy slipping away from the meeting, we can't know for sure until we do a complete sweep."

Jewel shook her head. And she had been feeling sorry for herself. But she was safe now and the others were in trouble. She ruffled her wings, feeling them respond. Sluggish, but it was there. They were reacting as needed and that was all good. She could fly David to where they needed to go and get there ahead of the others. Goran would likely be doing just that. An air attack at the same time as one from the ground would be best. She might not be in fighting form, but she could do reconnaissance from the air.

Goran could kick ass. She was still feeling a little like her ass had taken a beating, but she wasn't down or out and if her friends needed her, then she was going to the rescue. Regardless of what David wanted.

Lord knows they'd all taken part in saving her sorry butt several times.

David put away the phone. "Come on. Straight upstairs to the main chambers. Sian is coordinating a full-on attack. We're needed up there."

Jewel turned and raced up the first flight of stairs. "I'm all for helping, but if you think I'm going to stay here and attend meetings while you're off helping our friends, forget it."

He groaned. "Why can't you see reason?"

"Why can't you see my wings are back and that gives me a huge advantage?"

"Maybe and maybe not. If you go down from a silver bullet, then what?" he snarled. "My sister can't save you then."

"Ha, she can't save *anyone* from silver."

David realized just how much of Tessa's newfound skills Jewel had missed hearing about. He took the next few flights of stairs to itemize the things she'd done. After the first startled look, Jewel had gone silent.

When he finally ran down and ended with, "And that's the hard and dirty version,"

She shook her head and said, "Poor Tessa."

David spun to look back at her. They'd reached the main floor. "Why?"

"Because everyone is looking at her to win the day. She's just a girl like me. She can't save *everyone*. It's impossible. She can't be expected to consistently develop like this. There has to be time for her body, her mind, and her emotions to catch up." She shook her head. "At some point her defenses will be down, and someone somewhere is going to see that window of opportunity and take advantage of her."

Jewel stared up at the man that meant so much to her and added, "And it's likely that's one attack she won't be able to recover from."

CHAPTER 5

TESSA HADN'T BEEN sleeping. At least not fully. There was a part of her always tracking what was going on around her. She had to wonder if deep sleep was lost to her now. It would be a shame. But it seemed like she could never let go. Never fully relax.

Was that Deanna's energy? The result of understanding how easily Deanna had taken her over, *or* was it something else – like the massive amount of energy she could feel flowing through her? She didn't know, but it was strange to consider not needing sleep again. But if that was true, why was she tired?

The answer came to her in a flood. Because she hadn't let the energy inside. She needed to reach out and access the energy, to utilize it for herself. Not keep it available in case someone else needed her, but to understand she had needs, too. And to realize the energy available was never going to run out. There was no limited supply of usable energy. She needed to take off for a few weeks. Preferably with Cody.

Her old life was gone. Her human schooling – history. It had only been weeks since this nightmare, but she'd been fooling around there anyways. She could write the final exams without having attending this entire year. If it mattered to her, she'd write them, graduate, then figure out what to do. Now she was more vampire than human anyway. She didn't think she'd care to get her human school certificates. Hell, she didn't even know what happened to her school friends. Were they safe? They were supposed to be, but look at Jared.

Neither could she see her future this way. What was she going to do with her life? She wanted to spend it with Cody, but she also understood that Deanna's presence had changed something for him.

And for her.

Fear that it was going to break them up slid up her throat.

She sensed when Cody lifted his head from where he'd been reclining and twisting to stare at her. They were waiting in the parking lot for Motre to return since she'd woken up.

"Tessa?"

She hated that caution, that fear that it might not be Tessa anymore. It would take time for him to understand. But she didn't want him to need time. The bitch was gone, damn it.

And she froze. The bitch might be gone, but the language and anger were new for her. It wasn't Tessa. She relaxed. It was new. But it was a product of the last weeks. She couldn't stay sweet and innocent and stupidly naive as she had been. She'd been through too much. And so had Cody.

"Hey," she said in a soft voice. "I'm awake. Not sure I'm ever going to be able to sleep anymore. More like drifting in and out."

There was a smile in his voice as he shifted close and placed a hand on her shoulder. She loved that physical connection. Unable to help herself, she turned and kissed his fingers.

"You were so tired," he murmured behind her, his warm breath tingling her ear. She wished they weren't waiting for Motre to rejoin them. She'd love a hug.

"I'd love a hug, too," he whispered and kissed her cheek.

It wasn't quite what she'd been looking for, but she'd take what she could get.

She nuzzled closer, needing this moment. "Thanks for staying with me in here."

"I won't be leaving you again," he whispered. "Ever. I seriously wondered about spitting Deanna with a silver spike when she was in control, but I couldn't hurt you."

"If you ever think that she has such strong control and that I can't regain control, and you think that's it – she's now me – kill her," she said solemnly. "That's not how I want to live."

"What's not how you want to live?" Motre asked from the driver's door. "Look at you two. Leave you alone for five minutes and you're making out."

"I wish," Cody muttered as he retook his seat. "Do we have a game plan?"

"Yes, Sian is on it. Attack planned on the coordinates. Your fathers are both in the game and David has found Jewel."

"Oh thank heavens," Tessa cried out in joy. "I was afraid she'd been drugged again."

"And she might have been, but she's not showing any signs of it yet. When you see her again, be sure to check out her energy."

Motre tossed something in her lap then handed several sticks to Cody. "You eat, and Cody, stuff these somewhere for later, just in case."

Tessa stared at the granola bars in her lap and grinned. "Thank you." She snipped open the first one and took a big bite, her stomach growling in anticipation.

"That's why I was so long," he said in exasperation. "It's

not something routinely stocked at Council Hall."

She nodded but couldn't talk. It was Cody who answered, "Well, they will now."

Motre nodded, handed him a chilled blood pack, and said, "That's for us. We'll need to feed before we go into battle."

"Are we waiting for anyone else to join us?" Cody asked. "Or can we go and check out the location?"

"That's exactly what we're going to do." Motre started up the engine then stopped and looked at Tessa. "As long as you're up to it."

She nodded. "Let's go and kick butt – again."

Cody laughed at Motre's huge grin. Motre, like everyone else, had fallen under Tessa's spell. So easy to do. His cell phone was going steadily with texts between David and Sian and his father. He watched as they came in so fast he didn't have enough time to read them.

"So the Human Council is sending in three teams as well."

He glanced up and caught Tessa's wince and Motre's glare in the rear view mirror.

"They didn't help last time, but they might now as they should have a better understanding of what they are up against."

"Maybe." Tessa nodded. "As long as I'm not babysitting them."

"It would be good to have help. Our resources are dwindling. Several of the foreign dignitaries are leaving. They want to go home and clean their own houses out."

Cody wasn't surprised, but the thought of how much damage the dignitaries could be up against during their absence was mind-boggling.

"They could be going home to complete clans wiped out or turned," Cody said. "They need to get home and fix it now."

"But it's also not good for us if we lose all the able-bodied men we saved." Motre said. "We need more backup,"

Cody, his gaze caught on Tessa's face, wondered at that. She was thinking about something – only what? "Tessa?"

Motre took his eye off the road to glance at Tessa quickly. "What's the matter?"

"Nothing. We don't need the help, and they should all go back and clean their own house. We need to do the same thing ourselves." Her voice was low, hard. And she was staring down at her cell phone. "At least if David is correct. It appears that our friends were kidnapped from the lower levels of the Council Hall itself."

Right. And he'd forgotten that. Shit. "You thinking more moles in the Council?"

But then how could there not be?

"Or they have had the run of the place for years and when they needed an instant place to set up camp on short notice, it was ideal. If it was used by people on the Council, like Gloria for instance, then they could have been using the Hall for decades. Do we even know how big that place is?"

"I wonder if there are any blueprints of the building we can check out?" Cody asked. He started texting the one person he knew who could get that information fast enough. "David is there. He could find out for us."

"Too bad Ian isn't." Tessa turned to smile at Cody. "He's a wizard on a computer."

Cody froze and slowly raised his head to look at her. "Do we know exactly what those three were up to when they were snatched?"

She frowned. "No idea. But I bet they stumbled into something they shouldn't have. Jared was with them, and we know how much the blood farm has been trying to get him back into their clutches."

"So all three would be a coup for them and might help them gain favor with the ever-changing hierarchy of bosses above them."

"And your mother," Motre said. "How does she fit into this?"

"No idea," Tessa said. "Whatever she is doing will be to save Seth. I just don't know how far she'll go to save him."

"The drugs have affected her, so who knows?" Cody said apologetically.

"So she took more. Right, that makes sense," Motre muttered.

"She might have, but only if she thought she could control their effect on her. Otherwise, it doesn't make any sense. If she only took a partial dose, she might be able to do just that." Tessa sat forward in excitement. "That would actually make sense."

Cody shook his head. "Tessa, I know you want to believe in her, but she took more drugs. Doesn't that sound like a junkie to you?"

He caught the look on Motre's face, the single eyebrow shooting to the hairline.

"No," Tessa said, but instead of being mad like he'd expect, she sounded sad. "Mom is all about saving Seth. So we might not like her methods or understand her reasoning, but I do believe she's doing it because she doesn't see another option."

"If they believe she's trying to infiltrate their organization, they'll kill her," Motre warned.

"And she'd say that it's what she had to do and if she died doing it, then she died." Tessa leaned her head back. "So let's find her before it comes to that."

Cody let his breath out in a whoosh. "How far away is it, Motre?"

"Another ten minutes," he said. He changed lanes and turned on his signal. "This should lead to where we want to go. The road had a lot more traffic since the big blow up."

"Blow up?" Tessa asked. "Where exactly are we going?"

"The GPS signal is coming from the valley beside Moltere's Mountain."

She turned in shock to stare at Cody. "Really?"

Cody nodded. "That's where the GPS signal stopped."

She slumped back to her seat. "Damn. I swore nothing could be left alive in there now."

"I don't think it's there as much as it's in the same general location. That would make sense. You found the one place that went up inside the mountain and you came out at the top in the snow region. It's on the list of places to clean up and out, but I don't know that anyone made it there yet. The hospital became a priority once we realized our friends and family were all in trouble instead."

"I'd forgotten about that place. It was at a much higher altitude than the other blood farm."

"Do you know for sure that you were in a blood farm? Or maybe it was just offices? It seems ludicrous to make the blood farms so far apart." Motre turned to glance at Cody. "Unless it was a new one they didn't have up in operation yet."

"I think that's why they were hunting humans when they caught Jared. They had new blood farms and needed new livestock."

"So we've taken out the old ones and now we need to find

the fresh stock again." Motre nodded. "Makes sense."

"But we found one of the new farms that wasn't finished yet. So it could just as easily be the one she escaped from was an original and it was difficult to move the blood so they built new ones. And maybe after blowing those ones up, they were forced to return to the original facilities until more could be built."

"All of it is possible. I almost want to blow up the entire area," Tessa said quietly. "But if there are people we can save, then we need to. Our numbers are declining. If we don't stop this, then it's over for us. Maybe not today or next year, but they have the capability to grow armies, and when they have enough, they will unleash them on us."

Cody felt her shudder from the back of the van. Tessa had been through so much already. Just the thought of this mess never being over made him tired now. He couldn't imagine what life would be like in several decades if this continued. He wanted life to return to the pre-blood farm era.

In that case, Tessa said, *we have to wipe out ninety percent of the vampires around us.*

☙ ❧

"I'M NOT STAYING behind," Serus growled. "You heard Sian. Rhia is there. I need to find her and stop her."

"You won't know which side she is on. You'll want to believe her but won't understand if she's your Rhia or the drugged one. And she's likely to stab you in the back," Goran warned.

"I know, but I don't have a choice. She is my heart. She's doing this to save my son." Serus stared out across the bright sunny sky. "Damn, we'll have to drive."

"I know. And that's already a problem if they have any kind of lookout. We won't be able to approach quietly."

"Then let's hope they don't because we're coming regardless."

Goran grinned. Serus smiled. It was good to be back with his friend. He wished he was with his daughter too, but the whole family was splintered. He'd like it to be otherwise, but at least she had Cody with her. David was safe here now and his wife Rhia, well, he understood what she was doing even if she didn't.

❧ ❦

DAVID SHOOK HIS head. "No way am I staying here. That's my mother and my sister out there. Someone needs to be on their side."

Sian looked to be ready to pull her long beautiful hair out. He glared at her. "You know someone needs to help Mom. The other vamps are going to kill her on sight. So few believe she's not been turned and most would say kill her just to be sure. You know that."

"Your father has gone for just that reason. I've got two units verging on that location," Sian cried. "But someone needs to figure out what's going on here. Those three people – your friends – were snatched *from* here. And we need to know how to make sure there's no one left here that isn't supposed to be here."

Jewel tugged on David's arm. "Sian does need our help."

He turned to look down at her in frustration. She'd been the one who wouldn't stay before, now he was going to have to stay too? Finally he relented. "Fine."

"Thank you," Sian said in relief. "I really do need the

help."

And that made David feel all that much worse. "Sorry, I just hate to be left out of the fighting." He grinned as both Sian and Jewel rolled their eyes at him. He snagged up Jewel's arm and tucked it into his. "Okay…" He paused to consider their first move when his phone went off. He pulled it out and read the message in surprise. "Cody and Tessa suggest we find blueprints for the Council Hall and do a full sweep."

"Now that is something I can help with." Sian walked to an empty computer desk on the side and brought the machine up. She quickly logged in and opened up several folders. "These are the original drawings of the building."

"Who'd know about these?" David asked, sitting down beside her to look. He clicked on one folder and a big blueprint rolled up. "This thing is going to be hard to read on the monitor."

"Blow it up," Jewel said. "Then print it off in sections. We can pin the whole thing on that wall."

David looked at the wall she pointed at and back again. He nodded once. "Great idea. Let's do it."

∽ ∾

RHIA TOOK A deep breath then pushed the door open. And found it full of vamps all eager for enhancements. She wanted to give them a quick boot up the rear. What was wrong with them that they weren't happy with who they were? Enhancements wasn't going to make them better, it was only going to make them different. And considering how different, she didn't understand the enthusiasm.

She frowned at them. Surely they weren't old enough to make this decision. The part of her mind that was clear was screaming at her to tell them to run. To get away from here. And the part of her mind that was like a gray ooze in her head was screaming at her to drug them up now before they had a chance to change their minds. This wasn't the room she was supposed to do first. That was the good part of her mind. She was trying to delay going to Ian and Wendy, but she also knew if she waited, someone else would do the job.

The vamps stared at her. "Now what? We just had our blood taken," one of the vamps lounging in front of her said. "The other woman said our blood would have to be checked before anything else."

She nodded. "I'm in the wrong room. Sorry."

With a cold smile, she left and closed the door behind her.

She heard one of the men say, "Wow, who the hell was that? She didn't look quite right."

She wanted to laugh and cry at the same time. It was not the first time she'd heard something derogatory about herself, but it was the first in a long time. She couldn't blame him, she was a mess and now with part of her fighting the drugs, she was a bigger mess likely than she even realized. Good for him for seeing something was wrong. Maybe he'd reconsider his own pathway here.

He didn't have to take the drugs. These kids had come here voluntarily. In that case, they could all disappear and no one would know or care. Well, the blood farm would care. They'd probably turn the kids into unwilling participants. Rhia didn't think anyone was allowed to leave – ever.

The door she was looking for was outside. She reached a hand in front of her and found it shaking. She clenched her fist and stared at it. This was a turning point. She knew and cared for the people on the other side of the door.

How she handled this was important.

For everyone.

She opened the door and stepped inside.

∂ ∽

IAN WATCHED RHIA survey the room, ready to fight.

He caught his breath.

Rhia turned to face him and smiled. A sad smile, but it was definitely a smile. "Hi, Ian."

Ian let out a shaky breath, his gaze wary as he studied the mother of his best friend. She'd been through it these last weeks, but then, so had he. He'd had the same drugs coursing through his veins as she had, only she might have had more. And he'd missed out on the brainwashing system she'd been put through. He could emphasize, even sympathize, but no way in hell could he condone her helping the bad guys.

"Rhia," he acknowledged with a head tilt. "What are you doing here?"

"I came here to help you," she said. "The trouble is I don't know if you know what that means."

"Maybe the better question is do *you* know what that means?" he responded warily, his attention tracking her movements. She was a powerful vampire and older than him, as in way older. He was also hampered by respect for someone he knew. And respect for the relationship they'd had up until now.

The haggard look on her face damn near broke his heart. Seth's actions had hurt so many people. He understood she felt guilty, but he wasn't in the same camp that said Seth was completely innocent. At one point, Seth had signed up for this. At what age, and had he done so without influence, he didn't know. But Seth was brilliant. And maybe he had been just naive and stupid. But somewhere along the way, he'd gotten in too deep. Rhia might be able to save the boy she remembered, but Ian was afraid the man he'd been hearing about was past saving.

"I need to find Seth," she said, articulating carefully.

Why was she speaking so oddly? He studied her, looking for signs of drugging. "Are you still taking drugs?"

She opened her mouth to speak then snapped it closed. She appeared to be struggling as to what to tell him, then her shoulders slumped. "I took a little. Enough to try and get the information I need to find him."

"And if you get sucked into this morass instead of saving him?" he asked gently. Inside, his mind was screaming. Why? How could she? She'd seen so much damage from the drugs. Had been drugged herself. She wasn't likely to recover from another dose.

"I had to try."

And oddly enough, he understood. "Then how can we trust you?"

Her gaze shifted to look across the bedroom as if to look across the distance between them. He hated to see her so torn, but she was an unnatural vamp in that she took to mothering like humans and not the cold survival strategies that most female vampires adopted. "I'm hoping you'll help me," she said quietly. "As I'll help you."

That was the last thing he'd expected.

CHAPTER 6

TESSA WATCHED AS they drove to a place that had nothing but harsh memories for her. She slowly, methodically chewed her way through her third granola bar. They'd been talking earlier, but the closer they got to the destination, the more silent they'd become. The three of them had faced death so many times already that in a way, it had become the norm. For all of them. Her family, Cody's family, their friends and clan members. Now they were heading into battle yet again. It's not that she was tired. She understood now that so much of her fatigue was mental, emotional. Not physical. At the moment, the melancholy was dominant. Not bad. Not sad. Just reality.

There was a sense of needing to move through the emotions and not trying to avoid them. Maybe that was part of maturing, or maybe it was just a reaction to the massive stress she'd been under and the changes wrought in her own psyche. She'd grown, changed so much. And now she didn't know what to think. But the sight of the collapsed mountain brought back much that she'd hoped to never revisit. How so very appropriate that she was here again. It was like nothing ever changed...just the people caught in an endless loop that did. She had. Cody had. Everyone she knew had.

"You okay?" Cody asked her quietly.

She nodded. "I am. Just not impressed at where we are."

He looked over at the new formation of the mountain beside them and nodded. "Both good and bad memories."

Motre snorted. "You're a sick person if you can find anything good from this place."

Tessa grinned and reached for Cody's hand, overjoyed to find his already there reaching for hers. She knew what good had come from this place.

Focus on that, he whispered in her mind. *All the rest are dark details that will fade over time. We have each other. That's what's important.*

Thanks for that.

No problem.

And damn if she didn't sense a warm hug wrapping around her. God, she loved that. That sense of being part of an intimate twosome and knowing that others *knew* but that they didn't really *know.* How could anyone if they weren't part of it? Weren't one of the two? It was so damn special.

Did all couples feel this way?

She hoped so. But with the mindspeak, it made the connection so much deeper. So much more intimate. There was no way to hide anything from him. And maybe that was the way it should be. Honesty on all levels.

She smiled, realizing how much better she felt already. Just knowing he was there for her had pushed the melancholy away.

No. Her smile widened. It hadn't pushed anything away. His presence had helped her walk through it – and leave it behind.

He was a blessing.

"We're here," Cody announced, holding up the GPS.

She looked around. "There's nothing here."

"Maybe, but according to the GPS reading, this is where

their last location registered. In fact…" He stopped talking as Motre shut off the engine and opened his door. "As there is nothing here, I'm going to suggest that we are right on top of them."

The clouds had filled the sky, making it safe to walk. It was almost dark enough, but the late afternoon sun was still a problem. Tessa frowned. The clouds would help a little. It wasn't a problem for her, but for Cody and Motre…

"Which makes sense considering the number of tunnels riddling this area." Tessa turned to look at where they were in relationship to the mountain they'd brought down and the cliff she'd jumped from. It had to have a connection here. In fact, as far as she could tell, and she'd be the first to admit she might be wrong, but it looked like they were between both of them. The mountain she'd escaped from into the snowy peak rose sharply behind her with a valley near the toppled mountain. These vamps had done an incredible amount of work over the last couple of centuries to make this happen.

"Okay, but how do we access it?" Motre asked. He stood, hands on his hips, and surveyed the area. "There are no hills, doors, trapdoors, mine entrances, buildings, or anything obvious to show an entrance."

Cody walked the area with his GPS tracker. "They are definitely below us."

"How deep will that signal register?" Motre asked. "Will it read six feet down or a hundred feet down?"

Cody frowned, looked at the tracker, the ground, then the tracker. "I'm not sure it would read below the surface at all."

"Then why are we here?" Motre asked in exasperation. "It's obvious no one else is here, so why do you have a GPS signal unless it was registering below the surface?"

⁂

CODY STARED AT Motre. "I have no idea."

Tessa strode to the left, catching his attention. He watched as she bent, twisted, then straightened. He nudged Motre, who turned to watch, too.

"What is she doing now?"

"Likely checking to see what energy is here now and who might have been here before. But I can't say for sure."

"The things that girl knows how to do…"

"The things she's learned how to do," Cody corrected, watching as Tessa backed up, as if trying to get a different view of where the vehicle had parked. "She didn't know how to do any of this before."

"And that just makes it all the more fascinating. So many vamps would kill for her skills."

"Another reason why they want her DNA – so that they can figure how she is doing this. Good luck though as none of her siblings can."

"Do we know that for sure though? What sent Seth on his pathway?"

"A very good question." Cody studied Tessa, loving the ease with which she moved. The graceful movements as she searched for answers. She was truly beautiful, but it was the inside Tessa shining though that made her who she was. And that just reminded him of that Deanna bitch. Was she gone? Could he count on it? The last thing he wanted was to be kissing Tessa and have that old crone be on the inside playing games with him. That had already held him back, even if he hadn't been ready to acknowledge it. But she wasn't exactly what he wanted in his life. He wanted his Tessa. Not a Deanna/Tessa combo.

That incident had freaked him out. What he had to figure out was how he could tell when it was one or the other. If he could do that, then it wouldn't matter as he wouldn't be fooled anymore.

Definitely something worth learning. He studied Tessa, trying to see the energy she talked about so much. If he could see the energy shift when Deanna took control, then he'd do fine. But he had no idea what that looked like.

But you do inside, she whispered in his mind, reminding him once again that they were two parts of a whole. He could feel an odd discomfort that she'd heard his thoughts, but it was better this way. To know for sure was imperative. Otherwise, the doubts would poison what they had. And he didn't want that.

Ever.

Look not at me, but past me, she whispered. *The energy is there on all things but almost impossible to see if you are looking at it straight on.*

He frowned and looked past her. He almost let out a cry of surprise when he realized that he could see something out of the corner of his eyes. Not clear enough to understand or close enough to capture for a better look, but a distinct waviness to her form.

That's the energy, she said with no small amount of satisfaction. *The trick now though is to see it all the time and to identify mine from someone else's.*

He tried to look at the tree branch and the rocks on the ground, but for all his efforts, he couldn't see anything.

The only thing he had seen was a wired softening to her outline.

Apparently I suck at this, he said, grumbling.

No, you don't suck at it, she said gently. *I'm not sure why I see the colors and energy clearly, but apparently not everyone does.*

Except Deanna.

She saw some stuff. I don't know exactly what.

You could check though, right? he asked quietly, sensing her reluctance but not sure why.

I could, but not right now. We have friends we need to rescue.

He nodded in understanding. She was scared to look. Scared to open up the Deanna can of worms and find more than she was ready to accept.

"Ideas then?" Cody turned to Motre. "We have several teams converging on this spot in less than an hour. What exactly are we going to do to find an entrance to this underground mind?"

"If it's even here," Motre said. "If your GPS isn't registering below ground, then chances are good the cell phone was tossed here to throw us off."

"Doesn't matter if it was," Tessa said. "The cluster of energy moves this way." She pointed to a small rise ahead. "There is likely an entrance close by."

Motre shook his head. "We don't really have time for likely at this point. We need to know for sure."

She smoked him with a look. "Let me rephrase that. There is an opening over here according to the energy."

A sharp crack ripped through the air, a bullet striking the ground between Motre and Cody.

Cody hit the ground, screaming, "Find cover, now."

He lifted his head to find Motre behind a small dip in the ground. He searched for Tessa.

There was no sign of her.

GORAN HATED TO drive when he could fly, yet the light was fading enough that he'd likely be able to do his thing soon enough.

By the time they reached the coordinates given, then maybe he could. For the moment, he was stuck in the back of a big Council vehicle that carried a team of four men and Serus. But like him, Serus looked as uncomfortable as hell. Good. Why should Goran suffer alone? This was ridiculous. He poked Serus in the ribs and nodded outside. There was only a small window higher up on this rig, and it used dark glass to keep the light out. "It's getting dark."

"Not dark enough," his buddy growled.

"Almost," Goran said cheerfully.

"So, we're still stuck inside." Serus slumped in place and glared at the driver.

Goran grinned. He felt better already. Serus had been moody since leaving, his thoughts heavy on his wife. So this way he had something else to grouse about. All good. He grinned at the men sitting stone-faced across from him. He barely recognized them. They were part of Motre's security detail but having never used any himself, he didn't recognize the faces.

He closed his eyes to slits as that thought drifted into his mind and wallowed. If he didn't know who these men were, how could he be sure whose side they were on?

He couldn't.

Serus, do you recognize these men, he asked using mind-speak.

He loved that Serus never shifted from his slouched position nor turned to look at the men in question as he answered, *No. I was about to ask you the same thing.*

Do we know where we're going? Goran asked, wondering if

they were being led into a trap.

Roughly where we rescued Tessa after she escaped into the snow and jumped down the mountain.

Goran tried to track that information in his head. He'd flown her out of there. And it hadn't been all that far away from Moltere's Mountain that they'd blasted. *Son of a bitch. Are we thinking that they are at a new blood farm?*

New, or an old one being brought back into service out of necessity, Serus growled, adding, *or one we missed.*

Made sense. *But what if the guys with us are part of the blood farm?*

Serus's answer was succinct and clearly to the point as ever. *Then we're giving them a lift home. Permanently.*

❧ ❦

RHIA STRUGGLED TO control the two warring parts of herself with each other. "I'm struggling here, Ian. I'm trying to help you and help myself."

"Then why are you here?" He nodded at the medical kit in her hand.

"They sent me to take your blood."

He shook his head. "They already have samples. They don't need more."

She stopped and considered his words. "Maybe they were destroyed."

"And maybe they came here wondering if we'd try to kill you and if you would kill us."

"As a test?" She shook her head even as the other part of her snapped inside her mind, *You know they are suspicious. You know they need to find out for sure if you can be trusted, so of course this is a test.*

She looked down at her kit. "What am I to do then? I have to return with blood or they'll know."

"Take mine. They've already got it in their database, so that will just confirm who we are. Leave Jared and Wendy alone."

He waited quietly for her to sort out the ramifications of handing over the blood of only one person.

"We won't have much time to get away if they get onto us," she warned. "It might not be enough time to get away at all."

"It will be if the vials are mixed up with others. They'd have to test them all before they conclude you didn't get blood from the three of us."

She frowned. "That might work."

He waited with that gaze of his, that much younger gaze that had now hardened over the life experiences he'd been through himself. She suggested, "The men beside us have given blood, but I could go and take more."

"Do that first," Ian said. "That will give these two a little more time to wake up." His gaze glittered as it locked on Wendy. "What did they do to her?"

"I think it was just a hold they used to knock you out. They didn't hold you long enough, so you're awake early. They are expecting the three of you to be out for at least another hour or so."

"Good, that's our window then." He thought quickly, then rolled up his sleeve. "Take a vial from me, and then go take more blood from the men beside us. That will mean they've got the blood needed and won't send anyone else for a while."

A bit confusing, but Rhia thought she understood his thought process. She nodded. "Might be the easiest at this point."

She quickly pulled out the needle from the bag and plunged it into his arm.

"How much time do you need to get the information on Seth?"

"An hour," she said firmly. "That's the time we have, then that's the time I need. No more, no less."

"And if you can't get it in that time frame?"

"Then…" She stopped, unable to speak. "You have to understand. Failure is not an option."

Ian nodded. "That doesn't mean it won't happen."

❧ ❦

JEWEL PINNED THE last piece of paper on the wall. This was it. David studied the wall. The whole blueprint blown up and cut into twelve segments then printed now placed back together on the wall. He had a different perspective of the Council Hall now. This place was massive.

"What do you think?" Jewel said when she stood back and studied the image.

"I think this place was built to sustain a war and house the entire vampire clan."

"It's not that big." She laughed at him until she saw where he was pointing. "What is that?"

"A long tunnel that says under Main Street."

"But where does it go?" she cried out. "It's a single tunnel."

"And could be connected to three quarters of the city."

"Or…" She turned to face him. "Maybe the hospital?"

"All those floors and tunnels…unbelievable."

"Exactly. Do we have access to the blueprints of the hospital? Other major centers? Teams are on their way to the mountain," she cried. "What if that was a lure to get everyone away from the Hall? How hard would it have been to have taken the cell phone and drive it up there and drop it? Set a trap there and lure everyone away from here."

He stared at her in shock. "They'd take control of Council Hall before anyone even knew what had happened."

Shit. "We need to talk to Sian, like now."

CHAPTER 7

TESSA HIT THE ground rolling then got to her feet and ran. There was energy where the shooter had been, but there was a part of her that was already registering that none of the energy was familiar. It wasn't Wendy, Ian's, or Jared's, so who? She dashed for cover then jumped high and hard over the top of where the shots had been. And came down in front of the vamp lining up for another shot.

Shit.

She threw herself to the left then kicked out and...missed. She shook her head and took to the air as the vamp tried to line up on her. She kicked a second time and this time took the gun out of his hand. She landed and stabbed her nails into his gun arm. He cried out, his left arm coming up to grab at her neck when she swung upwards with her spare hand under his chin and let her claws on that hand extend. He screamed as she tossed him out into the remaining sunlight as it peeked over the horizon.

He blew to ash, but not fast and not hot, more of a slow roast. It was terrible. Motre, his coat over his head, ran forward and stabbed the suffering vamp with a stake.

This time he blew to ash like normal.

Motre glanced over at her. "Are there more?"

"No," she said. "Not only that, the three of our friends were never here. There's no sign of their energy."

"So a trap?" Cody crawled out from under the vehicle where he'd rolled to get away from the bullets and held up a cell phone. "We were led here like pigs to the slaughter."

"With only one gunman?" Motre sounded insulted. "That's shameful."

Cody shook his head. His phone rang. Tessa took a last look around as Cody answered his phone. She couldn't quite hear the conversation, but her mind was struggling to put all the pieces in place. One gunman only, so either they didn't need more, or had more men on route, or they needed the men somewhere else and couldn't afford to leave more than one man here right now. But why would they need the men elsewhere?

She froze.

"Tessa," Cody's sharp urgent voice called her. "That was David. He thinks this was a trap to lure everyone away from the Council Hall. A team is enroute here with the ancients and every other able-bodied man plus a top-notch human military team. Sian is trying to contact everyone."

Shit shit shit…why hadn't she seen it?

"They are going to take over Council Hall," she screamed, jumping toward him. It took two leaps and she was at the vehicle. Both men scrambled inside to stay out of the waning sun's rays. She leaned inside, her voice bubbling over with excitement. "That has to be what they are doing. It's the perfect plan."

Cody's phone rang. Then Motre's rang. Tessa shook her head. They needed to move and fast. They knew what was here and how to get inside of the blood farm, but they could do that afterwards. The Council Hall was a strategic location. They had to hold it.

She walked around to the driver's side and motioned for

Motre to move over. He was needed to coordinate their next move. Her best option was to drive.

Action was better than talking any day.

She grinned and fired up the engine. And froze. How did she know to drive? She didn't know. Did she? Or was this Deanna's knowledge? She shifted the gear shift, desperately trying to not show the other two the change in her demeanor. It's not that Deanna was in control, but somehow she'd instinctively accessed Deanna's knowledge base. Then she'd done it many times before and likely would again. Letting her energy use the memories of an experienced driver, she turned the vehicle around and started back the way they'd come.

Hortran, is this the right way to do this?

She didn't know why she was asking him, but it seemed the thing to do. He was like a wise council member in her mind and yet he could just as easily be that relationship to Deanna. *No, he was her brother.* That's why the two were so close. Hortran had been born decades ahead of Deanna and raised in the Ghost way.

As that knowledge flowed through her, she smiled. There was a lot to be said for having centuries of information at her fingertips. The driving showed she also had centuries of skills available as well.

Thanks, Deanna.

No answer.

Good.

Hortran, you still here?

A brief mellow wave washed through her. It wasn't much, but it was enough.

She hit the gas pedal and drove them back to the Council Hall.

They were ten miles out when she caught sight of a

Council vehicle up ahead. "Cody? Motre?"

The men stopped their conversations and peered through the windshield.

"No idea."

She slowed to a stop and waited for the other vehicle to come toward her. "I wonder if the ancients are in there?"

"No idea," Cody said. "Quite possibly. Father would fly rather than drive, but it's just not possible for him to do that yet."

The vehicle slowed.

That was when she realized she'd stopped in the middle of the road with no place for the other vehicle to drive around her because of rocks. There was no room. Given that the sun was an issue, the other vamps weren't likely to leave the vehicle and come talk to her. She'd have to go to them. "I'm going over. But I can tell you right now, I don't like anything about this."

"Don't go," Cody snapped. "If they are rebels, then we'll take them out."

"But how do we tell?" Motre asked. "They can't get out because of the sunlight and the way she's parked, they can't drive close enough for the two of us to talk."

"Right. Time to change tactics." Tessa said. She unbuckled and twisted in her seat to climb through to the back of the van. There she opened the back panel door and jumped out. She landed on the roof then jumped across to the roof of the other vehicle and down to the ground behind it. In a flash, she had the back door opened.

And saw black energy everywhere. She kicked out and slashed wildly as the men struggled to fight her off from the inside.

Suddenly there were only two men standing.

The ancients.

Her father groaned. "Damn it, Tessa, we were looking forward to doing that."

She snorted. "Right. Then how about you take out the driver and the passenger before we get rained on with silver bullets?"

His grin turned feral as he turned to the front cab. The men there were pinned inside by late sunlight and couldn't reach the men in the back because of the cage-like divider. Tessa watched her father dispatch both men efficiently.

Goran looked pissed.

She grinned at him. "Sorry, Goran. They should have been yours."

"Your father should be at the Council Hall and resting," Goran growled, but he was eyeing the smug look on Serus's face with a satisfied smile of his own. "Nothing like a good dust up to make you feel better, huh?"

Serus grinned. "Always."

"Good," Tessa said. "Because we have lots of dust ups to come."

She quickly explained what they'd figured out. "We still don't have a location though for Mom and the others."

Serus closed his eyes briefly, then said, "We have to protect the Council Hall. So many foreign dignitaries are there resting up before leaving. They might be in fighting form, but if they get more drugs…"

"And lots have left, too," she said. "But we have to go back. At least we have a short window where the enemy won't know we're onto them, but that's the only advantage we have. They'll step up their timeline when they realize the tables have been turned."

The men scrambled into place at the front of the truck.

"We'll meet you back at the Hall," Serus called out.

She nodded and spun back to where Motre and Cody waited for her.

"Hey wait," her father called out. "Did you drive that van?"

She laughed and said, "Yeah, but I had a little help."

CODY HOPED SHE was kidding. He studied her face as she crawled into the back of the van with him. He waited until she was settled and Motre, who'd taken the driver's seat, was driving forward.

"What did you mean?"

She didn't pretend to misunderstand. Instead she beamed and said, "I used Deanna's and Hortran's knowledge to drive."

He stared at her, his mind swirling with the concept. Then he remembered that she hadn't known how to drive before as her father had delayed teaching her. David had finished his training, but her father had been holding back on hers. Still, she'd driven down from the mountain perfectly. And neither Motre nor he had even considered it as anything other than normal. She did everything with skill now. Interesting. *But it was you in control?* he asked carefully, studying her face and looking for something to say it was Tessa, not Deanna.

She grinned. *Absolutely. I was using her knowledge to drive. And it was so easy and natural.*

And weird, he added dryly. *I know that probably sounds like a good thing, but it needs to be something you use with control.*

She nodded comfortably. *Agreed. But this time it worked*

out just fine.

And no sign of Deanna?

She shook her head. *None. The good news though is that I did sense Hortran inside. So he's still with me.*

Cody studied her, wondering how that could make her so happy. The thought of that creepy Ghost living inside of him made his skin crawl. *And that's a good thing?*

It's a very good thing. Her voice was calm and controlled. She believed in what she was saying. But she had before too. And look how well that had worked out for her.

He decided to ignore it for the moment, but inside rose the same damn question as to how could he tell for sure when it was Tessa? And once again, he came up blank.

"Cody," Motre said. "Call David and see if he managed to find a connection from the hospital yet. I'm wondering if one of our teams shouldn't go in from that direction. Catch the bastards between us in the middle."

Tessa gasped. "Oh. Deanna's memories say there is a long tunnel going from where she was a prisoner through town and ends up at Council Hall. All part of the plan to protect our species in case the humans destroyed the world above."

The thought of the planet being a victim of mass destruction was a sobering thought. Vampires didn't need much to survive, but they did need blood of some kind and if all the humans and animals died, then they would too. Unless they had...blood farms.

He leaned back, wondering if that's how this mess all started. They could manufacture plasma now, but there would always be the purists who wanted the real stuff. And in the event of a catastrophe happening, then the blood farms and potentially the plasma were all the vampires needed to survive.

For the first time, he understood the drive to keep the

species alive. They might not all deserve to survive, but there was no doubt that they needed a place in the event of something major happening on the surface.

"Let's go to the hospital and come in from there, Motre," he said. "If we divert a couple of teams in our direction as backup…"

"Right. You got a way to tell who's on our side and who's not given that Tessa just annihilated men I thought we could count on?"

Shit. Why was this never easy?

Tessa reached over and grabbed his hand. "We're better off doing this ourselves. If anyone comes our way and they are on the wrong side, then they are going to radio ahead to the others and our element of surprise will be gone."

He nodded. He knew that. He'd just hoped that for once, things would be easy. Still, if he had to go to war with only a few people, the ones he was with were the best. "We need to tell the ancients."

She nodded. "They can decide where they want to go. With us or back to the Hall."

"Send them to the Hall," Motre said. "It's going to get ugly there. And the ancients are the best at cleaning house."

❧ ❦

"THE HALL? WE'RE to go to the Hall and they are going to the hospital. How the hell does that work?" Goran growled. "What does the hospital have to do with anything?"

"They will have a reason." Serus lay with his eyes closed, listening to his friend as they drove behind the others.

"Then ask them so we know, too."

But he didn't have to. His phone was going off steadily as

Tessa explained. He never understood why they didn't just pick up the phone and call. No, that was a generational thing David had tried to explain to him years ago. It's not that young people were averse to talking on a phone, but they were faster and more comfortable texting.

Well, he wasn't.

Still, he could read, and as he scrolled through the texts from his daughter followed by several from his son, he explained the gist of what the kids had found out to Goran.

"I think we always knew that the hospital was connected underground to other parts of town," Goran said in a contemplative tone. "The trouble is I think we as a species have forgotten more than we know about our heritage. Isn't someone supposed to be keeping track of that information at the Council?"

Serus looked over at Goran. "That was Gloria, wasn't it?"

The two exchanged glances. "That would make sense then."

"She had access. She'd known about the other facilities. She was the leader on this side of the blood farms. Too much to hope that she'd been the only leader."

"No, there was definitely someone above her."

Serus agreed. "So they are going to the hospital to come in from that side. And we're to go directly to the Hall." He brightened. "This day is getting to sound better and better."

Goran snorted. "Now that we have a fight brewing, it is." He glanced over at Serus. "Unless the kids get the bigger fight."

Serus glared at him. "No way. Make this thing go faster. If we're there first, we get a bigger piece of the pie."

With a shout of laughter, Goran gunned the engine and shot the vehicle down the road as fast as it could go.

❧ ❧

DAVID, ARMED WITH a copy of the blueprints clipped together and Jewel at his side, headed downstairs. They were on a time crunch and somehow it had taken twenty minutes to get the information they needed, and yet this had been so complex with so many updates that the time had whipped past them while they were trying to figure out how to even plan their next move. They'd sent the information they'd gathered to everyone they needed to, including the Human Council via Sian. What they were attempting to do was avoid sending out the information to the blood farm people. The last thing David wanted was to have those assholes know that they were onto them.

It was going to happen eventually – no way to avoid it, unfortunately, but every minute they could steal without the enemy knowing was a gift. He hit the stairwell and raced down. He wasn't a flier or a jumper, but like his mother, he was agile, fit, and damn fast. He was taking full landings in one jump, and Jewel was hampered because her wings couldn't open in the confined space. She was struggling behind him. He didn't want to slow down, but...

Looking behind him, he checked on her condition.

She snorted. "Keep going. I'm fine."

"You should be recovering from your ordeal," he snapped. "Not racing toward a war."

"Ha." She laughed. "I'd rather be doing this."

He shook his head and made sure she didn't see his grin. He loved that about her. The let-me-at-them attitude. Still, he worried about her. She was more than willing to do this, but was her body ready? She'd been through hell at the hands of those assholes. It couldn't happen again. He planned on making sure she stayed safe this time, but he couldn't be everywhere.

She had to help him by being careful.

At the last set of stairs, he held up his hand. "This is the bottom floor according to the blueprints."

"Right. But that doesn't mean we can know for sure that more weren't added at a later date."

"Let's not go there." What a thought. There was enough here to start searching the building without considering renovations that might have been done in the years since. "This is what we have to go on, so let's trust that for now."

She nodded. He opened the door and peered out. "I don't think I've ever been down this low."

"I'm not sure many have," she said. "It's clean though, so there must be regular maintenance done on this level."

"I think the whole place is cleaned weekly," he answered in an absent voice as he studied the empty hallway. The good thing was they were at one end of a long hallway. A decision he'd made early on. There were staircases on all four corners of the H-shaped hallway pattern. That meant four exits and four entrances. That meant four escapes for them and the others. He wanted to be methodical about this. With Jewel holding his hand, they quickly went door to door and checked the rooms. Most of the doors were unlocked and opened to show empty rooms. The four rooms on the left were empty. Jewel noted the location and they kept going. After completing that side, they moved down the main corridor, with David running ahead to check and Jewel keeping track of the results. On the entire floor, there was only the one locked door. Jewel contacted Sian. On her orders, they returned to the door, and with the help of a master key that required several patient moments of fiddling, they managed to open it. David stood in the middle of the room. It was empty. But it was damn small. As in way smaller than every other room on this floor. He knew they were supposed to be the same. The blueprints had shown that, and his visual exam had confirmed they were all approximately the same size.

So why this one smaller, and why was it locked?

"You know, it could be as simple as realizing this room was different, so keeping it locked stopped the confusion and anyone needing a room could use any of the others."

"Yet the room where they were testing the chemicals in Bart's canisters was also small."

She studied the room, then walked to the far corner. "In that case…" And she found a hidden door in the shadows. "This is the matching door to that room."

David grinned and reached for the handle. "What do we have here?"

⌘ ⌘

RHIA WALKED BACK to the main center, her arms full of tubes of blood. She'd gone back to the room of male vamps and grabbed several more from them. Another tech had walked in while she'd been there and sent her out, a frown on his face. But he seemed to ignore her as he called four names from his list. She walked out before she had an understanding of what he was doing there.

Back at the center, she put the vials in with the others waiting, making sure the vials were in no special order, and sat down at the closest computer. It was not connected to a main server. That was going to be her next problem. Finding the computer that would be connect her to the databases – in an hour.

"Rhia, come over and work on this computer please," the tech she'd just seen in the room said. "I need that one to process this new information."

Willingly, she switched to the computer he pointed out in the corner. It was on and running, but the monitor was dark. Still, as she walked to where she was supposed to be, she clicked the keyboard to bring it up out of sleep mode and opened the network. Of course, it needed a log in. Damn. That's the one she needed to be working on.

She studied the computer screen in front of her.

Then reached down and pulled on the network cable separating the end from the wires. Instantly her screen went black. "Huh, sorry, I can't. This one doesn't appear to be working."

He looked up at her, distracted. "What? Really? We had problems a few days ago, but I thought they were fixed."

"It's not letting me get on the network."

"Damn." He nodded at the one she wanted and said, "Use that one."

"What about a log in," she said in a light voice. "I hate the damn things. Can never remember mine."

"Use mine," he snapped and reeled off a series of numbers. "Then get someone in to fix yours."

"Will do." She smiled to herself as she logged in. "Thanks."

"Doesn't matter what password we use. We all have access to the same shit," he muttered. "How am I supposed to get anything done without any help?"

"There's always too much to do," she sympathized.

"Only since the bastards took out our facilities. Getting the numbers back up is a huge problem."

She nodded but struggled to keep her face from showing

too much interest. She needed to know what he did. But how without raising his suspicions?

He groaned and pushed his chair back. "I got that done. On to the next problem." He walked over to the vials of blood at the side and started fiddling with the machine. "It's going to take time we don't have to process this batch. We should have invested in new equipment a long time ago." He continued to lament his lot in life while Rhia listened with half an ear. She had the computer up and was trying to get into the database to look up Seth's information without him seeing what she was doing. At the same time, she was trying to look busy so he didn't question *what* she was doing.

Finally finding the patient list, she typed in her last name.

And up came every damn member of her family.

The drugged part of her mind shouted for joy. *See, they are all here. That's great.*

The other part to her mind screamed in horror. What was this? Why were David, Serus, and Tessa here? Surely they hadn't been drugged – had they?

CHAPTER 8

W ALKING BACK INTO the hospital that they'd left only
hours earlier was weird enough, but going to the bowels
of the building where they'd met Hortran and Deanna was
downright scary. And she had no idea why.

"Tessa?" Cody's warm voice washed over her. Lord, that
man knew her inside and out. Always when she was feeling
off.

She didn't know what to say to explain the funny emptiness inside her. Only it wasn't empty, it was more a feeling of
a black hole. Empty but not empty. As if something somehow
was ready to blow.

"I'm fine." She offered him a small smile. "Or I will be,"
she amended, "when I realize why I feel so off down here."

Motre, who was walking ahead slightly, said, "Maybe it's
because this was Deanna's and Hortran's world."

"Right," Cody said, slipping an arm through Tessa's as if
to ward off any nastiness.

If Motre's comment was right on… "So not *my* sensation
as much as I'm tapping into Deanna's memories of this place."

"Did she have bad memories here?" Cody frowned.

"I'm sure they are mixed. She was a prisoner for a while
until she managed to turn the tables on that. I'm sure anger is
one of many emotions she felt over the centuries." Still, it was
an idea, and one she needed to consider. Hortran's memories

were also here, not that she'd investigated much of his. It was enough at the moment to deal with Deanna's overpowering energy. The sense of wrongness was the bigger concern.

"I think…" She paused, stopping in place. "…we're not alone."

Motre froze up ahead. "What?" he said urgently. "Can you see someone?"

"No, I can't…" She winced, knowing how this would go down, but continued anyway. "I can sense them."

Both men spun to look at her. She shrugged and added, "I can't explain, but that's the weird feeling inside."

"Where are they?" Cody studied her features. "And can you tell us who or what or how many?"

Lord, she loved him. He continuously gave her reasons to love him a little more each day. Acceptance. What a glorious thing. With a happy sigh, she said, "I think there are several, but I can't tell from the size of the energy ball if that means three or four."

She frowned, trying to sort out the feelings. "They aren't quite here yet. As in I'm sensing their approach like a wave of energy coming towards us."

"That implies they know we're here," Motre said. "How could that be?"

"Easy, the cameras," Cody snapped. "Damn it, we forgot about those."

"Doesn't matter," Tessa said, marching forward. "They'd have found us soon enough anyway."

"But we would have more warning," Motre protested. "There's only three of us. What if there are dozens coming at us?"

Cody snorted. "Bring them on. A dozen is nothing."

Motre glanced from him to Tessa and back again and

smiled. "Right. I forgot for a moment."

Tessa laughed. "I'm not perfect, but there are some things I can do, and fighting is one of them."

"You just keep track of the energy and we'll do the rest," Cody said. "You're tired. And we're going to need that energy of yours later to heal the wounded."

Right. Funny how she'd forgotten about that. Or had it been Deanna's thoughts that had dominated? Tessa was all about healing. Deanna figured it wasn't worth the time and effort. Better to kill them all off or let them die on their own. The world was too crowded as it were.

She motioned to the left of them where a solid wall existed. "They are coming from that direction."

Cody stared.

Motre raised his eyebrows.

She sighed. "Honestly."

They walked through the large room into a narrow hallway. She held up her hand, feeling the ball of darkness flying toward them. "I still don't have a clue what this is," she admitted, "but it's coming very fast and is now very close."

Cody shifted his position until he was on the far side of her and Motre on the other and waited. She held up her right hand and said in a low voice, "They are coming. Three. Two. One."

And she dropped her arm.

All hell broke loose.

CODY HAD NO idea what the hell hit him, but he was lifted up off his feet and tossed to the floor a dozen feet away and he never saw it coming. Or what it was.

Then he heard it growl.

His heart froze. *What the hell?*

He studied the wolf-looking animal crouched in front of him. Had that *been* a German shepherd? Were the assholes now turning dogs into killer…what? He didn't even know what to call this animal. The wolf jumped him, its teeth ripping and tearing at Cody's coat then pants. Cody tried to get free when a second animal launched onto his back, dropping him to his knees. Cody struggled. There was nothing to grab and when he did finally grab the first one and throw him across the room, the animal was launching at his throat instantly.

Motre screamed as an animal bit into him.

"Use the silver," Tessa cried, her voice loud and piercing over the din of the animal howls and grunts.

Cody finally managed to pull the silver stake out of his pocket and stabbed the one trying to bite his neck through his coat collar. Instantly a wave of black dust surrounded him. How? Why? There was no such thing as a vampire dog. At least, there hadn't been before.

He was relieved that they responded to that age-old defense and wished he had one of the UV light weapons so he could blast this whole pack at once. The first animal lunged again. Cody dropped to one knee and stabbed it as it jumped. That one disappeared just like the other one. Now emboldened and pissed, Cody went on the attack and swiped and stabbed the last few animals attacking Motre.

Tessa. He spun around to see her staring, crouched on her knees, eye to eye, growling right back at the largest canine abomination he'd ever seen.

"Jesus, Tessa, what the hell are you doing?"

"It's not his fault."

Motre joined Cody to stare at Tessa and the last animal alive in the room.

"What's not his fault?" Cody hated to admit it, but his breath was ragged from the surprise attack.

"What they did to him," she said in a low, even tone.

"You're forgetting something," Motre snapped. "They turned these dogs into killers."

"But they don't want to be. It's not who they are inside."

And Cody realized something else. This strong beautiful woman in front of him was still the gentle, caring Tessa that had gone after her own people to save a friend. And now that she'd come up against a dog that had been abused by the enemy and turned against her, she was still trying to save it.

"You can't save it," Motre cried out in frustration. "We just killed the rest of these evil bastards."

"I can see its energy. It was bigger than the others. They gave him the same amount of drugs as the others instead of basing it on body weight."

Cody shook his head, trying to understand. "So he's not turned?"

"He's been turned into this, but the original dog is still in there."

"Dog or wolf?" Motre snapped. "Even if you could fix him, he's still going to be dangerous as hell."

"Maybe and maybe not," Tessa said quietly. "What if I could heal him?"

And she lay down on the cement floor in front of the dog.

Both Motre and Cody jumped forward to protect her, but she held up her hand. The dog stopped bristling and snarling. He walked over slowly to stand over her.

With his breath caught in the back of his throat, Cody could barely stand still when the dog, calmer, not so killerish looking, whimpered and lay down beside her.

And laid its head on her ribs.

"Holy crap," Motre whispered.

Cody watched as she gently reached out a hand and stroked the dog's fur and seemed to continue the stroke out into the air. And he understood. She was moving the darkness away from the animal. Cleaning it of the damaging poison that had turned it into a killer. The dog slowly turned less black and more silvery gray as Tessa worked. The animal whimpered several times while she worked.

Just when Cody figured that Motre was going to say something about being short on time, Tessa laid a hand on the back of the dog's neck and slowly sat up. The dog's head slid down to her lap, but he made no move to stand up and leave. Or to stop her. Sitting, Tessa checked out the dog's energy a little further.

"I think he'll be okay now."

"Think?" Motre scoffed. "The penalty is high if you're wrong."

"Not really. Just a bite. And I'll heal."

Talking quietly to the dog, she carefully stood up. The dog stood up with her, apparently not willing to be separated. Cody stared down at the huge dog and wondered what had happened to it. "What could they have done that turned these dogs into killers? And surely there would have been easier weapons. Although it is hard to imagine one with greater shock value."

"It's the genetic experiments and drugs," she said quietly. "They are growing some, snatching others off the streets, and perverting them into this. But this guy appears to be slowly recovering. I wonder if he wasn't as badly treated or hadn't been under their control for very long that I could still see the essence of who he was."

"Well, how about you shoo him away and let's get moving?"

The dog slowly turned his massive head to stare at Motre, a horrific growl sliding out the back of his throat.

Whoa.

Motre hastily shifted back several steps.

Tessa casually reached down one hand and placed it on the dog's head. He subsided instantly.

Cody stared at Tess. "Did you just tell it to stop that?"

"Sure. He's well-trained."

Motre snorted. "That's what you call it?"

She smiled. "He's less certain of you because he can feel your fear."

"And can you feel his fear?" Cody asked curiously. "He's huge and dangerous if you can't control him."

"I don't know that I can control him, but I can communicate with him somewhat."

"If he goes after me, I will kill him," Motre snapped.

"If he goes after you, it will be because he's afraid that you'll go after him and he's only defending himself."

This was an interesting twist. "What are you going to do with him?" Cody asked. "I'm not sure you can keep him as a pet. He's hardly pet material. Look at the size of him. His head is almost at your waist. The jaws on that thing..." He left the sentence unfinished. The other dogs hadn't been quite so big or so bad-looking or as mean-looking. But they'd been deadly. And they'd been killed. He had no idea what to do with the dog now. And would it even die the same way as the others had? "Why did the dogs die by silver? That makes no sense."

"It's the genetic material they injected into the dogs," she said. "Vampire blood. Makes them hungry for more, and yet is affected by silver and sunlight the same as we are. They are trying to make these animals perfect so they can replicate them. I'd say these were the first ones tested, so they don't know how the injections work on them yet."

"The spikes should have made them bleed out as any normal injury would to a dog, not explode like vampires though."

"I'm wondering if they didn't switch the blood in their veins with vampire blood," she said quietly, staring down at the massive dog beside her. He seemed content to wait for her to make the next move. He wasn't exactly sure yet, but he suspected she had gained a pet.

"Can we go now?" Motre strode in the direction the dogs had come from. "I'd like to make sure there are no more of those psycho animals to scare the bejesus out of everyone at the Council Hall."

"Good point." Tessa walked to the door. The dog remained sitting where she'd left him. Cody watched and wondered. Tessa got to the door, turned back to the dog, and raised an eyebrow. She looked at him and said, "Well?"

And the dog loped toward her like an obedient puppy—only ten times the size.

Jesus. Could this day get any weirder?

Cody fell into line behind the dog. If Tessa wanted him to walk beside her, that was too damn bad. Until he knew that dog wasn't going to hurt any of them, he'd stay where he could keep an eye on it.

And then, if need be, kill it fast before it could do any more damage.

RHIA KEPT HER eyes down on the desk and shuffled through papers and the long list of instructions. As she read the detailed notes, it occurred to her that they must have a hell of a problem training staff here if they kept such perfect instructions. Had they managed to make heavy inroads in the staff here or was this such a new department no one had experience so everyone in here had to be trained? And if people were moving from department to department, then an instruction manual like this was essential.

"Can you read my notes?" the tech asked. She realized there was a name card tossed on the desk she was sitting at. Barry. She studied his face. He looked like Barry. Then it could just as well be the last vamp she killed herself. "It's pretty clear," she answered.

"Good. I've rewritten that thing several times trying to dummy it down for everyone who comes through here when I need help. When we were in normal operation, then I could do all of this myself." He waved his hand around the room. "This was my domain. Now that we are losing so many people and animals, well…" He shook his head. "That just became too much. I'm only one man. And I'm good, but I can't do the work of five or six men."

He sat back down and stared at his monitor then groaned. "See, and now I just entered the wrong information on this person." He pinched the bridge of his nose. "I need sleep."

"Go," she urged. "I won't tell anyone. Crash in one of the many rooms here. You can't work like this."

He looked hopeful for a moment then studied the work stacked up around him. "I can't. There is too much to do and no one else to do it."

"How will they know if you take an hour and power nap? You can't keep this up. The integrity of the work needs you at your best."

He studied her for a long moment then turned his gaze to the doorway. "An hour might do it."

"If you sleep half that, it's as good as four hours. It's not going to replace a full day's rest, but it will power you up for a long time."

She smiled encouragingly at him. "I'll hold down the fort. If anyone comes looking for you, I'll tell them that you are collecting blood samples."

"Thanks." He stood up and stretched. "I am wiped."

He walked to the doorway. "Tell them I've found an anomaly in the system and have gone to the techs to track it down."

"Will do."

And he walked out. She listened to his receding footsteps and a few minutes after that to make sure no one else came in, then she minimized all the programs open on her screen and went to work. The information she needed was here somewhere.

She just had to find it.

DAVID OPENED THE door and stared at the old-fashioned set of cut stone stairs. "Well, well, well."

"What the..." Jewel gasped as she studied what appeared to be a narrow staircase leading straight up, with no end in sight. "That's not on the blueprints."

"That's likely because it was a builder's back entrance. In a building this size, particularly when it's as deep underground as this one is, the first thing that builders do is construct a way back to the surface in case of a major disaster." He walked to the bottom of the stairs and looked up. "There is no electricity in here."

"Do you think it goes all the way to the surface? Or just up a level?"

"If it were me, I'd make sure that it was accessible from each floor. We've checked this floor and marked down what we've found. Let's inform Sian in case we run into trouble. She'll be able to track us."

With Jewel sending texts, David closed the two doors and started up the stairs. He was loving this. If it wasn't for the thought of an imminent attack, he'd love to stay and explore some more. Unfortunately, his prime objective was to determine if this exit was really just that and if it had been used recently. He wasn't seeing dust everywhere, but down so deep it was still cold and there didn't appear to be any footprints on the cold stone ahead of him.

Making sure Jewel was right behind him, he climbed up to the first floor. Only there was no door. Damn.

He looked back at her. "I wonder if we should go back down and around and try to find this passage from the next floor up."

"Maybe. That's what we're trying to do in the first place. If this doesn't go from floor to floor, then it's not going to help us much at this point."

He nodded and motioned at her to turn around. "Let's be methodical. We'll come back."

"Right." She paused. "What can we do to see if someone traveled this way in the meantime?"

He grinned. "I've got something I can do." He bent down and using the little bit of dirt from several steps, he left a flat covering of sand on one step where a person wouldn't be able to miss stepping on it.

"That should show us." He nodded with satisfaction. His phone buzzed. He read the text and gasped. "Change in plans. Sian's gone missing. We're going back to the original plan and doing a floor by floor search for her."

⤳ ⤲

GORAN STRODE INTO the Council Hall, the delays chafing him. But it was the thought of having been sent to the mine with a truckload of traitors that really burned him. When he got his hands on Sian, he wanted to find out where the hell they came from and who ordered them to go with him and Serus. Someone had organized that team and he wanted to know who. Enough already.

The hall was once again alive like a battlefield headquarters. It made him nostalgic for a moment as he saw everyone scurrying around trying to accomplish something.

"We didn't think this through," Serus said at his side. "If we had Tessa with us here, she'd be able to see who the hell ordered those assholes to go with us to the mountain."

Goran grinned. So like Serus to match him in thoughts. "I'm going to ask Sian just that question."

"She won't know."

They strode over to the corner of the hall where Sian was usually to be found. Only she wasn't there. Serus did a slow turn in the middle of the room. "I'm not liking this."

"She could be just talking to someone in the main hall," Goran scoffed, but inside he wasn't liking this either. It said a lot about their current lives when they expected to find someone at their desk twenty-four hours a day and when they weren't there, to automatically assume that person would be in trouble. Goran fished out his phone and called her.

While Serus walked over to the doorway and stood staring out at the organized chaos, Goran waited for her to answer her phone. Finally she did.

"Sian?"

"Goran…" her voice dropped to a low whisper…"Help!"

And the phone went dead.

CHAPTER 9

TESSA STARED DOWN at the hulking animal walking calmly at her side. "What am I going to do with you?" she murmured. The dog was healing at a rapid rate, his energy swiftly becoming a calm blue all over. The jagged edges smoothed back down to a silky coat around him. She didn't see any permanent damage from the vamps' treatment, but she couldn't guarantee there wasn't any.

Her gaze lifted to Cody walking on the other side of the animal. "We need a name for him."

Cody's gaze slanted in her direction. "That implies you're going to keep him as a pet."

"It's not a case of me keeping him, it's more a case of him choosing to stay around me." She laughed. "Sounds stupid, I know."

"I don't know about that," he admitted. "If you are going to let him stay, then a name makes sense. How about Beast?"

The dog's huge head lifted and turned toward Cody. Cody glared down at him. Beast's gaze glittered.

Tessa reached out a calming hand toward both of them. "That's actually not a bad name. There's certainly nothing pretty or cute or tame about this guy. So Beast it is."

Out in front, Motre gave no indication he was listening. She knew he didn't approve of her 'pet' but like she'd said to Cody, it wasn't an option to get rid of him unless she killed him, and she wasn't going to do that. The dog had chosen her, and that's the way it was going to stay until something changed.

Motre paused, his hand going up to stop them.

Tessa slipped to his side and studied the shadows in front of them. They should be almost under the hospital. Shifting her vision until her vampire vision was piercing the gloom, she wondered what bothered Motre. She could see nothing.

Then she heard it.

Voices.

Keeping close to the wall, the three of them crept forward. She had no idea why she couldn't see any energy of people that were ahead yet the closer they got, the louder they became. Beast walked normally, showing no signs of being upset or antagonized by the presence of other noises. Interesting. She filed that away as a positive sign. She hoped she'd be able to let him live. If he turned on her and her friends, well…

A second tunnel appeared on the right. Tessa peered around the corner. There was the energy she was expecting. Giving a quick count before pulling back, she held up four fingers to the men.

As she turned back to face the enemy, Beast walked around the corner and headed to the vamps. Shit. She froze and crouched down. Slowly, not wanting to let the vamps know she was there, she peered round the corner and watched as Beast casually walked up to the first man – and bit him.

The vamp screamed and the others attacked the dog.

"Damn it," the injured vamp cried, holding his leg. "They promised us these animals would only attack the other guys. Not us."

But Beast was so busy growling and chomping at the other screaming vamps that the replies couldn't be heard.

As Tessa approached, grinning, Cody walked ahead of her and took out the injured vamp. Motre did the same for the two vamps who'd run in their direction to get away.

Tessa snorted. Not their best decision. Only the last vamp was screaming in terror as Beast loomed over him, his shoulder now firmly clamped in the animal's jaws. She gently lowered a hand to Beast's shoulders. "Thanks, boy. Let him go now."

Beast slowly shook his head, that piercing blue gaze glittering up at her.

Tessa, in a calm voice, said, "You're right. He's your prize. But we need to talk to him."

It was almost as if he raised his eyebrows in response saying, "So. What's stopping you?"

"Right." She crouched beside the prone man. "Talk. We need to know what the plan is."

"Go to hell, lady," the vamp snarled.

Beast, as if knowing what was needed, deepened his bite. Or maybe he just didn't like the tone of the vamp's voice. Tessa didn't, but it worked.

The man screamed, "Get him off me. Get him off."

"Why would I do that? You're trying to kill us. Beast is helping us. See, he doesn't like you guys much after the treatment he received in your hands."

"Not my hands," he cried out. "I didn't do this to him."

"He doesn't know that apparently. He's just going to treat all of you the same and kill you equally." Although how he could tell good vamps from bad remained to be seen.

"No, I'll talk. I'll talk," the vamp screamed. "Just get him off me."

"No, I'm not into playing games. I'm going to walk away and let Beast find more of your kind for him to extract a little revenge of his own." And she stood up.

"No." The man started crying. "Please. They said the animals would help us. That you'd all be so busy protecting yourselves from them that you'd not see us coming. It would give us the advantage we needed because you decimated our numbers so badly we don't have a big army anymore."

"So, what…" she cried out, "you created an army of deranged dogs?"

"Something like that." But his voice was fading. She crouched down at his side, her hand busy on his energy that had suddenly clouded with blackness. "What are you planning to do when you have Council Hall?"

"Keep it. It's the center. So much can be done from there. The bosses always planned to take it. Now…"

And his head fell to the side. Limp. That's when she realized that there was a thin silver thread rippling through his system. Poison. She glanced over at Beast and saw it was coming from his mouth. Around the big fangs.

"Beast, let go."

And without argument, he did and backed up two steps where he lay down, his head on his paws. She looked back at the dying vamp. "They put silver into the dog's teeth?" she asked incredulously. "So they can kill us that way?"

The vamp, his face twisting in a macabre fashion, gasped out, "Not much. Only a little at a time can come out. Dogs are supposed to hold on until the silver is enough."

His form turned black and crispy and he broke into a crumbling ash pile.

"The dogs can kill with silver?" Cody asked in horror. "How many did they create?"

"Likely as many as they could. Council Hall needs to be warned. They'll have to kill the dogs on sight."

"I'm calling Sian," Motre said. "She needs to warn the others."

Tessa stood up and walked over to Beast. She didn't even know what to think now that she understood what he'd done. She could see the silver in his energy now that he'd used it, but it was faint. Like there might be only one killer bite for each. What a thing to do to an animal. And the vampire community.

Horrific. And ingenious. No one would suspect it. Everyone was going to be scared of a pack of wild dogs, but no one was going to consider that their bite was going to be lethal. Not like this.

She held out a hand to Beast.

"Easy, Tessa," Cody said at the side. "We don't know anything about these animals."

But Beast sniffed her fingers then nudged her hand for some attention.

❧ ❦

THERE WAS SOMETHING fascinating and repulsive about the huge animal that walked at Tessa's side. Cody wondered how dangerous it was truly. That Tessa had healed him was the start of the unique bond between them, then the way she had done so had cemented that bond. Energy. It ran through everything apparently and by adding her energy to Beast's to heal him, the animal had accepted her as his – or maybe as an extension of himself. And what was that going to mean to those close to Tessa? Cody walked quickly at her side, his gaze on Beast. Beast had a raised hump on its back where the hair stood up in short bristles, and yet he was calm.

Would it help him to get closer to the animal? He didn't see how it would, but he didn't want it to come between him and Tessa either.

Rest your energy on his back, stroke it down his spine, she said in his mind.

How?

Just think it, she said. *In your mind, stroke his back in a calm, caring manner.*

Easier to imagine than do, but he did as instructed. There was no response from the dog, his gaze remaining on the path in front of them. Cody repeated the actions several more times. The hallway took another sharp corner and Cody stopped what he was doing to study the way ahead. Tessa bent down looking presumably at energy trails. Beast walked until he stood at her side. She smiled at him. He sat down, totally comfortable.

"So does he not sense any danger ahead?" Motre asked. "He doesn't look worried."

"Who said he was a guard dog?" Cody muttered.

Motre nodded. "An attack dog obviously, but having attacked and killed once, then what? He's just a big animal now?"

"The tracks keep going," Tessa pointed down the hallway, ignoring their comments. "But I'm afraid this is taking too long. We need to move faster. I'm going to jump." And she picked up her feet and in that peculiar ballet stride of hers, with arms out to the side, she took long running steps that was more jumping than walking and more gliding than flying but ate up the miles. Cody looked around. The tunnel was too narrow for him to fly. He'd have to run to keep up. At a nod at Motre, Cody raced behind Tessa. He'd love to take the lead, but it looked like Beast had gotten into the spirit of the hunt as he loped just ahead of Tessa. An odd couple for sure.

One long and lean and beautiful moving in a graceful flowing way, whereas Beast was a big-muscled, brutish-looking animal running with his tongue hanging out of that huge jaw.

Motre, running at his side, said, "They look like Beauty and the Beast."

Cody grinned. In school, they'd had to study Human fairytales. He'd always like that story. He wondered if any humans really believed in them.

Tessa slowed up at the end, then turned another corner and disappeared from sight.

Cody and Motre raced to catch up.

And heard Beast howl.

Shit.

☙ ❧

GORAN RACED THROUGH the main part of the Council Hall looking for anyone who had seen Sian and when. Everyone thought she was in her office, which meant no one had any idea of who'd taken her or when.

"Damn it," he roared. "How could you let her be snatched right out from under your noses?"

Taz came racing in the front door, his face ravaged. He still wore his hospital scrubs. Goran stopped him. "We haven't found her. Did she contact you? Did anyone?"

Taz shook his head. "No. She has to be here. She said that David had pulled the blueprints of the hall and that there were places no one seemed to know existed."

Goran nodded. "That's true. We will find her."

Goran's gaze was caught on a series of papers on the wall. He raced over. "These are the blueprints," he said excitedly. "She has to be here somewhere. She's only been missing for twenty minutes or so. We also have people watching outside to see if someone tries to take her away from here."

"Goran," Serus called, racing over. "I just spoke to David. They are on the lower levels. He said they found an old set of stairs on the bottom floor but there was no sign of anyone having used them. They are now on the third floor and moving up. No access to the staircase from the other floors, although the rooms corresponding to the one housing the staircase are all smaller, as if the access could have been put in but someone chose not to."

He glanced down at the phone in his hand. "He has Jewel with him."

"And Tessa? Cody? Any contact from them?"

Serus snorted. "Not from those two, but Motre checked in. Something about dogs given enhancements and silver implants so that their bites become lethal?"

"What?" Goran roared. "Are you serious?"

Serus nodded. "They are." He held up his phone. "Apparently Tessa had to heal a huge wolf dog animal and it's now with them. Motre is scared to death of it."

Goran stared at him. "She what?"

Serus shrugged. "You know as much as I do. However, remember all the people she helped? She figured that the dog deserved life after being mistreated and it was something she could do..." He let his voice trail off. Goran knew as well as anyone there just what his daughter would do at any given time.

"We have to find Sian," Taz said, bringing the conversation back to the present. "How many teams are out looking for her?"

A young woman standing off to the sides said, "Two teams have just gone to the two floors below us. David is coming up and looking, so we need to check this floor."

A group of vamps scattered. Goran hadn't even realized that they'd been circling around the ancients, listening. Remember Serus's words, he yelled. "Make sure you have something to kill wild dogs. Just in case."

Several people detoured to their desks to get weapons. He couldn't imagine. Vampires were animals and at the top of the food chain, but not one of them liked dogs or cats. Dogs were a hell of a good choice for the enemy to have chosen.

Facing four-legged enemies in battle was the last thing he wanted.

Taz turned and raced back to Sian's desk. "She'd have left us a message if she could have."

Back in her office, they studied the desk full of notes. Serus picked up the first page. "She's got a complete list of who went where and when. This page is the communications with the Human Council. They are on the way here too. Good Lord. Why?"

"Because they were supposed to meet you at the mountain, only it was a trap. She didn't know what to do so she detoured them here," Taz said. "But I don't know what she planned to tell them."

"She's got notes here. She's afraid the colleges and high schools are compromised."

Serus lifted his head. "The high school where Tessa and Jared attended is on this list."

Goran was barely listening. "So?"

"And the college. Human college and vampire college."

Goran turned to face Serus. "We knew that already."

"We knew about the vampire college. But what about the human side? What if the blood farm just picked those kids off one at a time?"

"Then we're talking all-out war. It's one thing to have some kids go missing and pay off the authorities, but not even those people can accept or deal with the public outrage when *all* the kids go missing."

"True." Serus studied Sian's notes. "She's done so much here. It looks like she's been working toward a big sweep. Take out all the strongholds at once."

"How many strongholds has she identified?"

"The hospital and yes…the Council. She also has the one high school circled."

"Why?"

"No idea, unless the teachers there or administrators have been bribed. We need to see if everything is okay there or if students have gone missing."

"When they clean the building out, do they sweep up the people that helped them and hang them in the blood farm too?" Goran shook his head. "That might be their eventual plan."

"It's all written down here." Serus tapped the notepad in front of them.

Taz walked over and studied the script.

"She's saying that *is* the blood farm's plan."

"And likely the reason she was snatched. Or close enough to it."

∂‍ ∾

WENDY OPENED HER eyes slowly. The white light had her slamming her eyes closed immediately. She tried to turn her head to the side and roll over but the pain…she arched her back and gasped.

"Easy, Wendy," Ian said quietly at her side. "We were

knocked out and brought to what appears to be another blood farm."

Wendy's eyes opened in shock. But it was Ian who was talking. She reached her arms out and struggled to sit. Ian lifted her and tugged her gently onto his lap and into his arms.

"Slowly," he said.

"How can we be back in one of these?" she cried. Only to then groan softly. "My head hurts."

"I know. It will take a few minutes before that eases up."

She snuggled in close for a few minutes. When she hoped it was safe, she opened her eyes and caught sight of Jared out cold in the bed beside hers. "He's here with us?"

"Yes. I'd called you to come and see what I'd found in the lower levels of Council Hall and while in the room, someone came up behind us. We fought and lost."

"Is Jared okay?"

"I don't honestly know," Ian said. "There is another twist to this mess too." And he quickly shared about Rhia's visit. "She's fighting the drugs and trying to save Seth and us."

Wendy bit her lip. She wanted to feel bad for Rhia, but the woman could have helped them already and had chosen to leave them locked in this room.

"She's not far outside, and we couldn't move easily while you were both unconscious." Ian said as if reading her thoughts. "We have to trust she won't deliberately hurt us."

Wendy tilted her head back and looked up at him. "Do you think she's the Rhia we know or have the drugs taken hold and she's one of them now?"

"I'm hoping she's the Rhia we know," he said calmly. "She spoke normally, and we hatched somewhat of a plan for her to get the information she needs and help us."

Wendy nodded. "I hope so. I won't want to but if she

hurts you, I'll kill her myself."

Ian grinned down at her. "So protective," he teased. "Who knew?"

Wendy reached up to stroke the side of his face, "You've been hurt enough. I just want to go home and have this over with."

"And that's exactly what Rhia and I want too." He stood up and set her on her feet. "To that end, let's figure out how you are doing. Can you stand? Walk? Run?"

Wendy tried to take one step, then a second. Each one was stronger, the room spinning less. "I'll need a moment or two, but I think I'll be fine." She turned to stare at Jared. "What about him?"

"I'm not leaving him behind," Ian said. "Not after all he did to help us."

"Right, well, you're carrying him. It's going to be all I can do to carry myself." Wendy bent and twisted, trying to limber up her stiff body.

She had to be ready to bolt and fast.

"So tell me. How are we getting out of here…and when?"

❧ ❦

DAVID RACED FROM door to door to door. They'd found three more locked doors. The first he'd finessed open with a credit card. It had been empty but looked to have been recently occupied. The second one was completely empty and was the small room that matched the one holding the stairs several flights below. He did a thorough check, but there was no other access door leading to stairs behind it. He wanted to break the wall down and open up to the stairs, but they had to be methodical about this. He'd bust it down soon if they didn't find Sian. The third door he'd made no attempt to open properly. He'd kicked it open. It had also been empty.

They met another group on the next floor. So far, no sign of Sian. David grabbed Jewel's hand. "I'm going to the hidden staircase," he said. "Let's make sure no one else has been there. We need to find out where it comes out."

"I'm coming too." Jewel said.

Without saying anything to the other group, David bolted down the stairs to the lowest floor. There they made their way to the small room and staircase. Taking one last look around, David led the way upstairs. And stopped.

There was one big footprint in the sand David had left behind. He took a quick picture, then stepped over that step. Someone had gone ahead of them. Now he had to find out why.

CHAPTER 10

TESSA FELL TO the floor under the crushing weight of several vamps. Damn it. She'd been so locked onto the idea of the men being ahead of her, she hadn't seen the assholes drop from the ceiling on her as she passed below them.

Beast howled. With a vamp on her back and another kicking her in the gut hard, she groaned and damned near went over-extended. The vamp fell forward as if following the pull of energy. By the time he hit the floor, he was dead. Her nails slashed the front of the man lunging at her, pulling his energy toward her as she shifted.

It's not how she'd thought to use Hortran's energy, but damn, it worked. It was hard to get into his mindset to use his trick when she was already under attack.

An attack that had happened so fast she'd had no chance to pull her normal tricks.

From the corner of her eye, she saw Beast attacking yet a third man. Then a fourth. How many of these assholes were there? She lunged upright, twisted, and tossed the man still hanging on her back toward Beast. Beast lunged and snagged this man by the throat.

With six attackers down and Cody and Motre racing toward her, she bent over and caught her breath. What the hell had she done? Something about Beast's presence at her side was soothing, reassuring, and she'd just taken off not even thinking of a surprise attack. And she should have.

Still, she'd survived and gotten away without a scratch. Which was more than she could say about the vamp currently dying in Beast's huge jaws.

She walked over to him. "Easy, Beast. He's done. Let him go."

Those glittering eyes glared at her, reminding her that he was an animal and this was his prize. "He's not going to taste very good," she said in low, calm voice. "He's been enhanced, and that's done all sorts of nasty things to his flesh."

"That's disgusting," Motre said as he studied the animal and the dying vamp. "I'd take a silver bullet over being eaten any day."

Cody frowned at Beast. "He can't be allowed to think he's the alpha in this group."

Motre snorted. "Personally, I'm thinking a bullet is a kindness for both of them." He waved at the other dead men on the ground. "How did they get the drop on you, Tessa?"

"Because I was a cocky fool," she muttered. "I was jumping, thinking what fun it was to have Beast beside me, when the assholes dropped from the ceiling on top of me."

The two men looked up to see enough of a carved depression out where the men had been able to snug up against the ceiling. There might even be handles for them to hold onto. Tessa wasn't sure. She shook her head. How long had they been there?

"Wow. New tricks every day," Cody said. "We need to get rid of these men," He motioned at the three on the ground.

Tessa watched as Cody carefully avoided looking toward Beast and his prize. He didn't want to know if the dog was actually going to eat that diseased vamp or not. Beast needed sustenance as well, except she really didn't want him to eat that vamp.

She pulled a silver stake out of her pocket and walked over to Beast. He growled at her. She ignored him, but kept her hand ready in case he lunged over the spoils of war. She'd pull his energy and have him drop in place if he did.

She reached down and stabbed the vamp on the ground.

Instantly, he flared into coals and turned to a glowing process over thirty seconds or more. She'd put it down to genetic modification and the damn drugs.

Beast whined and dropped his head on his paws.

"Poor guy. He was yours, wasn't he? But he'd make you really sick." She rummaged in her pockets and came up with a granola bar. She unwrapped it and offered it to the dog as a consolation prize. He took it gently from her hands and crunched through it in no time.

"There is no way you're going to be able to feed that dog granola bars and still have money left in your pocket. He's huge and will eat a ton."

"Maybe, but he also took out vampires." She smiled at Cody. "That kind of loyalty is hard to buy, and at the price of a granola bar, it's damn cheap."

Cody grinned. "Okay, but don't say I didn't warn you."

She rolled her eyes at him. "We've lost enough time. Let's go."

And she immediately resumed her ballet jumping down the hallway. She didn't dare let her senses relax now. It was a good reminder that she wasn't infallible. That she needed to always be on alert down here.

For some reason she had been getting cocky, and that so wasn't her. Her next jump faltered as she realized one possible reason for that shift.

Was Deanna still inside? Affecting Tessa's judgement? Tessa couldn't feel her, but she knew the woman was powerful enough to stay hidden. Had Tessa only injured her and now after a certain amount of healing Deanna was strong enough to reappear and cause Tessa trouble? Surely not. And if she were, then what? The last thing Tessa wanted was to have that witch take over again.

Just the thought of it was like a fatal punch in the gut. It couldn't happen. She didn't think Cody would ever trust her again if that happened. It was hard for him now. He hadn't really kissed her since that episode. And she missed his touch. Cody ran past her just then, his concerned gaze studying her. She smiled at him and picked up the pace, making it a competition as she glided past him again.

She missed those moments of intimacy. But she also knew that those moments were for the two of them. And two of them only. Deanna was a damn ugly third party intruder.

And she was no longer welcome in Tessa's personal space. It was one thing for her energy that housed the experiences and knowledge of her long life, but it was another if her presence intruded on that one special thing Tessa had created and treasured beyond all else.

Her relationship with Cody.

THEIR PROGRESS WAS steady – and cautious after the attack from the unexpected direction.

Cody stayed close to Tessa the whole way, Beast on her other side. Cody worried about her. She'd been a little off after the ambush. He understood. She hadn't seen it coming.

It was a whole new day out there again. He glanced at Beast. And how.

He shook his head. That the enemy had actually brought animals into their sick world was just wrong. What next? Wild animals? Bring in cougars and bears? That didn't bear thinking about.

His phone rang. He glanced down at it without breaking stride. "David and crew have gone back to the hidden staircase. David said tracks show someone went up while he was searching the Hall for Sian."

An odd strangled sound came out of Tessa's mouth. He glanced over at her, caught hot pinched lips, the paler than ever skin, and the increased speed in her jumps. "David can handle himself."

She half smiled, shot him a quick glance in thanks, and nodded. But she didn't ease the power back.

They should be under the Hall anytime now. Outside of the one tunnel, there'd been no other branches off the one they were in. He wished someone could have continued down their original pathway. It would be nice to finally map everything at once and do a full sweep of the place. Even now, it wasn't out of line to consider that someone could be coming up behind them.

He glanced behind, but it was just normal blackness. Of course it was. It would be that way even if they were being followed.

Tessa slowed to a walk, her breathing easy and controlled. He stopped at her side. She walked slowly forward, her gaze intent on something ahead of them. He looked and saw nothing but he knew she'd tell him when she figured it out.

She took another step. And stopped. Looked behind them then back forward. And frowned.

"Problems?" Motre asked quietly.

She shrugged. "Doesn't feel right."

"Meaning?" Cody studied her face, sensing her unease but not knowing where it was stemming from. "Your memories or Deanna's?"

The startled look she flashed his way reminded him of how much she had to keep track of. And that division between her and Deanna was just one of them.

"Mine," she muttered. "I think."

"Then maybe access hers."

He watched as she half closed her eyes and did something inside that massive intelligence of hers. He couldn't imagine all the knowledge and power that was available to her now. He was glad for her. It was the last thing he wanted for himself. But for her...that was huge. He wondered how the Council would handle her when this mess was over. She'd not been allowed to attend Council meetings before. He thought Serus had tried to get her in. David served as an apprentice now, but Tessa had barely counted back then. As of now, though, it was a whole different story.

"Okay. The tunnel up to the Council Hall should be up ahead." Tessa said, relief in her voice. "Not more than a few yards."

Motre walked forward, his gaze searching. The tunnel appeared to end after he'd been walking for less than five minutes.

"Did Deanna's memories allow for a way up?" Motre asked as he slowly spun around, his hands on his hips studying the walls that appeared solid all around him.

"Not really. She went up and down here on a regular basis for decades."

Cody frowned.

"Most likely from when vampires lived in the shadows and not openly like they did now."

"Then how about you show us the way up?" Motre stopped moving and tilted his head, waiting for her to respond.

Tessa closed her eyes and slowly turned around in a circle.

Odd. He figured she was looking for energy. Although if this place was deserted and had been for a long time, there'd be no energy to see.

She opened her arms and slowly stretched, as if prepping for a sprint or something. He exchanged a confused look with Motre.

And just when he was about to ask Tessa what she was doing, she turned to the wall in front of them and walked into it.

As in right into it.

As in disappeared from sight.

Into the damn wall.

❧ ❧

DAVID HATED TO think that someone was coming and leaving the Council Hall all these years, making plans and planning attacks. While everyone in the hall had no idea. To the private amusement of the enemy. He'd like to see these guys. Put a face to the men who'd been orchestrating his demise. The men who'd been laughing at them all for years. Decades.

Bastards.

"David?"

Jewel's anxious voice had him pulling out of his reverie. He'd been standing on a stair, hands clenched and his teeth locked. He let his pent-up breath out and tried to smile. "I'm fine," he said in a low voice. "Sorry, but the thought of these men playing us for fools moving around in the shadows like they have been is pretty irritating."

"I know, that's why we're doing what we can to roust them out. Let's keep moving. Sian has to be found."

Shit. He'd forgotten the real reason they were here. He smiled and raced up the stairs, calling behind, "Well, someone went ahead of us. Let's hope they have her."

❧ ❦

SERUS FOCUSED ON the job at hand. He wasn't much of a commander, being more rogue than a team player, but someone had been needed to step into the breach. He'd been organizing the search of the Hall, had the Human Council going back to the mountain to check out the entrance where the shooter had been hiding, prepped in case it was an ambush, and doing his level best to kept calm and Goran in control. That bear wanted action.

"I'll go to the mountain," Goran said. "Meet the humans and get them into the blood farm. I can fly and be there in ten minutes. If it's another blood farm, I can take care of the guards and let the humans take down the rest. They can call for medical help and that will give Taz here something constructive to do as well."

Serus nodded. "Fine then." Secretly, he was relieved. He knew Rhia was out there somewhere. If Goran got to her first before the rest of the rescue party, he'd be able to save her. Serus had been trying to work his way around that problem when Goran spoke up. But the thing about Goran was you couldn't give in too easily. He'd refuse on the assumption you were trying to get rid of him and keep the fighting for yourself.

Serus would love to stop the fighting. If he had his family back. Barring that, he was more than willing to tear down every stronghold he could find and rip the assholes limb from limb to save them.

Goran slapped him on the back, then nodded to Taz, who'd collapsed at Sian's desk, his face ravaged by worry and said. "Good. I'm out of here then."

He walked to the front door. "Remember what Cody said. They were attacked by dogs. It's all too possible that could happen here."

Serus nodded. "I know. But let's hope it doesn't until you are back."

"Save some of the fighting for me. My trip is more of a babysitting job, but it's better than sitting and doing nothing here," he growled.

Serus shook his head. "Wish I were going with you."

Just then several young vamps came in to report.

Goran laughed. "I'm leaving while I can."

❧ ❧

RHIA CLICKED THE keyboard in a mad panic. Her window of opportunity was disappearing and so far, she'd found nothing. Hearing a door open, she glanced up then back at her monitor and froze. OMG. Who was that? An ancient? As in super old and almost bent over. She didn't have a clue who this vamp was or why he was in the condition he was in. Surely not natural causes. Drugs? Enhancements?

Her heart pounded, but she kept her face neutral and focused on the monitor in front of her. Seth's name appeared on the screen. His file had been saved to a special folder directly. Her son was still here in town but had been moved to some kind of secure location. She was desperate to find out where that was. The crone made his way over to the computer where the tech had been working and sat down as if he had the right. She knew that the tech needed her to cover for him...but the crone wasn't asking.

He logged into the computer and studied the information he brought up as if he knew what he was doing.

She relaxed slightly. The tech had only been gone about thirty minutes. She knew he could be back any moment, too. Her real concern was if someone could follow her, then track and see what she was accessing in the system.

She might have triggered some trip wires.

Dropping her gaze to the monitor, her fingers flew through the pages...until she hit a wall.

A firewall? Carefully, she tiptoed up to it, and then around it. A log in came up. She entered Gloria's name and the wall dissolved in front of her. Thank God. Quickly, she scanned the files and realized there was so much here she needed a copy of. This was it. This would completely destroy the blood farm. It was so damn comprehensive. Locations, names, dates, and times. They had a lot of this from Gloria's laptop, but it had been missing critical information. Information that she now had. But how to keep it? Where to download? Could she send it somewhere? Was there a key big enough? Surely not.

But maybe.

She knew Gloria's email address after having worked on her laptop enough. She quickly brought up the email program and started zipping files and attaching them. Adding her own name and Sian's as a blind cc, she worked hard and fast. She could feel her heart pounding in her chest, her throat locking down in panic. She dared not look up.

Then couldn't help herself. The crone suddenly looked up from the far corner. Panicked, she kept her face stone cold and locked down as she dropped her gaze to the monitor. She attached and sent file after file after file. She was grabbing more and more folders and zipping and attaching, sending multiple emails instead of just one. She was afraid the files would be too big and get hung up. Her cell phone was in her pocket. She was desperate to check if the material was arriving as planned. The sound had been turned off since forever so she'd have to log in and check. After she was done. This crone might figure out what she was doing, but he couldn't stop the process once she'd sent everything. And suddenly she was done. All the files behind the firewall had been copied and sent out.

She was shaking inside. Good Lord. She'd done it.

They were all out in cyberspace. And she was still alive.

There was a video icon on the top of her screen. She clicked on it. And froze. Dear God. The camera had zoomed in on a man lying on a bed. His arms were wrapped in gauze, tubes running in and out of his body.

She couldn't zoom in or out, but it wasn't hard to see the man's face.

It was her son – Seth.

"Did you find what you were looking for?"

Shocked by what she'd found and by the interruption, she looked up to see the crone walked over toward her. She smiled. "I did. I'm done now."

"In more ways than one, Rhia. Did you really think you could fool us?" He laughed. "We made you. We tracked you. And we can easily see if you're responding to your stimulus."

He lifted his hand to show her a syringe. "It's time for your next dose." He grinned. "You won't have any doubts after this as to whose side you really are on."

Slowly he straightened, his back uncurling, his shoulders widening. He grinned at her shocked gasp. "Yes, we are so much more than you will ever know."

"Who are you?" she whispered. "I almost recognize you. But it's as if you no longer look like the person I used to know."

"Ah, that's a good thing. I used to be good-looking, but I was weak. I wasn't as good as I could be." He approached slowly, his hand raised. "That's okay. I am now and getting better all the time. Soon you will, too."

And he threw himself across the room at her.

CHAPTER 11

TESSA LAUGHED AS she realized the wall was yet another mirage. Now that she'd walked to the other side of it, it all made sense. She turned and walked back out between the strategically placed slabs to see Motre and Cody racing toward her. "Hey, it's all good. The passage continues on this side."

"Damn tricky shit," Motre growled. "Why couldn't they do anything simple?"

"They were trying to stay alive, remember," she said with a grin. "I have to admire them. They constructed some pretty cool stuff." She motioned to the wall that wasn't a wall. "You'd never know this wasn't solid unless you walked right up to it."

"What's on the other side?" Cody asked as he walked through. She came through right behind him. "Stairs."

"Wow," Motre said. "Not just one set though, two."

"Right. So which do we take and where do they go?" Cody asked as he walked from one to the other looking for something.

"Likely different sides of the Council Hall, but it could also just go to the surface," she said with a shrug. "I say we split up and go up both directions at the same time but in that case, we should have done that back when the tunnel diverged."

"We need more men," Motre said. "Has anyone seen an

entrance to something like this from the top? How far down are we even?"

"It would be good to send a team through here from the beginning and have them go down both tunnels and report as they go. This tunnel hasn't branched off, but that doesn't mean the main one didn't if we'd kept going. There might have been several more," Tessa said absently as she studied the way the two different staircases rose up. "It needs to be done. And we need to map it as well. There are way too many secret doors and corridors in this place."

"Any idea which set of stairs is more used?" Cody said, walking to the right. "The steps are old. Cut stone."

"And the one over here is the same," Motre said. "Let's go up a few flights and see what we can find then come back down and report."

"You're on." Cody opened his wings and jumped upward into the spiraling staircase above.

Tessa laughed as Motre cussed him out good and ran as fast as he could up the set of stairs beside him. She waited, Beast at her side, wondering at the reason for two sets. In its time, she imagined the stairs saw a lot of traffic. She couldn't see much energy. More rats and mice maybe, smaller critters, but all the energy combined was so faint as to not be clearly discernible. Old wispy fog that had already dissipated from time. That brought up another point. Why hadn't she seen the vamp energy of those who had attacked her? She should have. She spun around. She should have checked the place they'd dropped down from. There had to have been an access point from above, or she would have seen their energy. Therefore they hadn't been down this way. They'd come from a passageway a floor above. She grinned. Interesting. These buggers were getting tricky.

Cody whooshed to a fast drop in front of her, a big smirk on his face when he realized that Motre wasn't there. "Beat him."

"Well, you did have the advantage." She laughed. "Did you see anything?"

"No. I went up six flights. No exits that I could see and no end in sight."

"Weird." They waited for Motre. Only Motre didn't return. Glancing over at Cody, she said, "I'm not liking this."

"I'm not either." And he jumped up, opened his wings, and gave a hard pull, disappearing up the columns of the twisting staircase.

She jumped up several stairs then several more, trying to make the distance between her steps widen to make her movements more effortless. She had a lot of jumping practice, but not so much up stairs. It was harder. More physically taxing.

She opened her arms and realized the curl of the staircase was tight enough that she could jump higher if she deliberately angled her efforts. She laughed as the stairs below fell away as she climbed higher and higher. She stopped and looked down, realizing how high up she'd come.

Beast was racing up behind her, anxious to not be left behind.

All this distance and she'd seen no exit. Why? Surely there was something along here. The men that had dropped down on her had to come from somewhere. Maybe a ventilating shaft? She took several shorter jumps, wondering where Cody and Motre had gotten to. Again, they hadn't had time to get very far.

She kept climbing.

Mentally, she reached out to Cody, *Where are you?*

I'm here.

She jumped again and again. *"Okay, this is getting bad. I feel like I must have passed you somewhere."*

No. The stairs end to an open room. Just keep coming. But carefully. The enemy snatched Motre off the steps and carried him up. Cody sighed. *When I flew up, they were expecting me.*

She froze. *Are you a prisoner?*

Not sure I'd use that term. Come higher and you'll see.

Am I walking into a trap?

Yes and no. He laughed, but it was a bitter laugh. *Don't suppose you still have Beast with you, do you?*

Yes.

Beast was climbing the stairs, but he was still a few flights below her. She could hear his footsteps, the nails clicking on the stone as he followed her. Cody should have carried him up with him.

Uhm, as much as I'd like to have Beast here with me right now, I'm not sure he'd have let me carry that fat ass up here.

He's hardly fat. And now that he's climbing all these stairs, he's going to be tired, she warned.

She stopped and waited for Beast to reach her. He wagged his tail and kept climbing past. In fact, he didn't look tired at all. He just powered forward. She walked at his side. They couldn't have much farther to go. Suddenly Beast raised that huge shaggy head and sniffed the air. And started to howl.

At the same time, he picked up speed and raced up the steps.

Mystified but knowing Beast's reaction was tied into whatever awaited them at the top of the stairs, Tessa ran behind the dog to the top of the stairs.

Beast jumped over the top. Instantly, horrific animal snarls filled the air.

Tessa crested the top and stared. Motre and Cody were pinned in an alcove but not restrained by anything as far as she could see. Then she caught sight of Beast. And understood.

Several big black cats circled Beast.

As in wild cats. Panther size. With long front fangs and claws that put hers to shame.

"Shit," she said in a fervent whisper. "Where the hell did these guys come from?"

"I was grabbed by a flying vamp about halfway up." Motre raced over to her. "He dumped me here, laughing his head off," Motre snorted. "I managed to hide in here until Cody came."

"And Cody came to the rescue, I see." Tessa giggled as she eyed the three cats. They'd make mincemeat out of Beast. She couldn't allow that though. He bristled at the felines, the hair on the back of his neck rising and his demeanor changing. He'd always been rough and dangerous-looking, but right now he was more demon than dog. She didn't know if she should jump in and help him or if he'd be insulted by her offer.

Still, there were three. He might be able to take one out, but he wouldn't be able to take on three without suffering some injuries. She walked closer. She needed to snag the energy spot and drop the cats before they could attack. It was not their fault. But unlike Beast, she couldn't see any of the cats' original energy. She didn't think she'd be able to save any of them. And that broke her heart. If she couldn't save them, she wanted to put them down as humanely as possible. Her world had become all about death and destruction.

The sad part was she'd become very good at it.

She strode confidently forward, stepping into the circle to

stand beside Beast.

"Uh, Tessa, that was not a good answer…" Cody called out. "Those cats are vicious. Not sure they've been fed or what they need to feed on at this point in their development."

"The blood farm has obviously developed more shitty animal experiments," Motre said, shaking his head. "These cats are unbelievable."

"True, but I find it reassuring." Tessa said, trying to keep her eyes on the cats. "If their numbers have been decimated to the extent that they have to resort to using cats and dogs for their fighting, then we are making progress."

"Not enough. Do you have any idea how many cats and dogs there are in this town," Motre snapped. "Soon no one will be safe."

She tilted her head, considering that. "It would be more effective to work with the rats instead. They run everywhere. One bite and the vamp is gone."

"Thanks for that," Cody snapped. "I was just thinking the dogs and cats would likely be the worst they could throw at us, but if they start with rodents, then we are in major trouble."

Tessa only half heard him, her gaze on a particularly lethal cat that had locked its gaze on her. She didn't dare let it out of her sight. But while she was tracking that big cat, she knew there were two more that could be getting ready to slice her back open. She dropped to her knees, her claws extending as the cat lunged. High and strong it rose.

But Tessa was ready, she flashed her hand through the energy right at the cat's heart region as it rose above her. Without a whimper, it crashed to the ground beside her, the long legs catching Tessa's shoulder on the way.

She scrambled back, her hand instinctively rubbing the

injury. The damn animal had big claws and one had cut her. Still, it was nothing compared to the damage the cat could have done and indeed what the others were still trying to do.

"Tessa!"

She spun around, catching sight of Cody as he bolted toward her.

"Behind you," Motre yelled.

She twisted. The second large cat had snuck to the other side and lunged at her.

Tessa cried out as claws and teeth found their mark. Then she was free. She hadn't had time to react before Cody tossed the cat to the floor beside the first one – dead.

"You okay?" He reached over and tugged her into his arms, pulling her hair back so he could take a look at her neck.

"I'm fine," she said. "It's just a scratch."

"But a decent-sized one," Cody snapped. "You could have let Beast deal with them."

"How fair is that?"

Cody spun her around to show her Beast standing over the last cat and calmly cleaning his paws. "He's not a normal dog. This is fun for him."

"He's a beast," Motre joined them, his voice admiring. "Like wow. He took that cat out like it was nothing."

"How could they do this to these poor animals?"

"Considering how they were treated, I'm sure death is a kindness to them. Beast would be in the same condition if he wasn't so damn big. But you saved him from that fate, and now he fights on our side." Motre shook his head. "Could our lives get any weirder?"

He kicked first one cat then the other. "Thankfully, they are dead."

"Good," Cody said. "Let's go find the flier that dumped

you for the cat's next feeding."

œ ∞

DAVID SLOWED DOWN after climbing stairs steadily for at least ten minutes. The stairs spiraled up as far as he could see, with no other doors and no windows to show if they'd made it above ground level or not. He'd seen no other footprints, but then, there wouldn't be. The cut steps were dry and hard and clean. He glanced behind but Jewel was staying close. He went around one more bend and slowed. The stairs ended. At a door.

He took a deep breath and studied the ground in front of them.

"Where do you think it goes?" Jewel asked.

"No idea," he whispered. He leaned forward and placed an ear against the wood. He couldn't hear anything on the other side. "Get ready."

The door opened silently, well-oiled and maintained even if it was a heavy plank door that looked more appropriate for a medieval castle than Council Hall.

He glanced behind to find Jewel texting the news to his father. As she had been every step of the way. David understood. They had the technology to keep in touch. Given the circumstances, someone needed to be alerted to their position. He peered into the darkness. It was a small anteroom. A place to get out of the way of the stairs and keep watch of people coming and going without letting their position away. Well, that worked for him too. He motioned for Jewel to join him then closed the door. Just the two of them almost filled the space. He pointed to the second door. The second door was more modern and had been replaced sometime in the last millennium. Good. That meant someone had been using the place. With a shrug and a warning look at Jewel, David opened the second door.

∂∾ ∽∂

SERUS HAD TO admit that being back in command wasn't so bad. If only those under him weren't pimply-faced kids.

Could they get any younger? He hoped not. He wanted seasoned warriors to lead. Hell, he wanted to be at the helm himself. Somehow the kids here had latched on him as their leader in Sian's absence and he was stuck. He couldn't let them down. He must be getting soft in his old age.

They were down to three able-bodied Councilmen, considering several had died and several were still battling drugs, leaving Goran, Adamson, himself, and Rhia, who no one else would count as being on active duty. They were going to have to reassess the Council when this was over. With any luck, he might be able to move David up the ranks. Although it should be Seth first. He frowned, hating to have that big worry back into his head. He'd seen his son's attitude and actions. That would need to be fixed before Seth was going anywhere good. He understood Rhea's point of view. She was a mother. One always had to make allowances for those. But he was a father, and he wasn't so damn sure what he'd seen had been drug-induced.

Like Goran had much to deal with over his son's traitorous actions and subsequent death, Serus was struggling to make allowances for his own son.

Besides, the council members only ever picked from vamps of honor. Those with decades, even centuries of service. Serus knew that Goran had hoped to put his son's name forward when the next position opened up. They opened up rarely. Most Council members served for centuries, and some much longer, like Deanna. He hated that name. She'd have been the next spot to open up. Given her age, it wouldn't have been much longer. A decade at the outside. Now look at the mess she'd left.

No, David wouldn't be eligible for a long time. But he could move higher in the hierarchy. And he deserved to. He'd shown himself to be a good man in this disaster. So had Cody. That would make Goran proud. They both had lost one son – permanently in Goran's case. Lucky for the two of them, both had sons who'd stepped up to the plate in a big way.

None of them would be the same after this.

The society wasn't going to be same. They'd all been affected. Their innocence destroyed. They'd be years pulling their world back together again. And it wasn't even at the point where they could yet. He was very much afraid that the worst was yet to come.

৵ ৶

INSTEAD OF ATTACKING, Rhia dropped to the floor and scooted under the big desk, coming up on the other side of where the crone stood. There was something in his profile that was familiar. But what? And who was he? She glanced around quickly, looking for a weapon. He had to be killed or there'd be no freeing her son. He'd send out an alarm and that would be it. She'd have the whole blood farm on her back.

"You're not going anywhere," the crone snapped. "Do you really think I'm going to let you walk out of here? No, you will be used as bait to bring the last two ancients on our list. We need Goran and Serus here." He shook his head.

"You don't even know me, do you?"

She stared at him. Then shrugged. "No, I don't." At the twist in his features, she added, "Who are you?"

"Resnick. I served as financial advisor to the Council for over a century. Not one of the Council. Just always on the outside. A useful add on, but never one of you."

Really? She didn't recognize him. Hell, his own mother wouldn't recognize him. He was nothing like the young man who'd attended council meetings to give updates on the business affairs. "What happened to you?" she asked in a compassionate voice. She waved her hand toward him in a helpless motion. "You look so...different." She winced at the fumble, but it was hard to come up with something not derogatory that wouldn't inflame him.

Too late.

"Oh, don't feel sorry for me." He laughed with a tone of bitterness. "I'm so much more than I was. I got in on the experiments early on. My brain functions faster and better than yours – of course it always did, but now it's a super model to your old, slow one. My physical body might not look the prettiest, but it's stronger, faster, and will outlive yours."

She blinked. "This is all from the drugs and enhancement experimentation?" She shook her head. "I gather you're not the poster boy for getting new younger vamps to sign up?"

The man who was a full century younger than her but looked several centuries older snarled, his teeth bared like a dog. Jesus, he was a mess. Putting him down was a kindness.

"Did you really think you'd be able to walk in here and take what you wanted and no one would know?" He slowly took a step toward her. "Your son is one of us. Always has been. Even now he's being given the enhancements he asked for. We saved him from you. He's a rising star in our world. And you are a dying star. Your time to shine is over. It is our time."

He took another slow step toward her.

"Where is he?" she said in a hoarse voice, her voice rising to a scream, "Tell me where he is."

"It won't do you any good." Resnick smiled at her – if that movement of lips over teeth was classified as a smile.

He glanced at his watch. "He'll be heading into the lab any minute. And you're so damn close. Almost close enough to stop it. Just a few doors away. But instead, I think we'll take you as a prisoner so you can see what he becomes and hate it. If I save you for him to kill, he'll thank me for it. You never knew him. Mothers are the last to really understand what they truly spawned."

And he sprang.

IAN COULD HEAR the horrifying conversation through the door, but he'd been so shocked he'd been slow to react. He shoved the door open, Wendy behind him. A shivering and trembling Jared stayed outside in the hallway. Finally awake, he'd been desperate to escape the room and once capable of standing, he'd tottered his way to the hallway. That's when they'd heard Rhia's voice. And Resnick's, a man Ian had only known by sight and not for many years.

Inside the room, Ian found Rhia, her back to him, with an unrecognizable Resnick on the ground, one of the syringes Ian had seen Rhia use before jabbed into Resnick's throat.

Words gurgled out of his mouth, but they were hard to decipher. Something about how they couldn't kill him.

Rhia cast Ian a hard look, making him grateful he was on her side. He held up a silver spike he'd taken to carrying full-time. In fact, he had several on him. Her gaze lit up and she nodded to the bastard she held down. Ian stepped forward and stuck him through the heart with the spike.

It was a tribute to the drugs that Resnick didn't go up in ash like earlier vamps. Nor did he sizzle and burn before blowing to ash. No, he smoked like a bad brisket, the stench making him gasp.

Rhia withdrew the stake and stabbed him a second time, this time in the throat. Rescind gurgled and smoldered a little more.

"That is so…" Wendy coughed then ran out of the room to stay with Jared.

Ian stared grimly down at the dying man. "He's not gone yet, is he?"

"No," Rhia whispered. "Going, but not enough yet."

Ian pulled out two more stakes and though it was grim job, they all needed this over with as fast as possible. Rhia took one and stabbed the messed up vamp in the chest. Ian stabbed him in the belly.

Finally, as if all the weapons pulled together, he shifted from alive and smoldering to crumbling parchment.

He missed the ash stage altogether.

Ian stood up. "Jesus, I hope to never see that again."

Rhia stepped back, reached out, and kicked the vamp's head. Or where it should have been. Ian agreed. They needed to make sure this bastard couldn't be saved.

She turned to Ian. "We have to hurry. They are about to give Seth the exact same drugs."

With that, she bolted into the hallway.

༂ ༂

GORAN LOVED TO fly in the early evening. Before, the vamps were all stirring and clogging the skies. Not that there were many fliers anymore. Deanna was right about the lines diluting. He loved to fly. Was delirious when he found out that Cody had wings. He'd loved taking the young'un on flights, teaching him to soar through the clouds and glide on a full moon. They'd been special days. He wasn't particularly paternal, certainly hadn't been with his first born – he couldn't bring himself to say his son's name. The tears would flow. He'd always been happy to know that he'd leave behind the best part of him. Now he realized there was only Cody, who was easily a better man than Goran. Or would be when he made it there. Goran's current goal – to do everything to make sure that boy lived a long healthy happy life and not turn to a group like those at the blood farm in search of something better.

Although it looked like Cody already had found so much better. Tessa was not who Goran had envisioned for his boy, but now he couldn't imagine anyone else.

They were lucky. Goran had espoused long relationships like Serus and Rhia, but mostly because he knew he was likely to never have one. He was envious of what they had. It had been odd to be so close to both of them and know that they shared something he had never experienced. And now Cody had already been blessed more in that area than Goran.

He was happy for his boy. But would Goran ever find a partner like that? Or was it not in the cards?

He gave a hard pull of his wings, loving the way the wind flew past his cheeks and butted up against his eyes. He adored being out here. This was a short flight, which was unfortunate, but after all the running around and fighting of this last few weeks, his wings were wanting a long flight. A few days to stretch and glide and forget about all this nightmare.

Change had happened so slowly over time that the world was different. He'd opened his gaze to where he was and was sad to see that in his head, he was still living decades ago. Vamps changed. People changed. The relationship between them changed. For the better in some cases. But he'd always flitted from one thing to another and now looking back, although passionate and fun, he'd missed out on the constant and enduring. With any luck, he had centuries more ahead, maybe, just maybe, there'd be time for him to find another partner – a love that lasted.

He glanced down to see the humans traveling convoy-style way below him. Did they know he was here? Were they stupid enough to shoot him out of the sky when he was their ally? And wasn't that partnership a surprise. Who'd have thought he'd be going to war with humans against his own kind? Not him. His phone went off. He rolled onto his back and glided so he could read the text without the wind in his face. It was from Ian. Goran read the long message in shock. He knew Resnick. Had known him for centuries. Or was that the senior Resnick? No, the younger one had been on the finance committee since forever. Hard to believe he'd been a traitor. Just the thought. The kind of information Resnick had been able to siphon off and feed to the enemy was grotesque. Not to mention he had access to steal their funds.

Had anyone looked into that?

He immediately texted Sian and asked. After he hit send, he realized there'd been no update on Sian's whereabouts. He didn't know if Ian had sent the same message to Serus but on the assumption too much information was better than none,

Goran forwarded the text to him at command central. He sniggered. Serus at a desk job…

With a shout of laughter at the thought, he did a series of somersaults in the sky and with a sudden burst of speed, he raced ahead of the convoy to land at the right spot. He stood arms crossed, waiting for them as they drove around the corner.

The humans had better understand he was leading them and not the other way around.

Or else.

CHAPTER 12

TESSA SLOWLY SHOOK off the effects of the attack and regrouped in her head. Beast slept at her feet. Then she'd been standing here as if in a fog for the last few minutes herself. "They were a trap," she said softly. "For anyone coming up the stairs. And we fell right into it."

"Our second one of the day," Cody growled. "We need to be more careful."

"There wasn't much I could do," Motre said in an apologetic tone. "The vamp swooped down behind me and snagged me before I understood what was happening."

Tessa nodded. "They are getting smarter. More organized. They have built an army and are learning how to lead them."

Cody glanced over at her. "We've done the same."

"We have." She looked at the set of stairs and the perimeter of the long circular column they were at the bottom of. "Interesting system. Why all the stairs?"

"And why the cats down here?" Motre said.

"I'm thinking the cats were new," Cody said. "The guys we killed down below probably warned his team we were coming. The cats were there as a backup measure."

"When Motre arrived, they probably considered him a good test case," Tessa waved her hand at the walls rising steeply above them. "Whoever it was is likely up there ready to attack again. And have already passed on the results of the test."

"They must wonder about Beast," Motre said, eyeing the sleeping dog at her feet. "He's not exactly their best effort."

"He might have been, but he also had enough of his original personality to fight this off. The other animals weren't likely so lucky."

She glanced at the other two. "We need to get moving. Ready?"

They both nodded, and she walked to the bottom of the stairs and shook her head at the height they'd have to climb. She took the first jump then a second and a third. Before she landed a fourth, Cody flew past her, carrying Motre on his back.

"Hey, that's cheating," she called out with a laugh. Then realized that Beast was coming behind her. "We'll be fine, won't we? We can do this together."

She picked up her pace and focused, willing herself up the miles of stairs. She didn't know how Beast's energy was but as they neared the top, she could see him falling behind. She stopped and waited for him. He was panting hard when he reached her. And likely needed water. Damn, they were ill-prepared to travel with a large animal. And he appeared exhausted. He lay down. His long body stretched across, covering several stairs as he struggled to catch his breath.

Tessa sat down beside him, happy to have a rest. "Hey, buddy. It's okay. A few minutes won't matter. They've already checked out what's up top. If it was important, Cody would have come down and gotten us."

If he could. She lifted her head and frowned. *Cody? You okay?*

I'm okay, he growled in her head. *Where are you?*

I'm resting with Beast. It's a hard climb for him. She didn't want to admit she was tiring, but...

I'll come and get you, he said instantly.

No, I'm not leaving Beast. She hopped to her feet and called to the dog. He got to his feet, valiant and willing. She hoped he was okay. "Come on, boy, let's get up this last set and then we can rest." In her head, she said to Cody, *We need to find him water. This has worn him out.*

Cody snorted. *Right. I'll look around up here but if you're not here soon, I'm coming to get you and Beast can either make it on his own or he gets left behind.*

She smiled down at Beast. "Don't worry about him. I won't leave you alone."

And moving slower than she'd like but still too fast for Beast, they made their way up the circular stairs. At the top, she stopped and stared. "What the hell?"

"Yeah, we climbed to the surface somehow and past the Council Hall level."

They stepped onto the top of a platform outside, stepping down at the Council Hall at the bottom of the hill they were on.

"We're on the hill behind the Council Hall?" She surveyed the huge building below her. "This is bizarre. In a way, it's also perfect from a strategic point of view. This is great for defense. And quick access to the basement. Another big plus."

"We must have missed a door," Motre said. "There has to be a way into the Council Hall. Doesn't make sense otherwise."

"There would have to be," Cody agreed. "But not likely well used for centuries."

"And we don't know where the other staircase goes or if there are others."

Tessa studied the hidden burrow where the stairs had

opened to. "This is really amazing. I never knew this existed."

"None of us did. The entrance is hidden by trees and bushes."

"Let's go back down and find the way in. We were expecting an attack to come from several directions. Instead there is no sign of anyone."

"Are we faster than expected?"

Motre snorted. "I doubt it. After the fighting we did, there's no way."

"So was the attack delayed?"

Tessa shook her head. In a low voice, she said, "Or is the fight already inside?"

"So back down from here or go down there," Motre nodded toward the parking lot ahead of them. "Best chance?"

"Or we split up and check out both ways," Tessa said. She hated the idea, but they were spread so thin their options were limited.

"No. No splitting up." Cody was adamant. "Look what happened last time. If we'd been together, Motre wouldn't have been picked up or the two of us pinned by the cats. No, we stay together."

"Fine. Let's go then." And she jumped down to the ground and raced toward the Hall.

❧ ❦

"HMMM, TESSA?" CODY called behind her, running as fast as he could. Of course he did. Where she led, he went. Wasn't it supposed to be the other way around? Hell, she'd been racing ahead of him since this mess began. It was all he could do to keep up.

"Tessa, do you have a plan?" he called.

Motre snorted at his side. "That girl doesn't know what the word means."

Cody grinned. "So true, but she's done well so far."

"That she has, but this Deanna mess has me worried."

"Me too. I'm also a little concerned that the Ghost is in there with her."

Motre shot him an odd look. "Doesn't that make you cringe? To think of someone inside you like that? It does me."

Cody wasn't so sure. He had Tessa inside his mind. It wasn't that far a stretch to imagine someone else doing something similar. It was important to make sure whoever the host was and who was the guest both understood the roles here. And followed whatever rules were set.

Not that Tessa, innocent and naive and who believed in the best of everyone, had even thought to set rules. Or was she assuming Deanna was gone? Cody didn't trust that witch at all. She was too dangerous.

He finally caught up to Tessa – of course she'd stopped outside the grounds to study the back of the building. There were many windows on the tall, castle-like building. Many turrets and rooms on every floor. It wasn't a castle, more a huge imposing mansion. He'd never really thought about the architecture of the building before, having taken it all for granted all these years. He stood and stared up at the roof, realizing just how vast it was.

"What is in all those rooms?" Tessa asked, puzzled. "I've gone down several floors, but never up."

"Several of the ancient council members keep rooms here, and the oldest of them keep apartments on the top couple of floors."

"How many ancients are we talking about?" she asked, puzzled. "I thought Deanna would be classified as one, and she wasn't living there. Why not?"

"She had problems with many of the other members and still had a partner. My understanding is the other ancients are single, very old, and that this has been their home for so long I'm not sure anyone remembers that they have lived elsewhere."

Motre stood with his hands on his hips. "I'd forgotten. How the hell had that happened?"

"Because we deal with those active on the council assuming that they were the only ones. I think there is one more who is so old he doesn't attend meetings anymore. Like Deanna, but I can't be sure."

"Was Deanna's partner ever part of the Council?"

"No," Motre said. "I think he tried to be and was refused. He turned his back on them after being rejected."

Tessa nodded. "Is there any benefit to trying to communicate with whoever lives up there?"

Cody frowned. "I don't think…"

"But if we don't know who is up there, then how can we know that?" she said. "More than that, if the Hall is being attacked, are they safe?" She studied the soaring building.

"If vampires prefer the dark and deep depths of the earth, why would someone choose to be living up there?" Motre said with a frown on his face.

"True. Look at it. Location-wise, it's more suited for humans."

Tessa snorted. "Yet as a way to come and go without anyone knowing, I'm thinking a flier lives there."

She walked a few steps closer. "I'd like to know for sure."

"You might," Cody said, "but there are other priorities. Like Sian and keeping the Hall safe. We can do a full-on check after we know where we stand."

As they stood and studied the building, Cody could hear sounds of vehicles approaching at high speeds. "Sounds like we're just in time for a little action ourselves."

"About time," Motre said. "I'm wanting a little payback for that cat luncheon someone tried to invite me to."

At that, Cody laughed. "You're too ugly. Even the cats wouldn't touch you." He motioned to the side entrance that led to the main hall. "Let's go."

⤳ ⤳

GORAN WATCHED AS the humans exited the vehicle, guns out and forward. Had they been given any warning he'd be here?

Hey, Serus old boy, did you tell the Human Council that I'm vamp and I'm here to help them? Because they don't look like they want anything but to fill me with holes.

I'm calling them now.

Goran watched, eyes narrowed as a phone rang and the leader pulled out his phone. "Serus, what's up?"

He listened then turned to study Goran. "Ugly, huge, and dressed in black. Actually, he reminds me of you. Both of you were with your daughter that day when we were looking for the traitors in our group. We need her back to do more, you know that. If we can't find who's mixed up in this, we'll never stop it completely."

He nodded. "Well, let's get through this mess, then I want her to walk through the ranks and sort out the good from the bad. That's not negotiable. With your buddy here, we'll see what's down below. Anyone there is free game."

He hung up the phone. "You're Goran, I presume?"

"I am. Not only ugly and huge and dressed in black, but if you decide to turn those guns my way again," he said, "I'll take that as an insult and make sure you can't do so again."

He drew himself up to his full height and glared at the humans. "I'm here to help. You don't want my help, that's fine, I'm happy to leave."

The leader held up his hand. "Stand down. This is Goran. He and Serus are with Sian."

Goran watched with satisfaction as all the weapons were lowered. "Damn right."

He motioned beside him. "There's a ventilation shaft here. A ladder gives us access. Single file. I'll go first." And he led the way around the hill where the shaft had been cleverly concealed. It had taken him a few minutes to understand what he saw himself. The leader joined him and studied the metal structure completely overgrown on the one side. "I'd never have seen this on my own," he admitted.

Goran nodded. "I didn't at first either."

He took the first step down, slid around the large venting pipe, and started the descent.

❧ ❦

"SIR, DO WE have anyone coming to help us here?" A young female vamp stood in front of Serus. He lifted his gaze to study her, wondering what exactly caught his eye. She looked familiar, but he couldn't place why. "Do we need anyone?" he asked mildly. "What is our head count at the Hall now?"

She flushed. "I'm not exactly sure. So many are injured. We need to protect them."

"Sure we do, but they'd better be injured and not just avoiding what's coming as that's never going to be allowed." He glanced at the board where the layout of the rooms floor by floor had been filled in by Sian. "According to Sian, on many other floors, rooms are full of men leaving soon. If they don't get to leave today but need to help us instead, then too bad. They can leave tomorrow just as easily."

She flushed. "We didn't know, and without Sian to let us know, we let many of them leave."

"Interesting." Serus walked over to the board.

"Where are the men we sent back with the injured? There would be at least fifty able-bodied men to help us fight off an attack."

The young woman reached up and wiped off the names on several of the rooms. He frowned mentally, counting off the dozen or so that had left. He couldn't blame them. They weren't in on the finer details of what he and his own clan were up against right now, and most had been set up by their councils at home. "What about the Nordic team?"

"They are still here." And she tapped the board where one of the larger community rooms showed and said, "There are dozens of men here. They are recovering."

"Well, consider them now recovered," he said with a snort. "We're vamps. We need minutes, not hours to return to our full strength. Especially we need their fighting ability. If any say anything to you, you tell me."

She hesitated then said. "That's why I am here. They are bored and want to leave."

"And leave they can, after the attack has been neutralized," he said. "Sounds like it's time for a talk."

He strode to the door as the young woman ran at his side, trying to keep up.

"What's your name?" he asked.

"Talia."

He nodded. Her name meant nothing to him. But she sure looked familiar.

THE DARKNESS BEHIND the door was deeper and blacker than anything David had seen yet. The climb up had been dark without overhead lights or windows to lead the way. But this…it was as if the stone walls had been painted black. He could sense Jewel's unease and when she slipped her hand into his, he understood. Whatever was going on here had elevated the creepy factor.

Then he heard it. A soft moan.

Jewel dug her nails into his palm. He squeezed her hand reassuringly. In his other hand, he clutched a spike. He had no idea what was up there but whatever it was, it wouldn't have any defense against silver and he'd seen too damn much lately to get all cocky now. Especially with Jewel beside him.

Giving his eyes a few moments to adjust, he studied the small room they were in. And in the far corner, discarded for later…was it? He rushed to the vamp's side. Sian!

Jewel's gasp of joy resounded in the room. David searched for another door. Had she really been carried up the way they'd come or had someone found a different entrance? What were the plans? Leave her until later? Wait until the rush to find her was over then come back and move her? Move her where?

He gently ran his hands over her to check for injuries while Jewel struggled to untie her hands and feet. He couldn't see any injury, but that didn't mean she didn't have any. It was so hard to see in here. He gently stroked the side of her cheek. She lay on her side, her pregnant belly cuddled between her knees and arms as she lay curled in a protective fetal position.

"Sian, can you hear me?"

He continued to talk to her, trying to reach her.

"Jewel, text Serus. Let him know we found her."

"I already have."

"We might need help getting her out of here. I don't know if we should move her or not. I wish she'd wake up."

"The bastards," she cried. "Why would they steal her?"

"It's not the first attempt on her life, you know that. None of us are safe."

"It's wrong," she said quietly. "The baby doesn't deserve this."

"No, but many people won't be happy if it's born."

"It's still innocent, and I don't blame Sian for wanting Taz's child either." She glanced over at David. "They love each other. Taz is aging and her time with him is coming to a close soon. Of course she wants his child."

"And if the child is more human than vamp and she loses it young, too? Then is it still worth it?" David asked, studying her face. He'd never thought to have children. Down the road, centuries away, maybe. As he studied the moving belly in front of him and Jewel's hand so protectively held against it, he realize how ingrained it was in a woman's psyche to want a child.

"We need to get her awake and see if we can get her downstairs."

"David?" Sian's voice, low and slurred but easily recognizable, shocked them both.

"Sian, oh my gosh," Jewel cried. "Are you okay?"

She opened her eyes, but they were cloudy, unfocused. "I don't know. What happened?" She reached her hand down to her belly. She stroked the child within and smiled. "She's fine."

"She?" David asked worriedly. Who was Sian talking

about?

"My daughter," she whispered, smiling. "I can sense her. Feel her. She's okay. I was so worried..." and her voice broke.

Jewel wrapped her arms around Sian. "You're going to be fine. I don't know how you got here, but we need to get you back to the main hall. Taz is freaking out."

"Poor Taz," Sian said as they helped her into a sitting position. "This has been so rough on him."

"On all of us. Poor Serus is in command downstairs. I don't think he's enjoying it much."

David watched Sian's gaze widening as she digested his words, then her humor was followed by horror. "Oh no. We have to get back. He'll terrorize everyone to the point they will disappear and nothing will get done."

She struggled to her feet, wavered for a long moment as she took several deep breaths, then said. "Lead the way."

❧ ❦

IAN RACED BEHIND Rhia. He had no idea if she was to be trusted or not, but she appeared to have a plan and he was happy to go along with it – until it came to killing their own people. Then he'd see what she was up to. With Wendy behind him trying to urge a very groggy Jared along in their wake, Ian struggled to keep close to Rhia and not disappear too fast in front of the other two. No more splitting up.

"Rhia, slow down," he urged. "I don't want to get separated from the others."

She shot him one desperate look. "You look after them. I have to save Seth."

And she ran even faster ahead of him.

He slowed long enough for Wendy and Jared to catch up.

Ahead, he watched Rhia take a left. He looked at Wendy and she shook her head. "They gave him quite a cocktail. He's not doing so well."

Grimly, Ian eyed Jared. His skin was gray and his steps wove as he struggled to follow them. Ian had no intention of leaving the man behind, but this pace was going to kill them.

He walked closer and scooped Jared up into his arms. He was surprisingly heavy. But at least this way they could move faster and with Wendy running alongside, he raced after Rhia.

The left turn she'd taken was just ahead. He bolted around the corner after her and came face to face with huge double doors. He stood Jared up and leaned him against the wall. When he was sure he wouldn't fall over, he peered through the large windows.

Shit.

Rhia was backed against a corner, her fangs as long as he'd ever seen them and her eyes…well, she was going to save Seth, if that was Seth, or go down right now.

He had to help her.

CHAPTER 13

A T THE SIDE entrance, Cody jumped ahead to push the door open. It wouldn't move. He pushed it harder but it still wouldn't budge, then Motre jammed his shoulder up against the steel door.

It refused to move.

Tessa stood back a few feet. For some reason, and it had been building for a while now but she'd been trying to ignore the odd sensation, she'd been feeling slightly…woozy. The last thing she was going to do was faint. She had a reputation to uphold now, and fainting wasn't on the list of things she'd like to be known for.

Then again, she wasn't sure it was a faint that she was feeling. Just kind of off. While the men fought fruitlessly with the locked door, she closed her eyes and brought up her vampire genes, telling them to get rid of this sensation in the pit of her stomach. Instead, it made it worse. Frowning, she walked around slowly, trying to ease that sensation. She no longer felt like she was going to keel over but that she might lose the contents of her stomach.

What the hell…she took several deep breaths but this horrible sensation of wrongness…wouldn't go away.

She spun back to the men to realize that they had picks out, trying to unlock the door.

"Stop," she screamed.

Cody looked at her, startled, the knob in one hand and the pick already jabbing in. He withdrew and backed up.

Boom.

The door exploded.

Cody was picked up and tossed backwards. Smoke billowed up to engulf all of them. Motre flew several feet to the opposite side before landing hard. He lay still.

Tessa raced into the cloud to find Cody.

He lay on his stomach, his shirt ripped open and his back scorched.

She dropped to her knees. "Cody!" She poured healing energy into his back, willing him to sit up and say it was all okay. That he was fine. She reached down to his neck to search for a pulse and couldn't find one. Panicked, she rolled him over.

His heart chakra was black. Cold. She ripped his shirt open, searching for an injury. Something she could see to explain this, but there was nothing. Outside of shock and the fall, he should be fine.

Instead, his heart wasn't beating. The blood not pumping. She shot a bolt of energy against his heart, feeling his body jolt from the surge, but he still wasn't breathing.

She did it again.

Nothing.

Tears in her eyes, she kept pouring more and more energy into his body. What was the good of having any abilities if she couldn't use them to help the person she loved? Beast whimpered at her side.

Dimly aware of Motre struggling over to where she worked on Cody then dropping to his knees at his side, she heard him ask, "Can't you save him?"

"He's not responding," she said, unable to hold back the

tears.

In the very back of her mind, she could feel a weird knocking sensation. "What," she cried.

And realized it was Hortran.

Let me help, he whispered. *I might be able to save him.*

Save him, she whispered. *How? What more can I do?*

Watch...

Her hand lifted on its own accord and laid flat on Cody's chest. The energy around him bubbled up to encompass the two of them. The black energy of Cody's, the blue healing energy from Tessa. As she watched, her hand seemed to sink deeper and deeper into Cody's chest.

"Is this really possible," she whispered.

"It can't be," Motre cried out. "Your hand is in his chest."

That was when she realized she'd spoken out loud. And that for all the energy she could barely see through, he likely saw only a portion of what she saw.

Her hand slid all the way inside Cody's chest.

Now...you say you love him...

I do, she whispered in awe. Cody was in here. She was inside Cody. She could sense the tiny spark of his essence. She had no idea what had happened, but he was still there. A tiny spark only.

"The blast splintered his energy. He needs your help for him to pull the pieces back together again."

She blinked. "How?" She was beyond asking if such a thing was possible. Her gaze focused on Cody and the blackness in his system. She could get rid of that. She quickly pulled and tugged and wafted the darkness from his body, realizing that for her, he had no body. She couldn't see his form in a physical sense, only the energy that ran through his bones, the different energy that ran through his veins. It was like a 3D holograph where Cody had only lines. No form, no edges. At the same time, kneeling beside him, she realized she couldn't see her knees either. It was like there was no distance between what was Cody and what was Tessa. Nothing separating them. As if they were one together.

Remember, we are all one, Hortran said. *In this world, we are all made of the same stuff. This view of what you're seeing right now is the type of vision you need to connect with to cross that highway I showed you. You must see all the energy around you. Not just one layer. We are all layers. As Cody is connected to you, he is also connected to the ground beneath him. He does not start and stop. He does not only exist in his physical body. He is one of the world. One with the world. And so too are you.*

And how does that help him? she whispered, fat tears rolling down her cheeks. *He isn't breathing on his own. His heart isn't beating.*

Yes, they are. But they are moving to the same tempo of the life force around him. Cody is here and he is alive, but he's one with all things. You must ground him. Help to pull him back to his physical being.

I don't even know what you're talking about, she cried.

She sensed Motre at her side, but he was the same as Cody, energy zinging and zagging throughout his body. His brain was a huge orange ball of seething thoughts and emotions. Were they all like this? Her glance landed on Beast and she found her own answer. Yes. Only Beast's head was a wild violet color that deepened as he dropped his head to rest between his paws.

Yes. You are all energy. When you come to my state, my energy is weak as well. I'm using your energy to prolong my existence so that I can help you with your transition. But make no mistake, all energy is meant to go back to the source. And I will eventually too.

Help me save Cody first. Please.

I will help, but it's for you to do. He's lost. He's not even aware that something happened to him.

Was this a new weapon then? If it was, she planned to dismantle every damn one these assholes had created.

Possibly, but also likely that Cody at that moment was attempting to do something in his mind, maybe even communicate with you, and at the time of the blast, his energy was already reaching for you and it blew him further away than he expected.

Who knew that could happen? She stared down at the tiny spark of Cody, and she leaned forward and blew gently on the tiny light. Now that Hortran had explained, she could see the faintest of blue all around her.

Cody, she whispered.

Tessa?

She smiled through her tears. *He can hear me.*

Yes, he is you. As I am you. He needs your help before it is too late to stop him from becoming like Deanna and myself. He is too young for such a future, and you are too young to carry yet another.

I don't want him to be like you, she cried. *I want him back in his body, healthy, happy, and giving me hell once again.*

Then help him...now, Hortran ordered.

How? she cried.

Close your eyes and take control. This is energy, and you work energy. That is your destiny.

But I've never done anything like this.

It doesn't matter. Those who work energy must learn to control it. Or it will control you and as the world is energy, to save yourself, you must save him. Or all is lost.

She stared down the thousand blue bits floating around

her head, dimly registering Motre's grief at her side, and closed her eyes. She opened her arms wide and arched her back so her face was up to the sky. And she started chanting an old song. She didn't know where it came from. It felt like it was deep in her bones. She cared not as long as it did what she knew needed to be done. As her voice modulated to a specific tone, she sensed a change. Opening her eyes, she could see the blue vibrating.

Good, keep it up. Hortran said. *Take control of that energy and make it to what you want it to do.*

She needed the energy to pull itself together and heal Cody.

He will heal...don't stop.

She smiled sadly and kept it up. There was a weird sensation in her hands as she sang, a stronger vibration building of power.

Remember, you need to be detached and will it to happen. Casually. In control. Don't be sad. Don't be confused. Or angry. Be happy. Come from a position of love. Of being in the right. Let no one defy you because you are the one.

At that, her back arched more and the tempo in her head hit a fevered pitch. Suddenly, like an elastic pulled back and for as long as possible—she released it—whatever *it* was.

She dropped back onto her ankles and slowly opened her eyes. And stared. She could see the roots of the grass under Cody's back down into the ground and the working ants – rather, the energy of those critters down deeper.

She wasn't meant to be restricted by the physical. She wasn't meant to be locked into the now. She was connected to all things all the time. And Cody was a big part of that connection. With a deep releasing sigh, she waved her arms and ordered the cells to reform, to rejoin and rejoice in this connection. His connection. To refill the well that was Cody with his essence.

Like Hortran said. It wasn't a request.

It was a calm and caring, loving…order.

As she willed – her will be done.

❧ ❧

HOW DID ONE explain a sense of connectedness to all things – yet a sense of loss to the one thing that he really cared about? Tessa was still there. She was everywhere. He was everywhere, but she was a solid pulsing warm magnet. He couldn't get close enough. He was there but not there. He was part of her, yet separate. He was conflicted by all the mixed messages – and yet he was okay with it. As if he were taking a giant step in a new direction. One he was meant to travel.

Only did it have to be now? Emotionless and wondering at the state of finality to this, he posed that question more with a gentle rumination than expectation of an answer.

But an answer came.

No. It doesn't have to be right now. You have a choice here. You always have a choice. In this situation, you have more than you know. You are in a unique position. You can go on and be one with the world forever…

Or, Cody asked curiously, *what else is there?*

And if he had a choice, how did he actually take action on the choice he made? He was nowhere. Had no physical body. No voice to express his wishes. But he had a mind that could think – otherwise he couldn't make a choice and with a mind he had everything. Right. No, that was foolish. He gave a whimsical laugh.

How bizarre. Surely he'd wake up soon to find this nothing but a pleasant dream.

This is no dream, and there will be no waking up from this state unless you choose that option.

No waking up?

How did that work? And did he want to wake up? If he didn't, was this what the rest of his life would be like?

Your life would be over. This would be your existence, yes...and it would drift into more of a dream state than now. Your thoughts would become softer, less clear. You will care less and less until you dissipate into the world around you as the others who have gone before you.

A heavy sigh rippled through him, a rolling wave of feeling that washed through the whole area. Wherever he was, the air rippled.

A soft brush of another energy sent him into a gentle rocking motion. So peaceful here. Soothing. No war. No fighting. No friends. No Family. No Tessa.

He frowned. He couldn't leave her. She was his. But then she was here with him. Right? So it wasn't like he was leaving her?

Yes, as all things are here with you. But she isn't in the same endless state like you. She's alive and well and physically strong. In fact, she's stronger than ever. Of course, without you to protect her, to keep her strong when she missteps, to hold her when she's hurt...someone else will do that job. Someone else must do that job. She must always be protected. If it's not you, then the universe will put another in your place.

Cody's warning sense went off like huge flashing red lights. Someone else will be chosen to guard her? To spend their life with her? To be her loving partner? Hell no. That was his job and his job alone.

But if you're not there...

I'm there, he snapped. *Decision made.*

And pain like he'd never experienced before filled him, his back arching as his energy regrouped and his physical body started to pulse with life again. A guttural groan like he'd never heard before erupted from his mouth. He opened his eyes.

∂∞ ∞⟨

DAVID HAD WANTED to carry Sian down the stairs. She wouldn't hear anything of it. So he'd gone first in case she fell and Jewel had stepped into last place, with Sian safely tucked in between them.

"You sure you don't remember anything?" David asked for the third time.

"If I did, I'd have said something," she said for the third time. "Honestly, I remember being in the conference room with several councilmen and support staff then turned to walk back into my room. That's where I don't know what came next. My head hurts," she murmured. "So I presume I was attacked. I remember being tossed over someone's back and carried off. I thought I heard Goran talking to me, tried to warn him, but it's all mixed up and foggy," she added.

"Well, you didn't tie yourself up, and neither did you get up here on your own," Jewel said. "My concern is that we'll get you back downstairs to your room, but the person responsible will be able to blend in and no one will be the wiser. In fact, they are likely to be so solicitous of your welfare that we'd never suspect them."

"We'll have to look at everyone who is at the Hall and see where they were when you were attacked. Hopefully we can account for everyone but that bastard," David said with feeling. "Except he might have done this at someone else's orders."

"I'm sure they did," Sian said in a calm voice. "Think about it, every boss in the blood farm is looking for me. Wouldn't be surprised if there was a price on my head." She laughed. "Hope it's a decent amount. I'd hate for anyone to consider me an unimportant job."

"Hardly," David said. "And thankfully it appears they want you alive."

"They want my baby alive," she said, her voice thinning to a fine edge of steel. "Well, they didn't get me—and won't get her."

"And from now on, you get a personal guard," Serus growled, surprising them all from the bottom of the next landing.

David grinned at him. He hated to admit, but he was damn relieved to pass the responsibility of Sian over to the ancient. She had a better chance with him than anyone.

Serus took one look at her and snorted. "Of course you had to make your way downstairs on your own. Even though you're tired and sore."

Her smile faltered.

David was going to protest, saying that he'd offered to carry her, but the relationship between the two vamps was different. Caring. They'd been friends for a long time.

"I thought I could make it," she whispered, but her voice was fatigued. "But…"

Serus nodded and opened his arms. She stepped into them and hugged him tight. Serus swung her up into his arms and glided his way down the stairs. David and Jewel were hard pressed to keep up, as were the men that had come with Serus. By the time they made it to the ground floor and out to the hallway, David could see Serus already walking at the far end of the hallway. He shook his head, grabbed Jewel's hand, and ran to catch up. At least they'd found Sian before the bastards had a chance to hurt her or the baby. All in all, it was a good day.

❧ ❧

RHIA HISSED AND crouched, her gaze flitting from vamp to vamp. Like hell they were going to do to her son what they'd done to every other asshole in their world. He was hers, and if he'd gone bad and there was no going back, well, as hard as it would be, he was her responsibility and she'd punish him herself.

She wasn't going to allow him to become a twisted abomination of what he used to be.

"Damn it, Rhia, what's gotten into you?" the doctor cried. "He asked for this. You know he wants to be the biggest and the best."

"He's a kid," she cried. "Of course he wants that. But that doesn't mean we should give it to him."

"He's not a kid," the doctor snapped. "He's a respected member of our council."

For the moment, Ian was confused.

Seth had *never* been on the Vampire Council. What was the doctor talking about? Then as he heard a little more, he realized the doctor was talking about *their* council, as in a council that ran the blood farms. He didn't know what to do with that piece of information. There shouldn't be two councils, but the warring faction had created their own copy of the main vampire clans' government. In their need to organize, they'd copied their enemy while espousing their superiority. A fact that amused him. He doubted the doctor would appreciate that point.

Ian slipped around behind the others. He wanted to make sure it was Seth on the table. While the three people in his room had their attention on Rhia, he had a chance to look. And it was. With that confirmed, Ian stood and studied the man he'd seen around and would have been happy to have called a friend if Seth had shown any interest. But he hadn't. He'd been with his own crowd. Like every kid found their own friends.

He reached down and touched Seth's neck. Was he drugged? Would they have a problem getting him out of here? Not that he had any idea where here was.

The young man's pulse was strong, but he was out cold.

He studied the frozen tableau in front of him, Rhia glared at him and nodded to Seth. He realized that meant get Seth out—now. He bent, scooped the good-sized male into his arms, and walked back out the hallway.

He couldn't help Rhia this way. He could only help save Seth.

Wendy gasped when she saw him. She peered around him at the room and cried, "No."

She darted past him. Jared gave Ian a weak smile. "Hey, Ian. You found him, didn't you?"

"I did, but Rhia's in trouble." Ian didn't want to lay Seth down and have the man wake up and disappear on them, but he could hardly leave Jared in charge. Neither could he leave Rhia to face the three vamps.

Damn it to hell for shitty choices.

At a high-pitched howl, he spun around to find Rhia going berserk, but in a good way. She stabbed the doctor in the throat and was busy slashing and kicking the hell out of the other two vamps. Wendy jumped in and added her spike to the doctor's shoulder, and he disappeared into a pile of ash. As Wendy turned to help Rhia, Ian wanted to laugh. There was no one left to fight. The other two people were dead and gone. Rhia herself was slowly coming down from her fiery adrenaline rush.

Ian hoped she didn't come down too much. They needed her to be strong and fiery in order to get out of this hellhole. He had no idea where they were and with two of their group either down or so weak they couldn't move, Ian needed her help.

She burst through the double doors, her gaze wild until they landed on Seth still held protectively in Ian's arms.

"He's fine. He's still out cold though," Ian cautioned. "We need to get out of here and get him back home where *our* doctors can help."

She nodded and reached out a gentle hand to Seth's forehead. "And Tessa. If she can do what you all say she can do, we need her to remove all the black from his system."

Ian stayed silent, but he caught Wendy's worried gaze with his own. It might be well past the point of Tessa helping Seth in any way. And in helping him, she might just kill him.

"Let's go," Rhia called behind her as she strode forward. "We have to move it. Now."

❦ ❦

GORAN STRODE DOWN the tunnel. There were no pretty white walls or ceiling tiles anywhere. This was a ventilation shaft for something, but they hadn't had a chance to figure it out. He knew what was likely down here – after all, what else could it be? – but they hadn't seen any proof of it.

And they'd been walking for a while. He could hear the military grumble behind him.

So far, he'd been referred to as an old geezer, geriatric wannabe warrior, and a few other choice names. He didn't care. He was a vamp, and being a seriously old vamp, he could still run circles around the human kids.

He had no need to prove anything anymore.

Unless they called him old to his face. Then he was going to kick their ass.

He knew he'd been delighted to get out of the office and into the field, but this walking trip was hardly the type of action he was looking for.

Up ahead, he could see the darkness ease. There were lights ahead.

Holding up his hand for silence, he cautiously stepped forward.

CHAPTER 14

ESSA STOOD UP, woozy and disoriented but...*maybe* fine. She wasn't exactly sure what had happened and was fairly certain that what had gone on hadn't been done by her hand.

But she couldn't be sure.

Cody sat up slowly, his body moving in as graceful a movement as she'd ever seen. So weird. He'd always moved well, strong muscles functioning at their prime, but now there was a smoothness, a panther-like grace to him. As if everything was working better than before. She could see the blue energy vibrating through his system. There was a wonderfully coordinated rhythm to it.

From sitting, Cody leapt to full standing and gave a huge stretch. She watched him in wonder. Beast studied him, seemingly for the same reason. Cody...felt different.

"Hey," he said, that smile of his triggering warmth inside. She studied his blue eyes, melting a little more.

Hey back, she whispered in his mind. *How do you feel?*

Better than ever. Strong. Powerful.

What happened, she asked cautiously. *Do you know?*

Some. He gave her a crooked grin and said out loud, "I took a hit that affected my energy, scattering it everywhere. Someone in my head kept saying I had a choice. Did I want to stay there or want to come back here? To you."

She gasped. "Who said that?"

"I'm not sure," he admitted. He opened his arms and tugged her close. "But if I didn't come back, someone else was going to take my place in your life. Or I could come back and look after you."

He laughed at the look on her face. "I didn't argue. The thought of someone else holding you like this...I couldn't stand it."

And he tucked her up close against his heart and cuddled her. Held her. Cherished her.

"I'm so glad you came back then," she whispered. "I wouldn't have wanted to go on without you."

"Wouldn't have mattered what you wanted. According to the voice in my head, you are doing what you need to do. You are the One, and it was my job to stand by and protect you – in all ways."

She shook her head, finding it hard to believe. "Who could that have been?"

"I don't know," he admitted. "I wondered if it wasn't Hortran."

"Hortran? I don't even know what to stay." Motre was standing beside them, looking worse for wear, but his face glowed as he looked at Cody. "I thought you were done this time. What would we do without Tessa, huh?"

"I didn't fix him this time," she said with a big smile. "He did most of that on his own."

Cody laughed. "Well, I did, but it took Tessa to make it happen."

"What?" Motre stared at the two of them in shock.

Tessa listened from the circle of Cody's arms as he tried to explain.

She was still in shock herself. That he'd experienced such a breakthrough was wonderful. It helped him to understand much of what she'd gone through. There was no way to explain what she'd been through, he had to experience it himself.

As she listened to Cody's explanation, she wondered at what all he'd seen and experienced.

Motre, on the other hand looked...shell-shocked.

She grinned up at him. "Amazing, isn't it?"

Motre's gaze kept going from one to the other. "Well, I don't know what to think."

"I knew," Cody admitted. "But no idea that this was possible until I came so close to dying."

"Were you that close," Motre asked. "Really?"

"Yes," he said. "I was. Everything was so faint and thin and emotionless."

He shook his head slowly as if remembering. "There was a voice talking to me in a calm, natural tone and I could hear him clearly."

Motre shook his head. "Well, I sure hope that never happens to me." He turned to look at the door that had blown up. "What do we make of that? Was it a weapon?"

Cody glanced from the door to Tessa. "I think it was a bomb of some kind."

"I can't imagine anything else having that effect." She shrugged. "Then again, who knows?"

"Well, I'm not opening any more doors." Motre crossed his arms and studied the door. "Besides, if it was a bomb, why is the door still standing?"

"It blew open with the blast then shut again." Tess walked closer. She wasn't too eager to touch it either but given the blast had already happened, she couldn't imagine there would be much more danger involved. Then it was a whole new world again.

She reached out for the knob that was looking a little worse for wear but still attached.

"Easy," Motre cried, backing up several yards.

Cody stood beside her. "Go ahead, it's probably fine now."

"I was thinking the same thing." She grabbed the knob and tugged the door open.

And stared. Inside, the damage was much worse. "Wow, the floor and walls were blown to crap in here."

She couldn't imagine the damage if Cody had been any closer to the bomb. Or indeed if it had gone off at a different time.

She stepped inside carefully. The plaster was hanging drunkenly down from the ceiling and the walls appeared to have been torn off. There was wood underneath it, and although that appeared distressed, it was still standing. Good for the original builders. Who knew they'd be looking at protecting the structure against bombs? With Motre finally inside, the three, Beast at Tessa's side, gingerly walked down the hallway. This was a small side hallway specifically for this exit. She'd used it before when she wanted to get away from the noise and crowds of a gathering.

Sad in a way. She'd never felt a part of the clan before, and now she was an important member. At least she hoped some vamps thought so. It would be sad to consider that she could be an outsider again after all of this.

Then again, she no longer felt the need to be accepted. If she wasn't, then she wasn't. She was no longer a young girl with easily hurt feelings. She was a full-grown woman who felt a wrath she barely recognized building deep inside. If more of Council Hall was like this hallway, she might let that rage blow at that damn blood farm.

෧๏ ๏෧

CODY STUDIED THE blast zone in awe. It had taken a lot of balls to do this. Of course it was an insider job. Unfortunately, if there was one bomb, there was a chance there were more. They'd been expecting an attack from the outside of the hall, but he was afraid as he studied the blast radius that the enemy was still within the inner circle. How the hell was that still happening?

He walked down the hallway slowly. There was no sound. No music, no voices. No arguing. Council Hall was famous for its arguments. Right now, he'd do a lot to hear raised voices. Stealthily, afraid the Hall had already been taken, Cody slipped into the main chamber. The huge room rose above his head in a domed roof. He'd never really studied the architecture of the place before. But looking at it now and seeing the damage one small blast had done to the single hallway, he could just imagine the damage several of those charges would do in a room like this. All the floors above would collapse. He gazed upstairs. And who the hell was up there? Tessa was right. They needed to find that out.

According to David's text, they'd found Sian at the top of a hidden staircase. No windows to see out of, so it had been impossible to keep track of how high they'd gone or why. There were secrets to this building they needed to uncover.

He looked around the Main Hall. It was empty.

That room, the main community space, was never empty. Even if the place was shut down for a day or so, as soon as people entered, they were in that room. So that made no sense either.

He was filled with the sudden urge to see who or what was on the top floor of the Hall. He had no idea how to get there though. And the main floor was too damn silent to leave right now. Unless there was something that connected the two incidents?

"Where is everyone?"

"I have no idea." Tessa's tone was odd though.

He glanced at her, Beast as always walking calmly at her side. "You okay?"

She nodded. "I am. Slightly off, maybe, but not sure why."

"Good." That sounded better but not quite right. He studied her face. "Any more signs of Deanna?"

A shade of guilt whispered over her face.

"You did?"

She shrugged. "I'm not sure if I did or not. When you were having your experience, Hortran spoke to me. At least I think it was Hortran. But there was an odd energy there as well. I think it was Deanna's energy."

"So, her energy fills you." He lifted his eyebrow as he stared at her. "That shouldn't worry you."

Her sideways smile slipped out. "I know, but it was different. It wasn't like the energy of the memories. It was livelier."

"As in she was still inside you and capable of taking over? Or just that there was more liveliness because of the Hortran connection?"

She walked forward and froze, her foot off the ground. Her shocked gasp was hoarse, raw. More of a gurgling cough.

He raced to her side. "What is it?"

"It's Deanna."

"What? She's still there?"

"Yes, but so much smaller. Lesser. Weaker. But she is giving me a warning."

"About what?"

Tessa shook her head and groaned.

"Now what?" he whispered in harsh tones. "You're acting like you're in pain."

"I am. I tried to move closer to the middle of the Hall and she's...shocking me into paying attention?"

"As in a warning?"

Tessa looked puzzled. "Maybe?"

Cody turned to look toward the main part of the Hall. "I'm willing to listen to it." He looked behind him. "Do you have any idea how to get to the upstairs apartment?"

She shook her head, apparently struggling to pull her gaze from the Main Hall. He tugged her backwards slightly. Motre had stayed behind them. As Cody glanced at him, he realized that Motre was holding his hand to his head. Had the blast caught him, too? Damn it. Cody had been so involved in his own experience that he'd had forgotten to see if Motre was okay.

"Headache?"

Motre shrugged but he didn't pull his hand down. "It's getting better."

"Sorry, Motre." He quickly explained the warning and hesitation to go further into the building. "Do you know how to get upstairs?"

Startled, Motre nodded. "You want to check up there now?"

He nodded. "We can't go in that direction of the Main Hall. Something has gone wrong, and we need to know what we're dealing with."

"I haven't been up there in forever. Several ancients used to live there. But I don't think they do now."

Cody wondered. "Except someone is up there. We saw them."

"Was up there." Motre shrugged. "We don't know anyone is there now."

"Let's go find out."

⌒ ⌒

RHIA FELT LIKE this was a last stand.

She stood in front of the others, Ian still holding her son behind her. Wendy was supporting Jared. They were a sad lot. And she'd had so hoped they could escape without attracting any further attention.

But they'd come around the corner and there were four men filling the hallway – waiting for them.

Damn.

She was already tired.

But not tired enough to lay down and let these asses walk all over her. She hadn't come this far to lose now.

She gave a fruitless look at the men's faces in the hopes they weren't here with ill intent. But of course, there was nothing to register but their anger.

"There you are," she said in exasperation. "About time."

The man standing slightly ahead of the other three vamps grinned – if that's what the grimace barely covering the man's teeth was called. "You're going nowhere."

"Did I say I was?" She raised her eyebrow at him. "These men need help. I thought that's why you're here?" She frowned at them. "Hurry up. Both men are in bad shape. There should be beds already organized for them."

Two of the men in the back looked at each other. She knew she had them worried. But the big man in the front, well, he wasn't too interested in listening to her. And the fourth man, he wasn't looking at anyone. He looked more asleep than awake, but she got the feeling that he could be the most dangerous of all.

If she had Ian and Wendy's help, then this was doable. If she had to handle it all herself – not so much.

But they had to keep Seth and Jared safe.

∽ ∾

SIAN SAT DOWN on the chair Serus pulled out for her. Her legs were shaky and weak, her belly roiling with the lack of blood. She was tired and sore but so damned relieved. She was safe again. Unfortunately, she had no idea who had grabbed her, so she had no idea who to guard against. She'd been on her way to the office where several people had come and gone. But who could have snagged her and carried her out? And how had they gotten her past the main room? Someone would have seen her being carried away.

Surely.

"Sian," Serus asked her. "Are you feeling okay?"

"Now that I'm safe," she said in a low voice, "I'm much better. Thanks."

"Well, you don't look it," he said bluntly. "But I'm hoping you're well enough to handle the reins here again. It's not where I want to be."

She tried to laugh, but everything ached. "But you're such a great commander."

"No, I'm a commander in war. Not at communication central."

"But you do it so well."

"No, I don't," he said, his hands waving out in front of him. "I'd rather be strung up and flayed alive before I spend another day here."

She glanced around at her office. "I might be able to take the reins again, but not without help."

"And guards." Taz stood in the doorway, his face glaring at her. "Lots of them."

Tears filled her eyes at his beloved face. She opened her arms toward him. "And I just might accept them."

"You will or you're leaving town. That's two attacks. Two more than your body should have at this stage. Our daughter needs to be safe."

His voice, hard and lethal, brought slow tears tracking down her cheeks.

"She is safe. And she will stay safe." But her voice trembled with the effort to stay strong.

Taz rushed to her side. "I'm sorry, sweetheart." He bent over and gently wrapped his arms around her. "Take it easy. I'll leave the hospital and stay here with you if you won't go home."

"I can't go home," she said, her gaze hot and wet, willing him to understand. "She'll never be safe if we don't finish this."

Serus, his voice at the doorway, snapped, "We *will* finish this."

Nestled against Taz's big chest, she nodded. "Thanks."

"This isn't *your* fight, Sian. It's all of ours. We're all affected. Everyone has been hurt by these bastards. And no one will come out of this unscathed."

Sian stared at Serus. He was so strong and determined. He'd been through as much as she had. More with the problems dealing with Rhia and Seth. And then there was Goran. Both ancients had lost sons. She could only hope they recovered. But if she lost her child, she couldn't imagine trying to go on.

Her spine stiffened. She'd be damned if she let any harm come to her daughter while she was still alive.

"Go. End this. We'll hold down the Hall."

❧ ❦

GORAN DIDN'T WANT to go forward. Instinct was telling him to run.

He turned back to look at the men behind him, trusting him yet at the same time not. They had no reason to follow him and likely wondered if he was leading them into a trap.

Hell, that's what he'd be thinking if he were in their shoes.

But they didn't appear to be considering that as an option.

There was anger around him. They wanted a target and they wanted it now.

"Let's move on, Goran."

"There's something wrong here. It's too easy. I'm afraid it's a trap."

Someone in the back sneered. "Yeah well, I'm not afraid. Let me at them."

A roar of assent picked up around him.

The men wanted action. He understood, but he hadn't survived for centuries for being stupid. Something was wrong. But being the only vamp at the front of several teams of military men who he couldn't do anything to hold them back, well.

With misgivings, all senses on alert, Goran crept forward.

CHAPTER 15

TESSA TRIED TO take a step and couldn't. Deanna didn't want her to go upstairs. But why? She quickly told Cody. He stared. "What do you want to do?"

"I want to go upstairs," she snapped. "And I want to know what her problem is."

Motre stood off to one side. "Is she hiding something?"

"Maybe?" She didn't know. Right now she was pissed. She wanted to go upstairs, and she wanted to go upstairs now. That Deanna was doing something to warn her but not giving her a proper reason why was just making her angry.

Deanna, what is wrong? Why don't you want me to go up there? She stopped and closed her eyes, willing Deanna to speak to her. To give her the answers she needed. But Deanna wasn't talking.

"Nothing. Damn it. What does she want from me?"

Cody followed Motre, staying close to her side. "Are you really sensing her?"

"I don't know," Tessa said, frustration boiling over. "It doesn't feel like before, so I don't know. It's all different. She's gone, but there's that little bit left. I can't tell if I need to listen harder or if what she has to say isn't as important."

"Or it is, but she no longer has the power to get her message across."

Tessa studied Motre's insightful words. Unfortunately,

they were concerning. Motre opened up a large double door set. From the outside, it appeared to be part of the same ornate trim and not doors. She smiled as it opened to a wide staircase. "Wow. I never saw this before."

"Neither have I," Cody said. "But it's cool. It's twice the width of any other staircases in here."

"And very ornate."

He laughed. "I'm presuming that the ancients originally lived up here. It looks like the best of everything for them. Nothing scrimped."

"Back in the day when they were the elite." She laughed. "It's pretty fancy."

They started climbing. "I wonder how many people know about these steps."

"Not many. I'm thinking that whoever lives up here – if anyone lives here – likely has another entrance and exit. It allows them to move in and out quietly without being seen. To them, they might not even see anything wrong with that. Most vampires are loners. Private. If they could have a place like this," he waved his hands to the rich paintings on the wall and the big windows, "then who wouldn't want it?"

"It's familiar."

Cody stopped. "Sorry?"

"It's familiar to me." Tessa stopped and stared up the long staircase and the massive windows. "It's beautiful."

"Hmm. Back to that looks *familiar* part. Have you been here before?"

"No," she said positively. "I haven't."

"Then…"

"Deanna's seen it before. That's why. There's something that hurts her – maybe wants to hurt her – up here."

She felt Cody's gaze but refused to meet it. How could

she explain without going and accessing Deanna's memories? Memories she didn't want to access. She was scared to go there when she wasn't sure what had happened to Deanna. It felt like her presence was growing now. Getting bigger. Gaining in power. And the thought terrified her.

After all she'd seen and done, to think of Deanna gaining a foothold in her life and locking Tessa up again indefinitely was the private horror she'd been enduring in secret.

Not in secret.

This time she did look at Cody. *You knew?*

I could feel it, he said calmly. *And it's a fear that I recognized as it mirrors my own.* He reached out and grabbed her hand. *All the more reason to go upstairs and find out what bothers her here.*

And the others?

Motre called up from behind them. "I hear voices in the Main Hall. I'm going back down to see what's going on."

Tessa hesitated. She hated the idea of them splitting up, but she could hear voices too. Not angry confrontational voices. More conversation tones. So no fighting. But if she went back to the Main Hall, she'd have trouble escaping again. And she really needed to find out what was up here. There was a secret up here. And it related to Deanna. She snorted. Even if she did try to access those memories of hers, she wouldn't be allowed to. That was walled off. Private. Something she didn't have to try to know it wasn't going to work. In her mind's eye, she could see the filing cabinet locked and wrapped in chains. To not be opened – ever.

Well, Deanna *might* be able to keep her out of that set of memories – but she wasn't going to be able to stop Tessa from climbing up the Council stairs to the penthouse apartments.

Who was up there?

Sensing that Motre wasn't heading into any danger, she gave him a bright smile and turned to run up the stairs lightly.

Cody, as always, or rather, even more so now, was close behind. Beast ran at Tessa's side. At the top, she stopped and looked around. Beast growled, a low and hostile sound coming from the back of his throat.

She reached down a hand to calm him. She had no idea what was up here, but someone was.

And he stood in front them.

Only Tessa didn't recognize him. No one could. Not even a mother would acknowledge that face. She stopped and stared and realized something else. This man's energy wasn't black with poison. He was deformed from some other cause. He wasn't young like her and Cody, but not as ancient as Deanna. Yet he appeared older than the ancients.

She took a step forward, plastering a smile on her face.

He held up a hand. "Stop. You are not welcome here."

"Why?" Tessa asked, studying him playfully. She was sure she'd never seen him before. Yet he seemed to know her. "Who are you?"

"It matters not. I know who you are – what you are. The *what* you are is not welcome in my presence." For all his disfigurement, and she couldn't quite see how bad it was, there was an aura of power around him.

"Who are you?" Cody asked. "Why do you have a problem with her?"

"She is Deanna's vessel, and while I don't wish to kill her at this point, there are many of my friends who would do so instantly," he said coolly. "I can't protect her or you for long."

Tessa slowly drew herself upright. She could feel the anger, the injustice of it, inside. Deep-seated rage, pain, and...wow...fear.

Deanna was terrified of this man for some reason.

"Why do you hate her...me," Tessa asked quietly. "What did she do to you?"

He stopped and stared. "Why don't you ask her?"

No, Deanna screamed, her voice blasting through Tessa's head. *I won't talk about it.*

"She won't talk about it," Tessa said sharply, hating the uncontrolled edge to Deanna's anger. She was still too powerful for comfort. "But I can feel her anger and pain."

"Pain?" he mocked, his eyebrow shooting up. "She is not in pain. Hasn't ever been in pain in her life. She wouldn't allow it. She was the queen of all she commanded."

"And you," Cody asked his voice hard. "Who are you to her?"

The man gave a laugh that sent chills running down her back. "I'm Victor, her one and only son. And the one person she tried to kill and...failed."

❧ ❧

CODY STARED AT the deformed male in front of him. "Son?" He shot Tessa a sideways glance. "Did you know?"

"No," she said in a low voice, "And Deanna is getting angrier and angrier."

The man in front of them laughed. "Of course she is. My dear mother made a lot of enemies, and I'm one of them."

Cody watched him narrow-eyed. There was something going on beneath the surface.

Tessa? What are you getting over this situation?

I don't know. She's so angry. As in her energy is building—.

As in taking over, he interrupted in alarm. *You said...*

I know what I said, she snapped, her breath harsh and

choppy as she struggled with the inner onslaught. *This man…he is her son, but she doesn't really know him.*

How? he barked. *Did she raise him? Lose him? What's going on? You have the memories, so access them. This is important.*

I'm trying, she cried. *But she's blocking me.*

Cody struggled to keep his face calm and controlled. This man, whoever the hell he was, was studying Tessa with a hawk's intensity. Feral. He asked, "How is it you live up here?"

"Well, my dear mother arranged it of course. Been here since the building was erected." He smiled. "She owed me."

"Why?"

"Well, she did try to kill me."

"For a good reason, maybe," Tessa said, her words struggling to be understandable. "I think you tried to kill her."

"Sure. But only after she tried to get rid of me at birth. That's always good for a mother-son bonding."

Shocked, Cody asked Tessa, *Is that true?*

I don't know. There's so much rage in Deanna right now that I can't tell. Under the anger is pain. So maybe and maybe not. There are layers of deceit and anguish I can't see through.

"I made sure to celebrate your demise, dear Momma." Victor smiled, a cruel edge to his mouth. "And not even at my hand." This time there was real humor in his voice.

"Deanna says that's not true," Tessa said. "That you did have a hand in her death. That you've tried multiple times before your ceasefire and when she was at her weakest, you took her out."

The vamp's face turned icy cold, his misshapen features turning hard and ugly. "Well, isn't that nice to see she's still spouting lies and deceit even at the end." He laughed. "I hadn't planned on airing the dirty laundry but if she wants to get it all out…" He shrugged. "So be it."

He walked to the windows on the far side, the moonlight shining into the room. That's when Cody noticed the harsh limp, the wings. They were likely somewhat functional but he wasn't just deformed, he was disabled. *What the hell happened?*

Not sure, but I think there might be some truth to his words.

"She was young, about to be married. Only she found out she was pregnant." Victor said. "She tried to get rid of me before my birth. Then as the wedding was cancelled due to her carrying the offspring of another, she gave birth then tried to kill me again."

He turned to face them, the moonlight highlighting the scars on the face, the bone structure that wasn't quite right.

"And of course she killed my father. But I was saved by an old vamp who had known of Deanna's pregnancy. She spirited me away to the other side of the world. It was centuries before I understood the real story." He glared at Beast, whose low howl was climbing in volume. "I found out on Nan's deathbed. She told me what had happened. I made it my life's quest to make Deanna pay for what she'd done."

Cody had to wonder if any of this was true. Had Deanna done that? Even for a vamp mother, that was cold. "And yet you didn't succeed?"

"No." He stared out the window. "With time, the necessity seemed to not matter anymore. And with Nan gone, I was alone. When I'd finally found my mother, she'd married and moved on – happy to be childless."

Tessa, can you see his energy? Is he telling the truth? Is any of this real? Or more lies to make us believe something he's not?

I'm not sure, but I can't hold on. She gasped with the effort to retain control as the waves from inside slammed to be released. *She's so angry. She wants to speak.*

"No! If he thinks Deanna is in control, he'll try to kill you."

❧ ❦

RHIA BARED HER teeth and crouched. As a last stand, it wasn't much, but she had to fight. Had to survive. Or all of this was for naught, and she couldn't let that happen. Not to her boy or her children's friends that were helping.

The four men in front of her grinned. She frowned.

The leader nodded in the direction behind her.

Shit.

"Ah, Rhia," Ian said urgently, his voice low and hard. "We've got company."

She closed her eyes and bowed her head. Please not. *They might have a chance against four, but if there were too many more, they were lost.*

A sense of fatalism took over. She straightened and very slowly turned to look.

The hallway behind them was full of ugly-ass vamps.

They were not only outnumbered, they were surrounded by these men who were all enhanced.

They didn't have a chance.

❧ ❦

HE HAD NO idea what they'd found but up ahead, in a more trafficked area given the number of footsteps along here, they had to be coming closer to the blood farm.

This was where things got a bit dicey. He hoped the men behind him could follow orders. He wasn't getting a good vibe from the sight of the huge double doors ahead.

Excitement permeated the atmosphere behind him. He could sense their excitement. But he wasn't feeling it.

"What's his problem?" someone called behind him.

Another frustrated voice called, "Open the damn door already."

He stood, his arms open wide, his eyes closed, thinking this through. This could be a trap. The doors themselves could be armed. There could be any number of things behind that door – and not one of the possibilities crossing his mind were any good.

Several men behind him jumped forward and reached for the doors.

"No, wait,' he cried.

Too late. The doors opened and like two waves racing toward their destiny, they poured down either side of him. If he hadn't been bigger, taller, they'd have blocked his view. As it was, he could see all too well.

The men raced into a huge room filled with beds. Empty beds.

Goran stepped back out of sight but kept an eye on the men.

As they milled around looking for another exit, a voice from above called down. "Welcome. Choose a bed, boys. It's the last one you will ever see."

IT COULDN'T END like this. Not again. Not when they were so close. He knew he was Clarissa's only hope. And not much of one at that. It was bad enough that she'd been take while trying to find out about her friend. Now he'd been taken trying to help her. What a nightmare. Look at him, he could barely stand on his own. Rhia was the most capable of them all. Wendy looked like paste and Ian, hell, he was the strongest of the lot and he was carrying Seth. Jared still struggled to believe that this was Tessa's brother. He understood a lot of what had gone on, but not all. He did understand the one major issue in front of them now.

This was the end of the line.

If they were taken now, then there was no help for any of them. Rescue would be down to Tessa and the rest of the gang – again.

Damn.

CHAPTER 16

TESSA STRUGGLED TO stay in control. Anger like a wall of red washed through her, taking everything she had to fight Deanna back down. Tessa knew this wasn't a fight she could lose, otherwise, Deanna could take over any time.

She had to win. But so far, the anger of Deanna's was taking over the much softer anger of Tessa. It was incorporating itself into her own anger, building herself up to be stronger and more powerful. Tessa wanted to win. Knew she had to win. But there was an air of desperation about it. Almost a panic. The memories of the last mess were sitting in her peripheral vision, threatening her with the reminder that she failed last time.

That she had been a fool and Deanna had taken her over by being what Deanna always had been – older, stronger, and so much more devious. Tessa tried to build up the anger to match Deanna, but she didn't have a lifetime of hurts and enemies to draw from. Her short-lived years were merely a blink to Deanna's centuries, who had anger plenty for both of them.

Give me your anger. I'll take it and make it mine, Deanna whispered. *Think of how easily I ruined your life. Think of what I'll do with Cody when I'm you and he's mine. He'll be my lover. Not yours. You'll be stuck inside for the ages while he becomes my man. His young firm body mine to do with as I please. Feel the anger at my words. Give it to me.*

Tessa wanted to laugh and cry at the same time. There was much terror and fear mixed with the anger. And her words, well, they'd ignited a maelstorm. *Cody is not and never will be yours.*

Her own rage built at the thought of this old crone taking what was Tessa's. Not just her body and her life, but her love. Cody wouldn't be able to free himself. He'd already fought to return to save her. He'd come back to protect Tessa, but there was no way he could fight Deanna.

Then the tiny whisper came, *but he could be.*

Hortran?

Yes. You can't let her destroy you.

You helped her to do this. How is it you aren't okay with her actions at this time? Tessa snapped. *You are just as responsible for what she's doing now as she is.*

Yes, but not for the reason you think.

You love her.

Of course. She's my sister. But I'm not blind to her. I helped her because she's right – you are the One. But you've had no training and as Deanna's past has come back to taunt her, you need help. Everything we do in our life has a cause and effect, and right now she's still trying to walk away from her actions. Like she always has.

Tessa's mind was split in different directions. One part on Hortran's words, another desperate to match Deanna's rage that she might win against her, and yet another part aware of the vamp watching the two of them in fascination. He held no weapons, as if content to see who'd win then take out the victor.

You can't match her anger. Her rage. She's done much wrong in her life. She cared not for the repercussions and did as she wanted. But your present has collided with her past, and there won't be a good end to this. She's never faced this – him. She never confronted him. He wanted revenge and held information on her that could destroy her and her husband. He had power over her. Thus, she feared him. Hated him and wanted only to see him die so that he couldn't hurt her anymore. But for all her actions, she is still a mother and knew she'd been in the wrong first. All those memories became a twisted compilation of fear, anger, and guilt.

Tessa was so confused. She got the relationship was complicated. She understood that Deanna had tried to kill her own son, but it had been eons ago. *Hortran, what difference does it make now? She's dead. Her husband is dead. She was trying to extract revenge for his death, but he's dead too. Everyone who mattered to her is dead.*

But her husband was set up to die by another. And that other is the one ultimately responsible.

Who?

Her son...

Tessa's gaze went to Victor, who was still standing at the window. But Hortran was still speaking, his voice low, fading.

...and by Victor's command...her own grandson. And he still lives...still hurts.

Grandson? Oh no. Who is her grandson?

A man raised on poison to hate her and who spent his lifetime creating something that would keep the line pure. To see her die as they all lived, bigger, better, stronger...and not deformed and disfigured like his father.

Shit.

She closed her eyes, caught in a bubble of frozen time, so much going on around her. So much caught up in this moment. Deanna's grandson was the one who'd created the blood farms. He was the one in the background. That shadowy figure that they hadn't been able to identify and had often questioned if he even existed. They'd caught and killed many of his minions…and never him.

He's there. He exists. You know him.

Deanna screamed in the background. *You should have killed him when you had the chance. And you had the chance. Now we'll take out my son first – I was going to let him live – my penance for my wrongs and for his penance to live so broken an existence – then we'll go after his son.*

No, Tessa said, struggling for calm. For sanity. For control. *I will make the decision of who I kill – not you.*

And Deanna screamed. It was a rip of rage like Tessa had never heard before.

But it was so like Deanna that Tessa knew it wasn't her own anger. In fact, hers had faded to the background like it always did. She wasn't a hard, cold, angry person. She loved animals and flowers and saved dogs from bad drugs and military men from vampire poison.

Exactly. Hortran said. *You must save yourself.*

How, she said, her mind already looking at her actions, Deanna's actions, and seeing that harsh divide. *She's not me.*

And you are not her.

You are…

She finished the sentence for him. *I am Tessa. And I must be true.*

Together, their voices blended into one as they said at the same time…*to me.*

Exactly. She felt Hortran's smile rather than saw it. *Worry not about Deanna when her anger blows out as she'll have nothing left – her life force has been used up in the conflagration. She'll sink back in here with me and spend the rest of her life realizing the life choices she made and how she could have chosen to be more like...you.*

And his voice faded away.

Cody whispered, *I just heard all that.*

You're different now, too. She smiled. *Because you spoke with Hortran, he can now speak to you.*

And did he help? Do you know what to do?

I do. She smiled and tilted her head back. *I have to be me. While I'm doing that, I need you to keep this guy away from me.*

I can do that, but what do you mean about being you? he asked cautiously.

I'm a healer, not a hater. And that means I have to heal my-self, and therefore Deanna. I can't win this battle with anger. Or fear. I can only win it with...love. As I have always done to help those in need. Being me means operating from goodness. Not darkness. Deanna crossed over a long time ago. Whether she wanted to return or not, I think once that choice is made...it's almost impossible to return.

In the background, Deanna raged. Now all Tessa needed to do was to show her the love inside her pain. Somehow.

Cody. I love you. I just wanted to say that. And she closed her eyes and said, *let this war rage. I will win. But it might take a little bit.*

And she dove into the red wall of rage.

WAIT, CODY CRIED. But it was too late. She was gone.

He didn't understand what he was seeing, but it's as if there was a red haze in his mind.

There had to be something he could do to help her be-sides protect her from this bastard. He studied Victor, seeing the pain in his features, the shiver to his frame against the window as he leaned and watched Tessa. There was also a deep satisfaction permeating his features.

"How is it you want this young girl to suffer for your hurts?" Cody asked him bitterly. "Tessa did nothing to you."

"And I've done nothing to her...yet."

Cody studied the older man, realizing he was already dying. His disability was taking its toll on his body that didn't heal well. He had not long to live. And like his mother, he wanted to see justice done before he was gone. "You're quite a pair," Cody growled. "A chip off the old block."

Victor glared at him. "I am nothing like my mother. She's a cold heartless bitch."

"And you think you're so much better?" Cody snorted with disgust. "I think not. You helped your son create this monstrosity of a blood farm, hurting thousands of humans, and for what?"

"A better life. A simpler life. An old-fashioned life. One of clean lines, with no more of this mixed breeding. Enough abominations. We are a pure race. We should be living to our noble standards."

"And yet your mother was an ancient. One of the strongest and purest of lines." Maybe mental instability was part of the disability because none of this made any sense.

"And she bred to another ancient, her uncle. And I was the result. They bred like animals when they wanted and where they wanted. Did you ever think about the ancients of old – how few of them there actually were? How did they procreate? Inbreeding causes birth defects like I suffered with. Nan had the same fate as I. But someone helped her, so she in turn helped me."

"And yet you procreated." Cody didn't get that. If he was

so against random genetic breeding, why would he risk perpetrating the same genetic faults he carried?

"Only after much testing. My DNA was only compatible with one female out of hundreds we tested. And I managed to produce a small healthy, whole offspring with her." The older vamp shuffled forward. "The child was perfect. He was what I should have been."

"And the mother?"

The vamp waved his hand. "She is dead. When I realized she couldn't breed a second child, then it was important she not be allowed to breed again. Her genetics couldn't go to another line." He shrugged. "So of course I killed her."

Cody swallowed. Victor had killed the mother of his child because she couldn't provide him with more children. Yet he didn't see the similarity to his own mother? And they thought humans were a terrible species. He wondered if vamps should be allowed to live at all. Look at this animal and what he'd created.

"And your son. Has he founded a dynasty for you?"

The old vamp grinned. "He has indeed."

Only there was something off in his voice. As if Cody wouldn't like what he meant. But as he went to ask him, he realized the air had thickened, like tiny sparks flying with every breath.

Beast whined deep in the back of his throat.

Tessa and Deanna. The air swirled around Cody, tension filled him so tight he felt he would snap if he moved even the slightest bit.

Fascinated and horrified, he watched, catching tiny glimpses of life on the other planes. Planes he'd touched and felt himself. There were bits and pieces, but the explosions were small and red, like micro-fireworks going off. As if

Deanna was losing control and in her frustration, blasting at the only person she could reach – Tessa.

And yet, he could sense Tessa in there this time. Strong. Stalwart. Calmly standing on the side of right.

Where she always stood.

That was one of the many things he admired about her. She knew the difference between right and wrong. She knew her own morality and ethics and held herself accountable. She wasn't crying, hiding, or cheating. She knew what she had to do and she was doing it.

Her way.

He smiled.

"You can't help her," Victor cried. "They are both going to die today. I didn't plan it. But that's going to be the outcome."

"No," Cody smiled at him. "You don't understand Tessa. She is so much more than Deanna."

"No," the vamp cried, hobbling closer. "She can't win. It's not possible. She can't be allowed to live on in Tessa."

Cody stepped in front of him. He'd been through this once with Bart, and he wasn't going to let that happen again.

No one was going to hurt Tessa.

"When Tessa defeats Deanna, your mother will be relegated to the archives where she belongs. Along with your uncle."

The crippled vamp shuddered to a halt. "Uncle? I have an uncle?" He bent over as if from a blow. "Not possible."

"Well, you do, but he's a Ghost. Well, he *was* a Ghost," Cody amended. "Tessa carries him as well. She's trying to keep them as part of a living historical archive."

"Hortran? The Ghost?" Victor asked in a daze. "He's my uncle?"

Cody could sympathize. It was a lot to understand all at once.

"I thought Hortran was her lover," Victor whispered.

"No," Cody snapped. At least, he hoped not because that was just plain wrong. "He was her brother."

"Then I carry his DNA as well." the old vamp brightened. "We thought the Ghosts were gone, and yet here I was carrying that genetic marker all this time."

"You might be, but maybe not," Cody knew nothing about DNA and genetic markers. "And besides, so what if you do?"

"Then we can reproduce it in the lab," he cried. "Don't you see? I thought he was her lover and I was angry at her, because I could have been whole and have that genetic marker as well if she'd chosen a better father for her child." He waved his arm adding, "Instead, this entire time I had it already."

"*Maybe* you have it," Cody snapped. "And maybe not."

But Victor beamed with the possibility. "Maybe not, but there were markers in my DNA that I didn't know, didn't understand. And now I do. I have to go to the blood farm. I have to start the testing. We have been after the Ghost DNA since the beginning," he cried, taking a step toward Cody. Beast howled. Victor paused.

Suddenly the air, as if a calm after a storm, cleared.

Tessa spoke up – a smiling, wholesome-looking Tessa. Although weak and tired, she looked... normal. "And what good would that do you," she asked Victor in a low voice.

"We can create the perfect race." Victor laughed. "All births will be controlled. There will be no more abominations like myself." His eyes turned black. "No more like you..." and he ran toward her in as fast a gait as his crippled leg would allow him.

Beast sent out a chilling warning again.

Cody stepped in front of Tessa. "You will not hurt her."

"She can't be allowed to live," he whispered. "Surely you see that. She's not perfect."

"You're wrong," Cody snapped. "She is perfect."

Victor shook his head. "Then you are damaged too." He glared down at Beast beside Tessa. "And that thing is an abomination."

Beast, his hackles rising as if he understood, growled.

Behind him, Cody turned to see Tessa staring at Victor with distaste. "You will not touch my pet," she snapped. "Or else…"

"Tessa? Are you…okay?"

She released a heavy sigh and straightened, letting her shoulders slump as if released from tension inside. "I'm fine. Deanna burned through her anger faster than I thought. The more love I poured over her, the more pissed off she became. She lost control quickly – now she's only bits and pieces of what she used to be. Like her brother." She smiled at the crippled vamp. "In fact, I'm more than fine. And now I can see everything."

Waving an arm at Victor, she said, "Don't worry about Hortran. You don't carry his genetics. The Ghost DNA is lost to you."

"No, that can't be."

"It is," she said. "Ghosts were trained. Not born. You don't have what it takes."

Victor, anger flashing on his face, rushed across the short distance between them, but Tessa, in a move reminiscent of Hortran, waved her hand, bringing him to his knees. Beast lunged forward.

Eye level to the dog, Victor glared at the animal. "He

needs killing."

"Tessa?" Cody wasn't sure what he was to do with this. "Does Beast get him?"

"No," Victor cried, pulling out a UV light weapon from his pocket. "Do you really think I'd be here without protection of my own?" Holding it up for them to see, he turned it on.

Only it wouldn't turn on.

Tessa laughed. "Did you really think I'd let you have a working model of one of those? I saw the battery on it a few minutes ago."

She turned to Beast and said, "Are you sure you want him?" She shook her head. "He's going to make you really sick. But not just yet."

Beast, as if understanding, growled in eagerness.

She grinned at him, then turned to Cody and added. "I know how now."

"How what?" he asked, struggling to keep up with the switches in the conversation. "What do you know how to do?"

Tessa gave Victor a fat smile. "You know, don't you?"

Still on his knees, his legs too weak to help him get back up, he shook his head. "No, you can't hurt him."

"Hurt who?"

"My son. You can't hurt him," the cripple cried.

"This son of yours is the one running everything," Tessa said. "And I will have to kill him. He's someone we all know. Someone on the Council. Someone who helped us – is even now helping us to 'win' this war. All the while he's laughing inside."

Victor pulled out a different weapon, this one tipped in silver.

Beast lunged at the crippled vamp.

"No!" Victor, using the large silver knife, stabbed himself in the throat. And blew to ash in front of them.

Cody stared. "Damn it. We needed information from him."

Beast whined and lay down beside the ash.

"No, we didn't." Tessa pulled out another granola bar and offered it to Beast with a big grin.

"But we don't even know who the son is," Cody cried. "We can't kill him if we don't know."

"Except for one thing," Tessa said, with a bright happy smile of the Tessa he'd fallen in love with, making his own heart smile. More than just smile... his heart recognized the color, the tone, the feel of her energy. It was his Tessa. He could recognize her for who she really was now.

Thank heavens.

She linked her arm with him, reaching up as if to kiss him. She whispered, "I do know who he is. And now...I know how to win this war."

And sealed her promise with a kiss.

Author's Note

Thank you for reading Family Blood Ties Books 7–9! If you enjoyed the book, please take a moment and leave a short review.

Dear reader,

I love to hear from readers, and you can contact me at my website: www.dalemayer.com or at my Facebook author page. To be informed of new releases and special offers, sign up for my newsletter. And if you are interested in joining Dale Mayer's Fan Club, here is the Facebook sign up page.

If you'd like to read about other books I've written, please turn the page.

Cheers,
Dale Mayer

Family Blood Ties Series

COMPLIMENTARY DOWNLOAD

DOWNLOAD a ***complimentary*** copy of TUESDAY'S CHILD? Just tell me where to send it!

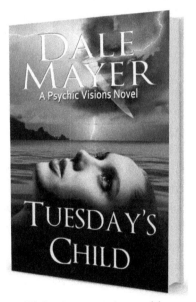

http://dalemayer.com/starterlibrarytc/

Dangerous Designs

Drawing is her world...but when her new pencil comes alive, it's his world too.

Her...Storey Dalton is seventeen and now boyfriendless after being dumped via Facebook. Drawing is her escape. It's like as soon as she gets down one image, a dozen more are pressing in on her. Then she realizes her pictures are almost drawing themselves...or is it that her new pencil is alive?

Him...Eric Jordan is a new Ranger and the only son of the Councilman to his world. He's crossed the veil between dimensions to retrieve a lost stylus. But Storey is already experimenting with her new pencil and what her drawings can do – like open portals.

It ...The stylus is a soul-bound intelligence from Eric's dimension on Earth and uses Storey's unsuspecting mind to seek its way home, giving her an unbelievable power. She unwittingly opens a third dimension, one that held a danger-ous predatory species banished from Eric's world centuries ago, releasing these animals into both dimensions.

Them...Once in Eric's homeland, Storey is blamed for the calamity and sentenced to death. When she escapes, Eric is ordered to bring her back or face that same death penalty. With nothing to lose, can they work together across dimen-sions to save both their worlds?

Design series

Gem Stone (a Gemma Stone Mystery)

A juvie kid trying to stay on the right path stumbles into trouble...

Gemma takes her camera everywhere. From juvie hall to a halfway home, the new hobby gives her a focus she'd never had before and... hope in a future. Until she takes pictures of something that could get her killed.

And not just her...after she and another juvie girl are chased by a stranger to the halfway home that same night, the other girl goes missing and Gemma knows she needs help. But who can she trust?

Not the authorities that's for sure. Trusting them is impossible for a girl with her damaged history, and besides, who cares about a troubled kid...especially when trouble just naturally seems to find her.

In Cassie's Corner

Faith and loyalty are tested as a young girl learns what it is to believe – in herself, in her friends, and in life after death.

Cassie's best friend, bad boy Todd, is gone. Gone as in dead. Gone as in he's now a ghost.

But she doesn't realize that when he wakes her in her bedroom and begs her not to believe what they say about him. It's not until the next day when her parents tell her about the accident that she learns the truth...

The police believe Todd was living up to the family name, drinking and driving and coming to a predictable end. It's up to her to find out the truth and clear his name.

Todd is shocked at his sudden change in circumstances...and angry. He struggles with his new ghostly reality, realizing all he's lost as he watches his brother build a relationship with Cassie as the two pair up to find out what really happened to him.

The truth isn't always pretty, and Cassie has to be stronger than ever before. Especially when the whole world seems to be against her.

About the Author

Dale Mayer is a USA Today bestselling author best known for her Psychic Visions and Family Blood Ties series. Her contemporary romances are raw and full of passion and emotion (Second Chances, SKIN), her thrillers will keep you guessing (By Death series), and her romantic comedies will keep you giggling (It's a Dog's Life and Charmin Marvin Romantic Comedy series).

She honors the stories that come to her – and some of them are crazy and break all the rules and cross multiple genres!

To go with her fiction, she also writes nonfiction in many different fields with books available on resume writing, companion gardening and the US mortgage system. She has recently published her Career Essentials Series. All her books are available in print and ebook format.

Connect with Dale Mayer Online

Dale's Website – www.dalemayer.com
Twitter – @DaleMayer
Facebook – facebook.com/DaleMayer.author

Also by Dale Mayer

Published Adult Books:

Psychic Vision Series
Tuesday's Child

Hide'n Go Seek

Maddy's Floor

Garden of Sorrow

Knock, Knock...

Rare Find

Eyes to the Soul

Now You See Her

Shattered

Psychic Visions 3in1

Psychic Visions Set 4–6

By Death Series
Touched by Death – Part 1

Touched by Death – Part 2

Touched by Death – Parts 1&2

Haunted by Death

Chilled by Death

Second Chances...at Love Series

Second Chances – Part 1

Second Chances – Part 2

Second Chances – complete book (Parts 1 & 2)

Charmin Marvin Romantic Comedy Series

Broken Protocols

Broken Protocols 2

Broken Protocols 3

Broken Protocols 3.5

Broken Protocols 1-3

Broken and... Mending

Skin

Scars

Scales (of Justice)

Glory

Genesis

Tori

Celeste

Biker Blues

Biker Blues: Morgan, Part 1

Biker Blues: Morgan, Part 2

Biker Blues: Morgan, Part 3

Biker Baby Blues: Morgan, Part 4

Biker Blues: Morgan, Full Set

Biker Blues: Salvation, Part 1

Published Young Adult Books:

Family Blood Ties Series
Vampire in Denial

Vampire in Distress

Vampire in Design

Vampire in Deceit

Vampire in Defiance

Vampire in Conflict

Vampire in Chaos

Vampire in Crisis

Vampire in Control

Family Blood Ties 3in1

Family Blood Ties set 4–6

Family Blood Ties set 7–9

Sian's Solution – A Family Blood Ties Short Story

Design series
Dangerous Designs

Deadly Designs

Darkest Designs

Design Series Trilogy

Standalone
In Cassie's Corner

Gem Stone (a Gemma Stone Mystery)

Time Thieves

Published Non-Fiction Books:

Career Essentials

Career Essentials: The Résumé

Career Essentials: The Cover Letter

Career Essentials: The Interview

Career Essentials: 3 in 1

CPSIA information can be obtained
at www.ICGtesting.com
Printed in the USA
BVHW040808031220
594767BV00019B/400